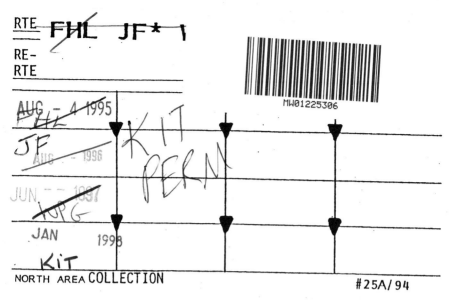

THE STEPSON

Other works by the same author,
translated into English
and published by The Marlboro Press

QUICKSAND
A SINGULAR MAN

EMMANUEL BOVE
THE STEPSON

TRANSLATED FROM FRENCH
BY NATHALIE FAVRE-GILLY

THE MARLBORO PRESS
MARLBORO, VERMONT

Originally published in French as *Le Beau-fils*
Copyright 1991 by Critérion, Paris

The publication of the present volume has been made
possible in part by a grant from
The National Endowment for the Arts.

Manufactured in the United States of America.

Library of Congress Catalog Card Number 93-80765

Cloth: ISBN 1-56897-004-8
Paper: ISBN 1-56897-005-6

THE MARLBORO PRESS

MARLBORO, VERMONT

THE STEPSON

ONE

It was well before the war, in 1904 to be exact, that Mlle Annie Villemur de Falais made the acquaintance of Jean-Melchior Oetlinger. She was twenty-one years old. She had been enrolled in a painting class for several months, though neither at Julian's nor the Académie des Beaux-Arts, but rather at an academy situated in the rue de la Grande-Chaumière, a choice of which she was proud because it left no doubt that hers was a true vocation. Like the other students, she admired the Pre-Raphaëlites. Every now and then her brothers, her girlfriends, and even her father would come to observe a life class from the doorway, somewhat embarrassed when the model was a nude man, but afraid to say so for fear of seeming prudish. Annie was a tall, fair-haired young girl, self-conscious about her beauty the way people in certain professions sometimes are about their youth. After repeated pleas, she had obtained her family's permission to rent a studio at the top of the rue d'Assas. Every week she organized little parties there. Her fellow students, for the most part impecunious foreigners, were always joined at these by a member of the Villemur family, who attended to ensure that everyone behaved respectably. It was at one of these teas that the academy's treasurer—to whom Mlle Villemur had taken a liking because, like all treasurers, he had been chosen from among the neediest students of the class, and she had preserved the habit of compassion instilled in her by her upbringing—brought along one of his friends, a gloomy man of about thirty with a pointed beard, rather ceremoniously attired in a morning coat. He was the son of a professor from Mulhouse who had been known for his Francophile sentiments. When the professor died in September of 1895, Jean-Melchior Oetlinger, who had turned twenty-one in February of that year, his older brother, Martin, and his younger sister, Catherine, sold their father's house and moved to Paris, where the boys intended to continue their studies and the girl to facilitate her brothers' task by running the household for them. They found an apartment in the rue Pierre-Nicole, with two rooms and a kitchen. At first, they remained perfectly united. The young girl did not go out. The two brothers parted only to attend their classes. If it happened that one of them wanted to visit a museum, he would tell his brother, who would then consult Catherine. Finally, when all had agreed, but not before, they would allow themselves this entertainment. As their entire fortune consisted of a modest inheritance that had to last them through the end of their studies, they instinctively stayed close to one another, both out of economy and to steer well clear of the temptations they had heard spoken of in their youth. But before long, Jean-Melchior had begun to allow himself small acts of treason. Bit by bit, he had grown bolder. The dangers he had been warned about began to seem less fearsome. He had a delicate constitution, an indolent nature, and was not made for steady work. Laziness and lounging about suited him far better than the rigorously scheduled life-style of the rue Pierre-Nicole. When, four months later, he fell in love with Ernestine Mercier, a woman who, between the ages of seventeen and thirty-one, had lived with a succession of different men, always with the hope that each of her lovers would be the last, he hesitated to admit it for a long time. It was only when he no longer had any choice that he finally revealed his liaison.

Martin flew into a terrible rage. Jean-Melchior had not yet learned that when we withdraw from an association, it is held against us by those who remain, even if our doing so is advantageous to them. He was ordered to choose. For an entire month he was unable to make up his mind. He would grow feverish every day at five in the afternoon. He loved his brother and his sister more than anything in the world—more, much more, than Ernestine Mercier—but she represented pleasure, a thousand things his family could not give him. Finally, when it became clear to him that he would have to choose, that he could not procrastinate much longer, he packed his trunk, embraced Catherine lingeringly, and asked Martin to forgive him. Avoiding sentimental considerations, the latter discussed money matters with him. It was agreed that he would be given what was his by right, and that his share of the rent would be deducted from this amount. Jean-Melchior then went off to join Ernestine Mercier.

She had not been expecting such a proof of his love. For the first few days, therefore, she dared not ask Jean-Melchior in what sort of situation his actions had left him. She endeavored to appear worthy of the feelings she inspired. But when she learned that Jean-Melchior had a bit of money, and that he intended to live modestly in order to be able to finish his studies, she began to mock him. She convinced him that one was only young once, that no one knew what tomorrow would bring, that one had to make the most of life while one could. They moved to a comfortable hotel, and no longer took their meals in modest restaurants but rather in *brasseries*, where they lingered until three in the morning in the company of noisy friends. In spite of this, she aspired to becoming a respectable bourgeois housewife—but only later, when she had met a man she really loved.

Because of his mistress, and above all because of the fever brought on by the slightest effort he made, Jean-Melchior had all but given up his studies entirely. He got up late and frequented Ernestine's friends, with whom he had nothing in common. As for his future, he was unable to imagine what it might bring. He was living from day to day, constantly pursuing Ernestine with his jealousy and his tenderness, and, at the slightest vexation, retreating into a stony silence that lasted for days at a time and from which he would emerge abruptly, embittered but still enamored. After a year, he had almost nothing left of the share of the inheritance Martin had given him. He was forced to contemplate living more modestly, all the more so as his health was beginning to show the effects of his unsettled life. They rented a small apartment, furnished it simply. On a suffocatingly hot night in August of 1897, Ernestine said to him, "We have been inspired." He did not understand what she meant. She refused to explain, but during the night, in the bed that she called her "domain" and had made into an accomplice, one which, to her eyes, had as many traits as a living being, she told Jean-Melchior, in an unbearably simpering fashion, that he was going to be a father.

From then on, not a day went by without her reminding him of the duties now incumbent upon him. The number of these seemed to increase endlessly, in spite of which she never lost sight of the principal one—to wit, that he was going to have to marry her. And yet, she had no one to blame but herself if Jean-Melchior no longer wished to get married. He had asked her once, not because it was what he wanted, for when he had left his brother and sister nothing could have been further from his mind than starting a family, but because of the scruples he retained from his upbringing, which made it difficult for him to conceive of love without marriage. In relieving him of those scruples, which he had been only too pleased to abandon, Ernestine had not foreseen that the arguments she was using to do so would one day be turned against her. As for Jean-Melchior, he could not believe that the same woman who had mocked his proposals when he still had his inheritance and it would have been very much to her advantage to marry him, was sincere in her desire to get married now that he was penniless and had no better prospects than giving a few German lessons. He therefore answered her distractedly every time she raised the question, having been convinced by Ernestine herself that this issue of marriage was unimportant.

At the end of April 1898 a child was born and given the

name Jean-Noël. As the couple's financial situation had grown ever more precarious, Jean-Melchior turned to Martin for assistance. When the latter learned that his brother had spent everything he had and was living with a woman with whom he had just had a son, he told him never to come back to the rue Pierre-Nicole. From that day forward, Jean-Melchior's problems multiplied. Apart from his family, toward whom his feelings had not changed, and whose harshness saddened rather than angered him, he knew only students, who were filled with youthful generosity but unable to either help or guide him. In spite of the obstacles that were becoming increasingly difficult to surmount with each passing day, and despite Ernestine's insistence, he refused to take a steady job, for it had become clear to him that his only hope of extricating himself from the fix he was in lay in finishing his studies. From time to time he would give a lesson or accept a nondescript job, which he would abandon after two months. The life they were leading destroyed any desire Ernestine once had of becoming Jean-Melchior's wife. Marriage was associated with happiness, and entering into it in their present circumstances would have been distressing. Several years passed, marked by poverty and bitterness. The relationship between Jean-Melchior and his companion grew ever more strained. She reproached him for having given her a child in spite of knowing that he lacked the means to support it. If she was so unhappy, it was because she had been hopelessly naïve and had believed in all his promises. She constantly threatened to leave him, and if he failed to beg her, grief-stricken, to do no such thing, she would begin to sob, saying that he did not love her and was doing everything in his power to get rid of her.

Jean-Noël was already seven years old when Jean-Melchior was introduced to Mlle Villemur de Falais. The world he glimpsed around the young girl and the carefree atmosphere that reigned at her studio had an extraordinary effect upon him. He saw Annie again. One day, when he found himself alone with her, he told her the story of his life. It moved her deeply. From the start, she had felt drawn to this sickly man, and was astonished by his sincerity. Although she hardly knew him, she was neither suspicious nor fearful of him. In her eyes, he represented everything she did not know, and the fact that she felt absolutely safe with him in spite of this filled her with pride.

Six months later, when Annie spoke to her family of her desire to marry a young man she had met at the academy, which was not strictly speaking true, she encountered unwavering opposition. Her father forced her to leave the academy and give up her studio. He forbade her to see all the friends she had made outside of the family, with no exceptions. Endless complications now arose. She loved Jean-Melchior. In her eyes, he was an exceptional man, superior even to the artists she had admired. When she had told him of her father's anger, hadn't he said to her that above all else a young girl had to respect her family's wishes, and that if he was so unhappy himself it was because he had failed to do just that? Unbeknownst to her parents, she continued to see him. When they discovered this, they found it hard to believe. Hadn't Annie always been perfectly frank with them? She had never concealed anything whatsoever. There was a great scene at the Villemurs' home in the avenue de Malakoff. It was necessary to establish whether Annie really intended to marry a sickly young man from Alsace, who had no money, no future, and had already fathered a child. She replied that those were the very reasons why she loved Jean-Melchior. M. Villemur realized that his daughter would not yield. For a moment, his face took on that expression seen in men who are at war with themselves. He asked Annie to follow him. He went into his study. He was extremely calm. Nevertheless, he brushed his perfectly aligned fingertips across his eyebrows more often than usual.

"You wish to get married," he said evenly. "That is your right. But I must ask that you introduce me to the man whom you have chosen."

"I wanted to on several occasions. You always refused."

"I've now changed my mind."

[6]

The meeting took place. As soon as M. Villemur laid eyes on Jean-Melchior, he realized immediately that the hope to which he had been clinging had been fanciful. How could he have allowed himself to believe that this M. Oetlinger would be any different from what he had imagined? Here before him stood the lackluster individual whom he had reconstituted on the basis of what Annie had told him, a sickly-looking fellow trying to give himself the appearance of an artist. When he was alone with his daughter once again, he did not even think it useful to convey to her the impression Jean-Melchior had made on him. He confined himself to telling her that she was free to marry M. Oetlinger, that he would give her her dowry if she did so, but that she should give up any idea of seeing her family again. With that understood, she was free to leave the house that evening.

While Annie continued to struggle with her parents, for these scenes were followed by others of a similar nature, Jean-Melchior was quietly preparing Ernestine for a separation. He had, in fact, long been wishing for one. After the birth of Jean-Noël—which is to say from the moment Ernestine had showed signs of becoming genuinely attached to him—he had begun to dream of regaining his liberty. Before he could do so, however, he needed to provide for the material well-being of the woman who, to hear her tell it, had given him the best years of her life. This had proven to be impossible. As time passed, they had drifted further and further apart, and although he had not been lying when he had passed himself off as a free man on his first visit to the rue d'Assas, he was nonetheless as much a prisoner as he had been at the beginning of his liaison. Free—yes, he was. Every morning, on the pretext of looking for money (which he rarely found), he would leave his mistress and return home only after she was asleep. But transforming this moral separation into an actual one would be as monumentally difficult as though they had been closely united, for Ernestine pretended both that she was deeply attached to him and that she adored their child, whom she treated badly.

e day after Jean-Melchior's meeting with M. Villemur,
ded to address the matter openly. He told Ernestine
that Jean-Noël was growing up, that he had reached an age at
which one begins to remember what one sees, that it had
become necessary to think seriously about his education, and
that, as a result of this and because he had no other choice, he
was planning to make a marriage of convenience. He added
weakly that life is such that we are often forced to sacrifice
our feelings to other concerns. Ernestine flew into such a rage
that it became necessary to attend to her as one would a child
racked with convulsions, with the result that when calm had
been restored, the contrast with the cries and threats which
had preceded it created the impression that she had given in.
But Ernestine had not resigned herself. A month later, in the
same manner as the first time, she announced to Jean-
Melchior that she was pregnant. He refused to believe her; he
took her to see a doctor. She was telling the truth. Mlle Villemur had just left her family and taken a room in a hotel
whose name, Hôtel des Grands Hommes, had amused her
whenever she had crossed the place du Panthéon. He went to
see her there and told her what had just happened for fear she
might hear about it from someone else, insinuating that it
was a hateful lie. He was not convinced of this, but as he was
no more convinced of the opposite, he railed with such indignation against what he called a desperate maneuver that Annie believed him, in spite of being deeply humiliated. "That
woman will stoop to anything," she said.

In the springtime of 1906, Jean-Melchior and Annie were
married. Whereas the Villemurs took a dim view of their
marriage, the Oetlingers were deeply impressed. To escape
from Annie's parents, therefore, who in spite of their feigned
indifference remained hostile, and from Jean-Melchior's
brother, who had suddenly been transformed, and from Ernestine Mercier, who continued to call herself Madame Oetlinger and talked about her pregnancy to anyone who would
listen, the newlyweds decided to settle in Nice, a town whose
climate would be excellent for Jean-Melchior and in which it

would be easy to obtain a proper education for Jean-Noël. When the moment came to fetch the child, however, new difficulties arose. In spite of the agreement that had been extracted from her in exchange for a certain sum of money, Ernestine Mercier refused to let him go. Jean-Melchior was reduced to carrying out what amounted to a kidnapping. It was a dramatic scene. Ernestine Mercier called in her neighbors to help her, told them of her condition, and of the inhumanity of the man to whom she had sacrificed her life. Everything was finally sorted out and Jean-Melchior was able to leave with his son, who was crying and trembling with fear.

TWO

M. and Mme Oetlinger had been living in Nice for nine years when, in the early days of February 1915, a telegram was delivered to their address. With neither an affectionate nor a comforting word, M. Villemur announced to his daughter that his youngest son, Bertrand, the only one who had not opposed Annie's wedding, had been seriously wounded. She left for Paris the same evening. M. Oetlinger accompanied her to the station. Standing on a platform beneath the enormous glass roof where every noise reverberated, jostled by soldiers on leave, wounded men, and nurses, Annie cried. It was the first time she would be separated from Jean-Melchior since she had married him. To be without him in such dramatic circumstances made her reflect upon the years they had spent together. She had a premonition that this moment marked the end of a happy period. In the next instant, she would be alone in the midst of a world from whose tribulations it had pleased her to think she had escaped, and which already seemed to be exacting its revenge.

A week later an entirely different woman stepped off the train. She hailed a porter and handed him her bags herself. No one would have guessed that her brother's leg had been amputated a few days earlier, and that he still hovered between life and death. "I have caused you a great deal of trouble, my poor Melchior," she said to her husband, who had come forward to greet her. She was alluding to the letters she had written him from Paris in which she had done nothing more than relate the events that had taken place during her trip. They took an open carriage. The evening was springlike. The horse set off at a walk. It was a relief not to be rushed any more, to be far from the war, breathing in air scented with the smell of burning wood and mimosa. Annie seemed indifferent. The self-possession she had displayed upon arriving, to reassure her husband from afar, had been replaced by an overwhelming weariness. She was wondering whether she had not made a mistake in marrying Jean-Melchior, whether her family had not been right after all in opposing the marriage. And yet it was not that her love had diminished as she had grown older. It had simply been transformed. Everything that had seemed so fine to her as a young girl—struggle, departure, exile with the man she loved—had been extinguished by day-to-day realities, the importance of which she exaggerated to herself. When she had suddenly found herself in the midst of her family once again, where it had always seemed to her that no such realities existed, she had had the impression that she was a renegade and had exempted herself from all of their suffering, whereas until then she had always thought the opposite was true, that she had left behind bourgeois security when she left her family. It had dawned on her that she had perhaps been blinded by love. She had been received most cordially. The fact that she had come alone, for she had no one to blame but herself if her husband could not be considered a member of the family, had hovered over the initial conversations. Afterward, no one had seemed to remember what had occurred in the past. One afternoon she had even gone to see her former maid, her darling Elisabeth, in a retirement home in Neuilly. Tearfully, Elsabeth had described the sadness which had reigned over the family after Annie left. Being surrounded by such benevolence had begun to make her feel remorseful. But such feelings were unfair to her husband, and she had put them aside immediately. One evening she had stayed with her father for nearly a quarter of an hour without either of them saying a word. Friends had come for news. Their duty accomplished, they had conversed at length with her. It had been hoped she would not leave right away. Attempts had been made to persuade her to stay in Paris. And what had touched her most had been when her mother, who was usually so cold, had asked her worriedly whether she was happy.

In the train on her way back, Annie had reflected upon all of this. Had she behaved as she should? Hadn't she left too soon? Showered with so much affection, should she not have extended her stay, if only to show that she had been touched by all the attentions shown her? Hadn't it been cold-hearted of her to return to Nice before knowing the outcome of Bertrand's operation? By taking leave of her family on the date she had announced upon arriving, by which she had intended to show she would not impose upon them, hadn't she responded to all their kindness with coldness? What was the nature of this grudge she held against her family? Hadn't they simply done their duty? Then, upon reflection, it seemed to her that she could not have behaved in any other way, not because she was of a nature to calculate the advantages to be gained from delaying a reconciliation, but rather because, in the course of her existence as a married woman, and despite her complaints, she had been proud to be exposed to the very troubles which, as a young girl, she had thought were reserved exclusively for artists, and above all because she had wanted it understood in Paris that, far from diminishing her, her marriage had improved her. The exceptional situation in which she found herself, Ernestine Mercier's pursuit of her and Jean-Melchior, the precautions they took to keep their whereabouts a secret—everything which, in a word, seemed to happen only to her—allowed her to cling to the illusion that she had a vaster experience of life than did her own father. She had therefore done well to leave on the date she had set herself. She had thus shown her family, more effectively than words could have done, that she had neither grudges nor regrets, that she had simply become a woman.

M. and Mme Oetlinger did not speak. Everything seemed light and distant to them. The stars appeared to have stopped climbing. They shone, each according to its own strength, at the level where the clouds passed by. Annie breathed deeply. Nothing remained of the people she had seen, of the things she had said. The horse's hooves and his bell, which was as big as an apple, sang in her ears. Lights were burning in all of the hotel windows. They were all the same, each illuminating the same room, a wounded man's room. Occasionally Annie's gaze would meet her husband's, and the two would then smile at one another. The mere fact of having been reunited after a week's separation would not have produced such contentment had the separation not been caused by a misfortune. This misfortune now brought the prospect of change; it brought what the couple had hoped for in some vague sense for years, all the more so since they had begun to fear they might face financial difficulties someday: the hope of a reconciliation with the Villemurs. Annie had not yet spoken of her father, nor of the welcome she had been given. Jean-Melchior did not dare question her. Soon they arrived at the avenue Félix-Faure. The wide street, lined with palm trees, shone in the night. The carriage stopped. Annie took her husband's hand. He raised his eyes. "We have arrived," she said in a lively voice. She was now reproaching herself for having envisaged the happy effects the misfortune in her family might have on her life.

In the month of May of that year, Bertrand died as a result of his injuries. Since her return, Annie had been corresponding regularly with her parents. They had not concealed from her the fact that Bertrand's condition was critical, but as each of their letters had been written with the obvious intention of pleasing her, the brother's condition had taken on the aspect of a pretext for keeping in contact, and all that had mattered was the way in which the letters began or ended. Thus, upon learning of Bertrand's death, and despite the fact that she must have been expecting it, Annie was as struck by the news as if her brother had just left her an hour earlier in perfect health. As she was preparing to leave, she received a second telegram from her father asking her to come to Paris as quickly as possible. This summons made her forget everything which separated her from her family. It was at that moment that the idea of having her husband accompany her occurred to her. But when she expressed this desire to him, she was startled to discover he was unenthusiastic about the idea. She asked him why this was so. After a moment's hesitation, he answered that she was mistaken, that on the contrary he would be very delighted to go with her.

If M. Oetlinger had briefly tried to avoid making the trip, it was because of something which had happened ten days earlier, and which he had not wanted to reveal to his wife. When the war had broken out, Annie's fears about the future had increased tenfold, and at her insistence he had reduced by half the pension he was paying Ernestine Mercier. Before the month of November 1914, was out, she had turned up in Nice. In fact, this was not the first time she made the trip: she had done so three times in the eight years that had elapsed since Annie and Jean-Melchior's departure. But the trip which concerns us here was exceptional in that, unlike the others, it made no provisions for a return journey. Considering it more prudent, in time of war, to be near the person who supported her, she and her second son had settled in Menton. As well as being close to Nice and the border, it was a charming little town, reputed for its climate, something Ernestine Mercier valued highly, for both she and Emile had constitutions as delicate as Jean-Melchior's. From that day forward, Jean-Melchior was exposed to every imaginable form of harassment. Everything served as a pretext for Ernestine to write, to level reproaches at him. There was one among these which surfaced constantly: M. Oetlinger did not seem to consider Emile his son. "All the same I can assure you," she would tell him in each of her letters, "he is well and truly yours." Jean-Melchior did not deny it. Nonetheless, he found it very disagreeable, especially as Annie had always refused to believe it. But Mme Mercier was not satisfied with merely writing. She used every means to try to harm the one who had abandoned her, a fact which she trumpeted loudly. After having been in Menton a mere three months, she had already made numerous friends. She passed herself off as the genuine Mme Oetlinger. The one who had taken her rightful place was an adventuress, and if she, Ernestine Mercier, had allowed herself to be supplanted, it was out of love, because she had pitied Jean-Melchior and had wanted to spare him material worries. These stories impressed the people of modest means with whom she associated, and she had great trouble restraining some of them from going to Nice to take up her cause.

It had doubtless been one of these overly devoted souls who had written M. Oetlinger a letter two weeks earlier— albeit without signing it— which warned him that Jean-Noël, whom he had not hesitated to favor to the detriment of his other son Emile, was leading a debauched life, had been seen at night in houses of ill repute, and had taken a girl of the streets as his mistress. The letter ended with reproaches that made those with which Ernestine habitually assailed him seem mild in comparison. Wasn't it shameful to take a child away from his mother only to then give him permission to stay out all night? Wasn't one justified in wondering if such a father was German rather than French?

M. Oetlinger had summoned his son. The boy we had seen in the arms of his father while Mme Mercier tried to snatch him away was now a tall, thin young man of seventeen. He had a bloated face, with that dull flesh that makes the pores visible. His teeth protruded slightly, so they were visible even when he was not talking. His whole being exuded an impression of sluggishness, timidity, arrogance. His forehead was as wrinkled as that of an old man; his features, especially his nose, were large. Yet this unprepossessing face had a sort of luminosity which came from his gaze, and which suggested that at certain moments this young man might be handsome.

M. Oetlinger had questioned his son gently, to avoid upsetting that thin-skinned prudishness he remembered having felt himself in the days when he still lived in Mulhouse. It had not taken him long to realize that, although the anonymous letter had exaggerated the facts, it had nonetheless contained an element of truth. Finally, Jean-Noël had confessed that once his parents were in bed, he sometimes left the apartment to go and meet a woman, whose name and address he divulged tearfully. Jean-Melchior calmed his son down, gave him to understand that he had not done anything out of the ordinary for a young man, and, although nothing could have been farther from Jean-Noël's thoughts in this moment of great embarrassment than his stepmother, added that he would never breathe a word of it, as though his son's shame originated in his fear that Annie would learn of his behavior. In reality, it was M. Oetlinger who most feared that Annie would learn what had happened. Although she found it natural that, even now, she should still be suffering as a result of Jean-Melchior's past faults or weaknesses, which in her mind were inseparable from the conditions in which she had married, any new problem infuriated her, whether caused directly or indirectly by her husband. For that reason, M. Oetlinger would have found it disagreeable if anything came to light for which his son could be criticized. But he would have found it far more disagreeable still if Jean-Noël knew of his fears. He had a profound adoration for the boy. He trembled at the thought that his son should even suspect his inferiority to Annie, and was anxious to preserve a prestige which, in spite of his best efforts, diminished with each passing day. For the past two years, Jean-Noël had been avoiding him, and when avoiding him was impossible, he dared not look him in the face. He was jealous of his father. He felt he was unworthy of Annie, and that if he had managed to make her love him, it had only been by concealing his true nature from her. The years had not made him forget the intimacy his father had shared with Ernestine Mercier. He clearly recalled the scenes that had erupted in the modest apartment in which he had spent the first years of his life: the arguments over sums of money which, even now, as a high-school student, seemed trifling to him; his joy whenever he had been taken to the rue d'Assas and, later, to that hotel which had seemed all the grander because of its proximity of the Panthéon, and, above all, the security he had felt whenever he was near Annie. Although he had been a mere child, he had sensed how different this unknown woman was from his mother, never raising her voice, living in the midst of books, colors, and objects which, like the little stuffed bear from Bern, had all seemed precious to him. Thus, when M. Oetlinger, upon receiving the letter we spoke of, asked his son to take him to the woman of easy virtue it alluded to, Jean-Noël did not view this as a desire to know the people with whom he associated, but rather as the attraction of a man, forced to live in a milieu not his own, to that which reminds him of his past.

A sort of procuress had greeted M. Oetlinger and his son, and without seeming at all surprised that two such dissimilar visitors would wish to speak to the same tenant, had asked them to wait in a small sitting room through the walls of which one could make out shouts and laughter. Then they were shown into the young woman's room. She received them wearing her dressing gown. Upon seeing the man who accompanied her lover, if one can grace a lovesick schoolboy with such a title, she sensed trouble. Above all anxious to avoid any problems, she pretended to be on no more than friendly terms with Jean-Noël. M. Oetlinger apologized for having disturbed her. Then, as if he had come to pay her a social call, he talked about trivialities, so that Jean-Noël, in spite of his embarrassment, wondered why his father, whom he had expected to be angry, had insisted upon this meeting. He was too young to understand that M. Oetlinger had willingly put himself in a humiliating situation only so his son's pity would afford him that which he thought he could not obtain in any other way.

A week later, on the eve of the day on which M. Oetlinger had resolved to return to see this woman alone in order to assure himself that everything was indeed over between her and his son, the news came of Bertrand's death. "And Jean-Noël, what are we going to do about *him*?" asked M. Oetlinger in the course of the evening. He was afraid to leave his son unsupervised. "It won't be the first time he's been left alone," replied Annie curtly. A question as natural as the one her husband had just asked her was enough to rekindle her fears about the future and make her apprehensive that she was going to be asked to make some sacrifice. But she stopped herself at once, not wishing to appear preoccupied with protecting her wealth on such a day. The following morning, in the same carriage that was to convey him to the station an hour later, Jean-Melchior took his son to the home of an English professor by the name of Stevenson. He had settled in France ten years earlier and now ran a small boarding school exclusively for English boys. Out of deference to Annie, however, he had agreed to make an exception. He had noticed long ago that M. and Mme Oetlinger were not of the same class. Thinking he was flattering her by doing so, whenever he found himself with Annie he would insinuate that he had guessed who she was. This was why M. Oetlinger had entrusted his son to him: such a choice, in his mind, was of a nature to soothe the irritation his wife displayed whenever she committed herself to taking on some new expense. And yet he had been wrong in this, for Mme Oetlinger had always been utterly indifferent to her admirers.

THREE

When M. and Mme Oetlinger arrived in Paris, they took a taxi to the Hôtel des Grands Hommes. Annie never looked back on the time she had spent there without picturing love in its most romantic aspects. Leaving the station, her intention had been to go directly to the avenue de Malakoff with her husband. She had even given the taxi driver that address. It was only after they had set forth that her plan of arriving with Jean-Melchior at the very moment Bertrand was about to be buried had struck her as impracticable, and that she had understood that it would be best to wait a few days so that M. Villemur could be prepared for the meeting.

She first accompanied her husband to the hotel, therefore, and only then went to meet her family. If anyone was overjoyed by this change of plans, it was M. Oetlinger. He was not at all put out that his meeting with the Villemurs was being postponed, although on the whole he would have preferred to go directly to the avenue de Malakoff, which would have been natural, rather than waiting for the moment Annie chose, which was going to seem somehow premeditated. How was it that his wife did not realize the awkwardness of her desire to thrust Jean-Melchior into the midst of her family on the occasion of an event as painful as Bertrand's death? How could she imagine that her parents would believe the reasons she wanted her husband to give for his presence in Paris, the most unlikely of which was that he had been so affected by Bertrand's death that he had insisted upon conveying his great sorrow to the Villemurs in person? In order not to irritate Annie, and in spite of feeling ill at ease at appearing at a time when they had other things to think about than being reconciled with him, he had accepted. But what were the Villemurs going to think of a man who appeared out of the blue, as if from a hiding place, at the very moment when he was the farthest thing from their thoughts?

The following day, when Annie returned, he expressed his fears to her. She dismissed them. The day before, she had made several allusions to her husband. He was in Paris. Bertrand's death had upset him deeply. Out of discretion, he had not wanted to make his presence known. In the days that followed, she continued preparing her father for Jean-Melchior's visit. After a week had gone by, M. Villemur finally understood what his daughter was trying to achieve. It struck him then that she no longer had the tactfulness he had so admired in her when she was a young girl. Had this change not been wrought by the man with whom she had fallen in love and for whose sake, even now, she was not afraid of offending her family? Thus it was that, when Annie decided the moment had come to bring her husband forward, she found, much to her surprise, that the welcome extended to him was no warmer than the one he had been given ten years earlier. In the aftermath of this attempt at a reconciliation, there was, for the first time since they had married, a certain unease between Annie and Jean-Melchior. The latter, who had shown no desire until then to see any of his former friends or even his brother because he had sensed that this would displease his wife, went off and, rather than wandering alone through Paris, decided to rekindle some of his old friendships. He saw his brother Martin again, who, word had it, had done very well. He found him settled on the second floor of a modest building in the rue Claude-Bernard, in an apartment that looked out over the inner courtyard. Like M. Oetlinger, that is to say for medical reasons, he had not been mobilized. Catherine, whose husband was at the front and who had been living with her brother and working as his secretary since the war had broken out, was overjoyed to see Jean-Melchior. "She is sick with worry. You ought to extend her your hospitality. The change, the sunshine, would lift her spirits," said Martin, taking advantage of the fact his sister had gone out. "I want nothing more than to make her happy," replied M. Oetlinger.

Mr. Stevenson, meanwhile, was keeping a particularly vigilant eye on Jean-Noël. The professor had not been advised to do so; he believed it his duty to preserve the other boarders from possible contamination. As for Ernestine Mercier, she had learned from one of her many friends of Bertrand's death and of M. and Mme Oetlinger's subsequent departure. Both of those events, which were none of her concern, perturbed her greatly, for in her eyes everything that went on in Nice was of fundamental importance. She was impatient to do something, to signal her presence somehow, as if such circumstances carried with them the risk that she would be forgotten. The idea came to her then to go and pay a visit to her son. She asked a M. Grimal, who looked after Emile's education a bit in addition to giving lessons in a private school, what he thought of her intentions. M. Grimal replied evasively. Mme Mercier's very unusual situation was also the principal reason for his having befriended her. Although he treated her as someone who had been unjustly victimized by powerful people, he nonetheless hoped that some day he would have a chance to approach those very people. Thus he took care not to compromise himself, so that if, for example, he was called upon to testify or to arbitrate some conflict later on, no one would be able to reproach him with this friendship.

Unable to restrain herself any longer, Ernestine Mercier went to Mr. Stevenson's establishment one morning, not as an abandoned mother, but as a woman who, although she has made a new life for herself, has nonetheless retained deep, tender feelings for the son she was forced to give up. She spoke with much affection, implied that she was from as good a family as the woman who had robbed her of her husband and her child. She even uttered these enigmatic words: "The day is not far off when you will have a great surprise," which, out of politeness, Mr. Stevenson pretended to understand. Afterwards she asked to see her dear child, and when he was brought to her, looked at him for a long time, pressing her lips together. Then, as if anything was permissible for a woman in her situation, she shed a few tears, hid her face in her hands, asked for a glass of water. Beet-red with embarrassment, Jean-Noël witnessed this scene rather than taking part in it. The following day he did not dare look up at his professor. He had never felt so ashamed. His only desire was to leave this boarding school, where it seemed to him that everyone was looking at him with contempt. Thus, when his father returned to Nice, the first thing he asked him was if he could go back to the avenue Félix-Faure. Surprised, M. Oetlinger tried to discover what had happened. Since Jean-Noël refused to speak, he questioned Mr. Stevenson.

"Nothing in particular happened," replied the professor, who regarded Mme Mercier's existence as a secret of which he should not have been aware.

Several days later, however, Jean-Melchior learned from his son what had taken place. He recalled Mr. Stevenson's attitude. Annie just happened to have telephoned the professor to invite him to tea.

"I no longer wish to receive him," M. Oetlinger said to his wife.

Because this surprised her, and because above all he did not want to divulge the reason for this change of heart, he told her that he had heard regrettable things said about Mr. Stevenson, upon which he carefully avoided expounding. Annie had blind faith in her husband's opinions. In spite of her friendly feelings for Mr. Stevenson, she smiled.

"The world is strange, isn't it?" she said. "Every day one hears of something vile."

When Mr. Stevenson began to notice Mme Oetlinger's coldness toward him, he thought it was due to the fact that he had received Ernestine Mercier, albeit against his better judgment. He recalled something she had said. "Monsieur Grimal, whom you know well, I believe, told me that you were a charming gentleman. I see that he was not lying." The professor's ill humor fell on M. Grimal, who learned of it through a third party. Although M. Grimal was not overly fond of his colleague, who earned more money than he did in spite of being a foreigner, he had no desire to be on bad terms with him. He sent him a long letter, adopting that lofty tone one uses to speak of disagreeable matters one has become involved in against one's will, writing of Mme Mercier and his occasional contacts with her. In no way had he been the one to suggest the steps she had taken. In concluding, he assured M. Stevenson of his distinguished and cordial sentiments and sincere devotion. Coming full circle, the affair found its way back to the woman who had instigated it. When Ernestine Mercier noticed that M. Grimal was now avoiding her, she no longer had any doubts that Jean-Melchior had maneuvered against her. She accused him of reproaching Mr. Stevenson for having received her as a gentleman should. By return post, M. Oetlinger replied that she was mistaken, that he had never even mentioned her name in Mr. Stevenson's presence. She hurried off to show this letter to M. Grimal who, exasperated, got rid of her as quickly as he could.

In the midst of this, Catherine arrived in Nice. In spite of the fact that trains were sometimes running several hours late, Jean-Melchior had gone to wait for her at the station to ensure that she did not go to the avenue Félix Faure. Since her return, Annie had been very despondent. Although she refused to admit it to herself, she had been counting a great deal on her last trip to Paris to make her family accept her husband. She had even envisaged that by the end of the war, and perhaps even sooner, Jean-Melchior and she would have made a permanent move back to Paris. Not only had her hopes been dashed, but a new, cold, formal relationship had been established between her family and herself. Annie had been struck by how strange and unpredictable fate could sometimes be. She had always thought that only the most perfect love could ever exist between her parents and herself, and now, without her being aware of how it had come about, she communicated with her family as if they were distant cousins. M. Oetlinger had therefore gone to meet his sister without telling Annie and, on the pretext that he employed no servants, had provided her with a letter to Ernestine and sent her to Menton.

On his way home, he congratulated himself for not having acted upon the fleeting idea he had had, as his sister got out of the train, of putting her up. He found Annie in a very bad humor.

"We must absolutely make a decision," she told him.

She began to talk of painting portraits, which would be a means of earning enough to cover their household expenses. What small income she still received could then be used for what she called their pocket money, the uses of which greatly exceeded what is normally understood by the term, given that they extended to everything which was not, as she put it, "housekeeping."

One afternoon, as she was on her way to the studio she had in the old town, her attention was drawn to a sign hanging from the door of a dilapidated house. An apartment was for rent. Abruptly, without thinking, she entered the building and sought out the owner. A man in his sixties, bent over a cane, came forward to meet her. He was dressed in a corduroy suit and wore a wide-brimmed black hat. His white beard made him look like an artist's model. Although she had never seen him before and could have nothing in common with him, he nonetheless made a great impression upon her. "I just read," she said respectfully, "the sign hanging on the door of your house." He led Annie into a sort of carpenter's workshop where five or six cats were sleeping curled up next to one another. She told him of her desire to rent a smaller apartment than the one in which she now lived. She feared bankruptcy. It was her view that she ought to reduce her expenses. Flattered and surprised by these confidences, the owner encouraged her to do so. She took her leave of him, almost joyfully, after he had promised that he would draw up a lease for her.

When she told her husband that she intended to rent an

apartment in the old town, he did not share her enthusiasm. He told her that her fears were exaggerated, that the war was nearly over, that things would work themselves out. Reassured, Annie did not keep the appointment she had made with the owner. He came looking for her. That was all it took to rekindle Annie's worry. She signed the lease. From that day forward, she felt better. Her peace of mind was short-lived, however. A week later, Catherine rang at the door of their apartment in the avenue Félix-Faure. When she turned up at Mme Mercier's with the letter from her brother, the latter had cried out, "Now I've seen everything!" After all that had happened, how did Jean-Melchior have the effrontery to ask her for a favor! Nonetheless she had not dared send Catherine away. She had taken her in grudgingly, as if she were someone who had only been prevented from taking up sides against her by circumstances. Chilled by this welcome, Catherine had tactlessly neglected to pay sufficient attention to the grievances being aired by Ernestine, with the result that, from the very next day, the latter had begun using the slightest pretext to lose her temper. Life had become unbearable, and Catherine had come back to Nice.

Contrary to what one might have expected, Annie received her husband's sister amiably. But when she learned that she had not come to Nice on her own initiative, that Jean-Melchior had invited her without saying a word, she shut herself up in her room. M. Oetlinger tried to go to her. The door was locked from the inside. He knocked several times. Annie finally let him in. Her eyelids and the shadows beneath her eyes were swollen but dry. It was only toward her cheekbones that one could make out damp traces which revealed she had been crying.

"She has to stay," she said to her husband, before he could say a word.

She was full of remorse. She regretted having given in to a fit of bad temper. Didn't this young woman have worries too? Wasn't her husband at the front? "Forget what I said," she added.

After dinner, tender and transformed, she suggested to Jean-Melchior that they go out. It was a hot evening. A warm wind came off the sea, slowly rocking the palm trees, which seemed part of a stage set, illuminated by the streetlights and the passing cars. Jean-Melchior had taken Annie's arm and pressed it against his side as they walked. Although their hips were touching, she walked, as always, slightly ahead of him, looking straight ahead. They walked along the promenade des Anglais, crossed the place Masséna, and took the avenue de la Gare. It was not late. A crowd of people had gathered in front of the *Petit Niçois* to read the communiqué. They sat down, as they liked to do, at the terrace of a large café. Suddenly Annie said, "I ought to telephone him." "Who?" asked Jean-Melchior. She did not reply. He understood then that the man in question was the famous M. Duncan she had been talking about for months and who, she claimed, was ready to pay her a fortune if she would agree to paint his portrait.

"So you really haven't noticed that this Monsieur Duncan makes fantastic promises to everyone, for the very good reason that he is a sordid miser."

Annie was struck by her husband's pallor. Rather than answering, as she had intended, and telling him he was mistaken, she looked at him for a long while, filled with worry. At that moment, a waiter approached M. and Mme Oetlinger. He was a tall, young, blue-eyed Swede, with a slightly lopsided jaw. Annie, who liked to recognize marks of distinction where no one else would think to look for them, squeezed Jean-Melchior's hand. He raised his eyes and was overwhelmed in turn by the waiter's beauty. "How old are you?" he asked him.

For the next few minutes he asked him all sorts of questions, while Annie looked on, amused. Then he wanted to know if he had children. The waiter replied that he had a little girl. Hearing that, M. Oetlinger extolled the joys of having children, with the result that the handsome waiter, after having taken a minute to assure himself that his interlocutor was not making fun of him, joined in this ode to paternity.

As they left the café, Annie began to laugh. "Why are you laughing?" asked her husband, who knew very well that she was laughing at his curious habit of seeking out paternal feelings in men who seemed least likely to have any.

FOUR

The next day, Jean-Melchior did not get up. He had been feverish throughout the night. For years, it had been his custom to drink as many as ten glasses of water before going to bed. When she left her family, Annie had been too young to have learned anything about the symptoms of illness. This abnormal thirst had never worried her. That morning, however, she called a doctor. In the afternoon, M. Oetlinger had an X-ray taken. He had several lesions on his lungs. What was more, he was diabetic. They needed to get him to Davos as quickly as possible.

In accordance with his father's wishes, Jean-Noël was entrusted to a Parisian family whose members had long been intrigued by the life of M. and Mme Oetlinger. The apartment was closed up, with the kitchen and one room left accessible to Catherine, who was going to stay on, there having been no time to make other arrangements for her.

Annie had always surrounded herself with nondescript people whose admiration for her spared her the minor tribulations of daily life. During the ordeal she now faced, M. Saglioni proved that the respectful devotion which he had always shown Mme Oetlinger was sincere. M. Saglioni was an old native of Nice, the son of tradesmen and a tradesman himself. He dabbled a bit in politics, had once been a town councillor, and was still president of an association to promote tourism. That evening, she hurried over to see him. In her panic, she not only told him about the current crisis but also about all of the problems that were overwhelming her. M. Saglioni's eagerness to be of assistance was increased tenfold by such a mark of trust. He reassured her. "Let me take care of it," he told her several times. He even offered to ask of one of his friend's lawyers what the best means of reducing Mme Mercier to silence would be. Mme Oetlinger found that she had to curb his overly zealous impulses, for she had no desire to do battle with a woman like Ernestine at such a difficult moment. She asked M. Saglioni to pay Mme Mercier a small amount of money every month and keep her informed of Jean-Melchior's condition. She instructed him not to divulge her new address under any pretext. She asked him to go to the avenue Félix-Faure from time to time, when he was not busy, and make sure that everything was in order there, that Catherine did not want for anything, and, to this end, gave him a key to the apartment. She also gave him the name of the family to which Jean-Noël had been entrusted so that he could inform the young man in case of some misfortune. She told him about the lease which she had been foolish enough to sign a few days earlier and asked him to do everything in his power to have it rescinded. In a word, she put everything in his hands, even the formalities to be completed at once at the Préfecture and the Swiss consulate. Two days later, accompanied by a nurse, she took Jean-Melchior to Davos.

M. and Mme Montigny had been living in a pretty property not far from the avenue Félix Faure for the past three months with their daughter, whose husband, Adrien Bérard, had been mobilized, and the latter's son by a previous wife who had died in childbirth. The boy was a school friend of Jean-Noël's, and it was through him, in fact, that the Oetlingers had become acquainted with the Montigny family. They had left Paris when the city had come under air attack. In search of relations as soon as they arrived in Nice, they soon sympathized with Annie and Jean-Melchior, who struck them as being what they referred to as Parisian types. Wasn't it agreeable, when in the provinces, to meet broad-minded people with whom one could converse, and with whom one had so many tastes in common?

Any excuse served them as a pretext to invite the Oetlingers, and preferably Annie. Thus, when she had gone to see them at Jean-Melchior's urging to ask them to take in Jean-Noël, they had accepted most willingly.

A month later, Jean-Noël, to whom no one had revealed the seriousness of his father's illness, and whom the Montignys were allowing to do as he pleased so as not to be outdone in liberal tendencies by M. and Mme Oetlinger, a situation he exploited by not returning to the lycée although he was about to face his examinations for the baccalaureate, managed to find Gisèle again. Much to his astonishment, he learned that, until he had been taken ill, M. Oetlinger had seen the young lady nearly every day, had taken her under his wing, signed her on at a charitable organization, and that thanks to him she had been hired in the slightly incongruous capacity of companion to an elderly Englishwoman. At first Jean-Noël thought that all of this was an invention. But Gisèle was able to supply him with so many details, in particular about his own family, that he soon stopped doubting her. That his father could have associated with a woman like Gisèle, obviously behind Annie's back, filled him with shame. It was so typical of his lack of dignity, which Jean-Noël found as afflicting as his mother's vulgarity. In spite of his humiliation, however, he resumed his liaison with Gisèle.

One day, she asked him to take her to the avenue Félix-Faure. She was curious to see where M. Oetlinger and Jean-Noël lived. He hesitated. The insinuations this young woman had made about his father had wounded him, and he realized that a visit to his parents' home would give rise to others. But Gisèle was so insistent that he yielded. Catherine let them in. The apartment was closed off, and Annie had put all the keys away in a desk that stood in the front hall. Jean-Noël managed to open it. For half an hour, he led Gisèle through the darkened apartment, without understanding what interest she could possibly have in trailing from one room to another. At last, to Jean-Noël's great relief, she announced she wanted to go. Just then, the buzzer that connected the apartment to the name-board downstairs under the arch near the entrance rang. For a moment he lost his head. What if it were his father, or Annie! But Gisèle, extremely self-possessed, had already opened the front door. "I'm going down," she said. "That way, no one will know we were together." A minute later, M. Saglioni, who had passed the young woman on the stairs but who suspected nothing, rang at the front door, which was opened by Jean-Noël, who had meanwhile closed and locked all the doors and put the keys back into the desk. M. Saglioni was startled to find the young man in the apartment, but made no connection between this coincidence and the person he had just seen on the stairs. "I needed a book," said Jean-Noël, signaling to Catherine to back up his story, even though he had never exchanged more than a few words with her. Wasn't she a member of his father's family? And because of that, wasn't she expected to do what was asked of her? But as soon as Jean-Noël had left, M. Saglioni interrogated Catherine. She told him what had happened. He recalled the young woman he had passed on the stairs. He briefly thought of telling Annie what he knew, but then again, didn't she have enough worries? Nonetheless, he went to pay a visit to M. Montigny and told him what he had learned quite accidentally. It so happened that M. Montigny had just received a letter from Annie. She wrote that the end was near and, no doubt because of her suffering, failed to mention Jean-Noël. "Poor woman!" said M. Saglioni after reading the letter, his tone of voice implying that Mme Oetlinger had further reasons to be unhappy.

Following this visit, everyone became much more guarded around Jean-Noël. As his greatest fear was that the Montignys would learn that Annie was not his mother, he grew convinced that Mme Mercier had carried out the threat she had made two days earlier. She had come to wait for him after school to ask him for Jean-Melchior's address. M. Saglioni had already refused to give it to her, which had sent her into such a rage that she had gone so far as to say that Jean-Melchior was fit as a fiddle, and that this illness was only a pretext to rid himself of her. Ordered to divulge the address, Jean-Noël had given in. Ever since, he had been afraid that, far from being grateful to him, Mme Mercier would use the absence of M. Oetlinger, who was the only person who could stop her, to broadcast the fact that she was his mother. As a result, it never occurred to him that there might be another reason for the change in the Montignys' attitude toward him. He was paralyzed by the same embarrassment that had overcome him at Mr. Stevenson's. Every meal was an ordeal. He thought he intercepted contemptuous smiles. From one day to the next, he stopped speaking to the young Bérard boy, his school friend. But whereas his suffering was confined to his vanity, his father, meanwhile, was slowly dying. Annie no longer left his side. From time to time he had lucid intervals. The first thing he would ask, then, was for news of Jean-Noël. She would answer that he was working diligently, that everyone was proud of him. One evening, as she was praising the young man, knowing that was what he most liked to hear, he interrupted her. Haltingly, he told her the story of his son's liaison with Gisèle and begged her to take great care, after his death, not to let Jean-Noël associate with the wrong sort of people. This tale so surprised Annie that at first she failed to comprehend that it had happened some time ago. When this became clear to her a short time later, she had to leave her husband's side to cry, not because she was hurt that he had hidden Jean-Noël's unseemly behavior from her, but because she had been struck by the contrast of the importance it would have had in her eyes several months before with its insignificance now, in the face of death. In the days that followed, as if her problems needed to multiply for her to perceive them clearly in the midst of her suffering, Mme Oetlinger first received a letter from M. Saglioni preparing her for the unpleasantness which awaited her upon her return, and then two others: one, rather cold, from the Montignys; the other from Ernestine Mercier, in which she hypocritically pretended to be moved by her son's love for his mother. Hadn't he given her the address she needed? The letter ended with the announcement of her impending arrival, saying that M. Oetlinger needed her care as much as that of a scheming woman. This last threat was only to trouble Annie for a few hours. That very evening, which happened to be the autumn equinox, as a gale blew over the mountain above them, Jean-Melchior breathed his last.

A few days later, M. Saglioni, the Montignys, Mme Bérard and Jean-Noël went to meet Mme Oetlinger at the station. On the platform, everyone talked about the woman who was being so cruelly tested. M. Saglioni even allowed himself a certain display of emotion. He pointed out, and was entirely supported in this by the Montignys, whose feelings for Annie did not justify their having taken the trouble to turn out in such large numbers, that it was perhaps better for Mme Oetlinger that her husband had died. He had not been from her milieu. There was no denying, certainly, that they had been a devoted couple, but hadn't that union been achieved at the cost of sacrifices made by Annie alone? Whereas now, once her grief had passed, one could imagine that she would lead a life more in keeping with the upbringing she had received. It was difficult to guess what she would choose to do, but she should be encouraged to go back to her family, in spite of how sorry all of them would be to see her go. The war was bound to end one day. A new life could then begin for her. Who was to say, she might even come back to Nice later.

The train entered the station. Strung out along the platform like sentries, the members of the little group each watched one railway car. When Annie appeared, dressed in black, thinner and even more beautiful, the honor of being the first to greet her fell to M. Saglioni.

"How are you, dear M. Saglioni? How is everything here?"

she asked immediately, to demonstrate that she was perfectly composed, and that the others need not involve themselves in her suffering.

M. Saglioni drove her to the avenue Félix-Faure, while Jean-Noël, in spite of the efforts he made to stay with his stepmother, found himself sent back to the Montignys.

It was only a month later, as Annie was organizing her departure, that she noticed that a number of objects she cared for had disappeared. She called M. Saglioni. It was then that he recalled, not just his chance meeting at the avenue Félix-Faure, but something else which had happened a few days later and to which he had paid no particular attention at the time. While visiting one of his friends, a hotelier, he had seen crossing the lobby the young girl Catherine had told him about. He had asked who she was. "She is the maid of one of our guests," he had been told. "In fact, that reminds me, the woman complained that she could not find one of her rings." M. Saglioni immediately made the connection between that disappearance and the ones Mme Oetlinger had just brought to his attention. He went back to the hotel, where he learned that Gisèle Orlandini had been hired on the recommendation of M. Oetlinger. Everything now became clear to him. This Gisèle must have worked for M. and Mme Oetlinger. During that time she had appropriated the objects which were now missing. He was, in additon, almost certain that her relations with Jean-Noël were rather different from what they should have been. The next time he saw Annie, he brought her up to date on the results of his investigations. Mme Oetlinger did not recall ever having employed a servant by the name of Gisèle, and for good reason. He specified that she was tall, dark-haired, and very pretty, and that there could be no doubt whatsoever about her, as she had a recommendation signed by M. Oetlinger. Annie grew pale. She suddenly remembered what her husband had told her about Jean-Noël's affair. Something had gone on, something about which she wanted to know nothing more. She answered that in fact she did remember Gisèle, who had been extremely trustworthy, and added that, furthermore, she had since found the missing objects. To change the subject, she asked M. Saglioni if he had met with the owner of the apartment she had rented. M. Saglioni, who tried to conceal anything from Mme Oetlinger which might upset her, was forced to confess that the owner refused even to discuss canceling the lease. "It doesn't matter," said Annie, who was anxious to be left alone.

It was only after she had restored some sense of order to her life that she agreed to let her stepson come back to live with her at the avenue Félix-Faure. Ever since learning that he had a secret life, a man's life, and especially since this had been confirmed to her by M. Saglioni, it had struck her that she lacked the necessary authority to guide him, and that it was best to leave him where he was, which, incidentally, was far from pleasing to the Montignys, who were beginning to fear, as Mr. Stevenson had done for his boarders, that Jean-Noël was setting a deplorable example for their grandson.

Annie soon regretted having been so quick to take Jean-Noël back. Before leaving Nice, she was absolutely determined to clear up any affairs she had in abeyance, so as not to leave anything behind that could be held against her someday. This was born as much out of her concern not to seem ungrateful to all those who had shown her their kindness as it was to ensure that, in future, she would never find herself in the midst of such disorder again. M. Saglioni was doing everything in his power to help her settle her affairs. He tried to appeal to the sentiments of those who had some claim against her by depicting Mme Oetlinger as a woman who had been a victim of her own generosity throughout her life. As there had been complications at every turn—the importance of which she exaggerated to herself to such an extent that, each time, she put off her departure—she had thought that she could very well leave Jean-Noël with the Montignys, which would have spared her the ironic comments her stepson never failed to make concerning M. Saglioni's dedication. Jean-Noël could not bear the gentleman and his constant shortness of breath. He believed he was responsible for the fact that Annie took no notice of his advice and wanted none of the protection with which he would have been so proud and happy to surround her.

Finally, in January of 1916, after a great many problems caused by an incapacity of ten years' standing to take charge of her own life, Annie left for Paris, accompanied by Jean-Noël.

FIVE

M. and Mme Villemur were so overjoyed to have Annie back, and free once more, that for the first month they hardly noticed the presence of Jean-Noël. Nor, in fact, did Mme Oetlinger try to impose him upon them as though he were her son. For example, if her father asked her to make some observation to the young man, she would comply without feeling at all put out. She was anxious to make her parents understand that she was not going to burden them, either with her grief or with what remained of her marriage, which was not to suggest that she had any regrets whatever. As for Jean-Noël, he was filled with pride at finding himself sharing such a luxurious style of life and had adopted the attitude of a son who knows his mother has suffered from her family's injustice but who, like her, has forgiven them—notwithstanding which he continued to harbor a certain grudge against them.

One evening, without looking up from the newspaper he was reading, in other words as if the question were of no importance, M. Villemur asked him whether he had any family in Paris. From the start, Annie had imposed certain conditions if he was to come to the avenue de Malakoff with her. The most important of these was that there was to be no mention of the past. She had also instructed her stepson never to discuss her, or Jean-Melchior, or Mme Mercier. He therefore avoided answering the question. Claiming that it was merely out of curiosity, M. Villemur pressed him, forcing

Jean-Noël to search his memory. He had an uncle, and an aunt, he thought.

"But don't you have a mother?" asked M. Villemur.

"I don't know," answered Jean-Noël, blushing furiously.

M. Villemur found this a most amusing reply, one that even a child would not have produced.

"What do you mean, you don't know if you have a mother?"

Jean-Noël, growing redder by the minute, brought out a confused explanation. He had a mother, but he did not know her. When he next saw Annie, he carefully avoided mentioning this conversation, all too aware of how ridiculous he had sounded. Shortly thereafter, Mme Villemur's older sister, Mlle Yvonne de Falais, who had not seen her niece since the latter's marriage, came to Paris for a few days. She was a prying, wicked little woman in whose eyes Annie was nothing less than a monster. "What a handsome boy!" she said when Jean-Noël was introduced to her. Then, taking advanatge of the fact that Mme Oetlinger had left the room, she bombarded him with questions. This time Jean-Noël, who was less intimidated by Mlle de Falais than by M. Villemur, sidestepped them without difficulty. All the prouder of himself for having felt so ashamed the day before, he told his stepmother about the interrogation to which Mlle de Falais had subjected him. Annie complained to her father.

"Tante Yvonne," she told him, "is too curious. Papa, you know what I told you when I first arrived."

She reminded M. Villemur that she had begged him to ensure that she be left alone, and that he had given her his word. She was no longer a young girl. She was thirty-three years old. She had just lost her husband. She was suffering. She felt no shame in saying so. She would never try to hide the fact that she had loved Jean-Melchior. She asked only two things: to be left alone and in peace.

M. Villemur did his best to calm her. He even promised he would have a word with his sister-in-law. But from that point on he grew suspicious of Jean-Noël, even though the latter was quite harmless: his only ambition was to be regarded as Annie's son, his only fear, just as in the years he had spent in Nice, was that his mother appear. Therefore, when he recognized Mme Mercier's childish handwriting a few days later on a letter addressed to him, he began to tremble. She was informing him of her return to Paris. She had not yet recovered from the news of Jean-Melchior's death; she needed to be comforted. She was asking her son to come see her. She expressed her surprise that he had not come to Menton before leaving Nice. Doubtless he would never have bothered to get in touch with her had she not written to him first. Jean-Noël's initial thought was to tell his stepmother. Upon reflection he did not do so. Annie lost her head if she so much as heard Mme Mercier's name mentioned. That night, he slept poorly. What should he do? If he did not go to his mother, she would come to him. The mere thought of such a prospect gave him unpleasant hot flashes. If he did go, it would have to be in secret. He decided that the wisest course of action would be to show the letter and do as he was told. But when he reread it, his attention was drawn to this passage: "I don't think it was the Scheming Woman who prevented you from coming to see me in Menton. In any case, I will find out. If she did, you will both regret it." No, he could not show Annie this letter. The best thing to do was for him to go to the address Mme Mercier had given him. At eighteen one is no longer a child. He would know how to reason with his mother. He would promise to help her later. Now that his father was gone, he would replace him. It was his desire to take on all of M. Oetlinger's responsibilities. Hadn't he already fancied, immediately after Jean-Melchior's death, that this desire was going to be fulfilled?

When he went to see his mother, the first thing she asked him was whether Annie had been informed of his visit. He answered that she had not.

"Are you ashamed of your mother, then?" she cried.

She burst into floods of tears. She and Emile could not possibly survive on the sum of money she had been given. It was certainly no accident that M. Oetlinger had been taken abroad to die. Now it was easy to say he had left no will.

"If you are a good son," she went on, "you will demand that I be given what is due me."

Jean-Noël replied that he would like nothing better than to do just that, but he thought it would be awkward, for Annie did not like to be told what she was duty-bound to do. He fully realized that by letting his mother think he agreed with her, he had adopted an ambiguous attitude.

"If you don't demand it, I will." With that threat ringing in his ears, he left. As soon as he was alone, he reproached himself for having allowed such a situation to develop. Finally, he made up his mind to speak to Annie, but rather than simply telling her the truth, he thought it artful to depict the meeting he had just left as a humorous incident.

"She is in Paris!" cried Mme Oetlinger.

A week earlier, she had received a long letter from M. Saglioni. He had settled everything. However, he warned Annie to be on her guard against Mme Mercier. When he had gone to pay her the five thousand francs which Mme Oetlinger had given him for this purpose, she had cried out: "It's a hundred thousand francs I'm owed! When you steal a woman's husband, you have to pay. She won't get the best of me. You can tell her." Such threats did not have to be taken seriously. Ernestine Mercier had no recourse against Mme Oetlinger.

"And did she tell you she would come here?" asked Annie.

"That would have been a bit much!" replied Jean-Noël, laughing.

Mme Oetlinger was far from sharing her stepson's optimism, and when the next day she received a letter from Mme Mercier filled with grievances, one of which was that Annie, not satisfied with having stolen her husband, was now preventing Jean-Noël from seeing her, it struck her that his optimism had served only to conceal his obvious complicity. She called in her stepson and read him the letter. It seemed the poor boy was being held against his will, that he longed to be with his mother.

"That's not true!" cried Jean-Noël.

Annie, upon whom sincerity had no effect, refused to listen to him.

"If you have any criticisms to make of me," she told him, "then address them to me, but I beg of you, spare me any more letters like this in the future. My dear child, you know perfectly well that I have always done everything I could to ensure you would be happy."

She added that she was perfectly willing to accept the fact that he might have desires which he chose not to reveal to her. If he thought that it would be easier to fulfill these if he was free, she would have no objection to his leaving the avenue de Malakoff. But if he stayed, he would have to see to it that his behavior did not become a source of embarrassment. She had already put herself in a delicate position on his behalf. "Don't think that because my father says nothing to me about you, he is overjoyed to have you living in his home." In fact, M. Villemur had made no secret of his impatience for his son, Henri, to come home on leave. One of the latter's friends, a man originally from Bern, was now director of a laboratory located near the stock market. He was short of staff, and M. Villemur had thought that Jean-Noël might find a job there while waiting to be called up, since he had made no mention of enlisting. But nothing could be done until Henri's return.

A few days later, Mme Villemur had a long conversation with her daughter. It might seem astonishing that she had waited two months to do so. The reason for it was that, out of sheer contrariness, this capricious old woman always did the opposite of what was expected of her. Upon her daughter's return, in other words at the very moment when she should have been brimming with joy, she had seemed utterly indifferent, but now that life had resumed its course, she had, in the last week, become more demonstrative.

"I don't know," she told Annie, "if you are behaving as you should. Don't you think this young man, whom, as you told me yourself, your husband loved so deeply, is acquiring bad habits? I know that he is going to be a soldier soon, but shouldn't he be working in the meantime? He will certainly need to earn a living once the war is over. If he were to get a job now, in a bank for example, or in some commercial enterprise, he would learn a trade and make contacts that would be useful to him later."

Mme Oetlinger replied that she was entirely in agreement with this, and that in fact she and her father were only waiting for Henri's return to take the necessary steps.

"What's that! Henri is coming home on leave?" cried the old woman.

It was only then that Annie remembered her father's injunction not to speak of Henri's leave, for ever since Bertrand had been mortally wounded on the very day he was due to come home on leave, Mme Villemur had been convinced that a similar fate awaited her second son. That evening, Mme Villemur asked her husband why it was that Henri's forthcoming leave had been kept a secret from her. Once he had managed to calm his overwrought wife, M. Villemur took Annie aside.

"I begged you," he told her, "not to mention Henri. Why did you take no notice of what I asked of you?"

To atone for such an act of forgetfulness, Mme Oetlinger related what she had been told of Jean-Noël's visit to his mother. Then she produced the insolent letter Mme Mercier had sent her. M. Villemur grew pale with anger.

"This is unthinkable!" he said. "If the boy loves his mother more—which is his right, I would even add, his duty—all he needs to do is go to her. No one is preventing him. Quite the contrary."

But although she seemed to treat her stepson with indifference, Annie nonetheless felt duty-bound to be a mother to him, in memory of her husband. She asked her father to show some indulgence to a young man who would soon be going off to war. M. Villemur then rounded on his daughter. That evening, he summoned Jean-Noël to his study. "You have now reached an age," he said, "at which one can speak to you as a man. You are not unaware of the situation my daughter finds herself in vis-à-vis Madame Mercier. If you feel that your rightful place is with your mother rather than here, which, I might hasten to add, would be entirely natural, just say so. My daughter has suffered enough—and brought it upon herself, I might add—and deserves to be left in peace now."

In reply, Jean-Noël, who was anxious to please, admitted that he had been wrong. He had gone to see his mother because he had not realized what the consequences of such a visit would be. Then, because he thought he detected a hint of animosity toward Annie in his interlocutor, he added that she was in no way responsible for what had happened.

"Your young protégé seems eager to defend you," M. Villemur said to his daughter a few moments later.

She was wounded by her father's ironic tone. She then questioned Jean-Noël so harshly about what he could possibly have said to M. Villemur that the young man lost his composure. He began to cry. No one loved him. Everything he did was turned against him. Mme Oetlinger looked at him impassively. "Come now, Jean-Noël," she said, laying a hand on his shoulder, which made him cry all the more," be strong."

SIX

Jean-Noël's continued presence at the avenue de Malakoff provoked further incidents. One of these was particularly disagreeable. It took place in July. Henri had just arrived in Paris. During his previous leave, in March, M. Villemur had asked him to recommend Jean-Noël to Berthoud. Henri had refused, and no one had asked him what his reasons were; a man who risked his life daily owed explanations to no one. He had refused because although Jean-Noël was not yet old enough to be called up to serve, there was nothing to prevent him from enlisting, if only for the honor of the Oetlinger family, of which no member, to his knowledge, had ever served the French nation from which they had nonetheless all known how to profit so well. When Henri had seen him four months later, still ensconced in the midst of his family, he had been unable to conceal his ill humor. Thus, when he was told one morning that Mme Mercier was asking to see Annie, he rushed out to meet her himself. In a few words, he made her understand that she was not welcome at the avenue de Malakoff, and before she left, speechless with shock at the way in which she had been received, he pointed to her and told the servants to remember this woman, and to send her away if she ever had the audacity to come back.

Although she heard only her brother's account of this scene, Mme Oetlinger was nonetheless badly shaken. A few days later, Henri left to return to the front. She accompanied him to the station.

"If I have one piece of advice to give you," he said in the midst of the shouts and whistles, "it's to induce Jean-Noël to enlist. Look at me, I'm going. It's everyone's fate. See, I'm not the only one. If he's lucky, he'll come back, if not, too bad. In any case, it will be better for both of you."

The train began to move. Annie walked alongside it, keeping her brother company. Jostling for a place at the door, he added: "Don't think that I want everyone to have to go to the front just because I have to."

Upon her return, Annie did not have the heart to follow her brother's advice. If it occurred to Jean-Noël to enlist without her having anything to do with it, of course she would not try to dissuade him; otherwise, everything would remain as it was. But what was she to do with this boy? Ever since his mother's notorious visit, he had been receiving a letter nearly every week from Mme Mercier, which, although addressed only to him, was nonetheless written with the expectation that it would also be read by Mme Oetlinger. Jean-Noël, who wanted to make sure there would be no recurrence of the unpleasantness he had experienced, now turned over everything he received to Annie. Because of her stepson, she was being forced to think constantly about the past, when all she wanted was never to hear it spoken of again. Her family no longer made any remarks to her about Jean-Noël. She knew that their silence concealed animosity toward the young man. They were not going to forgive her for having brought a stranger into their midst. But hadn't she promised her husband to look after this boy? And even if she hadn't promised him, wasn't it her duty to do so? Nonetheless, it had become impossible for Jean-Noël to stay at the avenue de Malakoff any longer. She began to consider a number of ways in which she could part from Jean-Noël while retaining some authority over him, without which, as Jean-Melchior had said, he ran the risk of committing the gravest sorts of errors. None of her ideas withstood serious scrutiny. Mme Oetlinger could not ask any of her childhood friends to do her the favor of taking in Jean-Noël as a lodger. In spite of the hugging and kissing that had marked their reunions, there now lingered an uneasiness born of Annie's long period of indifference toward them. She had gone away as if she alone were brave enough to marry a man she loved. She had stayed in touch with no one. While they pretended to admire the courage she had shown, secretly they criticized her for her provincial manners; for the way she changed the subject whenever they spoke to her of the ten years she had spent away from Paris, which they were all curious about; for the young man who was with her now, and who looked like a child born of adultery. There remained her parents' and brothers' friends, like the baronne de Berthoud, the mother of Henri's friend, who claimed to be an aristocrat from Bern and now had to take in lodgers as a result of reversals of fortune she had suffered some fifteen years earlier and about which she was still given to conversing with anyone who approached her. But wasn't someone quite different needed to supervise Jean-Noël? Annie did not know exactly what transgressions he had been guilty of in Nice. Nonetheless, she was convinced they had been serious. Therefore, she could no more think of entrusting Jean-Noël to Mme Berthoud than to a boarding school, where he would have been surrounded by young men of his own age. To prepare him for the struggles that lay ahead, he needed to be given some experience of life, to be hardened, to become a man. Four more months were to go by, however, before he left the avenue Malakoff.

In the early days of December 1916, Annie was having breakfast with her mother one morning when the latter suddenly passed the newspaper across to her. A list of nominees for the Légion d'Honneur included the name Doctor Martin Oetlinger.

"Who is this Martin Oetlinger?" asked her mother.

"It must be Jean-Melchior's older brother."

Annie had a vague recollection of the man, whom she had seen on four or five occasions around the time of her marriage. He had made a rather bad impression upon her. He had stared deep into her eyes for a long moment, as if he wanted to bewitch her. He had asked her how a young girl of her class could love Jean-Melchior, though he had said nothing whatsoever that was detrimental to his brother. She had never related these conversations to her husband, and had been left with the impression that Martin was not overly fond of his younger brother. To learn that her husband's brother had been leading such a meritorious life eleven years later, at a moment when, although she had no regrets about having married, she was nonetheless aware of having been overly enthusiastic, made her reflect that she had judged him, as she had judged life, like a schoolgirl. How proud M. Oetlinger would have been, had he still been alive, of the honor his brother had just received, a brother he had always spoken of with admiration and respect! Annie recalled that when Jean-Melchior died, M. Saglioni had taken it upon himself to notify her husband's family. Had he really done so? Shouldn't she have written to Martin herself, ignoring the advice of M. Saglioni, who had recommended she not do so because he thought she was surrounded by people who were only after her money? It was not regret at recognizing a man's merits only after he has achieved renown which brought on these pangs of conscience, but rather the idea that Martin would be an excellent guardian for Jean-Noël. The latter was due to be called up by the draft in four months. Had it been only four days, she would still have gone, as she did the following day, to the rue Claude-Bernard. After being made to wait for half an hour, she was shown into Doctor Oetlinger's office. He was now a man of forty-five. He greeted Mme Oetlinger coldly, as if the only possible reason for her visit must be to ask something of him. Annie immediately turned the conversation to Jean-Noël. He was now a grown-up young man, about to turn nineteen. She emphasized the fact that she was not his mother and that, as a result, she had no power over him. She then spoke of Jean-Melchior, of his dreams, his illness, the battles she had fought with her family in order to marry him, and the utter helplessness she had felt when he died, which had prevented her from writing to anyone. Upon her return, her father had made her feel welcome, but nonetheless she was in an awkward situation. Finally, she asked Martin Oetlinger if he would not take charge of Jean-Noël until April, when the 1918 recruits were due to be mobilized. This did not imply that she had no interest in the boy's fate. But wouldn't it be wiser? A single woman had so little influence on a young man.

"Why," asked the doctor, "does this boy quite simply not go back to his mother?"

He pretended to know nothing of his brother's contempt for Ernestine Mercier. Annie reminded him of the sort of woman she was, and of how Jean-Melchior, if he were still alive, would have suffered at knowing his son was in her clutches. M. Oetlinger replied that this was mere conjecture. As his brother was dead, it was difficult to know what he would have said or thought. And besides, life was life. One's dreams did not always come true. In fact, Jean-Noël was old enough not to need anyone's advice. He was a man now, and neither his uncle, his mother, or even Annie could prevent him from behaving badly if that was what he wanted to do. Although Martin Oetlinger was expressing himself in measured terms, he was nonetheless deriving considerable pleasure from ridiculing his brother's aspirations and playing the part of the superior man in Annie's presence.

"I don't understand terribly well," he went on, "what it is my brother hoped to make of his son."

And yet, he was no stranger to the fact that life was made of ups and downs. It was true that the unfortunate Jean-Melchior had been utopic, had dreamt of the impossible. The situation he had left behind was so muddled that there was no need to look further for proof of his incompetence, and yet his desires were now being treated with the utmost respect!

Annie did not dare interrupt Martin Oetlinger. She found him unpleasant, with the air he adopted of a man who knows he has been spoken ill of but who, conscious of his worth, pretends not to care. "Since you took the trouble to come,

Madame, I will gladly give you a bit of advice; that's all I can do," he said to her.

Annie returned home with a heavy heart. She no longer had her husband to make her forget life's little irritations through his charm and kindness. That day, by a singular stroke of fate, M. Villemur imparted an idea to her which, according to him, had just struck his fancy. "Why don't you tell Jean-Noël to go back to his mother's?" In order to convince his daughter, he used virtually the same arguments as Doctor Oetlinger had. Jean-Noël had become a man. A woman, even his mother, could no longer have any influence on his character.

Annie refused to hear any more. She had spent too many years believing that Mme Mercier was a harmful person to bring herself to let her take Jean-Noël now. Her husband appeared before her eyes. He seemed resigned, and yet at the same time there was something reproachful in his gaze. No, it was impossible. The next day Mme Villemur, who had been drilled in what to say, tried in turn to convince Annie, appealing to her daughter's feminine sensitivities and emphasizing the fact that as Jean-Melchior was now dead, any bitter feelings from the past ought to be forgotten. Ernestine Mercier might not be as bad a mother as everyone thought. Who was to say that the day she was reunited with her son might not be the most wonderful day of her life? Mme Oetlinger was unyielding, and Jean-Noël continued to live at the avenue de Malakoff. She had not, however, given up hope of persuading Doctor Oetlinger to look after Jean-Noël, if not immediately then at least at a later time. "I would like you to go see your uncle," she said to Jean-Noël one day. He told her that he would. She then wrote M. Oetlinger saying that she had persuaded her stepson to come to see him, which made her very happy, as she thought it her duty to put him in touch with people who could have a good influence upon him. Jean-Noël, however, kept putting off the visit. He was ashamed of anything that had to do with his father's family. Annie insisted several times. Having grown weary, she wrote the doctor again, as if he were a long-standing confidant, and complained of Jean-Noël's unwillingness. Martin Oetlinger was much annoyed by this second letter. The previous day he had written Annie to inform her that he had heard nothing from his nephew. This sign of life, which he sent a fortnight after having received Annie's first letter, betrayed an obvious desire to remain in contact with her. Annie, who had just sent him her letter, thought it unnecessary to reply. A week later, she received a new letter from Martin Oetlinger. He thanked her for having written, alluded to the fact that their two letters had crossed in the mail, and, without specifying a reason, asked if they could meet. A few days later, he came to the avenue de Malakoff. Ushered into a sitting room, he pretended not to notice the objets d'art and to be interested only in the real merit of the person with whom he was conversing. As if eager to make it clear that this visit concerned only Jean-Noël, he immediately explained his reasons for coming. He could do nothing for his nephew. But he did have a friend. In that opulent Villemur milieu, he was proud to be able to say that he, too, had people to whom he extended his charity. This friend had just been declared unfit for military service. He was experiencing great financial difficulties. He would be happy to take charge of Jean-Noël. Of course, and this was said in the tone of one general speaking to another general about a soldier, he would have to be given some financial assistance. At this, Annie became wary. She had heard it so many times in her life. After the doctor had left, she told her father what had just transpired, but in such a way as to make the offer her brother-in-law (how she hated that word!) had made seem unhoped for, so that M. Villemur would not suspect, as she had done, that Martin Oetlinger had something to gain from the fact that one of his friends was taking Jean-Noël in as a lodger. In spite of his impatience to get rid of Jean-Noël, M. Villemur told Annie that even though they were discussing the son of a man of no consequence, he would not turn him over to a stranger without first knowing something about him. He asked her for more information about the doctor's friend. Although Annie was unable to supply any, M. Villemur, who felt that from the moment he had voiced his disapproval he had done his duty, declared a few moments later that there was probably no cause for concern since this friend had been recommended by Jean-Noël's uncle.

Annie therefore went back to the rue Claude-Bernard. On the twentieth of January 1917, she and Jean-Noël were taken by Martin Oetlinger to the home of the very deserving friend we just mentioned. After having exchanged a few words with him, she left, leaving him her stepson. But several hours later, using the most banal excuse imaginable—to wit that he wanted a breath of fresh air—Jean-Noël went to the local army command post in the rue de Lille, not to volunteer, as it was now too late for that, but rather to enlist in anticipation of his call-up date, though without exercising the option this gave him to choose his branch of service.

SEVEN

Jean-Noël was assigned to an infantry regiment from Reims that was then headquartered in Brittany. He was just learning how to execute an about-face on the parade ground when he came down with the mumps, with the result that, even though he had signed on ahead of time, he shared the fate of the young men of his year who'd been called up. In July he arrived with them in the war zone. In October he was sent to the regimental depot. A fortnight later he went up to the front lines. In February of 1920 he was discharged. He had spent just over three years in active service.

Every time he had come to Paris on leave, he had been received most cordially by the Villemurs. During one of his stays, Annie had even painted a portrait of him wearing his helmet. Far from being considered a rash, impulsive move, the fact that he had anticipated his call-up on the very day when he was to have taken up residence in the home of Martin Oetlinger's friend had won him everyone's sympathy. He had regularly been sent "parcels." He and Annie had exchanged touching letters. But when he returned to the avenue de Malakoff wearing civilian clothing, the welcome he received was nothing like those which had been extended to him during each of his leaves in Paris. A very different atmosphere now reigned in the apartment, which he had described to all his army friends, winning the esteem of a few officers. The ponderous tranquillity that had added to the solemnity of the vast rooms, the memory of which still impressed him today, had been replaced by joyful animation. The phone rang constantly, friends came to call. Henri had been demobilized a few months earlier. A sister of Annie's had come to live at the avenue de Malakoff with her husband. M. and Mme Villemur entertained every week. It was in the midst of this revival that Jean-Noël saw Annie again. A month went by during which it seemed that never again would serious matters be broached. One day, however, she asked him what he intended to do with himself. When he seemed to hesitate, her face darkened. Banks, government offices, private enterprises were all in need of young men. The entire world was thinking only of rebuilding what the war had destroyed, and he had no plans! No, this could not be. She must have misunderstood.

"You know, my dear Jean-Noël," said Annie, changing the subject the way one does when wishing to remain pleasant in spite of having reasons for not doing so, "that there are quite a few of us now living here at home. Have you been back to the Hôtel des Grands Hommes, that hotel we lived in, if you remember, with your father? It was charming, wasn't it? You could rent a room there for now, and of course come and take most of your meals here."

Until the spring, therefore, Jean-Noël was able to maintain the pretense that he was a part of the Villemur family, and that he had only been asked to live outside the home for reasons of convenience. Annie had not spoken to him again about the future. More to forgive Jean-Noël his indecision than out of any sense of remorse, she regretted having been in such a hurry to know what his plans were and had decided to wait until he chose to speak about them himself. Time passed, however, and he remained silent on the subject. It was just when Annie had resolved to ask him what this silence was concealing that an incident between her and her stepson occurred. Among Henri's army friends there was one Annie could not bear, a man named Simon Wurtzel, whose father owned a number of tanneries in the Gobelins district. He was a ruddy man of thirty-six who was rather flattered to find himself a guest of the Villemurs. Upon learning that Annie had once been married to an Alsatian, he had hastened to tell her that he was originally from Mulhouse himself, and that in fact his father remembered an Oetlinger family very well. Try as Annie had to make him understand that this coincidence caused her no pleasure, he had nonetheless adopted a conspiratorial air around her that infuriated her. He sometimes brought his sister Odile with him, who was then nineteen, and as he had recommended that she be particularly amiable to Mme Oetlinger, the young girl thought it clever to imitate her brother. She was exceptionally beautiful, and the only flaw one could reproach her with was that she was a bit short. Jean-Noël had noticed her immediately, especially as she was one of the few young girls his age who came to the avenue de de Malakoff. It had not been long before the idea occurred to him that he might marry her. Judging by the way in which she was welcomed, Mlle Wurtzel doubtless came from a very good family. Moreover, he was not indifferent to her beauty. She sometimes gave him long, searching looks. Whenever she found herself alone with him, she was unable to conceal the turmoil she felt. One evening, during a party the Wurtzels were giving at their home at 123, boulevard du Montparnasse, Jean-Noël took her hand in his and told her that he loved her. They were both leaning on the balcony in the bedroom of Odile's younger brother, Maurice. It was eleven o'clock, and for the first time that year the night was warm. "Are you truly able to love?" she asked him.

After much hesitation, he decided to reveal his love to his stepmother. He did so with all the pride of a son whose independence has always been respected and who wishes to show that he has been worthy of this confidence. Wouldn't Mme Oetlinger be pleased that the example of her own marriage had not had any negative influence on her stepson, and that he had already understood that the way to happiness lay in not drawing attention to oneself? But Annie grew angry as soon as she heard him mention the name Odile Wurtzel. She did not wish to discuss those people. They thought that because she had once loved a man from Mulhouse she had to like them? It was only then that Jean-Noël realized that this marriage, which he had imagined would win him the Villemurs' esteem, would on the contrary close all doors to him. He was so surprised by this that he dared to ask his stepmother to explain further. She informed him that the Wurtzels were only received by her family because Henri had spent part of the war with Simon.

"I had no idea," said Jean-Noël.

Mme Oetlinger looked at him the way she did when she was not sure she had understood him correctly.

"What do you mean?" she asked him.

"I mean that if I had known, I would not have committed myself the way I did."

Now Annie lost her temper. Jean-Noël did not even love this young girl. So he had been thinking of making one of those marriages she had so often seen in her milieu, and which she so abhorred!

"Even had this young lady been from an excellent family," she said in one breath, "I would have been just as opposed to your marrying her."

She added that, at a time when there were so many fine and great things to be done, no strong, intelligent young man should be thinking of making a bourgeois marriage. What did he hope to accomplish by leading a coddled, pampered life with a woman who had money? Didn't he realize that the entire world was looking to the future, that all around him men were eager to tackle difficulties in order to reap the glory of having overcome them? And this was the moment he chose to court a tanner's daughter!

"Have you even thought of what you would like to be?"

"Yes," replied a slightly shamefaced Jean-Noël. "I want to finish my studies. I intend to study the law, as my father wished."

"And what are you going to live on while you do that? You know very well that I have no more money, and that I don't wish to ask my family for anything."

Jean-Noël made no reply.

"Listen to me," said Annie, calming down. "I'm not telling you this to be disagreeable, but you must find work. Once you grow accustomed to the idea, work will become indispensable to you. You have fought a war, you are a man. You're free. Everything will come right for you, but only on condition that you want it to. Of course, you will have to force yourself to do without certain things, and you will have to struggle; but think of the satisfaction you will feel years from now when, from the vantage point of the place you will have earned by your own merit, you look back upon the road you traveled."

Out of fear of meeting Odile, but also to show his stepmother that her advice, for which he thanked her, had nonetheless led him to the conclusion that she was not overly fond of him, he did not reappear at the avenue de Malakoff for several days. And yet, upon returning to the hotel every evening, he could not prevent himself from stopping to ask whether anyone had telephoned for him. Wasn't this the first time since being discharged from the army that he had gone so long without seeing Annie? Was she worried about him? Finally one morning, he found himself rushing down to the hotel's front desk. Mme Oetlinger was asking for him on the telephone. Without making the slightest allusion to her stepson's absence, she asked him to come and see her at his earliest convenience—assuming of course that this would not disturb him, for, needless to say, if he had something else to do, she could always wait. As he hung up, it struck Jean-Noël that his stepmother must think that if he hadn't been back, it was because he had been so struck by what she had said that he had immediately found himself a job, and that he already had no more time to himself. Annie's first words to him, in fact, were to ask if he had found work.

"No," he replied ill-humoredly.

"Fine, in that case, I am going to suggest something to you."

She went on to tell him that she wanted him to meet one

[56]

of her friends, a manufacturer. She'd had a long conversation with him a few days earlier, but wanted to be sure her stepson was free before making an appointment. Jean-Noël said nothing. The mere word "manufacturer" had made an unpleasant impression upon him. He failed to understand why Annie was so eager to see him employed, or why she was opposed to the idea of his pursuing an education.

"Tell me which day suits you," continued Mme Oetlinger, "so that I can make an appointment with this gentleman."

Jean-Noël hesitated before answering.

"You understand," added Annie, "that I have to be absolutely sure you will come. This man is very busy."

"I'm free all the time," said Jean-Noël provocatively.

"Shall we say the day after tomorrow, if you wish?"

But just then, although there had been nothing to suggest such an outburst was imminent, Jean-Noël declared abruptly that he had no desire to work in a bank, or in industry, or in a government office, because he had just discovered that he had a vocation for painting. Mme Oetlinger was unable to conceal her surprise.

"Yes, I want to paint," he repeated, in a tone of voice he might have used to say he wanted to devote himself to charitable works, in other words one with which it was impossible to argue.

"You surprise me," said Annie after a long pause.

"I don't see why. What do you find so surprising in that?"

She looked at him as if he were unaware of the all the good she had done him and now wanted to hurt her. Nonetheless, she was able to guess what was going through Jean-Noël's mind. How could this boy, whom she had raised as her own son and about whose future she was so worried, behave so despicably? For he had not fooled her. If he was claiming to have an artistic vocation, it was only because he knew that, if she wanted to remain true to her beliefs, his stepmother would have to respect his choice. Hadn't she often said, when

Jean-Noël was still at the lycée, that she would never be like those parents who force their children into a career they have chosen for them, but that one should rather wait for their vocations to emerge and then encourage, and even help, them to pursue them?

"But," she asked, "have you thought carefully about what you are saying?"

"Certainly."

"You know, of course, that painting is not a diversion. You need to devote yourself to it entirely."

"I know that."

"Fine. In that case, I will do everything I can to help you fulfill your ambition. I will speak to my father about it this evening."

It was then that she recalled the hostility she had faced long ago, the difficulties she had had to overcome before being allowed to take classes at the rue de la Grande-Chaumière. What was M. Villemur going to say when he learned that Jean-Noël, too, intended to take up painting? Wasn't he going to think that she had been the one who had steered the young man in this direction?

"And yet this is the first time," she went on, "I have heard you mention this desire of yours. It's rather unusual to discover, from one day to the next, that one has an artistic vocation. What I find surprising is that this struck you so suddenly."

In spite of being convinced that her stepson was putting on a cruel and ridiculous act, Mme Oetlinger was endeavoring to treat him as if he were being sincere.

"I've been dreaming of taking up painting for years now," replied Jean-Noël. "If I didn't mention it earlier, it was because I was afraid you wouldn't take me seriously, that you would make fun of me."

That evening, as she had promised, Annie told her father about her conversation with her stepson, feeling rather embarrassed, for such a subject could not fail to remind her family of her own past. Wasn't M. Villemur going to think that she hadn't changed? Wouldn't he seize this opportunity to reproach her yet again for the marriage she had made? He did no such thing.

"I fail to understand," he said, "why you are consulting me. If Jean-Noël wants to take up painting, let him!"

M. Villemur could not have expressed his utter lack of interest in what might become of young M. Oetlinger more eloquently. When Annie next saw Jean-Noël, she told him of her father's indifference.

"But," she added, "it is of no importance. I will rent you a studio. Before long, you will be able to make yourself useful to a decorator, or an architect, as well as doing your own work."

"The fact is," said Jean-Noël, "I've changed my mind. Having thought about it, it would be better if I took up something other than painting."

As he spoke those words, he looked at Annie slyly. When he had spoken to her of his supposed vocation, he had thought she would oppose it. He could then have used her refusal to reproach her for treating him in the very way she had always complained of having been treated herself. But she had agreed to let him take up painting. For his sake she had even incurred her father's sarcasm. He had thus found himself forced either to take up an art he cared nothing about or to admit he had lied. It seemed that no matter what he did, his stepmother would always have the upper hand!

"What do you mean?" asked Mme Oetlinger.

He repeated that he no longer wanted to take up painting. This conversation was taking place in M. Villemur's study. Annie got up and, without saying a word, left the room. Thinking she would come back, Jean-Noël waited for several minutes. Then he was overcome by fear. Had he gone too far? He opened the door. The hall was empty. He could see two old ladies sitting in the drawing room. The thought of going to Annie's room crossed his mind. He did not do so. A few moments later, he was on the avenue de Malakoff, disgusted that his lie had served no purpose and resolved not to return until Annie asked him to.

EIGHT

When his father had fallen ill, Jean-Noël left the lycée just as he was about to take the second part of the examination for the baccalaureate. The day after having changed his mind, the first thing he did was write to his old school in Aix and ask them to forward his academic records to Paris. He was filled with an ardor made all the greater by his desire to show his stepmother what he was capable of. He would take the examination in June or October. Then he would study law. But after a fortnight he had run out of money and was forced to go back to the avenue de Malakoff. He asked Annie where his books were and pretended he needed nothing else. When the moment came for him to leave, however, and in spite of what it cost his pride, he was forced to allude to his financial difficulties. From his pocket he extracted the receipt for a registered letter from Aix. Annie had always been impressed by anything official. It seemed to her that her stepson was suddenly more grown-up. Nonetheless, she would have preferred that he launch himself, as she put it, into the fray. To her, it seemed a shame that, on the morrow of a war such as the world had never seen, a young man should choose to waste several years studying. Now was the time to stand shoulder to shoulder with men. Later on, everything would be as before, and the lawyer her stepson would have become by then would be no different from all the other lawyers in Paris. Nonetheless, struck by the change in Jean-Noël and captivated by his newfound decisiveness, she finally relented, for in the end the object of one's desire mattered less to her than the intensity with which it was desired.

At the end of June 1920, Jean-Noël passed the second part of his baccalaureate. In October he registered at the Law Faculty. He rented a small room in a hotel near the Sorbonne. He was spurred by his desire to please Annie. From time to time, he would go to see her. On those occasions, she carefully avoided asking him any questions. She was afraid that if she showed undue interest in what he was doing he might think he was he was being exceptionally valiant. She had sensed how proud he was. For his own sake, it was best that he consider his life as a student as nothing out of the ordinary. Like people who are aware that they are going to be given a gift but pretend to know nothing about it in order not to upset the donor, she avoided anything that related to her stepson's studies. If they began celebrating now, what pleasure would they have when he passed his first-year examinations?

But in the springtime of 1921 Jean-Noël, to his great misfortune, met a young lady by the name of Marguerite Ledoux.

Whereas he was twenty-three years old, Mlle Ledoux was twenty-eight. She was the only child of an officer who had gone on to become an auction appraiser at the Hôtel des Ventes and lived in a modest apartment with her parents, in the Rue Lacépède. Jean-Noël was quick to make friends with the young woman, who had a pleasant physique and in whose eyes he had a certain prestige because the first thing he had done was talk about the Villemur de Falais family. He had explained to Marguerite that certain family rivalries, which it would have taken far too long to explain, had been the cause of his decision to move out of the avenue de Malakoff, although this was, of course, only temporary. The young woman introduced him to her parents. It did not take long for him to win over those simple people, who admired his manners and the meticulous upbringing he had received. M. Ledoux could not understand how parents could be so unfeeling as to leave a young man to his own devices in this manner. Gradually, without realizing the risks he was running,

Jean-Noël acquired the habit of stopping by the rue Lacépède on the slightest pretext. He was always received like a young prince. Now that he was alone, he found these visits a welcome diversion. M. and Mme Ledoux, with that ridiculous spontaneity parents have when they leave their daughter alone with a boyfriend, never failed to leave the room, which always annoyed Jean-Noël, who was more interested in hearing himself flattered than in being alone with a girl he dared not approach for fear her parents would come back in. After having long refused, she finally agreed to come see him at home. But as she claimed that she was not allowed out in the evening and spent her days working at the Ministry for Liberated Regions, she would meet Jean-Noël in the morning. At eight o'clock, or sometimes half-past-seven, she would go up to his room. He would wait for her in bed. She would tease him about his laziness and then lie down next to him. Unfortunately, at about this time it happened that Mme Oetlinger decided to reenroll at the Académie where she had studied as a young girl. One morning in May, as the weather had been exceptionally fine for the past few days, the students decided that the following day, rather than staying shut up in the studio, they would meet at the Luxembourg station and go spend the day at Fontenay-aux-Roses. Annie was particularly fond of these excursions, which were undertaken not just for pleasure but to work. She enjoyed working with a group. "One has so much more enthusiasm," she would say. On her way to the station, she remembered that her stepson lived nearby. It was a magnificent morning. As she walked along the Luxembourg, deserted and silent but for the cooing of a few pigeons, it occurred to her that Jean-Noël must be in his room, reading with his window open wide. As a way of showing him, by merely stopping by, that while everyone might well have an occupation of his own, they were nonetheless all traveling along a road toward the same goal, she went to where he lived. She knocked on the door. He thought it was the maid bringing him his breakfast. Annie entered, then backed away instinctively. Marguerite was getting dressed while Jean-Noël, still in bed, his hair tousled, smoked a cigarette.

That evening, Mme Oetlinger wrote her stepson a long letter. In it, she said that she did not hold it against him that he had been idling for the past year, because it was her own fault. She should have understood sooner that a young man who is not urged on by necessity will follow the natural inclinations of someone his age, which are to do nothing and enjoy himself. This experience had been a lesson to her. She now considered it her duty to cut off the monthly allowance she had been paying him. However, she did not want him to be caught completely unprepared. She was now informing him, therefore, that in three months' time she would cease to provide for his needs, and that under no pretext would she ever again give him the slightest amount of money.

A month and a half later, Jean-Noël successfully passed his first-year examination. He had not seen his stepmother since the day of her visit. He was planning to do so now, only to have Marguerite announce that she was with child and that they must marry as soon as possible, for if not her parents would be so distressed it would kill them. At first Jean-Noël did not believe her. Ever since the day Annie had walked in on him with Marguerite, the latter had done nothing but bemoan her fate. She was dishonored. What was Mme Oetlinger going to think of her? The following day, Marguerite insisted that Jean-Noël come with her to the rue Lacépède. She claimed she had told her mother everything. He needed to come and reassure the poor woman. He did as Marguerite asked. But a few days later, when he realized that it was going to be impossible to extricate himself from the promises he had made, he took fright. What would Mme Oetlinger say if she learned he was to marry Marguerite Ledoux? He went to the avenue de Malakoff. The fourteenth of July holidays were nearing. He found Annie in the midst of preparing for a journey.

"How I would love to go with you!" he said.

"That would give me great pleasure," replied Annie, "but it won't be possible. I'm going to stay with friends."

Jean-Noël noticed that his stepmother had not looked at him once since he had arrived, that she had not even been curious to know whether he had passed his examinations. He was so hurt by this that he left almost immediately. He walked home. In six weeks Annie was going to cut off his means of subsistence, and she had not even asked what he intended to do when that happened. Rather than feeling defeated by such selfishness, it spurred him to action. He should take advantage of the modest affluence that marriage to Marguerite would bring to complete his studies. He would not see Annie until he had finished his studies, which would be his revenge as well as a means of ensuring that his stepmother did not learn of his marriage. With his studies behind him, he would reappear. It would be easy to justify himself then. A fault is never more insignificant than in a moment of triumph. Although Mme Oetlinger was now turning her back on him, she would help him regain his liberty. But he was unable to prevent himself from going to see his stepmother as soon as she had returned from her trip. He had imagined it was going to be difficult to conceal his relationship with Marguerite. This proved not to be the case. Ever since the day of her unannounced visit to the rue Cujas, Annie had considered her stepson was now a man. She would have thought it indiscreet to ask him any questions whatsoever about the life he was leading.

The marriage was celebrated in October. M. Ledoux himself rented a small apartment for the newlyweds in the rue des Bernardins, which is very near the rue Lacépède. His daughter's happiness reminded him of something far off in the past. He remembered certain difficulties he had faced thirty years earlier. He wanted the young couple to be spared these.

In February of 1922, Marguerite was delivered of a girl. Until then, Jean-Noël had not fully grasped the situation he was in. He had only one desire: to finish his studies. But when the child was born, he looked at the life he was leading with greater clarity. In spite of the thoughtfulness he was shown, in spite of the respect his connections with the Villemur family afforded him, he felt he was demeaning himself. He became increasingly irritable. Whenever his daughter cried, he would leave. If she happened to start crying again when he returned home several hours later, he would leave again.

He had just began his third year of law school when he met Mme Gabriel Mourier. She was wearing a carnation on her fur collar that day, and tiny spears of the fern surrounding the flower had fallen onto her bosom. She was a young blonde woman who clearly liked to be the center of attention and yet seemed to pay attention to no one. The amethyst she wore on her left ring finger—to scare away demons, she said—and which half concealed a wedding ring, the care with which she was dressed and made up, that delicate nature which made her unable to face rain, walking, contact with crowds—all of these made a deep impression upon Jean-Noël. In his eyes, she was from the same milieu as the young women he had so admired at the avenue de Malakoff. He told her about his life, or rather those parts of his life which he thought would give her an elevated impression of him. Laure, for that was her name, was moved by what she heard. She wanted to be a good influence on Jean-Noël. She insisted that he should return to his stepmother's, confess his errors, and beg her forgiveness. When he expressed surprise at the advice she was giving him, she added that Mme Oetlinger must certainly be a charming person and that he had doubtless hurt her with his young man's rough ways. Only much later did she speak of herself. So as not to oppose the will of her father, a country gentleman of the sort one no longer sees, she had been forced to make a marriage of convenience immediately after the war. Until her father's death, she had put up with this man she did not love, who was very rich and highly intelligent. Then she had gone to stay with her mother who, because she no longer wished to live where she had once been so happy and, in addition, needed to clear up matters relating to her estate, had sold her château and retired to Biarritz, where she now dealt in land and antiques. Laure had gone with her, but having found the life there tedious, and in anticipation of the day when she might need to earn a living, she had decided to come to Paris to study nursing.

Jean-Noël concealed Mme Mourier's existence from Marguerite as long as he could. But in January of 1923 this became impossible. One evening, when his wife was complaining because he had come home even later than usual, he suddenly blurted out the truth. Marguerite fainted. The noise he made carrying her into the bedroom woke the child. Marguerite came to, and so that her daughter would not be frightened, she began rocking her and singing while tears streamed down her face, perfectly aware of the contrast this created.

The following day, Jean-Noël tried to reason with her. If he was leaving his wife, it was in appearance only. He would never forget that he had a daughter. He knew that there was nearly nothing left of the small sum Marguerite had brought as her dowry. She told him that he was abandoning her just when she was about to be rewarded for the hardships she had endured on his account. He replied that she was wrong, that he didn't have his degree yet, and that even if he had had it, their problems would only be beginning. He finally left her, using a pretext as feeble as when he had gone to anticipate his military call-up. As soon as he was in the street, he hailed a taxi and went to meet Mme Mourier. That evening, Jean-Noël, who had lost interest in his studies a good while earlier, left with Laure for Nice. For weeks he had been singing the praises of the city in which he had spent so many years. They rented a room from which one could glimpse the sea. They ate in restaurants with fixed-price meals and, as Mme Mourier claimed to have a profound aversion to common people, would arrive when everyone else had already left. Occasionally they would take tea in one of the big hotels. Mme Mourier would speak then of the people her father had known, of those she knew herself, of the luxury in which she had lived until the time had come when she preferred being independent to being wealthy. From time to time Jean-Noël would think of Marguerite. He would see her again, stretched out on the bed, while her daughter cried. It had the effect on him of a hospital scene, and he would quickly think of something else.

When he returned to Paris, Jean-Noël did not dare go to see his stepmother right away. He had not stayed in touch with her. He was afraid that Marguerite might have gone to complain to Annie. What had happened while he'd been away? The mere thought that Mme Oetlinger might know he was married and the father of a little girl made him blush. But Mme Mourier, who was dying to be introduced to the Ville-murs, convinced him that Annie would be happy to see him again in his present situation—in other words improved by a woman of her own milieu—even if, in the meantime, she had learned what he had done. It was obvious, of course, that returning to the avenue de Malakoff would have been terribly difficult if he had not had the good fortune of meeting Laure. He therefore went to his stepmother's. She was as happy to see him as she had been the first time he came home from the army on leave. She seemed to think that his absence had been motivated by important reasons of which she, a woman, had no need to be informed. She asked him a number of questions about the legal profession and wanted to know if she should encourage the son of a painter, whom she liked a great deal, to study law. For she had taken up painting again, seriously, and had even rented a studio, whose address, her stepson noted, she omitted to mention. "You see, everyone is working," she said, laughing. Jean-Noël carefully avoided mentioning anything about his trip. He was afraid that his stepmother would reproach him, not for having interrupted his studies, but for having chosen Nice for his holiday. And yet he was bursting with desire to tell her. Now that his fears had been allayed, all he could think about was bringing Annie and Mme Mourier together. He was so proud of Laure that he imagined a delicious friendship would unite the three of them from the day Mme Oetlinger made her acquaintance.

"You know," he said at last, "that I deserve no credit for all the work I've accomplished."

"Why is that?" asked Annie, suddenly worried.

"Because I was encouraged by a charming friend, whom I would very much like you to meet," he went on, in such a tone of voice that it would have been impossible to make any connection between the charming friend he was describing and the woman with whom he had been surprised in his room one morning.

"I well understand," said Annie, "that a friendly presence may have stimulated you. But you mustn't say that you deserve no credit. If, as I hope, you are awarded your law degree three months from now, you will nonetheless have had to work very hard."

"That's true," said Jean-Noël, who had just remembered that he hadn't opened a single book since meeting Laure.

"As for the woman you just spoke to me about, I really don't think it necessary for you to introduce me to her."

But Jean-Noël was so insistent that Mme Oetlinger, who was secretly delighted that her stepson should be interested in someone other than herself, finally agreed.

The next day, still glowing from the welcome his stepmother had given him, Jean-Noël wondered whether he ought not to see Marguerite again. He was grateful to her for not having gone to see Annie. He wanted not to thank her but to assure her that he would protect her, that he would never allow her to want for anything, so as to avert the possiblity that she might change her mind. He did not dare, however, go back to the rue des Bernardins. Not long before his marriage, in the summer of 1921, he had seen his mother again. Marguerite's parents had wanted to meet her. "We fully understand that you don't have the same feelings for her as those you might have for someone like Madame Oetlinger," they had said, in spite of not knowing the latter any more than they knew Mme Mercier, "but don't you think she ought to be at your wedding?" After the young couple had settled into the rue des Bernardins not a day had gone by without Mme Mercier stopping in to see them, in spite of Marguerite's coldness. Jean-Noël therefore went to see his mother. She could speak to

Marguerite for him. She would organize a meeting. But Mme Mercier did not know what had become of Marguerite. She had gone to the rue des Bernardins several times, in vain. Marguerite had left without leaving a forwarding address.

"Didn't you go to see her parents?" asked Jean-Noël, worried.

"I also went to see her parents. They told me that they didn't know where their daughter was. And yet I had the impression they were lying, for they were very calm."

Jean-Noël related this conversation to Mme Mourier. Because it pleased her to think that the love she inspired was unassailable, she made a great show of insisting that Jean-Noël do everything in his power to locate his wife.

"You must go to the rue des Bernardins yourself," she told him.

Jean-Noël therefore went to his former place of residence, with the lingering fear that Marguerite might have come back in the meantime. There the concierge, after having carefully closed the door to her lodge, handed him a letter from Marguerite. She informed him that she had taken flight to Saint-Cloud, where she was now living in the rue Mission-Marchand. She did not want to see anyone, not even her parents. Because of him, she had quarreled with them. They had tried to force her to recount her woes to Mme Oetlinger. In spite of being in desperate straits, however, she had not wanted to harm the man she still loved, and whose return she would await until the end of her days. Jean-Noël was very touched by her letter. He replied the very same day, telling Marguerite that he thanked her from the bottom of his heart and that maybe, as she said, he would come back someday, but that he would certainly never leave her wanting for anything.

"In that case, you are going to have to interrupt your studies," said Mme Mourier after Jean-Noël informed her that Marguerite was entirely dependent upon him. "Had I been able to help this unfortunate soul, I would have done so, but I am in a very delicate situation myself. I wonder what my husband is going to say when he learns I am in love with you. I'd rather not think about it. In spite of the fact that we are separated, he is very jealous. It could be that he will take his revenge by cutting off the monthly allowance he has been giving me. Would you like me to go and see an old friend of my father's, a charming man who is a solicitor here in Paris? You could work in his office, for now, and be able to help your wife. As for the rest, we will always find a way."

And so it was that in the springtime of 1924 Jean-Noël began clerking for Maître Préfil.

NINE

As he'd been doing every evening for the past six months, before leaving the office for the day Jean-Noël knocked on the door of the little room in which Maître Préfil liked to retire. He was a friendly man of sixty-five. Mme Mourier had recommended Jean-Noël to him. The solicitor had made a note of her recommendation, and eight months later, with that pride which comes from keeping a promise contrary to all expectations, he had written the young woman to tell her he needed to hire someone and would be happy to meet M. Oetlinger. The introductions had been made. Maître Préfil had not wanted to spoil the favorable impression he sensed he had made by not forgetting what he'd been asked to do. He had received Mme Mourier and Jean-Noël as if they were doing him a favor by coming to see him. Courteous yet undeceived, he had sought to create the impression that it was agreeable to be in such pleasant company, and when Jean-Noël, who was eager to place himself, had alluded to his capabilities and above all to his family, or rather his stepmother's family, the Villemur de Falais, Maître Préfil had replied, as if he had not heard the name: "If Mme Mourier recommends you, you have my complete confidence."

That evening, Maître Préfil did not greet Jean-Noël with his usual good humor. He was sitting at his desk, holding his head in his hands. A kerosene lamp was burning next to him; he had sensitive eyes and could not tolerate electric light. Jean-Noël coughed several times. Finally the solicitor looked up.

"Are you feeling unwell?" asked Jean-Noël, with the serious tone he knew how to adopt when, having arrived laughing, he suddenly realized that he was the only one doing so.

"My son was wounded last night. I don't know how it happened. He was fencing and his opponent's foil struck him in the armpit. It wouldn't be at all serious but for the fact they fear the top of his lung may have been touched."

"Are they sure the lung was damaged?" inquired Jean-Noël, asking the question in a way that suggested he had once been wounded in the same manner.

"For the moment, no one knows anything. We have to wait for the X-ray."

"Would you like me to ask Monsieur Villemur for the name of his doctor?" he asked, rolling the double *l* of Villemur as he knew was customary among the upper echelons of Protestant society.

"Thank you. We are used to our old doctor. He has been looking after all of us for nearly twenty years. He has become our friend."

"Nonetheless, Monsieur Villemur's doctor is a top man," said Jean-Noël, who did not at all regret that Maître Préfil wasn't taking him up on his offer: for him, what mattered was not that this doctor be summoned—and indeed he had never heard him spoken of—but rather that it be recognized that he was, as he put it, a top man.

A cold wind was blowing off the place Clichy and down through the street of the same name, at the bottom of which Maître Préfil's office was located. Every evening, Jean-Noël walked to Mme Mourier's little apartment in the rue Laugier. This walk was the most agreeable part of the day for him. Jean-Noël's thoughts would turn to his youth, or rather to the years of his life he called happy, the years he had spent in Nice. He tenderly recalled the road along which he had walked to the lycée, lined with hotels that had been transformed into hospitals, and the apartment in the avenue Félix Faure. His father had been alive then. Jean-Noël pictured him with his morning coat, his white tie, and the wide-brimmed black felt hat he carried without denting it. He could also picture his father's study, a plain, light room with wicker furniture, filled with stacks of the brochures Jean-Melchior used to have printed, for he had always had some project he was trying to launch, and the studio in the old town where his stepmother had spent her afternoons. He had often gone to take tea with her. To enter her sanctuary, he had to cross a garden and climb a little wooden staircase, which was nearly vertical. Inside, the walls were covered with paintings, and the air was scented with methylated spirits, mimosa, and turpentine.

When he arrived at the rue Laugier, Jean-Noël thought he recognized his brother standing across the street from Mme Mourier's, in front of a little watchmaker's shop. It was, in fact, Emile, that child whose upbringing Mme Oetlinger had refused to take on because he had been conceived, if indeed he was M. Oetlinger's son, after she had already made the latter's acquaintance.

"Were you waiting for me?" asked Jean-Noël, pretending to be even more surprised than he was.

"No, I'm waiting for our mother. She's gone up."

As he spoke these words, he nodded upward in the direction of the apartment.

"And you, you didn't go up?"

Emile did not answer. He was now a tall young man of twenty, as tall as Jean-Noël, but so stooped over that he seemed much smaller. He was dressed in clean clothes. His overcoat was so old and threadbare, however, that one could glimpse bits of tattered lining protruding from the ends of the sleeves. His shirt had doubtless been made by his mother. It buttoned low on his neck. The collar was not attached to it, and there was a band of flesh visible between it and the shirt below.

"Come up with me," said Jean-Noël kindly, even though he had understood that if his mother had asked his brother to wait downstairs, it was because she wanted to ask him for money.

"It's not worth the trouble. She'll be right down," said Emile, without removing his hands from his pockets, staring shiftily at his brother all the while.

He did not like Jean-Noël. He could not forgive him for having been favored while he and his mother had lived, and continued to live, in misery. It was a sorry life the two of them led in the single room in the rue Mouton-Duvernet which they had moved into shortly after M. Oetlinger's death, and which they had been unable to leave since because they had no money. If Jean-Noël had really wanted to, he could have rescued his mother from this penury long ago, or so Emile believed.

"You needn't bother about me. Go home," said Emile, in a tone of voice he might have used to say, "Go and enjoy yourself."

Jean-Noël slowly climbed the four flights of stairs that separated him from Mme Mourier's apartment.

"Your mother is here," she said, opening the door, as if she were speaking of some enemy they had in common.

"Did you show her into the drawing room?"

"Yes. She is waiting for you."

"Do you know what she wants?" asked Jean-Noël in a whisper, as if he believed in Mme Mercier's devotion.

"Money, of course!"

He rubbed his hands together as he entered the drawing room, as if things were going particularly well. The room, half of which was taken up by a grand piano, was full of knick-knacks. His mother, who had just turned sixty, was perched on the edge of an armchair like old women in waiting rooms. She was wearing a black suit that she had made herself, the jacket of which resembled a soldier's tunic. When she saw her son, she got up, leaning heavily on one of the chair's armrests, and came forward to greet him.

"Please, don't get up."

"But of course, of course."

She looked at Jean-Noël with her small, lively, mocking eyes. Mme Mourier had drawn closer.

"Please remain seated, Madame."

Mme Mercier lifted both hands as if to say she no longer knew what she should do, and sat back down again. It was difficult to imagine that this woman could be anything but innocuous. And yet her entire life had been spent doing just the sort of thing she was doing now.

"Well!" said Jean-Noël, as he lit a cigarette.

She smiled as if her son, rather than encouraging her to speak her mind, had just said something terribly clever.

"No doubt there was something you wanted to ask me?"

"Yes," she said, with an incomprehensible air of astonishment. "I thought that rather than giving so much money to your wife, you could entrust your daughter to me. I can assure you that she would be better looked after, and it would cost you less in the end."

"That's out of the question."

"Why?"

She looked at her son and Mme Mourier in turn. Even though she did this as if she saw nothing, one sensed that she was registering each of her interlocutors' gestures.

"I tell you it's impossible," repeated Jean-Noël.

When, with time, Marguerite had understood that she had been abandoned forever, her love for her daughter had been transformed into an absolute passion. If the child cut herself, her mother, a living image of pain, would rush out like a madwoman and stop the first passerby to ask for help. These maternal feelings, of which she was a bit too aware and which she displayed with the intention of showing her husband that he no longer mattered to her, that he had been replaced, were supplemented by a variety of pedagogical theories. She claimed that children should be left alone to do as they pleased, to develop on their own, and that first and foremost their instincts should be awakened. She also thought they should be encouraged to believe in all sorts of fairy tales, and when Jean-Noël had asked her in front of their daughter a few months earlier what toys he could buy her for Christmas, Marguerite had given him such a look that he had fallen silent immediately.

Although there was no longer any question of love between husband and wife, she had nonetheless kept, like a souvenir one is never asked to return because of its trifling value, the habit she had once had of making herself obeyed by a mere look. She was raising her daughter to respect her father. He was somehow a part, or at least so she thought, subconsciously, of that fantastic element with which it pleased her to surround their lackluster existence. She hoped that some day—for the future played an important part in her life, and she never acted without thinking ahead to the reproaches her daughter might make to her in the years to come—Jean-Noël would come back to her, and that he would be proud to see that his child had been brought up just as well without his help as she would have been with it. Until such a day came, however, she would not tolerate the slightest remarks. She was convinced she was giving her child an excellent upbringing and wanted to be given entire credit for it, hoping thereby to show Jean-Noël that she, too, was not like everyone else. How, then, could Mme Mercier think that this woman, whom she knew, would agree to be separated from her daughter and accept that she be entrusted to a person she specifically disliked? Jean-Noël sensed that this was nothing but a way of asking him for money, and that his mother had no illusions about the response with which her proposal would be met.

"You know very well," he said, "that Marguerite will never agree to let you look after Annie."

Jean-Noël had named his daughter after his stepmother.

"That depends. If you make her understand . . ."

At that moment, Mme Mourier interrupted them.

"Nevertheless, it would be much better for your daughter," she said, as if, being a woman above all else, she always put the interests of children first.

Jean-Noël gave her a look one might give a close friend who, in a moment of tactlessness, supports one's opponent.

"Still, do as you please," she went on. "You know very well that I don't get involved in these matters."

She smiled as she uttered these words. It was her way not

to make light of another's troubles, but rather to imply, whenever one was burdened with some problem, that this problem was nothing but the consequence of a failing she had not only pointed out but also struggled to correct.

"What's to become of me?" cried Mme Mercier.

Her lips tightened as if she were about to cry. Although she had known it would never be granted her, she had been counting on this custody so that, when her son refused it, she could bemoan her fate and ask for something else.

Laure had discreetly left the room.

"Jean-Noël, you know that Emile can't work. He's not healthy enough."

Mme Mercier realized then that her son's friend was no longer in the room. Her lamentations stopped immediately.

"She has money, doesn't she?" she asked, in a different tone of voice, and as if the fact that she was Jean-Noël's mother allowed her to make such an indiscreet inquiry.

He did not reply. This scene embarrassed him. He nearly called in Mme Mourier so that it would have to stop. Offended in the way a young woman might be if she offered herself and was turned down, Mme Mercier grew harsh.

"You know that there are some things I've learned," she said menacingly.

Thinking that these things concerned Laure, Jean-Noël, who would have found it repugnant to hear Mme Mourier maligned in her own apartment, told his mother that he would accompany her, and that they could speak more freely outside. They left the drawing room. From her bedroom, Mme Mourier heard them leave, but she did not stir. On the staircase, Jean-Noël felt a sense of relief, albeit a fleeting one.

"It seems," said Mme Mercier, "that you've had your father's remains brought back, and that this has cost you several thousand-franc notes."

Jean-Noël grew pale.

"That's not true."

"Madame Mourier just informed me of it. For that, she gives you money, but for me, she gives you none."

"That is to say, I intended to do so, yes, absolutely. But I haven't done it yet, and if I do it some day, it will be with money that I have earned."

"And you want to throw your money out the window like that, while Emile and I, we have nothing!"

M. Oetlinger had now been dead ten years. It was only in the autumn of the previous year, however, after a visit to his stepmother, that Jean-Noël had thought of having his father buried in Paris. During the visit, while telling him about her holidays, Annie had mentioned that she had gone to Davos for a day, to put flowers on Jean-Melchior's tomb. From the natural way in which Annie had spoken of this pilgrimage, Jean-Noël had sensed that it had never crossed her mind that he, too, might have wanted to go to Davos. A few days later he had written to the cemetery, and had even taken a few preliminary measures, but the cost of this transfer had brought his project to a halt. Nonetheless, he had talked to Mme Mourier about it as if it were firmly decided in his mind, hoping to show her by this that, where his family was concerned, he owed no explanations to anyone and money was of no importance. Since then, he had been setting aside a portion of his salary and, like a man living with an obsession, was ostensibly depriving himself of pleasures. Laure had not dared to oppose a project that seemed born of such noble intentions. In spite of this, the theatrical quality of the enterprise was not lost on her, and she had talked about it to a few of her friends, even though Jean-Noël had asked her to keep it a secret.

When his mother and brother finally made up their minds to go, after he had promised he would send them money, Jean-Noël rushed back upstairs. He was angry. He could not bear it when people gossiped about him behind his back.

"Was it to be disagreeable to me that you repeated to my mother what I had asked you to keep to yourself?"

"Not at all. It was to be agreeable to you. You shouldn't hide your feelings. As it is, people have too much of a tendency to look down on you. And that's not surprising, if you conceal all the finest things about yourself!"

TEN

Although he had long been thinking of doing so, it was only in the last six months that Jean-Noël had begun seeing the Wurtzels again. It was then he learned that they had quarreled with the Villemurs. Although the news had disappointed him, for he'd been hoping the two families were on friendlier terms than ever, which, if Annie was to learn he was seeing Odile again, would have spared him from being reproached for it, he had been all the more warmly received for it. Wasn't he, too, a victim of the Villemurs' arrogance? He now went to the Wurtzels nearly every week, where he was treated almost like a member of the family. His relations with Odile had become increasingly familiar. He had confided in her, so she now knew everything about his life. It was for this reason that, the day after his mother's visit, after having lunched in a restaurant near his office, he went to the boulevard du Montparnasse.

The Wurtzel family was still in the dining room when he was shown in. Gathered around the table were M. Wurtzel, his young wife, looking very dignified, an uncle, Odile, and her two brothers, Simon and Maurice. They all received Jean-Noël with that feeling of satisfaction one derives from a well-timed visit. He became the center of attention. He was asked if he had eaten. He replied that he had. M. Wurtzel, however, who always suspected others of being unnecessarily ashamed, insisted that another place be laid. Jean-Noël raised no objections, but when a servant passed him a tray, he did not even deign to refuse.

"Well, then, you'll have a coffee and some of our kirsch from back home," said M. Wurtzel.

When everyone rose from the table, Odile motioned to Jean-Noël to follow her. He joined her in a small sitting room. She closed the door herself, while he lit a cigarette. "Well?" asked Jean-Noël, as if she was going to be in his arms in an instant. He was seeing himself as though in a mirror. The fact that he had left the Wurtzel family without anyone finding this unusual and without his having had to offer any reason, that he had walked through a part of their apartment on his own, as if he were walking backstage, and then entered this sun-drenched Louis XV boudoir, had intensified the feeling he had of being loved.

"What happened?" asked Odile, who had guessed, from some of the looks he'd been giving her, that something had taken place.

Jean-Noël did not answer. He had already told Mlle Wurtzel about his desire to have his father's remains returned to France. He had told her this with unimaginable pride, such an act implying that his father had been someone of exceptional importance. Now that he was faced with revealing that his pious notion had become a weapon turned against him, the way a politician's opponents might reproach him with some generous intervention, he took care to do so slowly; being in a hurry to defend oneself is a sign of an uneasy conscience.

"The fact is that she has told my mother everything," he said, avoiding, as he always did when it was possible, mentioning Mme Mourier by name.

Odile put on a distressed look. At heart, she accorded no importance whatsoever to the proposed transfer, which she thought a sort of whim, but she was first and foremost a woman and whenever she suspected that a man, even a stranger, cared deeply about something, she never raised the slightest objection. She had noticed long before that Jean-Noël had a tendency to think highly of himself and to glorify the very family which repaid him with indifference. She had also remarked that his motives for doing things were of an inferior nature. Nonetheless, she had always supported him.

"I'm wondering now what I should do," continued Jean-Noël. "Should I tell Annie everything, or conceal it from her? If I say nothing and she learns of my plan, she will hold it against me for having undertaken something she may have been intending to do herself, and she will be right. But if, on the other hand, I tell her the truth to avert an indiscretion, I run the risk of upsetting her needlessly. It may well be that I'm wrong, and my mother has no intention of doing me any harm."

Jean-Noël knew that he would cause Annie no distress, but rather that he would simply make her angry. He carefully avoided mentioning this, for what he wanted above all was that Odile, like his own entourage, should think that his escapades were a source of distress to Mme Oetlinger.

"It's most delicate," said Mlle Wurtzel. "Nonetheless, I do think it would be best if you spoke about it to your stepmother."

"Do you think that's best? I have no idea."

"Wait here for me a moment."

She left the room. Shortly afterward, she returned with her brother Maurice. He was a young man who attached a great deal of importance to his suits, his ties—in short, to everything that pleased the eye. Ever since Odile had become Jean-Noël's confidante, and especially since she had begun thinking of marrying him, she had felt the need for the support and approval of a member of her family. But she had dared reveal her plans only to Maurice, whose sweetness and kindness made her trust him. He was her younger brother, and while he didn't behave as such in their everyday dealings, he reverted to that status whenever something unusual occurred. For the next hour, the three of them sought to determine, rather confusedly, what conduct would be most fitting for Jean-Noël to adopt. It was finally decided that he should go to see his stepmother and speak to her candidly.

"But why is it that you thought of having your father's remains brought back?" asked Maurice as Jean-Noël was about to leave. He had wanted to ask the question from the start, but had only dared to do so after his participation in the discussion could justify his curiosity.

"It's entirely normal," replied Jean-Noël with some astonishment.

The truth of it was that he did not know exactly why he wanted to do this. What he did know was that he would have been overjoyed if, in a year, or perhaps two, Annie failed to find her husband's tomb when she visited Davos. He had played out the scene in his mind numerous times. His stepmother would arrive, laden with flowers. Failing to find the tomb, she would interrogate the caretaker. The latter would suddenly remember that a lone young man, rather tall, as far as he remembered, and seemingly disenchanted, had had the body removed. It was for this scene alone, which might very well never take place if Annie chose never to return to Davos again, that Jean-Noël had begun taking the necessary steps to effect the transfer.

"You aren't answering," observed Maurice.

When Jean-Noël had told Mme Mourier of his intentions, she had thought at first that he was lying, as he did so readily whenever he wished to embellish either the Villemur family or his relationship with them. But when she had understood—from the fire in his eyes, and the feeling of having accomplished a duty which emanated from him—that he was taking himself seriously, she had judged that the best thing to do was express her approval of his plan. Her approbation had been mirrored in turn by all the people to whom Jean-Noël had spoken of his intentions afterward, with the result that he became accustomed to thinking of himself as the defender of some noble cause.

"I know," he replied, looking at Maurice Wurtzel scornfully.

The following afternoon, following Odile's advice, Jean-Noël went to see Annie. He had been to see his stepmother two weeks earlier, during the holidays, to wish her a happy new year. "You need to speak to me?" Annie had asked. She had replied coldly to Jean-Noël's New Year's greetings. During the war, she had admired the young men who were giving their country "the best of themselves." She had a storybook conception of life, work, the future, ambition. A baker, for instance, in her eyes as in those of a child, was a sort of devil, but white, who labored while the rest of the world slept. As a result, she failed to understand how a young man on the very threshold of life, whose fate was therefore to struggle and make his way, could choose instead to conform to customs associated only with people of leisure. Although that was just what she did, she had an excuse. It was through no fault of her own that she had been brought up to follow those very customs. While she might well find them ridiculous, she was nonetheless constrained to observe them. But Jean-Noël, who had been to war, who had been fortunate enough, like all those men who had then gone on to greater things, to live in a time of troubles and difficulties such as the world would doubtless never see again—where on earth had he acquired this pettiness which no one had ever taught him?

When he arrived at the avenue de Malakoff, a valet showed him into the drawing room and then, a few minutes later, returned to lead him to Annie's room. Jean-Noël was filled with emotion, as he was each time he went to the Villemurs'. Weren't they his family, the family in whose bosom he would have so loved to reside? He was filled with a great sense of well-being as he entered Annie's room. It was a luxurious room, from whose windows one could glimpse the trees in the avenue du Bois as if they were in a nearby park. Books and paintings gave it that aspect which he had so admired in her studio in Nice. It was pleasantly warm. Perfectly centered in the distance, as if in a perspective purposely created for this effect, the reddened sun, drained of life, was on the verge of disappearing. The slight haze that hovered over Paris, the sun he had failed to notice a scant quarter of an hour earlier, were like the backdrop to some distant memory, and there he was, facing Annie, who wore a mink hat and was ready to go out at the end of this winter's afternoon. She must have been writing, for on her desk he saw an unfinished letter and the famous ivory pen which she had forbidden him to use in Nice.

"Sit down, Jean-Noël."

He grew increasingly uneasy. Whenever he went to see his stepmother, he took care to have some pretext for coming, for he had noticed that nothing displeased Annie more than a visit for which there was no reason. This time, however, she seemed unconcerned with the reason for his visit.

"Do you know whom I was writing to?" she asked.

"No, I don't know," he answered slowly, so that he might take advantage of this greeting to regain his composure.

"To our friend Saglioni," she answered kindly, for at heart she liked Jean-Noël, and all it took to show her affection was for him to arrive at a moment when she was doing something that might be of interest to him, for instance, writing to someone he had known. On this particular day, Jean-Noël could very well have come for no reason at all. Consequently, he should have refrained from revealing one. When his stepmother was feeling cheerful, didn't it seem as if she knew there never was any real reason? For a moment, he thought of saying nothing, so as not to spoil her good humor, but it then struck him that he would not be able to come back before two more weeks had gone by. That was more than enough time for Mme Mercier to outmaneuver him. It would therefore be best to speak up now. After all, there had been nothing to suggest that Annie would react badly to his desire to have Jean-Melchior's remains brought back to Paris.

"I have something to tell you," said Jean-Noël.

Annie, so as not to be distracted, was talking to herself as she wrote.

"It is my intention," continued Jean-Noël, "to have my poor father's remains transported to Paris. He always said, if you remember, that he wanted to be buried in the cemetery at Montparnasse."

Annie straightened in her chair. She looked at Jean-Noël, first with surprise, then with anger.

"Have you gone mad?"

"It's the city he most loved," added Jean-Noël.

This time Annie could not contain herself.

"I know that. But that doesn't explain to me how you could entertain such a notion. It's enough to make one wonder whether you are in your right mind."

"I thought I was doing the right thing," replied Jean-Noël naïvely.

This last excuse, to the extent that it was one at all, failed to calm Mme Oetlinger. It was no doubt to show her that she had been in dereliction of her duty by returning to the family which had so loathed her husband that, without consulting her, her stepson had dreamt up this idea—for it would have gone no further than that, as she was fairly sure the intention existed only in his head—of moving his father's body. Was she really going to have to spend her entire life struggling with this boy? Oh, she had no regrets about having married against her family's wishes. She had been happy. The years spent in Nice had been the happiest years of her life. But today, ten years later, that happiness, in spite of being adorned with the poetry of the past, seemed to her the consequence of a youthful indiscretion, one that had been disinterested and fine, but upon which it was best not to dwell any longer.

"My dear friend," she said harshly, "you are already having enough trouble making your way in life without complicating your existence this way."

"You're right," said Jean-Noël who, now that he no longer had to fear his stepmother was going to discover that he had concealed from her something which nonetheless concerned her, wanted to change the subject.

Annie resumed writing. When she had finished the letter, she asked Jean-Noël, as if nothing had taken place, whether he happened to have any stamps with him. How he wished he had some! She looked at herself a last time in the mirror, then said to him as she opened the door,   "I'm leaving, Jean-Noël."

In the hall, seeing that her stepson did not seem to have decided to leave her, she extended her hand to him.

"Good-bye, Jean-Noël. I'm not going down right away."

Although this did not often happen to him, Jean-Noël began to feel sorry for himself as he made his way home. He thought it absolutely unfair that every time he had a generous impulse his stepmother reproached him for it. He even turned to his father as a witness. "If you were here, you would understand me and defend me," he told him, using the formal mode of address for the occasion. As he drew nearer the rue Laugier, he grew increasingly angry. Was Annie really going to refuse forever to see that he loved her, that she inspired all of his acts, even when they seemed directed against her? It was enough to make him think she loathed him. And yet, wasn't she adorable on some days? He was going down the avenue MacMahon when, for the first time, a marriage to Odile Wurtzel struck him as being acceptable. If for years he had made no effort to meet anyone, it was because, against all evidence, he had always hoped that some day he would be allowed back to live at the avenue de Malakoff. If he had resigned himself to working for Maître Préfil, to living with a woman as strange as Mme Mourier, it was because he had been convinced that, as soon as she could, Annie would take him under her wing. He could no longer turn a blind eye to the fact that he was deluding himself. Mme Oetlinger would never do anything whatsoever for him. This realization, which he should have come to long ago, made him deeply sorrowful. He felt alone, and abandoned by everyone.

When he arrived at the rue Laugier, he found Mme Mourier playing the piano.

"I beg of you, please stop. This isn't the time."

"On the contrary, there has never been a better time," replied Laure, alluding to the financial problems that she claimed were inevitable if Jean-Noël continued providing for both his wife and his mother.

He made no reply. He was irritated by the words spoken by this woman, who claimed he was the apple of her eye and yet made no attempt to conceal her desire to remarry an older, wealthy man.

"I am asking you to stop," he repeated.

She slammed down the cover of the piano and came to stand in front of him.

"You're not going to stop me playing music in my own home, I trust," she said, implying that thus far she had been the one to provide for the needs of their household.

This, in fact, was true. Jean-Noël turned over almost the entirety of his salary to his wife. There were times, when his mother became too threatening, when he asked Mme Mourier for money. Depending on her humor, she either gave it to him or refused. Jean-Noël had never discovered where her money came from. She claimed that her husband paid her an allowance, that he still loved her, that she had left him because she couldn't bear him any longer. At other times, however, it seemed that he had been unfaithful to her, that he had abandoned her, that she did not even know where he was. If, as Jean-Noël suspected, Mme Mourier was simply receiving a subsidy from her mother, why did she hide the fact? What strange pride compelled her to say that a man half dead with grief regularly sent her sums of money, about the amount of which she had never been consistent?

"It's not a matter of money," answered Jean-Noël. "I couldn't care less about money."

"I might understand your telling me that later, when I am remarried and have two or three generous lovers."

One could not have been more lacking in morals. In her eyes, the man she loved was a sort of accomplice. When Jean-Noël occasionally complained about the fact that she accepted money from her husband, she would laugh, as if to say he was trying to pass himself off as something better than he was. He wouldn't make such criticisms of her when she had found the much talked-about husband. Then, Jean-Noël would be able to give up his job. She would provide for all his needs. He would need to do nothing more than wait for her, smoking his favorite cigarettes, in a bachelor flat to which she alone would have the key, and which he would be allowed to leave only with her permission.

"Why," he asked, raising his voice, "did you talk about what I had asked you to keep to yourself?"

"I didn't think you would be able to hide anything from your mother," she said, knowing full well that the slightest allusion to Mme Mercier made Jean-Noël lose his temper.

He did not rise to the bait, but took a few steps, and then sat down near a window. Just as he had done in the small sitting room at Odile's the day before, he stepped outside of himself and saw himself clearly, this time in a small apartment near the Ternes, where a beautiful woman wearing a peignoir with a leafy design was berating him. He was aware of being the center of attention, which filled him with a certain childish pride. He was defenseless, dressed, like all gentlemen, in a dark suit; and yet there was conflict everywhere because of him. Soon afterward, the situation appeared to him as it really was. The life he was leading could not go on. Mme Mourier was becoming increasingly unbearable. That constant need she had to reproach him for things he didn't ask her for, and which she gave him out of generosity, would have been nothing had there been an end in sight. But hadn't Annie just shown him, a little over an hour ago, that she had no true feelings for him? If he had put up with Mme Mourier until now, it had been because, while waiting for he knew not what decision from his stepmother, he had not wanted to complicate his life further. He thought of Odile. After all, why not marry her?

It was not until three weeks later that Jean-Noël went back to the boulevard du Montparnasse. And yet, the day when he had gone to ask for her advice, Odile had said to him, "Come and tell me what happened right away." He had not done so. Of his quarrels with Annie and Mme Mourier he had retained most particularly the consequence, to wit the idea of remarrying. Ever since he had begun seeing Odile again regularly, however, he had always let it be understood that he would not marry her because of the Villemurs. In spite of everything, didn't he have to take their desires into account? They only appeared to take no interest in him. At heart, they loved him, far more than they were willing to admit. When his attitude had changed, therefore, he had wanted to attenuate what he considered to be a capitulation by not appearing overly eager.

"I had asked you to keep me informed," said Odile as soon as they were alone.

"Nothing special happened. That's why . . ."

"You could at least have come to see me, or given me some news."

She smiled as she said this, as if she bore him no grudge.

"That's true."

"And Madame Mourier, how is she?"

"Why do you ask me that?"

"What's wrong, Jean-Noël? Are you the one who's offended now?" continued Odile, smiling all the while.

"I'm not offended."

She drew closer to him and looked him in the eyes.

"Jean-Noël, even if we are not to be married, you must get a divorce. I am only telling you this in your own best interest. If you don't do so, you are lost."

ELEVEN

Every time Jean-Noël had gone to Saint-Cloud, Mme Mourier criticized him for doing so. He was really too kind. She failed to understand how he could have such consideration for a woman who allowed herself to be supported by a man who had abandoned her, and whose rival, moreover, albeit victorious, she was ashamed of being. When he set out for Saint-Cloud on a cold and rainy February morning, he therefore said nothing to Laure, especially about his intention of seeking a divorce. He did not take a taxi as he had often done in the past, not for the minor satisfaction of impressing Marguerite but rather for the much greater one of demonstrating that, in spite of his financial difficulties, he had not abandoned the habits he had supposedly acquired from his family.

He arrived just before noon. The wind had come up suddenly and was blowing in sharp, sudden gusts. He walked along the Seine, whose waters were so choppy that there no longer seemed to be any current. The trees were bowed over in all directions, as if the wind were coming from neither the east nor the west, but from everywhere at once. Dark clouds broke away from other, lighter clouds and filled the sky with so much motion that the embankments seemed deserted.

Jean-Noël was thinking only of Marguerite, however. How would she greet him? In spite of her silence on the subject, he knew that she had not forgiven him for having abandoned her. If she badgered him with requests for money, it was not only so that an innocent young girl should not suffer for the sins of her father, but also to make him understand the consequences of his wrongful ways. All she asked of her husband was money. If he shirked his obligations, she would be intransigent. Her own life no longer mattered. She had sacrificed it. Was it asking too much for Jean-Noël to sacrifice his material comfort in exchange? Shouldn't he consider himself fortunate to have escaped so lightly? Nonetheless, she had long hoped for a reconciliation. That was why she had preferred to break off relations with her family, which had wanted her to go after the Villemurs, rather than do Jean-Noël the slightest wrong. Later, she had regretted this generous impulse, which he had not even noticed. Time had passed, making reprisals difficult. She was bitter now, and pretended to want only one thing from her husband: that he do his duty. She never uttered the word divorce; she was waiting for him to bring it up first. Their roles would then be reversed. Everything she had endured would be worth having endured, just for that day. It would come, and that would be her revenge. Everything she had suffered, as much for her daughter's sake as to strengthen her own position, would at least have served some purpose. She would have to be compensated. There was not a court in the world that would dare deny her her rights, after the self-sacrifice and faithfulness she had shown. She had as much proof of her devotion as one could hope for. A hundred people would testify on her behalf. Whereas Jean-Noël had been living with a woman, and living off her money, which clearly showed his lack of morals, she had been raising her daughter.

Jean-Noël was worried as he turned into the rue Mission-Marchand, where Marguerite had rented a house whose modest proportions were in stark contrast to the size of the millstones its walls were built of. He sensed how strong Marguerite's position was, and how precarious his own. Hadn't he behaved with unforgivable carelessness? Whereas he was ill-prepared for battle, having thought of nothing for years but his own peace of mind, in the other camp everything was doubtless in order, his letters filed, his words remembered, his life well known. There would be an exact accounting of the monies he had paid, a crowd of devoted friends, not unlike those his mother had gathered around her so ably in years gone by, impatiently awaiting the call to arms. He recalled the day when Marguerite had begged him not to leave her. In spite of that, he had left, without even being particularly affected by his wife's distress. Was he going to have to pay now for his coldness? It wasn't certain. Marguerite was perhaps not the shrew he imagined. Perhaps he had more of a hold on her than he knew. Perhaps she too wanted a divorce, and was only waiting for him to bring it up first. Although he had been unyielding at the time of their separation, afterward he had nonetheless done everything he could to attenuate its suddenness. Immediately upon returning from his trip, he had undertaken to pay her a monthly allowance. It had often happened that he paid it late, but, if one were to judge his conduct impartially, it had to be said that he had never lost the sense of his obligations.

He was a bit comforted by these reflections as he rang at the gate of the little garden which fronted the house. A door opened almost immediately and Marguerite appeared. She was wearing an apron and had not yet dressed for the day. He entered the garden. Drying her hands on the apron, Marguerite came down the front steps. There was something hurried and friendly about her which reassured Jean-Noël. As if his arrival constituted some extraordinary event, however, before extending her hand to her husband she ran to the window and, climbing onto a garden chair, knocked on the pane.

"Come, come quickly, Annette. Your father's here."

The little girl appeared at the window. After a few seconds' hesitation, during which time Jean-Noël realized that his child considered him a stranger, no doubt because she recalled what her mother had told her, she tried to climb over the iron railing at the window, to hasten the moment when she would rush into her father's arms. Marguerite pretended to be panicky and stopped her. Seeing the importance given this little scene, and how quickly it served to turn their at-

tention away from him, Jean-Noël sensed just how superficial
was their joy at seeing him again.

"Papa!" cried Annie, throwing her arms around his neck
as fiercely as if she had done so right away.

"Will you please behave?" said Marguerite, whose remark
had no effect whatsoever, though this seemed not to upset
her.

This welcome was no different from all of the others he
had received here. It made the same painful impression upon
him. Wasn't he responsible for this mediocre life?

"That's enough. Go and play," said Marguerite.

The little girl's supposed love for her father evaporated on
the spot. Without giving another thought to the reprimand
she'd been given, she wandered off.

"It just so happens," continued Marguerite, "that she was
talking to me about you this morning, asking when you would
be coming next. Had I known it was going to be today, I would
have told her."

"She's grown again," said Jean-Noël as he entered the
house. As he reached the doorway to the dining room, he
turned to his wife and, by his look, asked if he could go farther, as a way of showing that he attached no importance to
his legal position as head of the household.

"Of course, of course, do go in."

She did not apologize for the disorder that reigned in the
room, and of which her own neglected appearance had provided a foretaste. Large spots of damp, caused by the proximity of the river, were visible on the walls. Clothing was strewn
everywhere. Scattered here and there were old-fashioned
things that suggested artistic pretentions—moth-eaten Indian
shawls, statuettes, earthenware jugs full of dead flowers, a
copper warming-pan hanging from a nail. It was freezing cold.
The chimney-flue was open, but the hearth contained only
the blackened ends of a burnt log. Marguerite noticed her
husband's look.

"I only burn wood now. It's much healthier for Annette.
But if you're cold," she continued, as if her husband, weak-

ened by the easy life, could not adapt to the rigors of the house, "there's nothing to prevent us from going into the drawing room."

"But why do you call her Annette?" asked Jean-Noël.

"I don't know. I like it better than Annie. It rhymes with pet, and coquette."

Without removing his overcoat, he sat down and observed Marguerite. She was paying no attention to him, not because she was occupied in restoring some order to the room, which would have been an admission that it needed it, but rather because ever since she had been separated from her husband she never looked at him, except in certain circumstances, when she stared hard at him.

"Perhaps you want some coffee?" she asked.

"Yes, if it's no trouble."

Just then, the sound of a drum was heard coming from the next room. "Will you be quiet!" shouted Marguerite. The noise continued. This time Marguerite paid no attention to it, for while other mothers took pride in being obeyed, she took pride in being disobeyed. Jean-Noël was then filled with sadness. What would become of his daughter as she grew up? If Marguerite had been more like other women the house would have had an entirely different appearance. But he had to remain silent. Whenever he had given any advice, it had been ignored; a man who has abandoned his family is not worthy of being listened to.

When Marguerite returned a few minutes later, she was carrying a small tray covered with a doily, though she had not used the opportunity afforded by her absence to tidy herself up at all.

"Be careful," she said. "My coffee is always very hot."

She seemed concerned only with fulfilling the duties of a spouse. Shouldn't Annette, as she called her, remain blissfully ignorant of the discord between her parents?

"I came because I need to talk to you," said Jean-Noël.

"Then talk," replied Marguerite at once. As she had some idea of what the matter in question was, she wanted her interlocutor to know that her conscience was untroubled, and that she would not stray from the code of conduct she had established for herself.

Jean-Noël now endeavored to make his wife, who interrupted him several times to say "Speak more quietly," understand that the life they had both been leading could not go on; that, moreover, it was as unpleasant for one as for the other; that Annie was growing up and this unsettled style of life could only be bad for her. He listened to himself speaking. It seemed to him that his voice was somewhat unnatural. Finally, he alluded to a divorce, which would set them both free. He stopped talking and looked at Marguerite, astonished that she had remained silent.

"You have nothing to say?"

"Ah! Forgive me," she said, as if she had committed some small misdemeanor. "I thought you hadn't finished. You're asking me for a divorce?"

"Yes."

"That's not possible . . ."

Very sure of herself, she paused, and then went on:

". . . because of Annette. If that poor little creature didn't exist, I would have asked you for a divorce myself, long ago. But she does exist, as you know better than anyone. And I have no right to deprive her of her father, in spite of my desire, believe me, to do so."

Jean-Noël understood that it would be best not to press his case further.

"We'll speak about it again," he said as he stood up.

"There's no point, I won't change my mind. I would rather you knew that now."

In the streetcar on his way back to Paris, Jean-Noël thought about what had happened. He had been expecting a negative response, but he had never imagined it would be so clear-cut. He had thought that Marguerite would begin by refusing, as a matter of form, but then give in soon afterward. It had not occurred to him that, although she had, in fact, lost her husband, he was still hers legally, and that this situation had gone to her head in the isolated life she was leading in Saint-Cloud. As long as Jean-Noël remained her husband, and he would remain so as long as she wished it, she could preserve, not the hope that he would come back to her, but that importance she imagined it gave her with obscure shopkeepers, and which she intended to retain. Jean-Noël blamed himself for his shortsightedness. Up to now, he had behaved as if only the present mattered. He had not deigned to give his wife any reasons when he had left her. He had treated her as if she had no rights over him, as if the fact of having given her a child entailed no obligations on his part. Now, just when he was beginning to understand that he would only be happy when his life was in order, he took note of the fact that Marguerite had led a blameless existence, that she was as protected by society as he was vulnerable to it, that the very laws which had made it impossible for anyone to force him to do anything against his will, which was something he had not realized before, now also made it possible for his wife to refuse to grant him a divorce.

TWELVE

The following day, Jean-Noël went to see Odile Wurtzel. He had spent a very bad night. Until two in the morning there had been so many thoughts spinning through his mind that in the end he had come to believe he would never win back his freedom. Every now and again Mme Mourier had asked him what was troubling him. He had told her that he couldn't sleep and left it at that. What was to become of him if he failed to break free of this ball and chain? He had even gone so far as to begin plotting his escape, like a prisoner. He would win over his wife's confidence, as if she were a guard. Then, when Marguerite was least expecting it, he would have her sign some paper—he didn't quite know what. Or then again he could try to compromise her, so that when the court heard their case it would find there were wrongs on both sides and annul the marriage, pure and simple. In the morning, however, nothing remained of these wild flights of fancy. Jean-Noël's thoughts had then turned to Mlle Wurtzel. She always gave him good advice. She had a reasonable way of seeing things, and never had he needed this more than now. In fact, Odile reassured him at once.

"But nothing could be more natural than your wife's attitude," she said with a smile.

She believed in the worthy sentiments that exist deep within each of us; if there were so many misunderstandings, quarrels, and injustices in life, it was only due to the fact that people did not know their own natures. To make them good, therefore, one needed only show them who they were.

"You have no idea," said Jean-Noël, "what this woman is like."

"She's no more wicked than any other. I assure you that everything will work out," Odile replied. "But tell me, Jean-Noël, why doesn't she want a divorce? If only for her own best interests, she ought to agree."

"For a great many reasons. The main one, I think, is that she believes I intend to get remarried to Mme Mourier, whom she holds responsible for her unhappiness."

Marguerite, like people who never venture outside their own circle, fancied that the only conflict there would ever be in her life was that between herself and Mme Mourier. She was convinced that her husband had not left her because he had grown tired of her, but rather because he had not known how to defend himself against the seductive wiles of a woman of easy virtue. When this woman decided to take another lover, which Marguerite had convinced herself was inevitable, it was possible her husband might come back to her. Therefore, when Odile said to Jean-Noël, with the abruptness of someone testing the waters, "After all, why shouldn't I go speak to your wife?" he did not think for a moment such a thing was possible.

"And yet, that would prove to Marguerite that if you want a divorce, it's for serious reasons."

She added that he could trust her, that she would act with the greatest discretion and not behave like those women who cannot conceal the satisfaction they feel when in the presence of a defeated rival. Odile was counting on this last argument to convince Jean-Noël. She was eager for this meeting, in large part because she was anxious to see Jean-Noël free, but also because she was curious to meet the woman who had preceded her in Jean-Noël's heart. He warned her that such an endeavor might very well defeat the purpose for which it was undertaken. It was important not to forget that, in reality, Marguerite had never given up the idea of winning her husband back. When she realized that everything was well and truly over between them, disappointment might make her more intractable than before. Odile answered by telling him, as she liked to do, that he knew nothing about the hearts of women. "Women," she told him, "never delude themselves in this way. They know perfectly well if they're loved or not." Nonetheless, Jean-Noël did his best to persuade the young girl that such a move could be perilous. It was useless. In fact, it seemed quite natural to Odile that a woman could imagine she was indispensable to a man, but she pretended not to believe it possible in order to emphasize the difference she wanted there to be between Marguerite and herself.

In the end, it was decided that, one day the following week, they would go to Saint-Cloud together. Odile's presence would serve to prove that if Jean-Noël wanted to regain his freedom, it was not in order to make bad use of it by marrying some street girl, but rather to settle down, to start a home and family. She would personally act as guarantor for the allowance Jean-Noël was ordered to pay. She would see to it that once he was free he did not lose interest in his daughter's future. He and Marguerite would part on good terms and everything would be for the best. It would be a show of bad faith on Marguerite's part if she refused to cooperate. Jean-Noël, who wanted nothing more than to be proven wrong, let himself be won over by her words. He even thought them uncommonly noble, a nobility, in fact, not lost on Odile herself, who remarked a few moments later that there were few young girls capable of doing what she was proposing to do.

But as soon as Jean-Noël found himself alone again, Odile's plan struck him as being so ridiculous that he was astonished he had ever agreed to it. There was no way he could go to Saint-Cloud with a lady friend. Marguerite would refuse to see him. Putting things in the best possible light, and assuming his wife failed to notice the peculiarity of such a maneuver, what would Odile think when she saw Marguerite, the little girl, the freezing, untidy house? He blushed. Wouldn't Mlle Wurtzel's love for him be diminished by the effects of such a visit? It was then that the thought of seeing his stepmother again crossed his mind. Maybe Annie was not as angry with him as he thought. It could be that she regretted the harsh way in which she had treated him a few days earlier. She might even be touched if it was he who made the first move. Aren't the people against whom we hold a grudge also the very ones from whom the slightest token of friendship touches us most? By recognizing the error of his ways and seeking forgiveness, wouldn't he make Annie come around? A new relationship would be born between them. If he won back his stepmother's love, what did Odile matter to him! A divorce would no longer be necessary then. He felt an immense sense of relief at the thought that his future no longer depended upon Marguerite. He was free. He would write to his wife. He was already composing the letter in his mind. "Dear Marguerite, as I left you it struck me that you were right, that we must not divorce, if only because of Annie . . . excuse me, Annette. She would certainly reproach you later for not having known how to keep her father for her. Whereas if we remain united by what you call the bonds of marriage, she will never be able to reproach you for that. So now you have what you want. We are married and will remain so forever. Unfortunately, as regards the monthly allowance I've been giving you, I am going to be forced to reduce it. Had we divorced, the court would have ordered me to pay you an allowance, the amount of which you and I would have agreed upon together. But by remaining your husband, which gives me great joy, as I don't need to tell you, there is no law which compels me to turn over the entirety of my salary to you. You won't be surprised, therefore, if in future you experience considerable difficulty in making ends meet."

When Jean-Noël returned to his stepmother's, she did not seem in the least bit surprised to see him again. She seemed to have forgotten all about her stepson's project. Newspapers were spread out on the carpet in her room. Sitting in front of a portable easel, she was painting some fruit she had placed on the corner of a table and behind which she had hung, as a makeshift backdrop, a piece of cloth which, although quite ordinary, was of a yellow hue she claimed never to have seen before.

"It looks very good," commented Jean-Noël, in spite of being terrified he would be badly received.

"Please, let's not talk about me. Let's talk about you instead," she said without looking at him while she continued to paint, as if, although she could not tear herself away from her work, she was nonetheless capable of carrying on a conversation.

Many a time Jean-Noël had heard this remark. It was one that Annie never failed to make when he committed the gaffe of showing some interest in her. While there was doubtless some degree of genuine modesty in her desire never to be spoken to about herself, the principal reason for it was her fear and dislike of flattery. So many people had set her apart, admired her, only then to betray her, that now, if Jean-Noël happened to pay her a compliment, it seemed to her that her stepson was only repeating what he had observed in his childhood in hope of obtaining, like those who had preceded him, she knew not what favors.

"Tell me what you have been doing lately," asked Annie.

As he was relating the details of an affair which Maître Préfil had entrusted to him, Jean-Noël suddenly had the feeling that his stepmother would never feel that love for him for which he would have given anything. She was not listening to him. From time to time, always without seeming to notice that he was there next to her, she would say, "Is that so?" He stopped talking, and it was only after a long silence that she asked him to go on.

"I've finished."

Annie looked at her stepson with astonishment. He was staring at her distractedly. He was thinking of Odile, of his divorce. The joy he had felt at no longer being dependent upon Marguerite had vanished.

"I didn't know."

"What I was telling you was not all that interesting anyway."

"Why do you say that? Everything is interesting when one examines it attentively."

"Naturally."

"This fruit here on the table. Nothing could be more banal. But think of what a Cézanne would do with it."

"I meant that what I was telling you was not interesting compared to something else."

"Which is?"

"Something the future holds in store for me. There will soon be a change. Unfortunately, I can't tell you anything more just now."

Jean-Noël was no longer trying to please Annie. On the contrary, although he held himself in check, he would have liked to provoke her. Why should he continue to measure his words, to fear her, since no matter what he said, no matter what he did, she kept this distance between them? Again he thought of Odile. Why shouldn't he say that he wanted to marry her? Ah, if Annie had been a mother to him, things would have been different. He would not have wanted to hurt her. But was he even able to do so? Preoccupied as she was with herself, was she even capable of caring about anything that did not affect her directly?

"That's too bad," said Annie, without showing the slightest curiosity about her stepson's enigmatic words. If there was one word she hated, because it reminded her too much of her poor husband, it was the word *change*. For what seemed the thousandth time, she had just heard it uttered by Jean-Noël. She pointed this out to him. He was taken aback.

"What exactly do you mean by a change?"

He did not know how to answer her right away.

"So, you have yet to understand that this word means nothing. There is no change. One does not wait for a change. In your mind, a change is some happy event. Well, no, a change is not a happy event. It's a lazy man's word, do you

understand? Never hope for a change. Take stock of it when
it has occurred, if that makes you happy, but that's all."

"It's that I intend to leave Mme Mourier."

Laure and Mme Oetlinger had met only once. This had
been through no fault of Jean-Noël's, who had done everything in his power to make the two women become acquainted. He had spoken enthusiastically about Mme
Mourier. He had given a thousand examples of her considerable energy, which was somewhat obsequious coming from a
young man himself so very unenergetic. But Annie hadn't
wanted to see Laure again. In spite of this, she had not concealed the fact that she had found her most agreeable. Since
then, whenever her stepson spoke to her of some plan or
other, she always asked him if he had sought Mme Mourier's
advice. Although there was no explaining this, in Mme Oetlinger's opinion Laure was a reasonable woman whom one
could trust and who was capable of teaching Jean-Noël the
respect one owes oneself. Although Annie now suspected that
all was not well at the rue Laugier, she continued to consider
Mme Mourier an ideal companion for Jean-Noël. She therefore expressed great astonishment when her stepson announced that he wanted to leave her.

"What on earth has happened now?" she asked. "You
can't be thinking of leaving Mme Mourier! I really don't understand your behavior. On the contrary, you ought to be
grateful to this person for everything she has done for you.
Since meeting her, you have improved yourself with each
passing day. She has the best possible influence on you, and
you talk of leaving her!"

Jean-Noël, like the young man who has not yet left home
he wished he was, selected among his reasons for breaking off
with Mme Mourier the one he thought most likely to appeal
to a mother. Mme Mourier was not the serious woman one
thought. She was married. Although she had no fortune, she
lived handsomely. She claimed, by turns, to receive her income from her mother and her husband.

Annie shrugged. Athough she had little doubt there was some truth to her stepson's explanations, the character she had fashioned out of Mme Mourier was far too useful to her to be discarded so easily.

"Why don't you believe me?" asked Jean-Noël.

"I do believe you . . . I believe you all the more for having no desire to be mixed up in all this business."

"You won't be involved in anything anymore," continued Jean-Noël, knowing that he was about to make his stepmother furious, "for I intend to get married . . . to have a home, a family," he added, using an expression he knew Annie favored.

"You aren't even divorced!"

"I will be soon."

"And what will you do for money? How are you going to live?"

"Oh! I have friends, a great many friends, who would be happy to help me out."

Annie grew pale with anger. Was Jean-Noël reproaching her for loving him less than these strangers did? Had he then forgotten that she had ruined herself for love? Had he reached the age of twenty-seven without realizing that she scorned money? She was on the verge of saying something like, "How dare you speak to me that way!" but because of her profound loathing for discussions that might remind her of those she had overheard, or just guessed at, during the years when Mme Mercier had harassed Jean-Melchior on a weekly basis, she said nothing. She pressed her handkerchief to her mouth. Whenever she was troubled she bit her lips; it was to conceal this that, unconsciously, she sought to hide them.

"It is my intention," continued Jean-Noël, "to marry Odile Wurtzel."

Annie, who had been taking long strides around her room, stopped suddenly.

"You wish to marry Mademoiselle Wurtzel?"

"Why not?"

At that moment something unexpected happened. Mme

Oetlinger's anger vanished. Very calm, her face composed, Annie approached her stepson. He had stood up. She asked him to sit back down.

"Listen to me, Jean-Noël," she said with unexpected tenderness, "there must be no further misunderstandings between us. You think that I don't love you. And yet, believe me, you are wrong. I have never paid more attention to everything you do. I would like you to be happy, to have a job worthy of your abilities. When I see you making a mistake, I ask myself questions, I wonder if I am not in part responsible for it. I should have done much more for you than I did. I should have watched over you, advised you, but a great many circumstances beyond my control made it impossible for me to do so! And even then, would I have been capable? Do you remember the precarious life we led in Nice? It was wartime. And those constant scenes your mother inflicted upon us. Toward the end, I was no longer myself. Then it was your turn, you went off to do your duty. When you came back, I should perhaps have kept you near me, but there were my parents. Between you and them, I no longer knew what I should do. It was impossible for me. And I so wanted you to show my family what you were capable of accomplishing. As always, it's because of our pride that we suffer. I thought a young man should get on in life without help. Now, let me speak to you from the bottom of my heart. You must not marry Mademoiselle Wurtzel. Believe me, I have more experience than you. You have already made one mistake with your first marriage. Don't repeat it. A marriage for money can never be happy. I, too, could have married a man I didn't love but whom my family would have loved. Today I might have children, a husband—unless the war had claimed him—a home, a life like that of so many other people. Rather than being considered slightly mad, I would be held in high esteem by my former friends. And yet, I have no regrets. Therefore how can you, you who have the good fortune of being able to lead a life of your own choosing, who will never have to overcome the obstacles I faced, want to marry a daughter of a

Monsieur Wurtzel? Do you realize that the two of you have nothing in common? She may be pretty, but what is that when measured against the course of an entire lifetime? A few years ago, I happened to see Odile's parents. Either you will put up with them and come to resemble them, or, as you've already done once before, you will leave."

Annie's voice had been filled with solicitude as she spoke, for, as she had just said, she loved her stepson in spite of everything. He might annoy her, there might be moments when she could not bear to be around him, but she had nonetheless watched him grow up. While uppermost in her mind, however, Jean-Noël's best interests were not alone in inciting Mme Oetlinger to oppose a marriage which, all things said, was not in the least dishonorable. The origins of Annie's antipathy lay in the fact that the Wurtzels and the Oetlingers had their roots in the same region of France, but this had been exacerbated by a second grievance of which Jean-Noël had been unaware. Shortly after his marriage to Marguerite, at a time, therefore, when he had ceased frequenting the Villemurs, Mme Wurtzel had died. A few months later, in spite of his childrens' hostility, M. Wurtzel had married a maid whom his dead wife had dismissed several years earlier, but whom he had carried on seeing secretly. M. Villemur, who had learned of this through his son Henri, had thought it very amusing. He had joked about it for several days, never considering for a second that there could be even the slightest correlation between that union and his daughter's marriage to Jean-Melchior.

"By remarrying," she went on, "you would be ruining yourself in my family's eyes. And that would be a mistake. I admit that they do not behave as they should toward you. I often point it out to them. But I am certain that one day they will understand how unfairly they have treated you and will try to make amends."

Jean-Noël was filled with joy as he listened to his stepmother. It had been years since Annie had spoken to him in this tone of voice. His happiness was so great that he allowed himself certain indiscretions. He recounted the visit he had made to Saint-Cloud, what Odile had suggested to him, and, to seem even more worthy of the interest Annie was showing in him, he weakly admitted that from the first he had thought Mlle Wurtzel's proposal unacceptable. Annie applauded this. Only a Wurtzel could have conceived of something so indelicate. That a young girl should even think of doing such a thing revealed a character of incredible vulgarity. In conclusion, she advised her stepson to visit Odile less frequently. He was not alone. He had a trustworthy, devoted friend in Mme Mourier. Of course, if this affair was to last for years and years, Annie would be the first to encourage her stepson to break it off, but Mme Mourier was far too intelligent not to realize that a marriage between herself and Jean-Noël was impossible.

THIRTEEN

One consequence of these recommendations was to make Jean-Noël write Marguerite a letter more or less identical to the one he had imagined. Then he telephoned Odile. He found it particularly disagreeable to have to see her again. But it had to be done. Hadn't he made an appointment to go to Saint-Cloud with her? Proudly, he told the young girl that, in spite of everything, he had wanted to consult his stepmother. He was not as alone in the world as people thought. In important circumstances, he had a true friend in Annie.

"You went to see your stepmother?" asked Odile, jealous that someone other than herself was playing a part in the young man's life. "I don't understand."

"The fact is that what we are proposing to do is very serious," replied Jean-Noël loftily. "If Marguerite were to take it badly, it could be used against me. It was both normal and necessary that I seek my family's advice."

"And you didn't ask Madame Mourier for her advice?"

Odile was finding it difficult to control herself. She could not understand how Jean-Noël could let himself be inspired by a woman who had always treated him so coldly.

"If I offered to accompany you to Saint-Cloud," she went on, "don't think it was for the pleasure of doing so. It was only to be agreeable to you, to do you a favor. If you would rather I didn't, I can assure you I won't insist."

Jean-Noël tried to convince Odile that although he was putting off the visit, this was only temporary, that he did plan to go one day, but that he needed time to make his stepmother accept the idea. Odile turned her back on him. Hoping to patch things up, he added, "You mustn't forget that Madame Oetlinger raised me. I owe it to her to obey her."

"Please, I don't want to hear about your stepmother any more. You know as well as I do that she doesn't love you, that she has never loved you. She has proven it."

Jean-Noël grew pale.

"I forbid you to say that."

"You can't stop me."

He left with the dignity of a man who cannot bear hearing ill spoken of someone dear to him. The next morning, he telephoned to apologize. But when Odile heard Jean-Noël's voice at the end of the line, she put the phone down. Throughout the day, the young man felt uneasy. He felt alone. Although he had been the one to upset Odile, it seemed to him that no one loved him, that already his stepmother was no longer thinking about what she had said to him, that she had resumed her occupations, and that, since he no longer even had the hope of getting married, things were worse than ever.

Mme Mourier had long since noticed the change that had taken place in Jean-Noël. She had blamed it on the worries caused him by "his families," as she said, "for I don't suppose," she had confided to a friend, "that he would stay with me if he didn't love me." And yet she was uneasy. As a result, she had got into the habit of going to meet Jean-Noël once or twice a week as he left work, thus reinforcing, by displaying her intimacy with the solicitor, the bonds that tied her to the young man.

Eight days had passed since Jean-Noël had last been to the boulevard du Montparnasse when Mme Mourier went to see Maître Préfil, that devoted friend whom, in spite of his age, she said she had always considered a child. It had struck her that her position vis-à-vis Jean-Noël would be strengthened if he were to learn, without any warning from her, that she intended to regularize her situation by asking for a divorce. In the waiting room, she found herself in the presence of a young girl who was almost entirely hidden behind a tall, narrow desk. As Laure was about to speak to her, the head clerk crossed the room. Upon seeing the visitor, he stopped and bowed.

"Would you be kind enough to tell Maître Préfil that I would like to see him," said Mme Mourier, with that satisfied expression she wore when a higher-up looked after her rather than allowing his employees to do so.

A few minutes later she entered the solicitor's office. He received her with his customary good humor, flattered as he always was when young women, and even young men, seemed to take pleasure in his company. After having questioned him about Jean-Noël in such a way that if Maître Préfil had been unhappy with him, she would have deplored the fact rather than defending her lover, she sat down on the arm of a chair, as if riding sidesaddle. Then, as if some bond existed between the two of them which authorized her to do so, she asked the solicitor to write, in his own name, a letter to her husband advising him to begin divorce proceedings. She hadn't the time to go into her reasons for not wishing to do so herself. Ill at ease, Maître Préfil told her that he did not know M. Mourier and that, as a result, writing such a letter was not within his province.

"I am asking you, Maître," she said, looking him straight in the eye.

"No, no, really, it's impossible," replied the solicitor, embarrassed at being forced to refuse.

"You could, my dear friend, make an exception for me."

Most fortuitously for Maître Préfil, this conversation was interrupted by Jean-Noël who, as was his custom, had come to take leave of his employer. At the sight of Laure perched on the chair in such a familiar fashion, he was unable to stop himself from thinking that she really was ridiculous.

"Aren't you happy to see me?" she asked, smiling.

She then continued talking with Maître Préfil, in order to show Jean-Noël that she was a friend of the solicitor's, as indeed of a great many other notables, and that as a result there was nothing surprising about the fact that he was so indulgent toward his employee.

On the stairway, she said, "Don't you agree that Maître Préfil is a delightful person?" which was the way she described all men who treated her with consideration.

Jean-Noël shrugged. Really, Mme Mourier was more and more ridiculous. They had walked a short way together when Emile, who had been waiting a quarter of an hour for his brother, approached them.

"Ah! It's you," he said, as if surprised to meet Jean-Noël, and without paying the slightest attention to Mme Mourier. "I was coming to meet you."

"Why?"

"I need to talk to you."

Mme Mourier had stepped away like a woman whose husband has been accosted by one of his subordinates. As Emile spoke these words, he looked over at her without moving his head, to make Jean-Noël understand that he wished to speak to him alone. He could even demand it. One doesn't hesitate for a moment between a brother and a mistress.

"Will you excuse me?" Jean-Noël asked Laure.

"Why certainly," she replied, her polite tone of voice laden with irony.

As she belonged to no particular community, which, in fact, made her suffer, she loathed clannishness with an assurance made all the greater by her vague feeling that there existed an entire category of people, whom she called intelligent, who would agree with her.

Jean-Noël led Emile to a café.

"Well now, let's talk," he said good-humoredly, as if he too had something to say to his brother.

"I'm not joking," replied Emile. "You wouldn't be joking either, if you were in our shoes. Obviously, you'd rather see nothing. And yet, given your situation, you could have done something for our mother and me long ago."

"What situation do you imagine I'm in?" asked Jean-Noël.

If he had kept the money he earned rather than giving it all away, he might well have been in that privileged situation Emile had just referred to. Yet everyone bore him a grudge, and everyone claimed he was selfish! In order to help Marguerite and Mme Mercier, he had been reduced to putting himself in Mme Mourier's debt. But that, too, was not enough.

"You won't convince me," said Emile, "that you have no money. You certainly have it when you want to court our stepmother."

Jean-Noël had just guessed at the reason that had provoked this attack, which was the desire he had had, and no longer did, to have his father's remains moved to Paris. Emile would not forgive him this. Wasn't he too the son of Jean-Melchior, as much as his older brother? As he had always sworn that Jean-Noël was nothing but a smooth talker, and that one couldn't count on him because he had gone over to the enemy side—which was to say the Villemurs—it was natural for him to find it shameful that the traitor should reap the honors of this initiative, at the expense of the faithful. For even ten years after the death of Jean-Melchior Oetlinger, the prestige the latter, by marrying a Villemur, had acquired in the eyes of a woman like Mme Mercier had not yet entirely disappeared.

"I'm telling you again that I have no money," continued Jean-Noël.

He was no longer bothering to conceal his ill humor. His thoughts had turned to Laure's ridiculous attitude at Maître Préfil's, the casual way in which he had sacrificed Odile's friendship, and Annie's silence ever since she had spoken to him so openly. He felt as if he were carrying a burden of heavy stones, that he wasn't allowed to put them down even for a moment. Wherever he went, he had to carry them with him.

"We've been patient so far," said Emile, remaining calm, "but if you're going to take it like that, then things are going to change."

Jean-Noël was greatly astonished by this insolence. His

brother was going too far. What was the meaning of this threat? He gave away everything he earned, and yet they thought this wasn't enough! Would he next be expected to turn to a life of crime?

"I earn a thousand francs a month," said Jean-Noël curtly. "I have a wife and child to support. I also have to live. How do you expect me to do any more for you?"

"You're under no obligation to give your wife so much money. And in fact, if you wanted, you could very well borrow some from Mme Mourier and from your darling stepmother. But you treat those people considerately. You'd rather leave us in misery, without enough money to buy coal. We've asked you time and time again to find me a job. You never have."

That much was true. But Emile had failed to say that whenever a job had been offered him, he had loftily turned it down. He was as good as his brother. Just because he had not been brought up the same way was no reason to offer him what had been spurned by others.

"You're afraid," Emile went on, "that I might compromise you with your beloved Annie, and perhaps you're also afraid that she might take some interest in me."

"Oh! That, no."

"You don't see that she cares nothing for you. She has done nothing but wrong by you and yet you admire her. She forced you to enlist, and then, when you came back, she didn't even look after you. And you get down on your knees in front of that woman!"

"Don't talk of things you know nothing about. Nobody forced me to enlist. In fact, this conversation has gone on long enough."

Jean-Noël called the waiter. He could no longer bear his brother. He had never before dared speak to him this way. Jean-Noël had thought that as soon as he showed a bit of toughness, Emile would back down. Instead, to his great astonishment, he had just realized that the young man was filled with steely resolve and that he, his older brother, did not intimidate him in the least.

"So," asked Emile, "what have you decided?"

"Nothing."

"Fine, we will act."

"What do you mean by act?" asked Jean-Noël scornfully.

"I will go see Annie. I will describe our situation to her. I will show her your letters, the ones in which you promise us sums of money that you never gave us."

It was this threat which Emile had been counting upon the most. A few years earlier, Jean-Noël would have begged his brother to do nothing of the sort. He would have offered him everything he possessed to restrain him. He did not flinch. Either his stepmother loved him, in which case this maneuver would have no consequences, or she didn't love him, and then what did it matter!

Emile spent the evening sorting through carefully tied packets of letters, which he had preserved as preciously as if they were papers related to the genealogy of his family, looking for those from Jean-Noël which could be useful to him and the one dated September 15, 1915, in which Jean-Melchior had written, a few days before he died, the phrases which Mme Mercier quoted nearly every day and which had become legendary, first in her eyes and then in those of her son: "Believe me, if something happens to me, you will not want for anything. A sum of money, of at least fifty thousand francs, will be paid you."

"I hope you're not planning to take that letter," said Mme Mercier when she saw Emile put it into his wallet.

"It's necessary."

"No, I don't want you to. It's not prudent. If you were to lose it, or if Madame Oetlinger were to tear it from your hands, we would have nothing left. We would be at their mercy."

FOURTEEN

Emile's face betrayed no emotion when he went to the avenue de Malakoff towards ten o'clock the following morning. The difference in the way he and his brother had been treated was so great, and the injustice of which he had been a victim so obvious, that he was ready to face the Villemurs with the same peace of mind as an innocent man called before an investigating magistrate. In spite of this, he felt uneasy when he reached the door to their apartment. He realized just how feeble the weapons he had at at his disposal were. Like an innocent man who finds the accusations leveled against him are being upheld in spite of his protestations, he was now aware that the truth is very little when it is all one possesses to do battle against an established power. Emile was not sentimental. He banished this thought from his mind, and when he rang the bell, it was as a man who is not going to let himself be intimidated. When the butler opened the door to him, he said that "Emile Oetlinger" wished to speak to Mme Oetlinger. The servant showed him into the hall and, after having asked him to wait, went to inform Annie. A few moments later, he returned and announced that Mme Oetlinger had gone out.

"In that case," said Emile, "I would like to speak to Monsieur Villemur."

The butler disappeared again, but rather than going to his master, he returned to Annie, who had asked him to keep her informed of the visitor's next move. Emile had been waiting for a few minutes in the library, which he had been shown into because it was the most isolated room, when Mme Oetlinger joined him there. Upon seeing her, he bowed slightly, without saying a word.

"I can think of no explanation for your visit."

"I have very important matters to discuss with you," said Emile, with a fervor as misplaced as that of a lawyer defending a petty thief.

"I have no time to listen to you."

"And yet you must, Madame. My mother and I can't go on living the way we have been. We have made sacrifices . . ."

"What sacrifices?"

"Do you think we haven't had to make any in order not to ask you for anything? But now, we've reached the end of our rope."

Annie was so surprised by these words that she was unable to stop herself from saying, "None of your sacrifices have anything to do with me. I have absolutely no idea what you're talking about."

"We are penniless, Madame. And you are to blame, as is my brother. If he hadn't duped us endlessly with his promises, we would have acted sooner."

From the moment Mme Oetlinger had come in, Emile had not once looked at the books, the tapestries, or the busts which filled the room, in order to demonstrate to the person he was speaking to that the luxurious surroundings made no impression upon him. He might not have been raised by Annie, but he was nonetheless Jean-Melchior's son. If distinction was an innate quality, there was no reason why he should have any less than his brother.

"My mother," he went on, speaking as if to an equal, "has never worked. It isn't now, at her age, that she is going to start. Her health is not very good. She needs peace and quiet, fresh air."

Whereas Jean-Noël was interested above all in showing off, Emile, who claimed that he knew what real wealth was, and who retained of bankers' biographies only the anecdotes relative to their apparent poverty, was only interested in ascertaining whether an expenditure did not exceed the means of the person making it, a quality of which his mother was inordinately proud.

"I really don't see why you are telling me this."

"Because had you not entered my father's life, and had you not prevented him from doing his duty when he wanted to, we wouldn't be in the situation we are in today. What's more, you know this perfectly well," continued Emile, who was taking great care to give his sentences a written rather than spoken turn of phrase. "Are you going to force me to remind you of the promise you made Monsieur Oetlinger?"

"What promise?"

"We still have the letter. I have it with me. I can show it to you. In this letter, which my father wrote to my mother several days before he died and which we consider to be the expression of his last wishes, he said that if he should die, you would take it upon yourself to make a payment to us of no less than fifty thousand francs, at the time. Instead of that amount, you gave us the miserly sum of five thousand francs."

"I never agreed to do any such thing," said Annie, "for the very good reason that I would not have known where to find that amount of money."

But Annie did not ask to see the letter. She had suspected Jean-Melchior of concealing certain expenditures from her, of frequenting people whom he had thought unworthy of bringing home but whose company he had nonetheless found agreeable. She had turned a blind eye to avoid learning anything that might diminish the image she had fashioned of her husband, an image that mattered all the more to her because she had been the one who'd made him leave everything behind. Now that she was back in the bosom of her family, her fear that she would learn of some deception was greater than it had ever been. To her, all those who had known Jean-Melchior seemed to be witnesses to some far-off sin. When in their presence, she trembled with fear that what was most dear to her, the memory of a love which had been embellished by the passage of time, would be taken away from her.

"I have come to ask you, therefore," resumed Emile, "to honor your commitments."

"What commitments! I have no more money. We spent everything I had, your father and I. Leave me alone. Please go. I have earned the right to end my days in peace."

". . . which riches bring."

"But nothing here is mine, nothing."

"That's too easy," continued Emile, speaking with that vulgarity which reappeared whenever he let down his guard. "Now that you've ruined my mother's life, and my own, you don't care what becomes of us."

This time Annie remained silent. She rang. The butler who had shown Emile in appeared almost instantly.

"Show Monsieur out," said Mme Oetlinger.

But although the servant respectfully pointed toward the door, the visitor did not budge.

"I will not leave."

Annie made a sign to the butler.

"Would Monsieur care to follow me?"

"I will first speak to your father," said Emile, raising his voice.

"My father will not see you."

Mme Oetlinger had barely spoken these words when M. Villemur appeared in the doorway. He came forward slowly, looking the young man over from head to toe.

"You wished to speak to me?" he asked him.

"Yes, Monsieur. I wanted to show you a letter my father wrote to my mother."

As he spoke these words, he drew his wallet from his pocket. But as he did so, Annie stepped between Emile and M. Villemur.

"No, Father, I beg of you, do not look at this letter. It is nothing but lies, hateful lies."

For a few seconds, M. Villemur stared hard at the young man, with neither scorn nor indulgence, but rather as if he wanted to penetrate to the very essence of his being. Then, without saying another word, he took his daughter by the arm, as if he needed her to support him, and left the room. After Emile had left, Annie, who had controlled herself throughout his visit, suddenly felt faint. M. and Mme Villemur made her lie on a sofa and inhale smelling salts. After she had come round, she went and locked herself in her room, refusing the assistance her parents wanted to continue to give her. It struck her then that Jean-Noël was indirectly responsible for what had just occurred. He was certainly capable of having boasted of the solicitude Annie had shown him a few days earlier. Every time she had acted in the interests of another, she had come to regret it. Had her stepson taken her generosity as a sign of weakness? Emile was Jean-Noël's brother, after all, and the latter had doubtless advised him to take advantage of the fact that Mme Oetlinger was well disposed. At last, she called Maître Préfil's office. As her stepson was not there, she could do no more than ask that he be given the message to come and see her as soon as he returned.

The reason Jean-Noël had been out of the office when his stepmother called was that he'd been on his way to the rue Mouton-Duvernet at that very moment, in the hope of stopping his brother.

When he'd returned to the rue Laugier the day before, he had suddenly begun to worry. However much he had tried to pretend that he had nothing to fear from Emile, he had nonetheless been dreading precisely what had occurred. Mme Mourier had been waiting for him with that impatience she always displayed when she knew Jean-Noël had just seen his mother or brother. Laure could not bear them: one was as lazy as the other.

"Your brother's been asking you for money again," she had said before Jean-Noël even removed his overcoat.

Shortly after Mme Mourier had left Jean-Noël with Emile at the bottom of the rue de Clichy, she had taken a taxi. The sooner she got home, the longer she would have to wait, and the more violent a scene she would make when Jean-Noël returned. It was not the fact that he was poor that she could not forgive Emile, or that he had a torn overcoat, or that he lacked qualities, but rather that he had none of that admiration for her which she claimed she could read in the eyes of certain passersby. Had he considered her a woman unworthy of being received by his family, since all he ever spoke about was family, she would have been unfazed if, on the other hand, he had displayed signs of some inner turmoil when in her presence. Emile, however, seemed never even to have noticed that she was a woman. She had saddled Jean-Noël with this boorishness, which was how she qualified Emile's indifference, in the following manner. There were two men in him: one who, because of his upbringing, his stepmother's affection for him, and the links that tied him to the Villemurs, had been able to seduce her; and another, less dazzling, who was indeed the son of Mme Mercier and the brother of Emile, and whom she now had to make do with.

"No one in my situation would ever have behaved as I have done until today," she had said. "I have done everything you wanted. I told myself that it was not your fault if you had such a family. But I can't go on any longer. If I have to see these people again, I would rather you take a room in a hotel. They make me sick. Surely your brother must know that if you help him at all, it's thanks to me, and that if you didn't have me, you would find it very difficult to give him anything whatsoever. And yet I'm not welcome! I am in the way when you and Emile want to have your conversations! It's unbelievable!"

These tirades, of which Mme Mourier made abundant use, would plunge Jean-Noël into a silence that sometimes went on for days at a time, during which he would think of disappearing without saying a word. On that particular evening, however, he had paid no attention to the flood of words. What he feared was far more serious. Was Emile going to carry out his threat? Jean-Noël's anxiety had increased as the evening wore on. Mme Mourier, whose tantrums never lasted long, had reverted to being gay and loving. From time to time, Jean-Noël had looked at her. He had been surprised to find that he felt friendly toward her. At heart she loved him, didn't she? He then thought of telling her what had transpired between him and Emile. And yet he hesitated. He had stopped confiding in her several months ago in order to facilitate the separation he was planning. But he was too tormented by the fear that Emile would go to the avenue de Malakoff, just when Annie had been so affectionate toward him. In the end, he had been unable to resist his need to talk about it.

"I didn't tell you that Emile wants to go and see my stepmother."

"That can't be!" Mme Mourier had cried out.

One would have thought that her grievances against Ernestine Mercier and the latter's younger son had never existed.

"Emile won't do that. Your mother will stop him."

"I doubt it."

"In spite of everything, your mother is a decent sort. And Emile, do you really think he is so wicked?"

Mme Mourier underwent a sort of metamorphosis whenever someone came to her with a problem. She had offered to go see Emile. Had Jean-Noël allowed her to do so, she would have gone to the rue Mouton-Duvernet as if there had never been the slightest discord between the Merciers and herself. The only time she had met Annie, Jean-Noël's stepmother had treated her like a person of great common sense, whose influence on her stepson could only be beneficial. Shouldn't she now show that she was worthy of this trust? In the end, she had advised Jean-Noël to visit his mother the next day and make her understand that if she allowed Emile to act, it would not be he, Jean-Noël, who would suffer as a result, but rather Mme Mercier herself, for she had everything to gain if her elder son remained on good terms with Mme Oetlinger.

The next morning, Jean-Noël had called Maître Préfil to tell him that he would not be coming in to the office. Then, at about ten o'clock, he had gone to the rue Mouton-Duvernet.

He had done so reluctantly. After the arrogant attitude his brother had adopted, the idea of seeing him again disgusted him. But now that he had asked Mme Mourier for her advice, he had little choice but to to follow it. Only half an hour earlier, she had given him some last-minute recommendations.

When he arrived at his mother's, Emile had already left. Jean-Noël concealed his annoyance. Mme Mercier was lighting a small stove that stood in front of the fireplace. A screen separated the two beds. "But no one knows it exists," she often said, "and you can imagine the tales people tell about me. They even went so far as to say that Emile, do you hear me, kindhearted little Emile, was my lover, that we were living as man and wife, that I tormented him. Oh! Your poor father, if he only knew!"

"Where is Emile?" asked Jean-Noël, as if mere curiosity drove him to ask her this question.

"I thought you'd seen him last night," said Mme Mercier, as if she suspected Emile of having lied to her when he had said he'd seen his brother, despite the fact that she was convinced he had been telling the truth.

"I did see him."

"Ah! That's better. I wouldn't have liked it if he'd been lying to me. But in that case, he must have told you that he wanted to go see the Villemurs."

"So soon, today?"

Mme Mercier made a gesture signifying that, where Emile was concerned, one never knew what to expect. When he had something in mind, it was difficult to make him think of anything else. He had been talking of going to see Mme Oetlinger for several months now. Had he done so? Mme Mercier had no idea. If she had no influence over the boy, wasn't Jean-Noël a bit to blame? How could a woman alone, and already old, govern a young man who, in living with her, found only worries, sadness, and complaints, all of them concerns so foreign to his age? Was it right to hold it against

Emile if he wanted to escape? He must certainly have gone to the avenue de Malakoff. And as if she had filed a formal complaint which now had to follow its course, Mme Mercier lifted her arms to heaven in a sign of helplessness.

"Are you sure of what you are saying?" asked Jean-Noël.

"Sure, no. It may be that he went for a walk. He never tells me what he's doing."

"It just so happens that I wanted to talk to both of you."

"He'll probably be back before lunchtime. Would you like me to make you a cup of coffee while you're waiting?"

"Thank you, don't bother."

Jean-Noël sat down. Whenever he went to the rue Mouton-Duvernet, he was overcome by an unpleasant sensation, that of having blood ties, in spite of everything, to all this misery. Even while he felt a mixture of shame and pity, he hoped that someday his mother and brother would come to resemble normal people. Had he had money, had he been able to earn enough, everything would have been so simple. He would have bought his mother a house in the south of France—if, of course, the climate agreed with her, for she had never been well anywhere—and he would never have had to hear about her or Emile again.

That morning, Jean-Noël was entertaining no such notions. He was so irritated that he felt he had nothing whatsoever in common with his mother. Wasn't it unbelievable that people always turned against him? He'd had enough. When Emile returned, he would tell him exactly what he thought of his behavior. "Had I never done anything for them," he thought, "I would understand." But hadn't he done everything he could? It was hardly his fault if he hadn't been able to do more. What made him even angrier was the thought that, if he hadn't existed, Emile would probably never have thought of going to the Villemurs. At heart, he alone was the reason for this maneuver. If they had even dared to do such a thing it was only because they knew that he was still in contact with Annie. They hated him and yet they used him.

It was nearly noon when he heard footsteps on the stairs.

Then the door opened. It was Emile. Slowly, he removed his overcoat and hung it in a corner. One guessed that because of the apartment's exiguousness, he had acquired certain orderly habits without which it would have been impossible to live in such cramped quarters. Without seeming to take Jean-Noël's presence into account, he approached his mother and greeted her respectfully, in order to show his brother that, although he had not had the benefit of Annie's favors, he had nonetheless been just as properly brought up.

"Jean-Noël has been waiting for you," Mme Mercier said to him.

Emile turned toward his brother and made a sign as if he had greeted him only a moment earlier.

"Have you just been to the Villemurs?" asked Jean-Noël, as if the question were of no particular importance.

"Yes," replied Emile, opening a drawer and taking out a packet of cigarettes that had been there for months. He no longer smoked, or rather only smoked on important occasions now, no one knew why.

"And yet I asked you not to go."

Emile did not reply. Turning toward his mother, he asked, "Did anyone come by?"

"No one," she replied, with such a questioning look on her face that her son was unable to avoid making some reply.

"I'll tell you about it later." Then, speaking now to Jean-Noël, he added, "You wanted to see me?" as if their roles had been reversed, and now it was the older brother who was constantly badgering the younger.

"Of course I want to see you!" retorted Jean-Noël, who was finding it difficult to control himself. "What did you go and do at the avenue de Malakoff?"

"I don't have to answer you. Why don't you go see your stepmother? She can tell you herself."

"I want to know now. I don't suppose you and Annie have any secrets."

Beads of sweat had appeared above Jean-Noël's upper lip. Other, larger ones, unevenly transparent, like drops of honey, trickled down his forehead from time to time. He was beside himself. Not satisfied with having taken this step with the express intention of doing him harm, Emile now refused to talk to him about it, doubtless to create the impression that Annie had confided in him.

"I am telling you again," said Emile, "that I have nothing to say to you."

Jean-Noël got up, took his hat, and moved toward the door.

"You can do whatever you like from now on," he said before leaving, "it won't trouble me in the least. On the other hand, I'm warning you that you can't count on me any longer."

He sprinted down the four flights of stairs and rushed headlong down the street to the place Denfert-Rochereau. He was furious with his mother and brother. Their conduct seemed odious to him. With every step, he wondered what on earth Annie could have said to Emile, and his brother's silence seemed all the more hostile for appearing to stem from the fact that the two had gotten along perfectly well. As he was about to enter a subway station, however, he was suddenly filled with remorse. Hadn't it been heartless of him to attack an aging mother and an ailing brother as he had just done? He reflected on the life they had led. Fundamentally, those poor people had legitimate reasons for being the way they were. In the course of their lives they had never known even the slightest joy. They had always been hidden away. Hadn't he, Jean-Noël, led a privileged life compared to that led by Emile, whom no one had guided, whose health was delicate, and who had suffered from being poor, all the while watching from a distance as his older brother was showered with favors and privileges?

Jean-Noël retraced his steps and slowly climbed the four flights which he had come down so quickly. He knocked at the door. No one answered. The key was in the lock. He entered. Emile was lying on his bed, his feet hanging over the edge, hiding his head in his hands. He was crying, while his mother sat next to him, talking to him. Whenever she touched his shoulder, he would push her away with his hand. She would then look at him fearfully.

"Look what you've done," she said to Jean-Noël, expressing no surprise that her son had come back.

Just then, Emile sat up.

"Why are you here?" he asked gently.

"She had him chased out by a servant," Mme Mercier shouted at Jean-Noël. "You told her to do that."

Emile laid back down, on his back this time. He was pale. His lips were slightly parted, exposing his damaged teeth. His face no longer registered either envy or bitterness. It was the face of a sick man, with neither pride nor ambition, and so distant that for a moment Jean-Noël had the feeling that this brother, of whom he was so ashamed, was superior to him by dint of his moral elevation.

FIFTEEN

By the time Jean-Noël left his mother and brother, not without having endeavored to lift their spirits by making yet more promises, it was already one o'clock. The streets were nearly deserted. As he'd already spent the entire morning away from the office, he hurried home in order not to be late getting back to work after lunch. He was no longer thinking of his brother, for he was quick to forget those from whom, momentarily, he had nothing to fear. Annie alone occupied his thoughts. What could possibly have happened at the avenue de Malakoff to so demoralize Emile, who was usually so imperturbable?

Mme Mourier did not have a telephone. There was one "for the building" in the concierge's lodge. As he passed by, Jean-Noël asked if there had been any calls for him that morning. The concierge didn't know. As soon as he was with Laure, he told her what had just happened. Then he ate quickly, with no real appetite. Mme Mourier asked him why he was in such a hurry. He answered that he had a great deal of work to do. Actually, he was anxious to know whether Annie had phoned him, but didn't dare admit it, for Laure had already several times expressed her surprise that, when she had something to tell him, Mme Oetlinger chose to call her stepson at the office rather than the rue Laugier. As soon as he arrived at the rue de Clichy, he was given Annie's message. Maître Préfil, however, had gone to the solicitors' guild.

Only towards five in the afternoon was Jean-Noël able to leave the office. Every now and again one of his shoulders

[127]

would twitch convulsively from fear and emotion. How would he be received? No matter how hard he tried to reason and convince himself that he was not responsible for Emile's impulsive actions, he still felt guilty. Visiting his stepmother in perfectly ordinary circumstances was enough to make him feel pangs of anxiety. He did not take the elevator. Slowly, he climbed the stairs, which were three times as wide as those at the rue Laugier, and illuminated by candelabra. In front of the door to the Villemurs' apartment, he leaned on a table for a moment, the table whose presence in the hallway he had once found so surprising. He was shown into the study. M. Villemur met him there a moment later.

"Have you come to see Annie?" he asked, and Jean-Noël, who remembered Annie's father as an authoritative figure, was struck by the gentle tone of voice in which he spoke.

"Yes, Monsieur."

"Have you been announced?"

M. Villemur sat down at his desk, without paying any further attention to the visitor, and after having put on a pair of spectacles, leafed through some bank documents. From the half-light where he stood, Jean-Noël observed him. M. Villemur's face was illuminated by a lamp that stood near him on the desk. It radiated calm. Even as he was filled with that pity which social power inspires in us when it serves only to accentuate our frailty, as with old or dying men, Jean-Noël thought how strange it was that this man, who could hardly be unaware of what had taken place that morning, and was perhaps even the one who had had Emile sent away, was behaving no differently than if he had been in the presence of a close friend. Occasionally M. Villemur would turn his head in the direction of the visitor, but, dazzled by the light shining directly beneath his eyes, he could not see him. Finally, M. Villemur got up.

"It seems to me that Annie has forgotten about you. I will go fetch her."

When he returned, after a rather long absence, he said, in

the same soft voice, "You know where her room is? My daughter is waiting for you."

This little scene had given Jean-Noël courage. If M. Villemur was being so friendly, nothing terribly serious could have happened. But when he saw his stepmother, he grew somber once again. Standing very straight and immobile in the middle of her room, she was quite clearly prey to some powerful emotion.

"I was waiting for you impatiently," she said to Jean-Noël, who came to a halt as soon as he stepped over the threshold. Far from soothing her, the several hours that had elapsed since Emile's departure had served only to increase her anger. "Would you please explain to me, very briefly, the meaning of all of this?"

Jean-Noël pretended to be surprised.

"Your brother came here earlier," she said, with the resolve of someone who has decided to pay no attention to the wiles of the person they are speaking to.

"I know," replied Jean-Noël. "I've just seen him. As a matter of fact, I wanted to ask what he'd said to you."

Annie had the impression that her stepson was putting on an act. Not only did he know why Emile had come to the avenue de Malakoff, he was doubtless the one who'd put him up to it.

"I fail to understand why you didn't stop him from coming, or at least why you didn't warn me."

"I just saw him now. I knew absolutely nothing about it."

"Ah! My poor Jean-Noël, if you had been here! He refused to leave. My father had to call the servants. I've never seen anything like it."

"He really refused to leave?" asked Jean-Noël, while thinking about the painful scene he had witnessed at the rue Mouton-Duvernet, which he felt guilty about keeping to himself.

"He spoke of a letter your father had written to your mother. Do you have that letter?"

"What letter?"

"I don't know, I don't know! How am I supposed to know? I'm asking you. Have you read this letter?"

"I've never heard anything about it."

"What! You see your family nearly every day and yet they've never mentioned this letter to you! Fine. The fact of the matter is, you know perfectly well who is at the root of all this business. I can't go on living this way. Now I am being hounded even here, in my father's house. People imagine I am rich, when the truth is I have nothing left. What is it you all want of me? Don't you think I've done enough for you? I cannot—do you understand me, I cannot—put up with any more of this. What I ask is that you all leave me in peace, simply in peace. That's not so much to ask, and yet I can't seem to obtain it."

"Why are you saying this to me? I understand you so well . . ."

Jean-Noël had spoken these last words in such a tone of voice that Annie, surprised, stopped. Her stepson's sincerity had struck her and, in spite of everything, even brought her a certain pleasure. Jean-Noël was not such a bad fellow after all. What she disliked in him were the impulsive actions and theatrical gestures he was occasionally given to. While there was no doubt that these sprang from childish, generous instincts, she nonetheless found them unbearable. They showed a lack of scruple, a desire to impose oneself in the name of supposedly high-minded sentiments, a tactlessness of which the most flagrant example had been his ludicrous idea of having Jean-Melchior's remains brought back to Paris. Annie was convinced that the reasons for her stepson's devotion to her had more to with what she represented than who she really was. It was for this reason that she bemoaned her fate, that she warned all those who approached her that she was ruined, for she was tired of playing the grand lady to ordinary people. It was becoming ridiculous. She aspired only to be treated like everyone else, neither better nor worse.

Finally, Annie calmed down. It was, after all, obvious that

Jean-Noël was deeply upset about what had happened, and that although he was in some sense responsible for Emile's visit, it was very much in spite of himself.

"I know," she said in a hushed voice, "that it isn't your fault."

"I am grateful to you for saying so," answered Jean-Noël, who, knowing how his stepmother loathed effusive displays, endeavored to speak these words in a steady voice.

"You have no reason to be grateful to me for anything whatsoever. If I didn't think this had happened through no fault of your own, I wouldn't have said it," she continued. In her mind, gratefulness was something one encountered only in dubious individuals who needed to be forgiven for their faults, and who were then grateful for the forgiveness shown them. As she was feeling well disposed toward Jean-Noël, and could only be feeling this way if he had behaved correctly, he had therefore not done anything wrong; as a result, there was no need for him to be grateful.

"I need to speak to you seriously. I did a great deal of thinking this afternoon. I am sure that you will agree with my way of seeing things. All this business must, do you hear me, absolutely stop. I find it extraordinary that ten years after your poor father's death I am still a target of your family's hatred. Life is no longer possible with that perpetual threat hanging over my head. Even though you are doubtless unaware of it, it is somewhat your fault. It would therefore be wise, I think, if you were not to come here for a certain period of time—a year, two years, I don't know, we'll have to see. While you may not pay any attention to what others think, your family, your wife, your friends, Mme Mourier, all of them are lying in wait to see what your next move will be. It is well known that I have taken an interest in you. In the minds of these people—and I don't mean Laure, who is extremely kind and is an excellent companion for you—I am a sort of charitable organization. I don't know everything they're thinking, but I am sure they imagine that I give you money secretly. They say to themselves: why just him? why not us as well? As a result of their envy they've come to hate us both. But as soon as we stop seeing one another, they will forget about me. I will go even farther: I think this will be good for you. You are twenty-seven years old. You need to become aware of your own worth. If, for a few years, you feel truly alone, and know that you have only yourself to rely upon, you will become more self-confident. That is just what you are most lacking, self-confidence. As for me, I will continue working as I have always done. Do you remember that atlas that amused you so much when you were a child?"

Mme Oetlinger had undertaken a project that was beyond her capacities. It was nothing less than an atlas on whose maps she would paint in miniature, on the very spot where they had occurred, all the greatest events in history from the very beginning of time.

Jean-Noël had listened to his stepmother most attentively, indicating his approval every now and again.

"Later on, when we have recovered 'our equilibrium,' our pleasure at seeing one another again will be all the greater," she concluded.

Mme Oetlinger thought she had expressed herself in the most reasonable terms possible in suggesting this arrangement to her stepson. If it never occurred to her that a separation under such conditions was somewhat inhuman, it was because throughout her life she had always considered that separation was, in and of itself, the best remedy for any misunderstanding.

Jean-Noël did not reply. What would become of him without his stepmother? Although there had always been perpetual conflicts between Annie and himself, she nonetheless remained the only person in the world he truly cared about. She was his entire family, his reason for living; because he loved her, and because she was his only connection with a milieu he longed to be part of but to which he was not admitted. If he was able to bear the mediocre life he was leading, it was because of Annie. Would he now be deprived of that respect which his connection with her afforded him, and which was so important in his eyes that he was happy only among those who recognized it? Was he going to become like Mme Mourier, Maître Préfil, the latter's colleagues, Emile? Until now he had been someone exceptional among his entourage, someone around whom hovered wealth and power—or so he liked to think. But tomorrow? In his darkest hours, he had never felt so lost. He had always imagined that he had the power to end his isolation. Today, Annie was the one who was leaving him, and so coldly that he hadn't even the strength to protest.

SIXTEEN

Jean-Noël replied evasively to the questions Mme Mourier asked him the following day. He was no longer in that frame of mind which had made him confide in a woman he was planning to leave. He was anxious that she not find out about Mme Oetlinger's decision, which was so humiliating for him. What would Laure have said had she known that he now had no ties whatsoever to the Villemur family, whose friend she hoped to become some day? Nonetheless, in spite of the fact that he kept silent, Mme Mourier noticed that he was concealing something. When she had some reproach to make, she liked to catch the person to whom it was addressed off guard, and therefore waited for a suitable occasion to complain of the strange way in which she was being treated by the very man for whom she had neglected all of her own interests. A visit from Mme Mercier gave her the pretext she needed. Pretending not to have noticed the delay with which she was doing so, the latter had come to tell her son, as if to unburden herself of a secret she knew perfectly well was no secret at all, that if Emile had gone to the avenue de Malakoff, it had been in the hope of being "reimbursed."

"Your mother is really not very pleasant," remarked Laure after Mme Mercier had left. "When I think that this woman comes into my home without even asking herself if she's disturbing me, that when she wants to speak to you, she draws you off into a corner as though I'm not welcome, I can't stop myself from thinking that I've really been far too kind. I would like you to tell me if you know any woman who would have been as patient as I have been."

It was just then it occurred to Jean-Noël that he ought to tell Laure the truth about his relations with his stepmother. Wouldn't this diminish him in her eyes, and thus make it easier for him to leave her? Anxious as Mme Mourier was for him to retain Annie's affection, she would have to be disappointed by this break in their relations. Jean-Noël was not mistaken. At first, she refused to believe him. Then, it struck her that what was happening to Jean-Noël was not unlike what had happened to her. He would now realize what families were like. For several days she pretended to be thinking of ways in which Jean-Noël could regain the ground he had lost. But when his passive attitude led her to believe that he was resigned to his fate, she surprised the young man by displaying renewed affection for him. They would go forward, hand in hand. They would reorganize their lives, stop paying out allowances. It just so happened that she was having some financial difficulties because of her husband and had been thinking of setting up a couture business. Why didn't they make a pact, while waiting for the day when fortune favored them? They were both already married. Shouldn't that fact draw them even closer together? Strengthened by the experience they had acquired, they would strive to make their way, independent in the eyes of the world, but secretly united.

Shortly after this, Jean-Noël received a letter from Marguerite in which she wrote that she would rather go begging from door to door than grant him a divorce, and that if he was to learn one day that she had led Annette to an early grave, he would know whom to hold responsible. Jean-Noël burned the letter immediately. Nonetheless it remained engraved in his memory. In spite of everything, he had been hoping some good would come of Annie's decision. Nothing of the sort had happened. Instead of being weakened, the bonds uniting him to Mme Mourier had grown tighter, so much so that, as the interests of their union had become his concern, a new worry had now been added to those already troubling him.

*　　*　　*

It had been three weeks since Jean-Noël had last seen Odile when he decided to go to the boulevard du Montparnasse one evening. Going there was disagreeable to him, not just because he was embarrassed to reappear after having stayed away for so long, but because the reason for his absence that would have excused him was the very one he did not want to mention. He now saw marriage as the only way out of the situation in which he found himself.

Everyone was delighted to see him again except Mlle Wurtzel, and he was only able to draw her away alone after having been forced to take part in a general conversation that lasted over an hour.

"You must have been wondering what had become of me," said Jean-Noël, as if there were nothing unusual about his absence. "Well, I had a great deal of work. Every day I thought of calling you, but would tell myself that I would come and see you the next day. The more time went by, the more difficult it became for me."

"That's where you're wrong," she replied coldly. "I wasn't wondering anything at all. I was simply thinking that you are very strange."

In reality, Odile very much wanted to marry Jean-Noël. She liked him, a bit because she had been charmed by him long ago, in the days when her family had been accorded the honor of frequenting the Villemurs, but more than anything because he had been subjected to the same disgrace as her own parents. She had liked his independence, the self-assurance he seemed to possess, his casual air, that disinterestedness which none of the young men who were introduced to her as possible candidates for marriage possessed. She had been flattered and proud to play a part in his life, to offer advice. But because she knew exactly what her own desires and expectations were, she did not want it to seem that she cared for him. They had been together for an hour when Jean-Noël, who no longer knew what to say, rose. M. Wurtzel was just then coming to give his daughter a good-night kiss before going to bed himself, and to warn her not to stay up too late. Jean-Noël was preparing to go when the thought of finding himself alone with all his worries made him want to know that he could at least count on the comfort of Odile's friendship.

"You must listen to me," he said without waiting for M. Wurtzel, whose voice was drawing nearer, to take leave of his daughter. "If I didn't come to see you sooner, it was because something very serious has happened between Annie and me. We've had a falling-out."

He was unable to go on.

"It's getting late, Monsieur Oetlinger. It's time you were going."

M. Wurtzel kissed his daughter and told her to go to bed.

"That's just what I was about to do," she said.

When her father had left her, she accompanied Jean-Noël into the foyer, chatting about banalities, but as she extended her hand to him, she added, now in a knowing voice, "Come back and see me tomorrow."

A long, drawn-out discussion then took place between Odile and Jean-Noël. They were so frank with one another that Jean-Noël even asked her if she still loved him now that she knew he no longer had any ties to his stepmother. She became indignant. "On the contrary," she replied, "it's only under those conditions that I could have feelings for you." He persisted, and asked her to look deep within her soul. For a few minutes, during which Jean-Noël pretended to be respecting her concentration, she asked herself whether the fact that Jean-Noël would not be seeing his stepmother again really diminished him in her eyes. "No," she said at last. "Not at all." Thus reconciled, they now had to consider the matter of his divorce. They were still discussing the matter long after M. Wurtzel had gone to bed. They finally took leave of one another after deciding to go to Saint-Cloud together the following Sunday.

Sunday came at last. Jean-Noël was worried about how Marguerite would react to Mlle Wurtzel. The weather was inclement and, like the last time, a strong wind was blowing. Jean-Noël had not been back to Saint-Cloud, although he had sent the famous letter he had been writing in his mind, to which his wife had replied a fortnight later with a threat to commit suicide.

"Perhaps we should make it seem as if we're coming because of that letter," said Jean-Noël.

But Odile made him understand immediately that she was not going to Saint-Cloud to play games. She was following her heart, and it was without any ulterior motives whatsoever that she was going to try to make Marguerite listen to reason.

Jean-Noël did not feel at all ashamed at the thought that an elegant and pretty young girl like Odile was about to find herself in the presence of an unkempt, slovenly woman who had already begun to run to fat and to whom, in addition, he happened to be married. He knew that Mlle Wurtzel possessed the attribute of never judging people by appearances and that, had he introduced her to an old, drunken hag and told her that she was his wife, she would have treated her with as much consideration as any other person she happened to meet. Surprising as this was, she was of the view that everyone is different, and that nothing could be more unfair than to judge people on the basis of their parents or their friends.

When they reached the rue Mission-Marchand, Jean-Noël pointed out Marguerite's house to Odile. A dozen or so children, including Annie, were playing in the little garden, for it was Marguerite's custom to organize gatherings of all the neighborhood children on Sundays. He hesitated before ringing.

"Where is your daughter?" asked Odile.

As he made no reply, she added: "We should ring. We can't stand here like this." Jean-Noël did as he was told. Then he made a sign to Odile indicating that they should wait until the gate had been opened for them.

It was Annie who came running. But when she spied a

woman she did not know, she froze for a moment, then ran back off again, crying: "It's Papa! It's Papa!"

"She's so untidy," remarked Odile. She liked children, and Jean-Noël was baffled by the interest with which she scrutinized his daughter, a bit as if she were the girl's mother and was seeing her for the first time after a long absence, without being recognized by the child.

"Maman, Maman, Papa is here, with a lady!" they heard her shout.

Almost immediately, Marguerite appeared beneath the little awning that sheltered the front steps of the house, an apron tied around her waist, her hair unkempt, a tie dangling from her neck, and wearing a sweater so stretched-out at the neck that her cleavage was clearly visible. Jean-Noël pushed open the garden gate, which was rusty. The children had grown quiet. Unable to avoid feeling embarrassed by his wife's presence, he moved aside to allow Odile to go in ahead of him. She had chosen a dark and very simple suit for the occasion, but one whose impeccable cut Marguerite could not fail to notice.

"Come in," said Marguerite, like a woman who has nothing to hide.

"Above all, we don't want to disturb you, Madame," said Odile gravely.

"Allow me to introduce you to Mademoiselle Wurtzel," said Jean-Noël.

"You are not disturbing me, Mademoiselle. Please come in," said Marguerite.

Odile stayed where she was, at the foot of the steps.

"Go in," repeated Jean-Noël.

This time, she did as they asked. The three of them made their way into the dining room that was in its customary state of disarray, for which Marguerite apologized.

"Every Sunday, as you can see, I organize a little gathering. The children have a wonderful time. Each brings his own lunch. They play in the garden. Then we all go walking in the woods together. So I don't do a lick of work on Sundays until they've gone."

Intimidated and yet intrigued by the visitors, a few of the children were standing motionless in a doorway.

"Go and play, my little ones, and be good!"

Jean-Noël had pulled himself together. Unless something unexpected happened, it seemed this visit would go very smoothly. Marguerite was receiving him more warmly than when he came alone, which was rather surprising. In her situation, which she seemed to find so very exceptional, didn't she need to be adaptable? If Jean-Noël had come back a week later with another woman, she would have received him in exactly the same manner. She had a daughter. It was her duty to accept everything, no matter how extraordinary. She was wise enough not to compromise her child's future. She knew her rights, and nothing would make her relinquish them.

"Do you want some coffee?" she asked her husband, using the familiar form of address, which made him blush.

He turned to Odile so that the answer would come from her. She declined. Marguerite did not insist. Jean-Noël could not put off the moment of speaking any longer without running the risk of seeming to dread it.

"I have come," he said, smiling broadly, "to discuss business with you. The last time, if you recall, I asked you what you thought of clarifying our situation."

"A divorce," interrupted Marguerite, so as to show straightaway that they could call things by their names, and that she would not let herself be influenced.

"Just so. If I've asked Mademoiselle Wurtzel to come with me today, it's because I know you don't have a great deal of trust in me, which is understandable . . ."

"I won't have any more in Mademoiselle Wurtzel." And turning toward Odile, Marguerite added, "I don't know you, isn't that right, Mademoiselle?"

"Your husband expressed himself badly," said Odile very gently, "or perhaps you misunderstood him. Do not think that I have come as his reinforcement."

"You would have been wasting your time."

"I have come because I have a great deal of affection for

Jean-Noël. When he told me the other day that you did not want to grant him a divorce, I thought that, in looking at your respective situations, you had not been able to do so with the necessary independence of mind."

"You were wrong."

"Let me finish. If Monsieur Oetlinger wishes to have his freedom back, in your eyes this can only be in order to do to another woman what he did to you, another woman who will doubtless not be as patient as you have been. Therefore you told yourself that if you were strong enough to resist him, he would be grateful to you for this later on and might even come back to you. This might indeed have been the case, of course, were it not for those never-ending questions of money."

Mlle Wurtzel then went on to intimate, thinking she was being very skillful by so doing, that Jean-Noël did not have what could be called passionate feelings for her, Odile; and that if the two of them had thought about marriage, it was out of the desire, on her part, to leave her family and, on his, to be relieved of the worries caused by his dependents and financial obligations. Such humility was not at all surprising. If it brought her closer to the distant goal she had set for herself, Odile was unconcerned at being the object of that scorn which the world heaps upon someone who expresses his gratitude to you for having struck him. But Marguerite was far more straightforward. She was not taken in by the little scene being played out for her benefit. The mere fact that it was taking place at all made a bad impression upon her. Rather than seeing a desire to please her in Odile's words, she saw in them only the selfishness and lack of feeling which one encountered, according to her, only in those rich and supposedly elegant circles where she imagined her husband spent most of his time. They were really all alike, these young society ladies: depraved, taking pleasure only in subtle games, and liking nothing better than to toy, out of perversity, with honest women. But in spite of the instinctive, automatic replies she delivered like so many cries from the heart, Marguerite showed no lack of deference, because from the depths of the poverty and solitude she had lived in for so many years, she had always thought that the day would come when that very world of which she spoke so disparagingly, while being proud of her connections to it through her husband, would need her. She had therefore received Odile without being at all surprised, as if she were owed this visit; for she had become like one of those upright civil servants who looks on helplessly at the scheming manuevers of those who covet his job, but from whom they must obtain his signature on a letter of resignation.

SEVENTEEN

Barely half an hour after arriving in Saint-Cloud, Mlle Wurtzel had taken her leave of Marguerite, to Jean-Noël's great
surprise. Nothing had been settled. Little by little, the conversation had drifted off into domestic details. It was not the
first time that Jean-Noël had noticed Odile behaving this way.
Whereas he had a taste for long, drawn-out discussions and
never left an interlocutor before being sure they were in perfect agreement, Odile, like a person who does not prolong a
visit for fear she is imposing, would get up and leave when
one least expected it. In ordinary circumstances, there was no
cause to criticize this way of behaving, but on that day her
actions had seemed somewhat cavalier. Hadn't Marguerite
become a very different person at the moment of this abrupt
departure? Convinced that she had proven she was exceptionally good-natured by receiving Mlle Wurtzel, she must certainly have been offended at being treated as if it were natural
she should welcome all of her husband's lady friends.

Once they were back in Paris, Jean-Noël pointed out to
Odile that it might perhaps have been more diplomatic to
wait for Marguerite to bring their meeting to an end. But the
young girl maintained that, on the contrary, they had done
very well not to linger. Marguerite would thus have understood that, although they wanted to reach an understanding
with her, they weren't prepared to yield to all her conditions
in order to do so. In fact, it was difficult to imagine how the
visit could have gone any better. "Your wife was very friendly

to me," observed Odile. Marguerite had paid attention only to the younger woman, as if Jean-Noël had not even been there. When Odile had pointed out to her that it was in her own best interest to agree to a divorce, for rather than living from day to day as she was doing now she would then be assured of being paid a regular allowance, the amount of which they needed only to agree upon, hadn't she said, after having sworn that she would never divorce Jean-Noël, that she would think about it, that she would give her answer in a few months' time, "when I have consulted my lawyer"? Wasn't it a success to have moved beyond emotional considerations? There would doubtless be a great many difficulties to overcome, but didn't money matters always sort themselves out in the end? "Your wife," said Odile, "is not at all the person you had described to me. On the contrary, she is a very reasonable person, terribly worried about her daughter's future, and who wants nothing more than to give you your freedom if, how-ever—and she is quite right in this—assurances are given her that she will not find herself in need."

But Odile was mistaken, if not genuinely so—for she had praised Marguerite in this way only to please Jean-Noël—then at least in appearance. A few days later, Jean-Noël re-ceived a letter from his wife, one that had certainly not been dictated to her by the lawyer of whom she had spoken. She wondered whether Jean-Noël had not lost his mind to have imposed upon her, and in front of their daughter, a woman who she had to admit was well brought up, but who was nonetheless his mistress. In fact, this person could not have much dignity if she had agreed to come with him. The letter continued with insults directed at Odile. If he wanted a di-vorce in order to marry a so-called young lady, he should at least have taken the precaution of never introducing her to his legitimate wife. Fortunately, her guardian angel had been watching over her. Had it not been for their visit, she might very well have agreed to a divorce, for although her own life was in pieces, she did not want to prevent her husband from rebuilding a life of his own. Now, however, everything had changed.

Jean-Noël did not dare show Odile the letter. As she asked him every day whether he had heard from his wife, however, he had little choice but to tell her about it.

"You would rather I didn't read it, then?"

"I tore it up," he answered, in spite of having put it into his wallet in anticipation of the day it might be useful to him. "But I remember everything it said. Naturally, Marguerite no longer agrees to a divorce."

"What reasons did she give you? Show me that letter, please."

She was so insistent that he finally gave in. After having read it she smiled, as though nothing it said had anything to do with her. Had she found herself with Marguerite at that instant, she would have behaved no differently than when they had been in Saint-Cloud. Nonetheless, she felt a certain satisfaction. Hadn't she now become the object of Marguerite's hatred, just like Jean-Noël? And didn't this in some sense give her the right to become personally involved in the matter of their divorce?

"Did you answer?"

"No. I wanted to speak to you first."

"Well then, you're going to act as if you hadn't said anything to me. You're going to send a very kind reply."

She then decided that Jean-Noël should write that very evening. He would appear astonished that Marguerite could have written him in this way after their meeting the previous Sunday. He would ask her to think about the offer she had been made, without seeming at all cross.

When Marguerite received this letter, she consulted, not a lawyer, but a warehouse manager and his wife who were her friends. They all drafted letters. Taking a bit from each, Marguerite wrote her husband that she had not changed her mind, that she still refused to grant him a divorce, and that later on he would be the first to thank her for this; but this time she expressed herself in much friendlier terms, so that it would be understood that the insults about Mlle. Wurzel her first letter had contained had been written in the heat of anger, in spite of the fact that she had waited four days before writing.

As soon as Odile learned of this latest letter, she declared that the situation had gone on long enough. As the kindness upon which she had been counting had proved ineffectual, they now had to resort to other means. They could not go on wasting their time this way. They needed to consult an experienced lawyer. Simon Wurtzel had a friend, Maître Herbst, who also happened to be from Alsace, and who would certainly be delighted to advise Jean-Noël. For fear that her family might learn of this consultation, however, she preferred that Jean-Noël go to see the lawyer alone, or, if this was disagreeable to him, to have Maurice accompany him. Maître Herbst would obviously suspect something, but at least they would keep up appearances.

Maître Herbst recommended vigorous measures. "I am sure you realize, dear Sir," he said, "that if you are the one asking for a divorce, and your wife is refusing, and she has done nothing wrong, you have very little chance of obtaining it. Has she ever been unfaithful to you? Has she ever publicly cursed you or struck you?" When Jean-Noël replied in the negative, he went on: "In that case, unless you want to accuse her of imaginary wrongs and have friends who are willing to serve as your witnesses, I can see only one solution: you must try to convince your wife to file for divorce herself. She must certainly be aware that if you fail to comply with the ruling handed down by the court—in other words, the maintenance payments it has imposed—you could be sent to prison, for a recent decree has made abandoning one's family a crime in the eyes of the law. I therefore think that the best thing would be for you and she to come to some agreement, and for you to make her understand how serious your situation would be if you failed to honor your commitments. If you like, I can give you a copy of the exact text of the law so that you can pass it on to your wife." Jean-Noël said that he wanted to think. His mind had just turned to Laure. Before producing texts of recent laws, even if these happened to be favorable to his wife's situation, wasn't it first necessary for Marguerite to accept the idea of a divorce? The details could always be settled later. But taking the offensive against his wife this way, with no warning, would be to provoke her. She was capable of coming to see him at the rue Laugier, of making a scene. And when Mme Mourier learned that he was seeking to divorce Marguerite, she would want to know why. He would be forced to admit that he intended to remarry. She would not rest until she knew to whom. How could he then stop her from going to see the Wurtzels, if she wanted to do so?

When he next saw Odile, he repeated what Maître Herbst had said to him and told her of his fears, particularly where Laure was concerned. Wouldn't it be for the best if he broke off with this woman before taking on Marguerite? Odile agreed. M. Wurtzel knew nothing of Jean-Noël's life. He had always been very friendly toward him. This was no time to jeopardize those feelings.

This conversation took place on Monday, March 13, 1925. Jean-Noël left Odile toward ten in the evening, promising her that before the end of the month he would ask Mme Mourier to set him free. Until then, he would keep her informed of everything that happened. They would also go back to Saint-Cloud together, in order to have a frank discussion with Marguerite. This time, they would discuss money and try to come to an agreement on the amount of maintenance she should be paid. They would surely be able to settle their differences. Odile would pretend not to know that Marguerite had written to Jean-Noël. Marguerite would therefore think he had not shown Odile her letter. She would feel that she shared a secret with her husband and might perhaps be flattered by this. In the meantime, Odile would make a few allusions to her family about her desire to marry so that if Mme Mourier came to the boulevard du Montparnasse in a fit of anger, the family would not be taken entirely by surprise.

Jean-Noël failed to find much comfort in all these fine

resolutions, however. His visit to Maître Herbst, the copy of the law the latter had wanted him to take, and the thinly disguised notice Odile was serving him all seemed somehow unreal. If he was hesitant, it was not because he feared that he was going to make another mistake, nor because he had misgivings. He was indifferent to everyone around him, to Mme Mourier and to Marguerite. While he had only a confused impression of the importance of the events taking place, the image of Annie had meanwhile grown very clear in his mind. In taking on these mediocre challenges without even being sustained by the idea that once they had been overcome he would be happy, wasn't he going to distance himself ever farther from the woman who represented his childhood, his youth, his entire life, and whose very severity seemed salutary in the midst of all this turmoil? Wasn't Annie the soul of disinterestedness, of simplicity in social relations, of disdain for everything calculated? But if he stayed with Mme Mourier, what would become of him? For the past few days Jean-Noël had been thinking he might go to the avenue de Malakoff on the occasion of his stepmother's birthday, which happened to be on the fourteenth of March. It had struck him that, after what had happened between himself and Mme Oetlinger, this would be a noble gesture. He would bring lilies, Annie's favorite flowers. He would speak to her for only a few moments and then leave as simply as he had come, thereby demonstrating that, while he understood what his stepmother expected of him, he was nonetheless still as devoted to her as ever. Mme Oetlinger did not like effusive displays, but rather what she liked to call contained sensitivity; emotion expressed by a mere detail touched her. This birthday might therefore be an opportunity to establish a new relationship between Annie and himself. If that happened, everything else would then become so simple! Odile, Marguerite, Mme Mourier, and Mme Mercier could fight among themselves; the last thing Jean-Noël would do was get involved.

EIGHTEEN

The following day, after leaving work, Jean-Noël went to the avenue de Malakoff. As soon as the front door had been opened to him, however, he was struck by the feverish activity in the front hall. Three people he did not know were speaking in hushed tones. Another stranger entered the sitting room. The butler, who ordinarily asked him whom he wished to see, said immediately: "Wait a moment, Monsieur. I will go call Madame." Shortly afterward, Mme Oetlinger appeared. She was pale. Her face was lined. Jean-Noël understood that something serious had happened. He came forward. His stepmother made a sign that he should wait. She exchanged a few words with the strangers, nodded, shrugged her shoulders, and even grasped one of their hands.

"Let's not stay here," she said as she came over to her stepson, looking behind her as if she were being pursued. "Come into the study."

She took her stepson by the arm—something she had not done for years—pulled him along with her, turned around yet again, and then, as if she had forgotten something, said, "Wait for me. Sit down. I will be right back."

Just then the front doorbell rang. Jean-Noël, who had not moved, looked inquisitively at the butler as he walked past.

"Monsieur is very poorly," murmured the servant, without stopping.

When Annie returned barely a minute later, she was even more distraught. She closed the door behind her and then, as if she were safe at last, stood perfectly still, her arms dangling limply alongside her body.

"What is going on?" asked Jean-Noël, not daring to seem at all informed for fear that, even in the present circumstances, his stepmother would reproach him for his being too familiar with the servants.

"My father had three strokes this morning. He just had a fourth. He has not regained consciousness yet."

"It can't be!"

"Oh, but it is, my poor Jean-Noël," continued Annie, as if she still found the strength within herself to console her stepson.

"Have the doctors been here?" he asked, immediately wondering why he had used the plural.

Although his dream was to live with Annie, and M. Villemur was the very person who made this impossible, he had never reflected upon the fact that the latter's death could, while perhaps not make his dream come true, at least give him some hope. It was not that Jean-Noël was an innately superior being and that such a thought could never have crossed his mind. The fact was that in his eyes Annie had remained M. Oetlinger's wife, and he had never imagined her being dependent upon anyone other than Jean-Melchior. Now, on this late afternoon, the happy consequences M. Villemur's death might have for him suddenly became apparent. At the same time, the necessity that he seem sincerely apprehensive about such a turn of events became equally clear to him.

"And what have they said, these doctors?" he asked anxiously, moving quickly and silently toward his stepmother, as if he did not want to be seen drawing nearer. She was sitting in an armchair and had hidden her face in her hands. From time to time, she wiped her eyes.

"It's dreadful," she said, extending a hand to her stepson, seeking a comfort in that physical contact which no words could have given her. Jean-Noël took the hand that was offered him, not knowing whether he should stroke it or merely hold it in his own. And yet he had become a different man. The fear of displeasing her, which usually paralyzed him, had disappeared. Like the memorable day when he had waited for Annie at the station in Nice after Jean-Melchior's death, he would have liked to protect his stepmother, to show her the extent of his devotion, and be shown in exchange that she trusted him at last.

"You mustn't give up hope."

He had the impression that Annie was suffering more deeply today than she had been that day in Nice. But wasn't he being unfair? When his stepmother had returned from Davos, nearly a week had already gone by since Jean-Melchior's death.

"Oh! No, I shan't give up," said Annie, who went on. "It's so sad! Just yesterday, he was looking forward to leaving Paris at Easter."

She could no longer contain herself and hid her face again.

"All hope may not be lost."

She did not reply. After a few moments, she raised her head, extended her hand to her stepson again, and with an expression so pained it seemed almost a smile, said, "You're a good boy, Jean-Noël."

The young man's ears, and then his cheeks, turned bright red. Did he really have as much heart as his stepmother thought? She was wrong. He was not as moved as he seemed. What would happen when she became aware of it? He squeezed Annie's hand. Then again, wasn't he maligning himself?

"No, he isn't going to pull through," continued Mme Oetlinger, as though talking to herself.

"You mustn't say that."

Annie gently drew her hand away to retrieve the little handkerchief she always kept tucked into her left sleeve. She closed her eyes and wiped them with it. Jean-Noël looked at her. Was a new life about to begin? If M. Villemur was to die, it was likely that his family would go their separate ways. Jean-Noël felt events taking on that joyful aspect they had

had in his youth whenever something very serious happened. The years he had just spent far from his stepmother seemed like a day to him. He had never left Annie; today was the morrow of their famous argument about his vocation as a painter. He was going to be assigned a new role. Mme Villemur would doubtless return to the provinces, to her family. And Annie, alone and free, would stay in Paris to devote herself to her painting. Perhaps then, with her family no longer there to prevent it, she would accept Jean-Noël living with her, would even be delighted by it. At that moment, it seemed to him that she felt a bit of love for him. He was infinitely grateful to her for this. Perhaps now she would love him like a son. He was no longer watching what he said, which made him more natural.

"I have to leave you for a moment. I need to go see what is happening."

"But of course," said Jean-Noël, forgoing the little silence with which he usually preceded his replies.

Mme Oetlinger was not long in returning, as distraught as when she had left.

"There has been no change," she said, without closing the door this time.

Jean-Noël sensed that he should leave. Like someone who has understood that there is nothing left to do but wait, Annie drew near a window, pulled back the curtain to look out over the avenue for a moment, then came back to the desk, where she touched a few papers with her fingertips.

"Jean-Noël, you can go now."

"I don't want to leave you," he said, as quickly as if he had spoken only one word.

Annie told him then that she was very tired, that she wanted to have a little rest, that above all he must not neglect his obligations on her account, and that she would never forget his solicitude. Jean-Noël moved toward the door. At that moment, Mme Oetlinger noticed the lilies that her stepson had put down on a little table when the butler had told him that M. Villemur was very poorly.

"These lilies, these beautiful lilies," she said. Looking away from them, her gaze returned to Jean-Noël, interrogating him.

"I had brought them for your birthday."

Annie breathed in their scent as if it were a consolation for all the sorrows in the world and then, putting the flowers back down on the table, she drew close to her stepson, took him by the arm as she had done when he had first arrived, and walked slowly with him toward the foyer without saying a word, as if, having just remembered it was her birthday, she was seeking to penetrate the significance of this mysterious coincidence.

It was nearly eight o'clock when Jean-Noël arrived at the rue Laugier. All along the way, he had been making plans for the future. He was in an agitated state, his eyes shining, as he told Mme Mourier what had just happened. As he had stated on a number of occasions that he was no longer seeing his stepmother, he did not want to admit that it had been his idea to go to the avenue de Malakoff. He therefore pretended that Annie had called him during the afternoon to tell him the sad news. As a result, he'd had no choice but to go there at once. "In fact," he added, "it's always been the way. Whenever we have quarreled, something has happened to patch things up between us."

It did not take Mme Mourier long to notice that Jean-Noël was talking too much about his grief for it to be sincere. Nonetheless she consoled him as if he were directly affected, there being nothing which could have flattered him more that day. Jean-Noël slept badly that night. He was so impatient to see day break that he could not lie still. He was constantly plagued by the feeling that terribly serious events were unfolding at the avenue de Malakoff and that, as he was not there to take part in them, he was going to be forgotten. Mme Mourier slept no better. She asked him several times if he would like some herb tea. Each time he refused so that Laure would begin to understand there was a possibility their relationship might change. She had to know that he would never sacrifice Annie to any love he felt for her. Tomorrow, perhaps, Annie might need him, might want him to accompany her on a journey. Nothing in the world could then prevent him from doing his duty.

Morning arrived at last. As soon as the hour allowed it, he returned to the avenue de Malakoff. Because he had a reason for coming, he felt none of his usual anxiety.

"Tell Madame Oetlinger I'm here," he said to the butler with great assurance.

He could already see himself walking freely through the apartment, making telephone calls, even receiving friends, surprising no one by his presence, neither Mme Villemur nor the other members of the family. When Annie joined him, her eyes reddened and her lips so pale that it seemed as if she had powdered her face awkwardly, he adopted a rather cold demeanor, hoping that this new attitude would make him resemble those young men who were the first to master their grief when their families were in mourning so that they could comfort their mothers and sisters.

"No change for the better?" he asked, almost as if he were a doctor.

As on the previous day, Annie tried to draw him into the study. In order not to be led away, he stopped after every two paces, the way people sometimes do in the street when they are being spoken to.

"Come, Jean-Noël. I beg you. We'll be more at our ease."

The door to the sitting room opened and he caught a glimpse of several people who seemed to be whispering to one another. How he wished that his stepmother had left him alone at that moment, had said to him, "I'll be back later" while he was still in the hall, onto which so many doorways opened and through which so many people were passing!

"My poor Jean-Noël," said Annie. "I am causing you a great deal of worry. You mustn't let this affect your work. Have you done everything you need to do?"

Jean-Noël would have liked to reply that there was nothing he needed to do, that even if there had been something, it would have made no difference. But he carefully avoided saying any such thing.

"I've taken the necessary measures."

The words were barely out of his mouth when Mme Villemur appeared in the doorway.

"Oh! Excuse me," she said upon seeing that her daughter was with a man she did not immediately recognize.

"Come in, Maman, come in. It's Jean-Noël."

The old lady did as she was told. She had already seen five or six friends. Making no distinction between them and Jean-Noël, she said, "So you came too?"

Jean-Noël bowed respectfully. Although he knew that Mme Villemur had never taken up his defense, she had nevertheless been very kind to him. Had it not been for her husband, she would certainly not have been against the idea of his coming to live at the avenue de Malakoff. Jean-Noël had interpreted her indulgence as a secret sign of sympathy for him. Whenever he was in the old lady's presence, therefore, he took particular care not to disappoint her.

"But of course, Madame," he said with that casual air he always adopted when with her, and which he believed was the reason for her friendly feelings toward him.

As Jean-Noël was no longer alone, Annie slipped away.

"Sit down, Monsieur," said Mme Villemur.

She was so overwhelmed that she was not entirely aware of what was going on around her and had retained of the dramatic events only the expressions of sympathy which had been pouring in.

"Thank you," answered Jean-Noël. "I would rather stand. But you yourself, Madame . . ."

"So would I. I have to be here, there, everywhere."

From the way in which she spoke these words, he understood that Mme Villemur was playing no part in the dramatic events, and that, shunted aside, she was wandering from room to room, which was why she had come into the study. He was greatly disappointed by this, as if he had been entrusted with the care of a child. He was forced to make polite conversation while so many important things were going on around him! It was with great impatience, therefore, that he awaited his stepmother's return, trembling whenever a hand was placed on the doorknob, which happened several times without anyone actually opening the door.

"Maman," said Annie when she reappeared at last, "your son is looking for you."

"Where is he?" asked Mme Villemur.

"I'll take you to him, Maman."

Mme Oetlinger took her mother's arm, and after having made a sign to her stepson that he should wait there for her, left the room with measured steps. Jean-Noël's feeling of deliverance was so great that he began pacing up and down the room. Time passed, however, and Annie did not return. Several times he thought of leaving the room and going to mingle with the people he could hear passing by outside the door. He dared not do so, however, and this only heightened the disagreeable impression that he was being kept off to one side. In the end, he was unable to resist his urge to leave the study. The large front hall was deserted; the door to the sitting room was open. He advanced. There was no longer anyone there. An overcoat had slipped off the chair over which it had been draped and lay on the floor. Through the curtainless windows, as transparent as water, he could see the bare branches of the trees in the avenue du Bois. He returned to the hall. Suddenly he heard the sound of footsteps, then that of a door.

"Don't go, please don't go," begged Annie. "They have just given him an injection. He hasn't regained consciousness."

She entered the study, followed by her stepson, and let herself fall into an armchair. There was the sound of voices drawing nearer.

"Close the door, Jean-Noël. I don't want to see anyone. I can't bear it any longer."

"I'll close it later."

"No, no, now."

For a brief moment, he could hear the murmuring sound

of a conversation being conducted in hushed tones. Annie was crying. He sat down near her.

"You have to be strong," he said, taking his stepmother's hand of his own accord.

"I know, I know," she replied with that astonishment we feel when we are reproached for lacking the very quality which we are most proud of possessing.

Just then the door was opened by Henri, who entered the room with one of his friends. While Annie continued to cry, Jean-Noël got up. Henri came to meet him without hesitation, extended his hand, and looked him straight in the eye without saying a word. When he turned to his friend at last, he made the necessary introductions in a very quiet voice, explaining that Jean-Noël Oetlinger was his sister's stepson. Then he moved toward Annie.

"Come now, Annie," he said, sitting down on the chair which Jean-Noël had just vacated.

As she made no answer, he took her by the shoulders and forced her to raise her head. Her eyes were swollen, her cheeks damp and blotchy. He took out his handkerchief, and with the care a husband might have shown, dried her face while murmuring consoling words. From the middle of the room, where he had remained standing with Henri's friend, Jean-Noël watched them, mesmerized. Why hadn't he, too, thought of drying Annie's tears? That act was so much more tender than anything he had done. Wasn't it exactly what he should have done? Now it was too late. And yet, with what love, what tenderness, he would have caressed Annie's face with his handkerchief! She had now risen. Henri was holding her in his arms. Her eyes half-shut, her head leaning on his shoulder, she seemed to have placed herself entirely in his hands. He made a sign to his friend, indicating that his sister would soon regain her composure. It was then that she spoke a few words which filled Jean-Noël with profound joy.

"You can go now, Henri," she said softly, detaching his arm from around her waist the way a young girl might have done. "I promised the nurse I would come back."

NINETEEN

M. Villemur's condition remained stable during the next few days. Toward six o'clock every evening, Jean-Noël would go to the avenue de Malakoff. He had not been in touch with Mlle Wurtzel since the fourteenth of March. Saturday dawned, which also happened to be the day he had agreed to return to Saint-Cloud with the young girl. As if he himself had been struck by a terrible misfortune, Jean-Noël announced to Odile as soon as he saw her that M. Villemur was at death's door. Mlle Wurtzel pretended to be saddened by the news. And yet she was surprised that Jean-Noël was making so much of an event that meant nothing to him, and that he was giving up his plans for people from whom, as experience had demonstrated, he should expect nothing. She did not dare point this out to him, however, for fear of seeming inhuman. But when she realized that the agitated state in which Jean-Noël found himself as a result of M. Villemur's illness was caused chiefly by the advantages he hoped to gain from a fatal outcome, her scruples vanished.

"Did you at least let Marguerite know that we wouldn't be coming to see her this afternoon?"

He replied that he had not done so, but that this was of no consequence.

"You think so!" said Odile, who thought Jean-Noël was behaving in a most cavalier fashion toward a woman he was supposedly trying to win over with kindness.

"I couldn't have known what was going to happen."

"Come now, Jean-Noël," said Odile, like a woman speaking to her husband.

Ever since they had been reunited, they had never spoken of their feelings for one another; these had to remain in the shadows until Jean-Noël was free.

"I have to go, they're expecting me."

"And yet," thought Odile, "you don't jeopardize your entire future just because a member of your family is dying."

"And when will I see you again?" she asked, certain that in his exalted state Jean-Noël would not notice how much she cared for him.

"How can I know?" he replied, raising his arms to the heavens and revealing some of the pride he felt at being unable to make any promises now.

"You will phone me, at least, to keep me informed."

He promised to do so and left as hastily as he had come. As soon as he arrived at the avenue de Malakoff he had a premonition that M. Villemur had taken a turn for the better. The sun was casting a yellow light over the stained-glass window in the front hall, a mysterious window he had never seen open. For a moment he thought he had brought this impression of gaiety, of tensions being lifted, in with him. Although he had grown familiar with the servants since the beginning of the week, the butler received him like a stranger, as if life were now going to resume its normal course, and led him into the study. When Annie appeared, he noticed immediately that she was much calmer than the day before. Normally she kept her neck covered, but today she was wearing a slightly low-cut dress. Her smooth hair shone. Instead of the handkerchief she had constantly been clutching, she carried a little evening bag.

"Things are much, much better," she said at once, as if Jean-Noël had been beside himself with anxiety and needed to be reassured as quickly as possible.

Hearing this, he blushed to the very tips of his ears.

"Ah! So much the better," he murmured, as if the great relief he was feeling made it impossible for him to speak.

Upon returning to the rue Laugier, he had the unpleasant surprise of finding his mother and brother there waiting for him. Laure was keeping them company. One would have thought that the misfortune which had struck the Villemur family had some importance for these people, and that it was a pretext for a reconciliation. Jean-Noël understood immediately from his mother's questioning looks that she had been awaiting his return anxiously, as if she feared for M. Villemur's health. But how had Mme Mercier learned of the events at the avenue de Malakoff?

In the days when Jean-Melchior had frequented Mlle Villemur's studio, Ernestine Mercier had fought to preserve her rights, which she considered equal to those of any married woman. She had schemed, and in the course of her machinations had made the acquaintance of Elisabeth, Annie's maid. Several years earlier, however, Elisabeth, who was by then quite old, had left the Villemurs. Thanks to the pension her former employers paid her, she now lived modestly in a small retirement home in Neuilly. Every Saturday she came back to the avenue de Malakoff for lunch, which she ate in the pantry. Afterward, to make herself useful, she would come into the apartment and serve coffee. She would exchange a few pleasantries with everyone, for she remained deeply grateful to this family, in whose employ she had stayed for over thirty years. Her devotion, however, did not prevent her from repeating everything she overheard to Mme Mercier. Although she was incapable of hurting a fly, she had always derived a certain pleasure from complaining about her masters and from being more intimately involved in their lives than she had been by merely serving them. As soon as she had learned of M. Villemur's illness, she had gone to inform Mme Mercier at once. The latter had immediately thought of what the consequences of this death would be. Annie would stand to inherit. It was certain that she would then give Jean-Noël some money. She might even acquit herself of the debt she owed Jean-Melchior's first wife, for she had never said that this debt did not exist: what she had said was that she didn't have enough money to pay it. It was therefore necessary to see Jean-Noël as soon as possible. Mme Mercier had already been waiting for him over an hour when he arrived. She had begun by concealing the reason for her visit from Mme Mourier, not wanting to betray her son in the event that he had said nothing to Laure. Mme Mourier had also kept silent, for similar reasons. After ten minutes of conversation, the two women had understood that each was deceiving the other. But Laure had not abandoned her friendly demeanor. She had nothing to fear. As the woman Jean-Noël loved, wasn't it she who would always have the upper hand?

"There's been an improvement," Jean-Noël said to Mme Mourier.

Ernestine Mercier gave her son a spiteful look. Wasn't he lying in an attempt to distance her? As for Laure, she seemed sincerely pleased by the news. In spite of this, she had not failed to envisage the advantages she might reap from M. Villemur's death. This was precisely why she had not been overly attentive to Jean-Noël the past few days, for she had a great deal of self-esteem when her interests were at stake.

The next morning, Jean-Noël received a letter from Marguerite. She had spent the entire day waiting for her husband, or so she claimed. She was not at his disposal. She was doing the best she could to raise his daughter with the means available to her. She never failed to take her out walking for several hours every afternoon. On Saturday she had been unable to do so. She did not want to jeopardize Annie's health because of Jean-Noël. He had done the child enough harm as it was. The entire letter had clearly been written in the heat of anger. Jean-Noël was surprised by this. Usually, when he failed to keep a promise, Marguerite said nothing, which was why he had not bothered to write. If that had now changed, it could only be because, now that she knew he wanted his freedom and needed her in order to obtain it, she had grown aware of her own importance. Getting a divorce was like getting married: you needed two people. As long as he had considered her his wife, she had been willing to accept everything, but at present she no longer had any reason to let him get away with what she had once tolerated out of love.

Jean-Noël burned the letter immediately and went out. A dazzling sun shone overhead. The place de l'Etoile, still wet from the previous night's rain, was deserted. The sort of white clouds one sees in paintings of battles trailed after one another at a great distance. The house Jean-Noël entered a few moments later was a house in mourning. M. Villemur had died at dawn.

Jean-Noël stared at Annie in astónishment. She was calm, even indifferent. He remembered then that he had been struck by this coldness before, when he had seen her just after the deaths of Bertrand and Jean-Melchior.

"How dreadful," murmured Jean-Noël.

A few weeks earlier, M. Villemur had sat at this very desk, with no idea whatsoever that his death was imminent. Jean-Noël could still see him, rising to go fetch Annie, removing his lorgnette as he always did whenever he stopped reading. That man continued to live on in his mind, and the fact that he was no more already made his former habits seem touching. While M. Villemur had never been anything more than a stranger to Jean-Noël, he nonetheless found it agreeable to imagine that he, too, had just lost someone dear to him. Wasn't the name Villemur nearly as familiar to him as the name Oetlinger? Was he deluding himself so much by imagining that this death marked a significant date in his life? What did the future now hold in store for him? He could not say, and yet he was certain that he was poised on the brink of great changes. Unfortunately, for the moment Annie was being as cold as ice.

"It would be best if you came back tomorrow," she told him.

The funeral took place the following Wednesday. Jean-Noël had been back to the avenue de Malakoff every day in the interim, taking advantage of the general confusion to stay for hours at a time. He arrived at eleven o'clock. Shortly before, he had been the object of an incident between Anne and Henri. Annoyed by her stepson's frequent visits, Henri had pointed out to his sister that everyone was wondering who this young man was, and that people had even asked him various questions which he had found it embarrassing to answer. Mme Oetlinger, who had been taking advantage of the circumstances to try to draw her stepson into the family, had been deeply offended that her plan had become apparent. Jean-Noël thus arrived to find his stepmother still flustered from having taken up his defense and better disposed toward him than ever. She asked him immediately never to come to the avenue de Malakoff again. She added that she herself was now going to live alone, which she was looking forward to greatly, and that she would then visit this house only infrequently, thereby leading him to understand that she had merely been transmitting the request she had just made. It was thus with none of the bitterness which such a ban would have produced in other circumstances, and with a heart secretly brimming with joy—for what greater happiness could Annie have given him than that of considering she had as many reasons as her stepson did to complain about her family—that he attended the funeral, not at his stepmother's side, but lost in the crowd. At the church of the Etoile, he left in front of the family after the ceremony. At that moment, he felt a twinge of regret that he was not among them. How proud he would have been solemnly to grasp all the hands extended to him! But he consoled himself with the thought that he could not have everything. As if arriving at the end of a long journey, he paused in front of Annie, whom he had almost failed to recognize under her veils. She kissed him twice, then hugged him, so that he quite forgot there were other people behind him. "Move along," she murmured, pushing him away gently. "Come back tomorrow."

Jean-Noël returned the following day—all the more promptly as Annie herself had been the one to invite him, and this against the will of Henri. The butler did not, as was his custom, ask him whom he wanted to see. He had clearly been given instructions and immediately led him to Annie's room.

"How happy I am to see you, my dear little one," she said. "You have been so devoted, your presence has been such a comfort to me."

"It was natural," answered Jean-Noël, who was hoping that his stepmother was going to complain about her family.

"Yes, it's true, it's natural; or rather, it ought to be."

Checking herself, as if not only did she have no right to say anything against her family but should not even think such things, she continued in a different tone of voice, "Now, my dear Jean-Noël, everything is going to change. This misfortune is going to transform my life. My mother will probably not stay in Paris, alone in this enormous apartment, for Henri, if he told me the truth, is going to be married. She will go live with her sister. As for me, my dear little one, I am going to work, work, work. I have neglected my painting these past few years. Do you remember my studio in Nice? How distant all that seems now, doesn't it? We all had so many illusions. Well, let's not dwell on that. We'll see one another at the rue Boissonnade."

"Rue Boissonnade?"

"Didn't you know that I had rented a studio in the rue Boissonnade?"

"No."

"That's right. I didn't want anyone to know. One can't live without a place in which to be alone, work, reflect, don't you think? As for you, you will come and see me when you wish. It's sad to say, but I'm going to be a great deal happier now. My family never forgave me for having married your father. Although I would speak up in your defense, no one ever listened to me. I didn't tell you at the time, but I thought it terribly unfair. But that's the past. One must never hold a grudge against those who don't see things the way we do. My family always believed in certain principles. They always thought of me as a sort of anarchist. To try to persuade them otherwise would have been pointless. So each of us remained entrenched in our positions."

While his stepmother spoke, Jean-Noël nodded his head constantly as a sign of his acquiescence. Her change of heart where he was concerned surprised him, but he was so happy that he was not even thinking of going further into the reasons which had prompted it. From time to time, however, he would be filled with a sudden fear that this unexpected interest in him was only the result of Annie's grief over the death of M. Villemur.

TWENTY

Because his stepmother had asked it of him as a favor, and so as not to make it seem that he was taking advantage of her grief to impose himself, Jean-Noël abstained from going to the rue Boissonnade for several days. During this period of self-imposed retreat, a fear began to gnaw at him: that in future, it might become even more difficult to approach Mme Oetlinger. Until now, whenever he had taken offense and left or been asked by Annie not to come back, he had suffered but never really worried. The avenue de Malakoff had always been there, a central point in his life. He needed only go back there to find, unchanged, everything from which he had been separated. Now it was different: Mme Oetlinger was free. Like a shopkeeper whose business relies on transient customers, he began to fear that she might disappear. The only bonds between him and his stepmother were those of adults united by friendship, a friendship that was at the mercy of an argument or a misunderstanding. Hadn't Mme Mercier come back to the rue Laugier? Hadn't she asked her son what he intended to do now that he was going to be rich; and hadn't he replied, out of vanity, that he had no idea, as if it were true an enormous change was about to take place in his life?

It was only a week after M. Villemur's funeral that Jean-Noël made up his mind to go and pay Annie a visit. This first meeting could not have been more cordial.

"Come in, come in," said Annie, who just happened to be making a pot of tea. Her stepson was hesitating at the door, stirred by a scent that had suddenly brought his entire child-hood back to him. He obeyed. A kerosene lamp covered by a Japanese lamp-shade illuminated the studio, throughout which were scattered little centers of activity. Here was a steaming kettle; there, a palette covered in fresh paints; in another corner, cups, a packet of sugar, flowers. He recognized certain pieces of furniture, a folding screen, and, on the desk, the ivory pen he had never been allowed to use.

"Do you take much milk?" asked Mme Oetlinger. She seemed younger, as if her stepson's visit were taking her back to the days of Jean-Melchior. And yet, she wanted to show that she had never changed, that in spite of the years she had spent living with her family, she had never lost her love of art and of that life she had once led, which meant so much to her. In this out-of-the-way studio no one knew about, she could at last be herself, and Jean-Noël felt she was doing him a great honor by accepting his presence in these intimate surroundings.

A month went by. Whenever Jean-Noël was free, he would rush to the rue Boissonnade. He had noticed that Annie no longer spoke to him as before, that she had stopped giving him advice it was impossible to follow. Although she had always been terribly reticent to talk about herself, she now discussed painting and her aspirations freely with him, as if she had become a sort of woman of action, involved in the artistic movement, since leaving her family's home. There was no longer any difference between Jean-Noël and herself. They were, each in their own way, striving toward the same goal.

But one night, when he returned to the rue Laugier, Mme Mourier greeted Jean-Noël in a fit of anger.

"So it seems you want to get a divorce!" she shouted. "You were carefully concealing this from me, you hypocrite. But it won't happen the way you think. I didn't sacrifice the best years of my life to you so you could leave me now. So the hard times were for me, and the good times will be for another woman. Now I understand why you no longer talk to me about your stepmother."

After Jean-Noël's visit to Saint-Cloud with Mlle Wurtzel, Marguerite's friends had insisted she go to see a certain Monsieur Large, whose rental agency had little by little been transformed into an office dispensing legal advice. She had explained her situation to him, then told him of the visit she'd had from her husband and Odile, which had prompted the businessman to say: "Well I never! He does as he pleases, your husband." The first piece of advice from M. Large was, "Above all, don't do anything." But when, after having written her husband the letter in which she reproached him for having made her wait in vain, she read in the newspaper that M. Villemur had died, it became clear to her that there was a connection between this death and Jean-Noël's desire to get a divorce. M. Villemur had undoubtedly been ill for some time. This, then, was the explanation for Jean-Noël's great haste. He would have preferred to regain his freedom before M. Villemur's death. If he had failed to come when he'd said he would, it was simply because by then it was already too late. Ah! She had done well not to let herself be taken in by Mlle Wurtzel, who was, without any doubt, merely his accomplice. It had been a well-planned job! Getting rid of the wife before M. Villemur's death would indeed have been to their advantage. Unfortunately, the latter had been unwilling to wait: he had not wanted to delay the moment he had chosen to leave this world.

Marguerite had immediately gone to see M. Large to inform him of this latest development. "Obviously," he observed once his client had finished speaking, "what you are saying is very possible. But it wouldn't be so astonishing if your husband really does intend to remarry. In that case, we should take the necessary precautions and find out as soon as possible how much maintenance we could ask for. The best way would be if I made discreet inquiries in Paris. You told me, I believe, that your husband clerks for Maître Préfil. That solicitor is not one of my friends, but I can find a way of seeing him."

This consisted, quite simply, of going to his offices in the rue de Clichy. Without identifying himself, M. Large questioned one of the other clerks, from whom he obtained none of the information he was seeking. Immediately after the mysterious visitor had left, the clerk went to tell his employer what had just happened.

Since the death of M. Villemur, Maître Préfil's friendly feelings for Jean-Noël had begun to wane. As we saw earlier, friendship played an important role in his life. As long as he had felt he was being helpful to a young man who was temporarily on the outs with his family, he had never made even the slightest critical remark to Jean-Noël. But ever since the death of M. Villemur he had begun to feel that his protégé had, as he put it, climbed up on his high horse. The next time he saw Mme Mourier, therefore, he was unable to prevent himself from making allusions to Jean-Noël's fickleness. It seemed he must have a hidden life. Hadn't someone come to the office recently, trying to extract information about him? Mme Mourier was so shocked that she insisted on questioning the clerk herself. It was then that she learned that the stranger who had come to the office a few days before was defending the interests of Marguerite. In this capacity, he had found it astonishing that Jean-Noël had gone to his wife's home in the company of his mistress.

"But who told you such tales?" asked Jean-Noël.

"I have my sources," replied Mme Mourier, as if she was surrounded by hordes of people who wanted nothing more than to oblige her in this way.

The two lovers quarreled bitterly, Laure demanding to know who the woman was who had gone to Saint-Cloud with Jean-Noël.

"I've guessed," cried Mme Mourier, who resembled Marguerite at times. "I would wager anything that it's one of those girls you rush off to see every evening. They are capable of doing such a thing."

Although he had never mentioned the Wurtzels by name, Jean-Noël had nonetheless told Laure, to impress her, that he frequented friends of the Villemurs, and out of the Wurtzel

family had created ten families he went to see, or so he
claimed, on successive evenings.

In the end, exhausted by Mme Mourier's shouting and
terrified by her threat that she would go and interrogate Marguerite in person, he admitted that it had been Mlle Wurtzel.
She had gone to Saint-Cloud with him only to do him a favor.
After all, what possible difference did it make to him what
happened now? The only person he cared about was Annie,
and in her studio, which was known to no one, she was out of
harm's way.

The following day, Mme Mourier went to the boulevard
du Montparnasse. She was very calm. She had received a very
different upbringing from people like Mme Mercier, Emile,
Marguerite. The steps she was taking had nothing in common
with the sort of things those people were accustomed to doing. She wanted only to come to the aid of a young girl who
probably had no idea that Jean-Noël was involved in a liaison.
But Odile was not at home. Mme Mourier was about to leave,
having refused to identify herself, when M. Wurtzel, intrigued, came up to her. He asked her what it was she wanted
to tell his daughter that was so terribly important. Laure did
not yield. She did consent, however, to divulge her name,
after which she left, saying that what she had to tell Mlle
Wurtzel was of no interest; for though she was not afraid to go
pay a call on people she did not know, she nonetheless liked
to think that she was decent enough never to do anyone deliberate harm. Not long afterwards, when Odile's father told
her that a lady by the name of Mourier had been asking for
her, there was no doubt in her mind that Jean-Noël had broken off with his mistress, which filled her with joy.

That evening, Laure carefully avoided telling Jean-Noël
what she had done, even though she was terribly proud of
having left as decisively as she had come. They dined together
as though nothing had happened. Jean-Noël had seen Annie
late that afternoon. She had treated him like a close friend.
Although he remembered the scene Mme Mourier had made

the day before, he was paying it no further attention, since she seemed to have forgotten it. It did not take long for his contentment and indifference to infuriate Laure.

"I saw your friend Odile this afternoon," she said abruptly. "You hadn't told me she was your mistress. So, while I'm faithful to you, you betray me."

Jean-Noël knew that Mme Mourier had no scruples about lying, and that to give herself the air of a great courtesan, she liked to utter deliberate falsehoods in order to learn the truth. And, in fact, a number of details proved that she was not telling the truth. Suddenly, however, she added: "And I also spoke to the young lady's father. How I wish you could have been there. You should have seen his eyes when he looked at me! As it is, they're not very attractive, with those blonde lashes and those little freckles, but when they look at you spitefully, it's enough to make you turn and run away."

Jean-Noël lost his composure. How could Laure have known of such a distinctive feature without actually seeing M. Wurtzel? It struck Jean-Noël that the only thing left for him to do was pretend to be dismayed, for the fact that he seemed quite happy was making Laure redouble her attacks upon him. He told her that he was deeply upset by what she had done, that he already had enough worries as it was, that there was nothing going on between him and Mlle Wurtzel.

When he went to work the next day, he found a note from Odile asking him to come and have lunch with her. He was surprised to find that M. Wurtzel greeted him most amiably. When he and the young girl were alone, she asked him whether he knew of Mme Mourier's visit.

"No," he answered.

She told him what had happened. She was convinced that Jean-Noël had broken off with Laure who, in a fit of pique, was trying to create a scandal. He carefully avoided disabusing her of this notion and pretended to fear the consequences of his supposed break-up. "It would be best," he said, "if we didn't see one another for a time." For ever since Mme Oetlinger had left her family, Jean-Noël, who now lived in anticipation of some extraordinary event, had been taking care to maintain a certain distance between himself and his entourage, in order to be able to respond without delay to the first sign he was sent.

TWENTY-ONE

During the next few months, Jean-Noël went to see Annie at the rue Boissonnade once a week, but never more, for fear she would grow tired of him. He almost always found her busy painting when he arrived. She would make a sign indicating he should sit down in front of her, for she hated having anyone behind her, and would continue to work for an hour or more without saying a word to him. If she happened to speak, it was only to herself, voicing critiques or praise as warranted by the fires of creation. Sometimes she would step back and squint while scrutinizing her canvas. Then Jean-Noël would feel that he no longer existed, and he derived no pleasure from the smile she bestowed upon him after those moments of concentration, a smile which seemed to say that it was not her fault if she took her art so seriously. He would follow his stepmother's work distractedly from the corner where he sat, waiting impatiently to hear the words with which she invariably ended each session: "That's enough for today." Fortunately, Mme Oetlinger was not always in a mood to paint. There were days when she claimed she was incapable of picking up a brush. On those days, she was much more cordial toward her stepson. She would talk to him about herself, about how her family didn't understand her. His role as confidant so pleased Jean-Noël that he took care never to interrupt her. She often asked him to accompany her to the avenue de Malakoff, where she would be going either to dine or to fetch some object that belonged to her. On those late after-

noons in the height of summer, Mme Oetlinger liked to dally
a bit. She was reminded of certain walks she had taken as a
young girl. She would take the boulevard Edgar-Quinet, passing beneath the railway bridge. Jean-Noël would advise her to
turn up streets he didn't know, hoping they would get lost.
And after leaving her at the front door to the building in the
avenue de Malakoff, he would make his way back to the rue
Laugier, filled with an unutterable sadness.

When he chose to visit on a Saturday, Annie would always be terribly busy. Everything needed to be ready for the
little girl who came and sat for Mme Oetlinger only on Sat-
urdays, and who was her favorite model. Although she was
barely five years old, Jean-Noël was jealous of the little girl.
Didn't Annie fret over her rather too much? Didn't she even
go so far as to leave Jean-Noël in order to walk the child back
to her mother's small haberdashery in the rue Saint-Jacques?

One Saturday in October, although he had come even
earlier than usual, he found the child already settled into the
model's chair, wearing a straw boater and holding a bunch of
grapes. Mme Oetlinger was so absorbed that she did not even
notice her stepson's arrival. After tea, she told him she had to
wait for someone and asked him if he would do her a favor
and take the girl back to the rue Saint-Jacques.

"Whom are you expecting?"

"A friend you don't know."

Taking enormous strides, so that the little girl had to run
the entire way to keep up with him, he acquitted himself of
what he considered to be a thankless chore. Upon returning,
he found the door locked from the inside. He knocked.

"Is that you?" called Annie. Upon hearing Jean-Noël's
affirmative reply, she told him: "Take the key, it's on the sill
of the little window. I'm getting changed."

He entered. The studio was tidy. Behind a curtain at the
far end of the room, a bathroom had been fitted up. Annie
liked this lack of comfort. Wasn't it fun to get changed this
way, in a makeshift bathroom?

"Make yourself some tea," she told her stepson. "I'll be ready in a minute."

A moment later she appeared in a black evening dress, with that particular air Jean-Noël so admired in people who have changed quickly but remain, beneath their new clothes, what they were a moment earlier, who are still fixing their hair while the door is already open and they are being called to go.

"Are you going out tonight?" asked Jean-Noël. This transformation, the cause of which was unknown to him, made him realize how superficial his intimacy with Annie was, even though he thought it had become so great since he'd been coming to the rue Boissonnade regularly.

"I don't know yet. A friend is supposed to come and fetch me, but nothing definite has been arranged."

Jean-Noël did not dare ask her any more questions. It seemed to him that the weather had grown gloomy. Suddenly, there was a knock at the door.

"Come in," said Annie.

There was another knock.

"Didn't you leave the key in the door?" Mme Oetlinger asked her stepson.

"No, it's here, I put it on the table."

Annie went to open the door. A man of about fifty, whom Jean-Noël had never seen, entered the studio. He had a prominent stomach. His complexion was rosy, like a child's, and he had a thin, blonde goatee. His bald pate was partly concealed by a long strand of shiny hair across which he ran his handkerchief as he mopped his brow, the gesture of a man accustomed to being alone. From certain details, like the little spot of blood on his false collar and the very new, very bouffant tie in the middle of his threadbare waistcoat, one guessed that although he was careless about his appearance, the visitor liked finery. Jean-Noël took an immediate dislike to him and, using a schoolboy's expression, decided that he was "ridiculous and pretentious."

"I was afraid of being late," he puffed, still out of breath from having climbed the single flight of stairs that led to the studio. "Isn't this charming!" he continued, looking around with a great deal of interest.

While he went on making remarks appropriate to the circumstances, Jean-Noël stood perfectly still off to one side, doing nothing to attract attention to himself.

"Jean-Noël," said Annie. Then, turning to the newcomer, she added, "My stepson."

"Ah! Yes, of course. I am very happy to meet you, Monsieur."

"Monsieur Charles Le Douaré has heard a great deal about you," remarked Annie.

M. Le Douaré had meanwhile resumed his inspection of the studio.

"You really do have a great deal of talent, dear friend," he said, pausing in front of a canvas as if he found it more pleasing than the others.

"Let's not talk about me. Do sit down."

For the next half-hour the conversation turned on banalities. Jean-Noël had seated himself on a sofa at the far end of the studio and, while pretending to be engrossed in a book of reproductions, carefully followed every one of his stepmother's and M. Le Douaré's words and gestures. What surprised him most was that Mme Oetlinger, who was normally so exacting when choosing friends, could have been at all interested in such a man. Wasn't he just the type of person she claimed to hate? How many times had he heard her say that one must be wary of men who wore rings? How often had he seen her mock characters who were flashy, oversized, untidy, and yet no more ridiculous than Charles Le Douaré! How was it that he came to call Annie "dear friend"? How long had they known one another? What role did he play in Mme Oetlinger's life for her to consent to receive him in this studio, which she said not a living soul was allowed to enter?

"But what is it you're reading there in your corner, Jean-Noël?" she asked suddenly.

He rose and walked toward them, smiling.

"I believe you are a lawyer," said M. Le Douaré.

He talked to Jean-Noël for several minutes, deferentially interrupting his flow of speech only when Jean-Noël spoke, and then, as if suddenly overcome with weariness, he turned toward Annie. In spite of this show of friendliness, Jean-Noël's antipathy had increased. He sensed that his stepmother was trying to please this man, and that he realized it. Whenever he expressed an idea, didn't he look at Mme Oetlinger at the same time, as if some bond deeper than conversation existed between them? Why did Annie tolerate such familiarity? But bit by bit light dawned on Jean-Noël. He thought he understood that the reason his stepmother liked M. Le Douaré came from the fact that she no longer believed in the ideas of happiness, sincerity, and independence which had led her to leave her family. She had replaced these with beliefs in her spiritual affections, of which she was as proud now as she had once been of the former.

"Perhaps you hadn't realized that it's nearly seven," said M. Le Douaré. "If you want to stop by your home, we should be going."

Shortly afterward M. Le Douaré, Annie, and Jean-Noël left the studio.

"Would you like me to drop you somewhere?" M. Le Douaré asked Jean-Noël. He refused. But Annie was so insistent that he finally agreed to let them drive him to the rue Laugier.

It was in a very foul humor that Jean-Noël returned to the rue Boissonnade a few days later. Laure had made several scenes and Mme Mercier had come to demand that he give her Annie's address, which he naturally had not done. But these problems were trivial compared to that raised by the appearance of M. Le Douaré. Jean-Noël thought about him constantly. Surely his stepmother could not be thinking of remarrying. And yet, would she have made an effort to please M. Le Douaré if he meant nothing to her? Jean-Noël had replayed the image of Annie in his imagination, smiling and attentive the way she was when she wanted to charm some-one—in other words, as she never was when in the presence of her stepson.

"It just so happens I was waiting for you," she said when Jean-Noël came into the studio. "I had a premonition you would come today."

They talked about painting for a few minutes. Jean-Noël, however, was thinking only of a way of bringing up the sub-ject of M. Le Douaré. Alone with her stepson, Mme Oetlinger might reveal her innermost thoughts.

"Monsieur Le Douaré seemed a charming man."

"In fact, I had been meaning to ask you what you thought of him."

"I found him charming," repeated Jean-Noël, who sensed he could not answer any other way.

"Indeed," said Annie, her voice suddenly serious, as if she had suddenly realized that she was speaking affectionately of a man who was not her husband. "But," she went on, "he is not just charming. There is great goodness concealed beneath that friendly, rushed, even slightly superficial exterior. And yet, he has as many reasons as I do to complain about his lot in life."

Jean-Noël was observing his stepmother. More than the words themselves, the tone of voice in which she had praised M. Le Douaré bore witness to her liking for this man. And yet Jean-Noël could not believe that his stepmother would not have kept it a secret if she was really thinking of remarrying. But what if, in fact, she wanted to accustom her stepson to the idea, what if the kindness she had shown during the past few months, rather than being a result of the secluded life she'd led since his father's death, was instead intended to prepare Jean-Noël for just such an eventuality? No, it was impossible. If Mme Oetlinger really intended to marry M. Le Douaré, she would, on the contrary, have arranged it so that her stepson knew nothing of her plans. Even supposing, which was doubt-ful, that she had thought it her duty to apprise him of her in-tentions, she would have gone about it in a different way.

"You seem to be very fond of this gentleman," said Jean-Noël, not without fearing that he might have offended his stepmother by calling M. Le Douaré "this gentleman." She seemed not to have noticed, however.

"Yes," she replied, as if nothing could be more natural, "I have a great deal of affection for him, because he needs it." Jean-Noël felt the urge to say, "What about me?" but checked himself. Wasn't Annie aware of how much her stepson loved her? And yet she preferred Charles Le Douaré's amiability and frozen smile to this love.

"But what exactly do you mean by having affection for someone?" asked Jean-Noël.

Mme Oetlinger looked at him and smiled.

"Come now, Jean-Noël, you're asking me questions that make no sense."

"I'm sorry, they do make sense."

"I understand you less and less, my dear little thing. Let's talk about something else, shall we? You haven't even asked me why my model isn't here today."

Jean-Noël's face remained stony. For the first time in years, Annie asked what was troubling him.

"Come now, what's wrong?"

He was pale. In spite of the fact that he was unaccustomed to it, he had not even noticed her solicitude.

"I would like to know," he blurted out, "if you are intending to remarry."

"That would be very foolish of me," she replied, still smiling.

Until that moment, it had seemed to Jean-Noël that his stepmother was receiving him at home, surrounded by objects that belonged to her, by canvases she had painted herself, but he suddenly saw her as if immobile and detached from everything around her, and the smile that had never left her face was as painful to him as if she had worn it at the bedside of a dying man. He said something which must have been insignificant, for his stepmother seemed not to have heard him. Later on, when he tried to recall the words he had spoken, he found he was unable to do so. There had been no link between them and his thoughts, and his only recourse had been to try to remember what he had heard himself say. So Annie had decided to marry again! Had she forgotten the man buried in the little cemetery in Davos? Jean-Noël now understood why she had not wanted M. Oetlinger's remains moved.

After leaving his stepmother, it struck him that the disagreement they had just had was far more serious than any which had come between them in the past. Although he had often quarreled with Annie, and had often thought he would never see her again, it had never been like this. An overwhelming sadness filled him, the sadness a man weighed down with problems might feel on the day the loss of his wife or child makes him understand that his problems were, at bottom, insignificant, and that it is only now that he is truly unhappy.

When he reached home, he carefully avoided speaking of what had happened, so that Mme Mourier's gloating would not exacerbate his suffering. After dinner, he tried to write Annie a long letter, but quickly abandoned the idea. He did not go back to the rue Boissonnade for two weeks, hoping thereby to show Annie he bore her a grudge. In the end, he was unable to stay away. It was absolutely necessary that he and his stepmother have a long talk. To his stupefaction, the concierge told him that Mme Oetlinger had left several days earlier and given no forwarding address. He refused to believe her. Mme Oetlinger kept nothing secret from him. She must certainly be in Paris; otherwise she would have told him. Like someone who feels that an order does not apply to him, and that he is being kept in the dark only because the person charged with enforcing that order has misunderstood or forgotten something, he tried for several minutes to obtain the information he thought the concierge was deliberately concealing from him. He was wasting his time. He hurried to the avenue de Malakoff. No one there was able to enlighten him. He was dreaming. Annie could not have left in this way.

Mme Oetlinger's disappearance had so shocked him that he had entirely forgotten he had come only with the intention of reprimanding her. So the only person he could now rely upon was himself! To the very end, Annie had treated him like a stranger. Afraid of showing himself again, he nonetheless went back to the rue Boissonnade. Until eight o'clock he paced back and forth, hoping that his stepmother would come out in the company of M. Le Douaré, which would explain everything. Finally, he went back to the rue Laugier. Upon reflection, wasn't it best that Annie had left? At least now he knew what he must do. If he had put up with being badgered by Mme Mourier, Marguerite, and Mme Mercier until now, hadn't it been because he'd been nursing the hope that one day Annie would ask him to resume that former life about which he constantly thought?

TWENTY-TWO

"We haven't seen you for quite some time," said M. Wurtzel, without seeming at all surprised, as if his friendliness toward Jean-Noël should not make the latter feel he was under any obligation to come see him regularly.

Before he had arrived, there had been talk that on Sunday Odile, and perhaps Maurice and Henri as well, might go to see some friends who lived outside of Paris. While M. Wurtzel exchanged a few words with Jean-Noël, Odile continued making plans with her brothers for this excursion. Between two questions, she finally looked over at Jean-Noël. He took advantage of this to make a sign indicating that he needed to talk to her. Although she had noticed that the young man looked more serious than usual, she pretended not to understand the meaning of his gesture and, as if her brother had just said something terribly witty, she started to laugh very loudly, visibly intending to show the recently arrived visitor that she had not been moping in his absence.

"You must listen to me," he said as soon as he was able to get away from M. Wurtzel.

She put on the same astonished look she would have adopted if a stranger had said this to her.

"I need to speak to you, it's very serious," insisted Jean-Noël, as if nothing could possibly be held against him once he had explained himself.

"I'm listening."

Odile did not consider herself at all flirtatious and was the first to scorn feminine wiles. Jean-Noël told her everything that had happened since M. Villemur's death, but when he came to his stepmother's desire to remarry, Odile, who had listened thus far as if from a sense of duty, suddenly grew animated and once again became the person she'd been when she had offered to go see Marguerite.

"That's impossible! Madame Oetlinger won't get married again," she said, although she had absolutely no reason for being surprised by this.

The news had filled her with joy, for if Jean-Noël was so hesitant to commit himself, wasn't it all due to this woman, whose importance he exaggerated?

"Unfortunately, it's true," said Jean-Noël, who was not taken in by Odile's feigned astonishment.

"Are you sure of this?" asked Odile.

She had noticed that the sorrow his stepmother's possible remarriage caused Jean-Noël was compounded by the shame he felt at having to talk about it. She felt sorry for him. If Jean-Noël had stayed away for the last few months, if he treated her with such casual disregard, it wasn't as some ordinary young man would have done, but rather out of absent-mindedness. It had not even occurred to him to apologize. Wasn't this proof in itself? She thus pretended to attach no more importance to her interlocutor's casual manner than he did himself.

"And yet I thought your stepmother loved your father very much," she said.

"Obviously," replied Jean-Noël, who wanted to justify Mme Oetlinger's actions by finding other reasons for them.

Odile was standing near a door. This door was open; it gave onto the sitting room, at one end of which stood M. Wurtzel, Maurice, Mme Wurtzel, and an old family friend who had just arrived.

"Papa," she said. "Can you come here a moment?"

M. Wurtzel did not hear his daughter.

"What are you going to tell your father?"

"I want to tell him what you just told me."

Jean-Noël seized Odile roughly by the arm.

"No, I beg of you, no, not a word of this to your family,"
he said in a state of high emotion.

When they saw each other again a few days later, Jean-
Noël and Odile discussed their own situation and made no
further mention of Mme Oetlinger and her plans.

"The most sensible thing," observed the young girl,
"would be for us to go see Maître Adrien Herbst together.
You've already met him. We'll ask him for advice. This time
we'll do things as they should be done."

Jean-Noël was horrified by the idea of going back to see
this lawyer, among other reasons because he knew he was a
friend of the Wurtzels. As Odile's family was not meant to
know Jean-Noël was married, Maître Herbst would be placed
in an equivocal position. Jean-Noël pointed this out to her.
Her surprise led him to understand that while Mlle Wurtzel
might have confidence in Maître Herbst's understanding of
the law, he was not, in her eyes, a man of great scruples, as a
result of which Jean-Noël felt his antipathy for the lawyer
increase.

It was not just getting a divorce Jean-Noël had to think of, but
also leaving Mme Mourier. One evening, speaking as frankly
as he had to Odile, something for which he had afterward
congratulated himself, he told Laure that his stepmother had
left without bothering to notify him, probably because ever
since she had decided to remarry, she found being around her
stepson disagreeable. By confessing to the truth and admitting
that he was now well and truly on his own, wasn't he regaining his liberty? Hadn't he become unwelcome, like a man
who'd been loved for his money and had now lost it all? He
pretended to believe so, though without undue exaggeration
so as not to arouse pity, which would have been to go from
one evil to another. He therefore kept his lamentations discreet. He let it be understood that he could no longer accept
a hospitality he would never be able to extend in return. Had
fate been kinder to him, he would have been happy to stay at

the rue Laugier. But with neither fortune nor family, he did not want to burden anyone.

"What do you intend to do?" asked Mme Mourier.

She had not been surprised to learn of Mme Oetlinger's sudden disappearance. During the past few months, Laure had been letting Jean-Noël cling to his illusions, but she had nonetheless wondered how a person like Mme Oetlinger could have taken any interest in such a young man. What she found surprising was that this escape, for it was an escape, had not taken place sooner. She preserved a very favorable impression of her one and only meeting with Annie. In her mind, Mme Oetlinger resembled her, in the sense that she was one of those exceptional people who do honor to their entourage. Therefore, she made no effort to conceal a certain satisfaction upon learning that she was gone. Jean-Noël was going to be forced to abandon his inflated opinion of himself. This would be a good lesson for him. But when he answered her question by saying that he intended to take a room in a hotel and try to rebuild his life, she grew angry.

"That's not true," she cried. "You want to marry Mlle Wurtzel. That's why you're trying to get a divorce. I repeat, you're wasting your time. I'm not Marguerite. You won't be able to do to me what you did to that poor girl."

Jean-Noël did his best to calm Mme Mourier. It was absolutely imperative that she not make another visit to the boulevard du Montparnasse.

"Fine," he replied. "I'll stay. But if you regret it later on, don't blame me."

Since Mme Mourier was shouting at him, he might just as well pretend to give in. He knew that Laure's angry outbursts always led her to reflect afterwards, and while she had a great many faults, failing to admit that she had been wrong was not one of them.

A few days later, he and Odile went to the rue du Louvre to see Maître Herbst. This was the first time they had ever done anything of an official nature together, and although neither one of them realized it, they already had the air of a newlywed couple. And yet Jean-Noël was far from feeling that peaceful happiness peculiar to such couples. He had retained a very bad memory of his last meeting with the lawyer. Hadn't Maurice introduced him as a friend, and not a future brother-in-law? And, in fact, what more could Maître Herbst do now, other than repeat what he had already told him? Odile, however, had high hopes for this meeting, and seemed convinced that it would clarify everything.

"How are you, dear Odile? So you haven't forgotten me?" asked Maître Herbst, who seemed neither to have recognized the young girl's companion nor to have made the slightest connection between this visit and the one Jean-Noël had paid him earlier.

"And you, Adrien, how are you?"

Five years earlier, in the days when Adrien Herbst did not yet have any clients, he had spent a good deal of time at the Wurtzels, and had hoped to marry Odile. But she, dreaming of greater things than a fellow countryman from Alsace, had refused. They had nonetheless remained very good friends. Adrien Herbst had eventually married, which had made Odile genuinely happy.

"But I know Monsieur," said the lawyer, smiling amiably at Jean-Noël, "and I think I can guess the reason for your visit. You came to see me with Maurice, didn't you? It was about a divorce."

Jean-Noël replied that he had indeed come to consult him about the steps he needed to take to obtain a divorce. Maître Herbst, who had the curious habit of pretending he could not remember anything, asked Jean-Noël to remind him of the facts. Jean-Noël, whose embarrassment at exposing all of the stages of a failed marriage to a stranger whom he suspected was hostile to his cause, did so in such veiled terms that in the end Odile spoke for him. She did so without any embarrassament whatsoever, and without omitting a single detail. Jean-Noël listened to her, and although every word she spoke concerned him, he had the feeling she was not talking about him. It was finally decided that the wisest course of action would be to write Marguerite and ask her to begin divorce proceedings herself, in exchange for which her husband would agree to pay her whatever maintenance she demanded.

"How much do you estimate you can pay your wife, Monsieur?" the lawyer asked Jean-Noël. He blushed. He had no money. He sensed that his interlocutor suspected this, all the more so since Mlle Wurtzel had done nothing to conceal the fact from him.

"Do you think she would be happy with a thousand francs a month?" Odile asked Jean-Noël. She so obviously hoped that this amount would be sufficient that it became clear it would fall to her to pay it.

"That's what I'm giving her now," answered Jean-Noël, increasingly embarrassed. "If she gains no material advantage from being divorced, I don't think she will ever agree."

"Let's say fifteen hundred," the lawyer, who found this bargaining quite natural, said to Odile.

Mlle Wurtzel appeared to hesitate. She looked at Jean-Noël. He had the feeling that even fifteen hundred francs would not be enough, but he didn't dare say so.

"She should accept that," he said.

"Do you really think so?" Odile asked him.

This time the lawyer replied. He thought that for now they could leave it at fifteen hundred francs. Although Maître Herbst was one of her older brother's friends, and because of this she'd always had great trust in him, Mlle Wurtzel suddenly found herself doubting his competence. Wasn't be being too quick to commit her? Shouldn't they consult someone else before making any decisions?

"What do you think?" she asked Maître Herbst. "Isn't it rather a lot?"

"No, it seems reasonable to me."

She turned toward Jean-Noël, who was becoming increasingly ill-tempered as this scene unfolded.

"Do you think that your wife will then leave you in peace?"

Maître Herbst interrupted her.

"Listen to me, Odile. I am going to have a letter typed for you. We shall then see if changes should be made. It will be much simpler this way."

He got up and went into an adjoining room.

"Maintenance of fifteen hundred francs seems quite reasonable to me," said Odile with greater assurance.

"I don't know," replied Jean-Noël, who was feeling so humiliated that he no longer wanted to express any opinion whatsoever.

Just then the lawyer returned with his secretary.

"I am going to dictate a letter, Miss."

Without once looking at her employer's clients, the secretary sat down in an armchair, a notebook balanced on her knees. Jean-Noël had lowered his head. He could not get used to revealing the details of a marriage that embarrassed him and which he had always done his utmost to hide from the world.

"The letter is to be addressed as follows: 'Madame Jean-Noël Oetlinger, rue Mission-Marchand, in Saint Cloud.' " Turning to Odile, he said, "Naturally, we don't mention you." In a different, friendlier, tone of voice, he added, "I told my wife you were here." He paused for a moment. "Madame," he began at last, pacing up and down as he spoke, "after a conversation I had with your husband, who has retained me to defend his interests without neglecting yours, it struck me that if you are opposed to a divorce, it is because you are concerned above all with safeguarding your daughter's future, as well as your own, which, I hasten to add, is perfectly legitimate. And yet you cannot fail to be aware..."

At that moment, Mme Herbst entered the office.

"Odile," she whispered, so as not to disturb her husband.

Mlle Wurtzel, who had been following the lawyer's every word, smiled abruptly and, getting up, went over to her friend. The two women began talking while Maître Herbst continued dictating his letter. Jean-Noël had blushed so many times since his arrival that he did not even think of hiding his face, which this dictation made in the presence of all these women had turned crimson yet again.

"Jean-Noël," said Odile, "I'd like you to meet my friend."

"Comma," said Maître Herbst for the twentieth time, forcing them to notice the pride he took in dictating the punctuation as well.

"Perhaps I ought to leave you," murmured Mme Herbst. "I can see that this is a serious matter and I don't wish to disturb you."

"Will you please read the letter," Maître Herbst ordered his secretary a few minutes later.

Odile signaled to Jean-Noël to come closer.

"It seems fine to me. What about you, Jean-Noël, what do you think of it?"

He had the feeling that the letter, which was curt and yet pompous, would make the worst possible impression upon Marguerite. The scene had made him so sick at heart, however, that he replied, "It's perfect."

Far from being convinced by this assertion, Odile was still wary. Finally, she too said, "It's perfect, in fact; yes, perfect. But if you don't mind, Adrien, I'd like to have a copy please. I will think about it and call you. I think that in an affair like this, one can't be too careful. You agree with me, don't you?"

When they had taken their leave of Maître Herbst, Jean-Noël nearly lost his temper with Odile. He sensed that she would never have dared to put him in such a ridiculous situation if he had not been weak enough to tell her his stepmother had left. But now, why shouldn't she! He thought of Annie. She was so different! She would never have stooped to discussing maintenance payments. Oh well, what had just transpired was of no importance. Once he was married and free from his worries, he would finish his studies, take up his profession. What difference would it make to him then that he had married a woman he didn't love? They would each lead their own lives. He would become friendly with the Ville-murs, and the day Annie reappeared, how surprised she would

be to find a strong, independent man rather than the unde-
cided, timorous young man she had left behind!

The Wurtzel family was one that lived in perfect har-
mony. It would never have occurred to any of its members to
undertake something of which they did not all approve. If
Odile had not yet spoken to her father of her desire to marry
Jean-Noël, it was not because she feared he would object, but
rather out of pride. She would have found it unpleasant to see
her family give its approval to a young man she knew was
married and who was, in addition, living with a mistress. She
had therefore preferred to wait until he was free. At Maître
Herbst's, however—and this was why Odile had asked for
time to think—she had been overcome by fear. It had struck
her that before committing herself it would be best to tell her
father, if not the whole truth, then at least what her intentions were.

"You know, Papa, I have some important news for you. I
want to get married."

"Ah! Very good, and to whom?" asked M. Wurtzel, without seeming in the least bit surprised. "Is he a good match, at
least?" he went on, teasing her.

"To Jean-Noël."

M. Wurtzel fixed a questioning look upon his daughter, a
look whose intensity made Odile abruptly aware that the
man who stood before her was her father.

"You know that boy hasn't got a penny."

Odile was not surprised by this remark. She was not unaware of the fact that money was the only thing which
counted for M. Wurtzel. She had suffered because of this, had
been humiliated many times in front of strangers because of
her father's constant fear of being deceived. But at the very
moment when she was telling him what she most cared
about, she no longer wanted to take such base considerations
into account. She extolled Jean-Noël's virtues like a young
girl who, in spite of knowing that her fiancé is penniless, is
convinced she is making a good match. The future looked
very grim in early 1926. Wasn't she proving she had great

common sense by putting more stock in a man's intrinsic worth than in what he possessed?

"Are you at least sure that this boy loves you?" asked M. Wurtzel, for whom what was most important was not that his daughter should love Jean-Noël but rather that the latter love his daughter. He then went on to imply that it was much easier to fall in love than it was to inspire a lasting love in someone. Odile replied coldly that she was certain of being loved, as if she had all the evidence in her possession necessary to prove this.

"Is he in good health?" continued M. Wurtzel. "You must be aware that marriage is a very serious matter for a young girl, that one can never be too careful. We can overlook the fact that this man has no fortune, although it's hardly a recommendation. But one needs to be sure that he has not led a dissolute life, had affairs the consequences of which you would have to bear—in short, that he is worthy of becoming your husband, of giving you children, of joining Simon and Maurice in running my business someday."

Jean-Noël met all these requirements. He was an honest, hard-working young man. Odile felt that she would be happy with him. She went on to emphasize the fact that the young man would be a useful addition to the family, but with a detached air, as if she herself had nothing to gain, wanting to show by this that it was perfectly natural for her to judge Jean-Noël from her parents' point of view as well as her own.

M. Wurtzel had risen. He was pacing up and down the room in a curious way, for he never took big steps, nor did he ever take more than a few steps in a straight line. Suddenly he stopped.

"I'd like to see him again," he said.

"Nothing could be easier."

"I want to see him immediately."

M. Wurtzel resumed walking. He had nothing more to reproach Jean-Noël for and yet something was bothering him.

"If this marriage takes place, your husband will have to

understand that your happiness is in his hands," he said, after a moment's silence.

"That's quite natural."

"Will he understand it?"

M. Wurtzel thought for a moment.

"As you have spoken to me so frankly," he said at last, "you won't hold it against me if I tell you exactly what I think. I believe, you see, that the way this boy has been brought up does not predispose him to becoming your husband. I must confess that I never thought of him as a son-in-law. I say this after having reflected upon everything I know about him. It seems to me that the influence the Villemurs have had upon him, and especially his stepmother, has not been particularly beneficial."

"He no longer sees them."

"That may be. Nonetheless, this boy has never given me the impression that he knows exactly what he wants."

"He managed to get an education in very difficult circumstances."

"First of all, he never finished. Second, I don't see what made his circumstances any more difficult than those of many others. But then, you're not planning to get married today, are you?"

"Oh! No."

"We'll have time to think, to observe him, to judge his behavior. For now, let's talk about something else, shall we?"

As soon as Odile left her father, the first thing she did was call Maître Herbst to ask him to send Marguerite the letter as soon as possible. Then she called Jean-Noël at Maître Préfil's to tell him she needed to speak to him and wanted to see him at six o'clock. She would wait for him outside his office. "Don't worry," she added, "everything is absolutely fine."

TWENTY-THREE

When Odile met him after work, Jean-Noël did not even bother to ask her what it was she had been so eager to tell him. She was not ruffled by his indifference. They had walked a short distance together when she announced proudly: "I have something to tell you which is going to make you happy. The letter went off."

Jean-Noël pretended to be overjoyed at the news. The day before, after leaving Mlle Wurtzel, he had reflected upon the events which had unfolded in Maître Herbst's office and wondered why Odile, who until then had seemed so impatient for him to obtain a divorce, had suddenly drawn back. The reason had soon become clear to him. Odile was afraid of committing herself before having some assurance, if not the absolute certainty, that her family would not oppose her marriage.

"I have something else to tell you," she continued. "I spoke to my father about you."

"Ah! I thought so."

"Why?"

Jean-Noël made a gesture indicating that he didn't know why.

"And what did you say to your father?"

"You seem to find this funny, and yet nothing could be more natural. We can't make commitments without knowing whether we will be able to honor them. I am free, of course. But that shouldn't make us imprudent."

At that moment a strange thought crossed Jean-Noël's

mind. If Odile was so eager for him to get this divorce, it was only because she was thinking of herself. Had there been some reason that made it impossible for them to be married, she would have been indifferent to the problems of the man she claimed to love. Although he realized this was perfectly human, he could not stop himself from saying, "In effect, our future is in the hands of your family."

"Not at all. Do you really fail to see that it is in our best interests to be on good terms with them? If that proves to be impossible, it doesn't mean that we won't get married. What's necessary, Jean-Noël, is for you to be very accommodating. You're going to start right now, by coming to the house with me."

"I was just there two days ago. There's no reason for me to go back."

"I'm asking you to do so for my sake."

Jean-Noël didn't yield. Odile asked him why he was refusing to do something so natural. He would not answer. So Mlle Wurtzel thought she was doing him an honor by consenting to become his wife, when in fact the opposite was true and he was the one doing her an honor by consenting to become her husband! How could she fail to realize that by forcing him to make a declaration so prematurely she was putting him in an equivocal situation, that of claiming to be genuinely in love with her when in fact he was not even divorced yet? If only because of her father, she should have been doing everything in her power to avoid just such a meeting.

"No," he said. "I won't go, because there is no reason for me to go."

Odile tried to persuade him that all she was asking for was a friendly gesture on his part. M. Wurtzel was very eager to see him again. He had been so conciliatory that she wanted to satisfy him on this one point. She added that she knew this was awkward for Jean-Noël, but that it was nothing more than an unpleasant moment to get through. Afterwards, the two of them would be left in peace. All of these arguments failed to budge Jean-Noël, however.

"As you are ill-disposed today," she said very calmly, "I think it best if I leave you."

Without saying another word, she walked away. It was the first time she had ever abandoned herself to a fit of temper, but in her mind this could have no regrettable consequences, because Jean-Noël was now too committed to back out. In fact, she had taken only a few steps when he caught up with her and took her by the arm.

"I'll come with you," he said.

She stopped and looked at him, smiling.

"You are stubborn!" she said, with that pride girls feel when they begin speaking like a wife to the man they love.

It was seven o'clock when they arrived at the boulevard du Montparnasse.

"My father must be in his study," said Odile, dragging Jean-Noël along in her wake.

By the way M. Wurtzel rose, came forward, and extended his hand when he saw the young man, Jean-Noël understood immediately that he was not being received as before—simply, freely, cordially—but rather a bit like a stranger, doubtless to make him understood that their former friendship would carry no weight in the negotiations which were to follow.

"I am happy to see you, do sit down," said M. Wurtzel, drawing up a heavy armchair. Without preventing the old man from going to this trouble, without even thanking him, Jean-Noël sat down and casually crossed his legs, as a way of showing he scorned such obsequiousness.

"Odile," continued M. Wurtzel, "I would like you to leave us for a moment."

She left, but not before giving Jean-Noël a knowing look, which the latter pretended not to have noticed.

"My daughter informed me yesterday that you wish to marry her."

Jean-Noël lowered his head as a sign of acquiescence, even though he thought this was not entirely accurate and that it was Odile, rather, who wished to marry him.

"That is, in fact, so."

"I want to tell you straight away that I have no initial objections to this marriage. You are almost a friend of the family's. We have always had a great liking for you."

Rather than being touched by these words, Jean-Noël found them unpleasant. They were not sincere. Objections could not be far behind. In order to play his role to the hilt, he was now going to have to defend himself. The mere thought made him want to leave. His position as a stranger being received as a friend one must treat with consideration seemed all the more ridiculous in view of the fact that if he'd been able to speak freely, he would have made it clear to M. Wurtzel in an instant that, contrary to what the latter believed, his future and his happiness depended only upon himself, Jean-Noël.

"However," M. Wurtzel continued, "—and I hasten to add that this is not a reproach—the rather exceptional circumstances in which you were brought up, certain family reasons that are none of my concern but I can guess at, have resulted in your having no resources whatsoever. As the idea that you might marry my daughter one day had never occurred to me, I must confess that I never thought of you as anything more than one of my childrens' friends, and that I never asked myself what you intended to do with your life. My daughter has informed me that you've begun studying law and are working as a clerk in a solicitor's office."

"That's correct."

"I have a feeling that is not a terribly well-paid occupation. You must be earning just enough to get by. But if you were to get married, how would you manage to meet all the expenses of a household?"

Jean-Noël was growing increasingly irritated. With no great enthusiasm, he declared that it was his intention to finish his studies and then begin practicing law. Without going so far as to look down on the Wurtzels, he had always behaved like a young man for whom material preoccupations were not a concern, whose family would ensure that he wanted for nothing. He was therefore deeply humiliated that M. Wurtzel was now asking him these sorts of questions. He would have liked to reply that he had been brought up never to discuss money, but he couldn't.

"And yet you must be aware," contined M. Wurtzel, "that at the moment members of the liberal professions are all struggling to survive. These are times which call for hard work. I need only look around to be reminded of this fact. My eldest son has many friends in intellectual circles. One of them, a lawyer, Maître Herbst—you may have heard of him—was just telling me that there is no new business, that the law courts are living, to use his expression, off old stock."

"I don't share your opinion. On the contrary, I think that the legal profession is one of those which will always have a raison d'être," replied Jean-Noël, who was so disconcerted by hearing M. Wurtzel mention the name of Maître Herbst that he wasn't even thinking what he was saying.

M. Wurtzel could not help but find it strange that Jean-Noël was defending a profession he had not yet taken up and which, in fact, he seemed in no great hurry to take up.

"I must tell you," M. Wurtzel went on, "that my wish, if I had a son-in-law, would be for him to become a son to me and be capable, like my other children, of taking my place someday. I will not be here forever. My business, as you know, is not doing well at all: money loses its value with each passing day. Where are we heading? I have no idea. What will become of the fortune we have so laboriously amassed? I cannot say. Hard work, more than anything else, is what's going to see us through."

"I understand you very well," said Jean-Noël, concealing the contempt he felt for a man who spoke of a "fortune so laboriously amassed".

"And yet, you implied earlier that you had no interest in business."

"Well, actually," replied Jean-Noël, who failed to see

[197]

where his interlocutor was leading and wanted simply to smooth things over, "if I get married, I would find it quite natural to enter the business."

No sooner had Jean-Noël left than a smiling Odile asked her father what he thought of her choice. He avoided answering so as not to hurt his daughter's feelings. She insisted. He then told her point-blank that Jean-Noël did not please him. She asked him why. He refused to tell her. At no moment in the course of the conversation he'd just had with the young man had he felt the slightest empathy for him. Although Odile's face darkened, it was only for an instant. She was twenty-six years old. Like all young girls who linger on in the bosom of their families, she was constantly battling, not against her parents' authority, but rather against her own instincts to submit to them. No one was going to stop her from loving Jean-Noël.

"This doesn't mean that the boy will never change," said M. Wurtzel, to console her.

In the wake of these events, Odile set about trying to mold Jean-Noël to her family's tastes, which was a far from easy task. She had only to ask him to do something for him to do the opposite. It must be said that he had a very bad memory of his visit with M. Wurtzel. He had come away with the impression that he was considered a schemer who wanted to marry purely out of self-interest. He was forced to acknowledge that appearances were against him. And yet, he had the feeling that he would never have dreamed of marrying Mlle Wurtzel if she had not encouraged him to do so. What he could, perhaps, be reproached with was allowing himself to be influenced when it was to his advantage. He now became increasingly touchy. While taking care not to carry this too far, he met all of Odile's efforts with a show of utter disdain for the Wurtzel family. The young girl, however, was patience incarnate. She blamed Jean-Noël's bad temper on his many worries. Arrogant as he was, mustn't it be painful for him to find himself in a situation so ill-suited to a young man who had been brought up as he had?

To Odile's great satisfaction, M. Wurtzel never again broached the subject of Jean-Noël. It seemed as if everything was going to work out for the best when, one evening, as he had done so often several years earlier, Maître Herbst telephoned at the dinner hour. "I would like to see you, Odile, as soon as possible. Could you come tomorrow morning, before I leave for the law courts?" Although her stepmother was within earshot, Mlle Wurtzel tried to find out what the lawyer wanted. "I cannot tell you anything over the phone," he replied. He then reverted to the tone of voice he had adopted at the beginnng of their conversation to add: "Give my best to everyone. If Henri is there, tell him to come and see me one of these days." Odile wondered whether she ought to inform Jean-Noël or whether it was best to tell him nothing. She finally chose the latter option, deciding that it was better to do on her own whatever could be done without him. She therefore went, not without anxiety, to the rue du Louvre. What had happened? Why had Maître Herbst refused to tell her anything over the phone? She was eager to know everything, but found she had to wait more than half an hour before he could see her. At last, a young woman showed her into the lawyer's office. With neither a smile nor a word of welcome, he got up and pointed to a chair.

"I'll be with you in a moment. I have so much work," he said, turning his attention to a thick file before him.

Shortly afterwards, he rang for his secretary, gave her an errand to run, then made a telephone call. Finally, one hand on his forehead and still not looking at his visitor, he went on:

"Now, I'm all yours, Odile. Let me see, what was this about? Ah yes, I remember."

He sat up straighter and, barely turning his head, looked behind him.

"I asked you to come today," he began without any introduction, in order to make it clear to Odile that the person now addressing her was the lawyer, "because I received a letter from that M. Large who says he represents the wife of your friend, Monsieur Oetlinger. I'll read it to you. 'In reply to yours of the thirteenth of May, I have the honor of informing you that Madame Oetlinger, who is concerned above all with the welfare and future of her child, does not want a divorce. Sincerely yours, etc.' "

"But that's dreadful!" cried Odile.

Maître Herbst made a gesture of helplessness. Then, after a period of silence during which he gave the impression of having decided there was nothing further he could do, he added, no doubt satisfied by the anxiety he had caused Odile: "But when I received this letter I thought of you. Aren't we old friends?"

"Yes, Adrien."

"You would have held it against me, wouldn't you, if I had let you down at the first sign of difficulty. I wrote to Monsieur Large. I asked him to be kind enough to come by and see me. He did so, and, after a considerable struggle, I was able to obtain the following. Madame Oetlinger will consent to file for divorce through me, which, mark you, is a very important point, on the condition that her husband, that is to say your friend Monsieur Oetlinger, agrees to pay her maintenance in the amount of two thousand francs a month and in addition agrees to reimburse her the amount of twenty-seven thousand francs, this being the dowry which he squandered."

By the emphasis Maître Herbst had placed on Marguerite's conditions, Odile sensed that he scorned the man whose wife made such demands.

"As we are at this person's mercy, it would be best to find her conditions reasonable, isn't that right?" asked Odile.

"That's entirely up to you," replied the lawyer. "I do not know what Monsieur Oetlinger's resources are."

"For the moment he has none."

"You yourself say 'for the moment,' " continued Maître Herbst, who remained enigmatic and distant so that Odile would understand he wanted to give her no advice other than that which was directly related to the divorce.

"In my place, you would accept these conditions, wouldn't you?"

"You mustn't ask me questions, Odile. You must know better than I what you have to do."

Mlle Wurtzel's annoyance was too visible for Maître Herbst to fail to notice it. Yet he did nothing to dissipate it. Even now, although by turning to him in the present circumstances Odile was making it clear that she had never considered him as anything more than a friend, not only did he have the impression that it would have taken very little for her to marry him, but also that she regretted she had not done so.

At lunchtime, Odile went to meet Jean-Noël at his office. When he learned of the demands being made by his wife, he flew into a rage. He thought it unacceptable that Odile had been notified before he had. What was the meaning of these secret meetings being held behind his back? He would not have been particularly surprised to learn that Marguerite and Mlle Wurtzel had met several times.

"I also came to tell you that you mustn't worry. If these are the conditions laid down by your "ex" (which was how Mlle Wurtzel referred to Marguerite), we might as well accept them. And three months from now, as Maître Herbst himself assured me, it will all be over and done with. The only thing which worries me is that I am going to have to sell some shares. It will be very serious if my father finds out."

There was something else that worried Odile. Jean-Noël was still living at the rue Laugier. Could anything be more foolhardy than touching off what was certain to be a scandal before Jean-Noël had even left Mme Mourier? The shares Mlle Wurtzel possessed were in her name; the dividends however were paid to her father. She finally plucked up the courage to tell the young man that, as he was going to have to leave this woman anyway, he might as well do so immediately. Oh! She was not asking this because she was going to have to bear the financial burden of his divorce, but rather so that everything would be in order. She would then be in a position to defend herself if her family learned she had dipped into her accounts. Jean-Noël, without perceiving what it was that offended him in these precautions, nearly answered that if Odile didn't trust him, it was pointless for them to think of getting married. But he said nothing. This seemed to him the wiser course of action. In fact, what he feared was that Mme Mourier, in the heat of anger, would go see M. Wurtzel.

"It's for that reason," replied Odile, "that I thought we should have told my father the truth right away. Don't you think it would be for the best? He will understand you, I'm sure of it. And that way, Madame Mourier can do as she pleases. It will be too late. What's more, you will feel you are in a more normal situation. Because at heart, the reason for the uneasiness in your relations with my father has to do with that situation, which you don't dare admit to him and which he perhaps suspects."

TWENTY-FOUR

A week later, by dint of insisting, Odile finally persuaded Jean-Noël to admit to her family that he was not only married and the father of a child, but was also living with a woman. These revelations made no effect upon M. Wurtzel. Ever since the young man had expressed his desire to marry Odile, he had ceased to feel any empathy for him. What difference did it make to him, therefore, if Jean-Noël was married or not married, if he had a daughter or didn't have a daughter! It never even crossed his mind to use this as a pretext for opposing the marriage, which was too much of a mismatch to be taken seriously.

Upon leaving their meeting, Jean-Noël felt utterly humiliated. That this confession, which he had put off for so long, could have so little effect on M. Wurtzel had given him an inkling of just how insignificant a figure he was considered to be. This indifference, by which Odile had been overjoyed, served only to prove that M. Wurtzel had never for a second thought his daughter's marriage was feasible. Until then, Jean-Noël had thought that being related to the Villemurs, if one could call it that, had given him a sort of prestige. That this should not be so seemed an affront, not just to himself but to Annie as well.

As soon as he found himself alone with Mlle Wurtzel, he was unable to conceal his vexation from her. "So no matter what happens," she replied, "you're always going to be unhappy! How can you fail to be delighted by the way in which my father just received you? Hasn't he just shown you how very indulgent he is? Do you know of a father who would have been so kind and understanding in similar circumstances?" Jean-Noël let himself be convinced. Having promised he would break off his liaison with Mme Mourier the next day, he left Odile.

At the rue Laugier, Jean-Noël was surprised to find the apartment filled with flowers, as if for some festive occasion. During the past few days, he had already noticed that Mme Mourier was doing her utmost to be pleasant to him. He had thought that this renewed affection was a result of the coldness he had shrouded himself in ever since his stepmother's departure. Laure was undoubtedly trying to win back the young man, and this was the very moment when he was going to have to leave her.

"Why the flowers?" he asked, hoping he had nothing to do with this embellishment.

"Today is an important day," she replied sadly. "Wait for me a moment."

He went into the dining room and was further astonished. The table was laid with Mme Mourier's favorite crystal and silverware. There were even flowers strewn decoratively on the tablecloth, just as when she invited friends to dinner. But the table was set only for two. None of the anniversaries Mme Mourier liked to celebrate fell on this day. Jean-Noël was wondering what the meaning of these lavish preparations could be when Laure reappeared. She was wearing an evening gown.

"What's going on?" asked Jean-Noël, more and more intrigued.

"You will understand later, my dear Jean-Noël."

She was very sure of herself. From time to time, she would go into the kitchen to give orders. Finally, they sat down to table.

"You know, my friend," she said in the middle of dinner, a moment she had obviously selected in advance, "that I have always been extremely fond of you. One doesn't live with a man for three years—and you may have forgotten it, but we have known one another for three years—without growing attached to him and feeling very sad at the thought of leaving him."

Soon afterwards Jean-Noël held the key to this elaborate production. While he had been living his life, concerned only with himself and his relations with the Wurtzel family, Mme Mourier had been doing a great deal of thinking. The hurt she had felt upon learning that he intended to get a divorce without telling her had been much greater than she had admitted. It was not that she had been afraid Jean-Noël really wanted to leave her; instead, his desire for independence had led her to the conclusion that he aspired to a more settled life. Then, there had been Mme Oetlinger's sudden departure. More than anything, that had changed the way she felt about Jean-Noël. He had told her so many times that his stepmother adored him that she had come to believe him, in spite of the fact that she had always had some reservations about Annie's love for her stepson. Older than Jean-Noël, dreaming of inspiring respect, eager to protect, she had come to believe that she was more appreciated by Mme Oetlinger, although she hardly knew her, than by Jean-Noël himself. During these last two years, aided by the young man's accounts, she had imagined to herself the nature of his relationship with Annie, and had become convinced that it was somewhat similar to the relationship she had with him. Nothing would ever come of this boy. With his stepmother there to stimulate him, there had been some small hope that he might change. But now that he had been left to fend for himself, it was more prudent to expect nothing in order to avoid being sorely disillusioned. She had then wondered whether she ought to continue to keep a watchful eye over Jean-Noël on her own. His disagreeable attitude had helped to convince her that she would never have more influence over him than Annie had enjoyed. The thought of leaving him had then entered her mind, but while that same idea had filled Jean-Noël with an iciness designed to make its execution less painful, it had, on the contrary, made Mme Mourier feel more tender toward him. For she gave the best of herself in her love affairs. In her eyes, the beginning of a liaison was no more more important than its ending. It was already sad enough that life should force you to leave a man you loved; why reproach yourself for having to do so? This was why she had wanted the day that was to mark the end of her love to be as festive as a holiday. Wasn't she grateful to Jean-Noël for all of the happiness he had brought her?

"I think it's best this way," she said. "Tomorrow each of us will go our separate ways. I say tomorrow, that's just a figure of speech. We'll stay good friends all the same, isn't that right?"

Hadn't Jean-Noël just promised Odile that he would be free by the morrow? He was so delighted, it did not occur to him that there was something indelicate about announcing, at the very moment when Laure was setting him free, that he had been about to ask her to do just that.

Extraordinary as this may seem, Mme Mourier was not offended. Love's repercussions on everyday life, no matter what they were, never failed to move her. Thus it was written that today was the day they must part. She looked at the flowers scattered on the table, the bouquets standing in vases. Wouldn't the two of them have been happy together if circumstances hadn't made theirs an impossible union? Tears, which she left untouched, ran down her cheeks. The following day, when Jean-Noël kissed her for the last time and, laden with suitcases, made for the door, she was filled with sadness as she watched him go.

Upon leaving Mme Mourier, Jean-Noël took himself to that famous Hôtel des Grands Hommes where he had previously stayed at various times in his life. It had been completely renovated and was under new management. Jean-Noël liked to play the part, in front of a new owner, of a client who had received special treatment from the previous owner. He found the first rooms he was shown so unsuitable and made such unpleasant comments about them that the bellboy went to fetch the owner and warned him of this client's peculiarity. In spite of this, Jean-Noël continued his tirade against the changes which had been made, and was finally told that if the hotel did not please him, he should go elsewhere. Ignoring these words, Jean-Noël took a large room with a double bed on the first floor that looked out over the square below. He closed the door, put his suitcase on a sort of stool designed for this purpose, and sat down in an armchair. It was nearly nine o'clock. He had just enough time to get to work. But what good would that do him? Wasn't Maître Préfil a friend of Madame Mourier's? Wasn't it best to abandon everything at the same time? The table Laure had prepared, with its crystal and its flowers, appeared before his eyes. At present, in the cold light of the hotel room, Mme Mourier's desire to be rid of him was the only thing the scene evoked for him. She had probably thought that there was little to be gained from remaining Jean-Noël's mistress now that he had lost his stepmother. Laure was no different from Ernestine Mercier and Emile. They, too, seemed to expect nothing more from him; it had been a long time since he had heard from them. Up to now, although surrounded by problems, he had at least derived some pride from knowing that people were counting on him and waiting for him to be in a position to keep the promises he made.

Marguerite had agreed to a divorce on the condition that she would be paid the twenty-seven thousand francs Jean-Noël owed her on the day she signed the petition. To attenuate the barter-like quality of this demand, Maître Herbst had organized a meeting between husband and wife in his offices. At first, he had informed only Mlle Wurtzel, to whom he spoke or wrote nearly every day. But when Jean-Noël arrived for the meeting, well in advance of the appointed hour and in the company of Odile, who, it had been agreed, would wait for Marguerite's arrival to slip away into the apartment where

Mme Herbst would keep her company, the lawyer spoke directly to Jean-Noël, as a way of showing that he was now dealing only with the interested party.

"Odile," he told her almost immediately, "I would like you to go now."

When she had left the room, he explained to Jean-Noël at length what attitude he should adopt, as if this affair was no different from any of the others he handled, and repeated the name Mme Jean-Noël Oetlinger several times, making the young man blush every time he did so. When Marguerite arrived, Maître Herbst went forward respectfully to meet her. Jean-Noël greeted her coldly, ashamed that this woman was his wife. Everything about her appearance was mediocre, both her clothing and that sly way in which she examined her surroundings, looking like a person who is not going to be imposed upon and who is prepared to leave at the first sign of difficulty. Maître Herbst sat down at his desk and, very calmly, began to speak. Jean-Noël was not listening to him. From time to time, he looked over at Marguerite. She occasionally interrupted the lawyer. She had no intention of being charmed by his fine language. Whenever he stopped talking about her, however, whenever her interests were not at stake, her attention would lapse and she would pretend to abhor discussions. She did not once deign to look over at her husband.

As soon as Marguerite was gone, Jean-Noël felt relieved. He looked at Maître Herbst. The lawyer was putting away his papers. "In three months, at the most, the decree will be handed down." He then got up and went to call Odile. She entered the room smiling. Jean-Noël had been expecting, goodness knows why, that she would thank him, but she seemed barely aware of his presence, engrossed as she was in listening to Maître Herbst's account of the meeting, and even in asking him for additional details. Jean-Noël waited a few moments, hoping that Odile would finally say something to him. When she failed to do so, he got up abruptly.

"I'm leaving," he said in an unpleasant tone of voice.

"Wait for me, Jean-Noël. I'll be finished right away."

"No, I'm leaving."

And he left, without Odile having done anything whatever to try to stop him. One would have thought that she found it entirely natural that this man, for whom she was willing to run the risk of falling out with her family, wasn't waiting for her.

TWENTY-FIVE

To make it impossible for Odile to find him, Jean-Noël did not go back to his hotel until midnight. There was a letter waiting for him there. He immediately recognized Mme Mourier's enormous handwriting. This was not the first time that she had written to him since he'd left the rue Laugier. She had already done so on two other occasions, to show him that she was still his friend. "I must speak to you, Jean-Noël. Please come tomorrow morning, before ten o'clock. I shall wait for you. It's to do with a matter of great importance to you." Those few words filled the entire page. Jean-Noël did not believe in this matter of great importance but he nonetheless went to the rue Laugier.

"Yesterday," said Laure with great pride, "I had a visit from your stepmother."

Jean-Noël turned pale. So Annie was in Paris! What had made her come to Mme Mourier's? One would have thought that, entrusted with keeping an eye on his stepmother, he had just learned that she was keeping dubious company.

"She stayed here for the better part of an hour. We talked a great deal about you," continued Mme Mourier, with that habit of liking to seem she was on intimate terms with the friends of the person she was speaking to.

"What did she want?" asked Jean-Noël nonchalantly. No matter what the two women might have said about him, wasn't he still Annie's stepson?

Mme Mourier ignored his question. She even changed the

subject, as if Mme Oetlinger's visit had merely been a pretext she had used in order to see Jean-Noël again. She asked what he was doing, if he was looking for another job. While she went on, Jean-Noël, exasperated at being kept in suspense this way, did his best to stay calm. Mme Mourier finally divulged the reason for Annie's visit: she wanted to say her farewells to her stepson before leaving on a trip. Having failed to find him at the rue Laugier, she had asked Mme Mourier to let the young man know that, until the first of May, he would find her, preferably in the morning, at the Hôtel Cambon, in the street of the same name.

When Jean-Noël next saw Odile, which was later that afternoon, the first thing he did was tell her that he had received a letter, not from Mme Mourier but from Annie, who was asking that he come and see her. Whenever she thought she had displeased Jean-Noël, Mlle Wurtzel could usually not rest until the disagreement between them had been resolved, and yet she was very cross when informed of this latest development. "Haven't you understood yet that your step-mother has never done you anything but harm?" Jean-Noël did not reply. "You will not go," she declared imperiously. This time, the young man replied coldly that nothing in the world would prevent him from going. Odile lost her temper. "You will have to choose between her and me." This ultimatum made no impression upon Jean-Noël. "You don't know how to distinguish those who love you from those who don't." As she spoke these words, Odile left the drawing room in her parents' apartment where this conversation had taken place, slamming the door on her way out.

Her temper tantrum did not last long. The following morning, a very different Mlle Wurtzel went to the Hôtel des Grands Hommes. Jean-Noël had already gone out. The night before, on his way home, it had occurred to him that he had been quick to leap to the defense of someone who would never be in the least bit grateful to him. His zeal had seemed pointless. Essentially, wasn't Odile right? Why was Annie interfering in his life now, if she cared so little about what became of him? Four months ago she had vanished without saying a word to him, as if he was a stranger. Why try to see him again? He was, however, unable to ignore her summons. Thus, at the very moment when Odile was asking for him at the hotel, he was crossing the Tuileries, where the lawns were shiny with dew on this bright, sunny morning. He was full of hope. Perhaps Annie had something important to tell him. Perhaps she wanted him to accompany her on some far-flung journey. She had realized that Charles Le Douaré's feelings for her were not as sincere as those of her stepson. It had struck her that the latter might be delighted to leave Paris with her. She was thinking of asking him if he was free. He was already imagining how the scene would unfold. Like every other time she had caused him great joy, she would do so without seeming to understand why he was so delighted. And so as not to displease her, he would accept with no show of enthusiasm.

When he was shown into the small sitting room adjacent to Annie's room, which was filled with trunks and dresses and through the windows of which he could see, shrouded in the morning mist, not the rooftops of some working-class neighborhood but rather the domes and terraces of central Paris, he was filled with such a sensation of well-being that he felt momentarily suffocated by it. Annie was standing near him, looking taller and thinner in her mourning clothes.

"I wanted to see you before leaving," she said.

"Where are you going?" asked Jean-Noël, astonished that he dared ask her such a familiar question.

"I don't know yet. In any case, we'll spend a few months in Florence."

Jean-Noël remained silent. Annie had not changed. She was still just as selfish, so selfish that she seemed unaware of the fact that the life she led was enviable. It did not occur to her that while she was preparing to leave for a city where, as she said so admiringly, there were Michelangelos in the streets, her stepson, the son of the man for whom she had sacrificed everything, remained alone in Paris, unloved and left to fend for himself.

"I am glad that you came. We are leaving, M. Le Douaré and I, the day after tomorrow."

When she had introduced Jean-Noël to M. Le Douaré, she had known she would be hurting her stepson. But she had carried on regardless. Wouldn't life have been impossible if she'd been forced to take Jean-Noël's susceptibilities into account? Today, she talked of going away with M. Le Douaré as if it had never occurred to her that the two men could be anything but friends.

"I have just learned," she said, "since I haven't seen you since, that you are no longer on such good terms with Madame Mourier. If that's true, it's a shame. That woman had a great deal of affection for you, and I think that she always gave you excellent advice."

"Some of it was excellent, as you say. Some of it was less so."

"What are you planning to do now?"

"I'll see. I don't know yet."

Annie looked her stepson in the eyes.

"Don't think that because you're free, you can now do whatever strikes your fancy. On the contrary, it's when we are alone, when no one is there to force us to do things which we often find disagreeable, that we most need self-discipline, without which we slide into ruin."

If Mme Oetlinger had changed the subject when Laure had tried to speak to her about Jean-Noël a few days earlier, it had been because she suspected there was some reason too shameful to mention for his having wanted to leave Laure. Either Mme Mourier had no more money or Jean-Noël was planning to marry into a wealthy family. Had Annie been certain that the latter was true, she would doubtless have told her stepson to leave immediately, for if there was one thing she abhorred, it was when people stooped so low as to associate love with personal gain.

"I am perfectly well aware of that," replied Jean-Noël. Annie smiled. She had not asked him to come in order to preach to him. In spite of everything, she felt affection for him. If she had disappeared so suddenly, it had not been because of him at all, but for a great many other reasons, for those secret reasons which she had always liked to have to seem to obey. It was to prevent her stepson from attaching undue importance to his solitude that she had gotten in touch with him again, but only on the eve of her departure, so that there would be a reason for their meeting, and so that Jean-Noël would not think his stepmother had any feelings of remorse whatsoever.

Odile had not left the vicinity of the Hôtel des Grands Hommes. She had returned there three times, in vain. In spite of her opposition, Jean-Noël must certainly have gone to see Mme Oetlinger. She was not waiting for him in order to reproach him for having done so, but rather to congratulate him. Wasn't yielding to him in order to emerge victorious the best tactic of all? There would be ample time later to make Jean-Noël understand how nefarious Mme Oetlinger's influence upon him had been. For now, there were enough difficulties to be overcome without adding new ones. Prejudiced as M. Wurtzel was, what would he say if he learned that his future son-in-law was still seeing Mme Oetlinger?

At half past eleven, Odile decided to go home. Her father was awaiting her impatiently.

"Ah! At last," he said. "Where were you? I've been calling everywhere."

"I've just been running a few errands," replied Odile, who didn't dare say she had spent the entire morning waiting for Jean-Noël.

M. Wurtzel did not reply. He pulled a letter from his pocket, handed it to his daughter, and said: "Read this. You will then explain to me what it means." Odile took the letter and turned scarlet at the mere sight of the stationery. It was a letter from her bank.

"So you're the one financing his divorce!" exclaimed M. Wurtzel, who was beside himself. "Not only does he have no money, what's more he needs a handout! Never in my life have I seen anything like this, never. It makes me wonder if you haven't gone completely mad."

"But Jean-Noël told you he was married."

"He told me he was married. But he didn't tell me that I was going to be paying for his divorce."

An extremely unpleasant discussion then took place between father and daughter, the purpose of which was to determine who exactly owned the shares M. Wurtzel had put in Odile's name.

"It's quite simple," said M. Wurtzel, calming down at last. "As far as I'm concerned, that money is now lost. You are going to write to Jean-Noël immediately, in front of me, telling him that you are breaking it off. If not, you can go join him straightaway."

Odile was shattered at having to take sides. She loved Jean-Noël, but throughout her life she had heard too much about the value of money and the difficulty of earning it not to feel some apprehension about abandoning her family for a man who possessed nothing.

"You can't ask that of me," she told her father.

Her only hope now lay in Jean-Noël. Had he been there, he might have succeeded in making M. Wurtzel understand that if he had acted this way, it was because it had been impossible to do anything else.

"Shall I call him and ask him to come?"

This suggestion only rekindled M. Wurtzel's anger. It was unthinkable that his daughter had dared ask her bank for an advance. Only a swindler could have influenced her to do such a thing. He now thought it his mission to save his daughter.

"That's it," he said to Odile, who could no longer hold back her tears, "have him come."

Jean-Noël had no idea of what awaited him and was still feeling the effects of his joyless meeting with Annie when he arrived at the boulevard du Montparnasse. Odile had taken refuge in her bedroom.

"I have just learned," said M. Wurtzel, "that you've been having my daughter give you money."

"Me?"

"Yes, you," repeated M. Wurtzel, adopting the mocking tone a judge might use when addressing an accused man clinging to his honor.

Jean-Noël blushed and blurted out several words by way of explanation. M. Wurtzel silenced him with a gesture.

"It's a way of behaving," he went on, with no irony this time, "to which I'd rather not give a name. Well, it's done now. As I've already told my daughter, I consider that money lost. But from this moment onward, I want you never to set foot in my home again, or telephone, or write, or speak to my daughter, no matter what the circumstances."

Just then, Odile appeared.

"Go away," her father said to her.

Jean-Noël was pale. He had been found in the wrong by the very people he most scorned. He lost his head.

"That was exactly my intention," he cried. Without even looking at Odile, he whirled around and stalked out.

"What happened?" asked the young girl in a pleading voice.

"The best one could hope for."

When she learned that it was her father who had provoked Jean-Noël, and that the words she had heard the latter speak had been uttered only in response to M. Wurtzel's angry outburst, she raised her hands to her temples and began to sob.

"If you don't apologize to Jean-Noël, I will leave," she managed to say a few moments later.

M. Wurtzel looked at his daughter in astonishment. Then he exploded.

"You will leave? Well then, leave, leave right this minute, do you hear me, right this minute! You might as well go join him!"

"No, I will not go join him," replied Odile, detaching each syllable as though it had never occurred to her that she might be interrupted. "I will not stop conducting myself like a lady just because I am being forced to leave my family."

TWENTY-SIX

When she left her family, Odile asked her friend Denise, a young divorced woman who had long been advising her to move away from home, if she could take her in. Two months passed peacefully. But a few days before the divorce judgment, Marguerite informed Maître Herbst that she was withdrawing her petition. An exchange of letters followed. They finally learned that Marguerite was demanding an additional payment of fifteen thousand francs. She was claiming that during the time she'd been married, she had been forced to sell the shares which constituted her dowry in order to meet the household expenses, and that buying them back now would cost her forty-two thousand rather than twenty-seven thousand francs. Although she admitted that she had agreed to a divorce, it had only been because her husband wanted one. Had she listened only to her heart, she would never have gone through with it, and she was asking in exchange that she not be constrained to go on endlessly claiming what was her due.

The divorce proceedings had been initiated a month earlier, and only another month remained of the obligatory waiting period when M. Wurtzel sought to see Odile again. He went to Denise's home. "I don't know if your daughter will be back this evening, Monsieur," the young woman told him rather uneasily, for having told Odile that, were she in her situation she would never go back to her family, she now found herself torn between a desire to be friendly and yet not to contradict herself. At that moment, the sound of a voice was heard in front hall. "Maybe that's Odile," she said, leaving the room and carefully closing the door to the drawing room behind her. It was indeed the young girl, in the company of Jean-Noël. "Shhh," said Denise. Then, taking her friend aside, she whispered, "Your father's here." Odile looked at Jean-Noël. "If you want to see him," continued Denise, "I'll take Jean-Noël into my room."

There were dresses lying across an armchair. "Always a mess in here!" she said, applying powder and perfume in front of Jean-Noël, as though he were one of her girlfriends. "This is all very troubling," she went on, taking a cigarette.

Jean-Noël offered her a light. She refused.

"I want my matches."

"What is troubling?" asked Jean-Noël without looking up, intimidated by Denise's casual manner and even more so by her beauty.

"These problems with M. Wurtzel," she replied. "Jean-Noël, you ought to use your authority to make Odile go back home. I'm honest, you see, since I've been saying just the opposite until now."

"I have no authority."

Denise, who was looking at herself in the mirror as she offered this advice, whirled around suddenly with a surprised expression.

"You're trying to tell me, *me*, that you have no authority over Odile? You're blind! Can't you see that she adores you?"

As a result of her father's visit, Odile went back to live with her family. M. Wurtzel had known how to speak to his daughter. He had told her that he regretted having been so intransigent, that since she had truly made up her mind to marry Jean-Noël and the latter was now finally free, he would raise no further objections to the marriage. What he had feared a few months earlier was that her feelings for the young man were volatile. He had then asked her if she thought Jean-Noël would be happy to enter the family business. She had answered that she was sure he would be, but without seeming to care one way or the other, so that her father would understand that even if Jean-Noël refused, she intended to marry him all the same. M. Wurtzel had reassured her. He was asking her these questions because her happiness was what mattered most to him. One never knew what tomorrow would bring. If money continued to lose value, what would become of her? It was important to think about the future, and, to the extent this was possible in such unsettled times, to take every precaution. Not only did he want to see the young man again, he wanted to get along with him, to treat him like a son.

When Odile informed Jean-Noël of her father's wishes, he showed no signs of being happy. Although he was not the sort to bear a grudge, by not being too quick to forget the affronts he had endured, as he put it, he was showing that he was a man of dignity.

During the weeks that followed he adopted the noble attitude of a man who has been insulted. In spite of this, not a day went by without Odile pleading with him to come to the boulevard du Montparnasse. Hers was a delicate situation. Her father was beginning to find it strange that his advances were being met with such loftiness. She was afraid he was going to lose patience with the different excuses she offered each time. She failed to understand why Jean-Noël was making such an issue of his pride, when doing so was clearly prejudicial to his own interests. In order to keep M. Wurtzel favorably inclined towards the young man, she had been reduced to talking constantly about the many good things he had done in his life. Among these, there was one in particular which she repeated over and over. It had been Jean-Noël himself who had forced her to return to her family. Had he not been so insistent, she would have stayed with Denise.

M. Wurtzel, however, pointed out to her that he found it highly unlikely that Jean-Noël had been thinking of pleasing him. "It's only natural," Odile had replied with great ardor. M. Wurtzel then implied that the young man had perhaps acted in his own best interest. Didn't he have everything to gain if his future wife remained on good terms with her family?

"How can you suspect Jean-Noël of being so calculating? If he was self-seeking, don't you think he would have tried to please you from the start?"

A few days after this conversation, Odile finally convinced Jean-Noël to return to the boulevard du Montparnasse. He was received there most cordially. Ever since his daughter had gone to stay with Denise, M. Wurtzel had understood that she would sooner leave him than give up Jean-Noël. At heart, he remained convinced that what she was about to do was a terribe blunder, but if her mind was made up, who was he to interfere? Jean-Noël was also very pleasant. Odile was so touched by this that the next day she expressed her desire to meet Mme Mercier and Emile. Although Jean-Noël was far from taken with the idea, she insisted. Wasn't it her duty to show an interest in everything that touched the man she loved, even if she displeased him by so doing? Jean-Noël had just been to the rue Mouton-Duvernet to announce his forthcoming marriage, not without a certain pride, for it was his view that his mother was incapable of distinguishing among persons of equal wealth. He was, however, mistaken in this. While Mme Mercier had always lived in relative isolation, she had nonetheless observed everything around her with that intelligence peculiar to people who see without being seen. She had raised her younger son in such a way that at present he all but believed it was only due to some administrative error that he did not bear the name Villemur. Thus, when Jean-Noël had pronounced the name Odile Wurtzel, Emile had pouted disdainfully. Wasn't Jean-Noël marrying beneath himself? Although Emile had never even approached the Villemurs, he now adopted the attitude he imagined they would have chosen in such circumstances, wanting to show by this that it had been unfair to shunt him aside, for he would never have demeaned himself by marrying a Mlle Wurtzel, and therefore at heart he resembled the Villemurs far more than his brother.

Shortly afterward, bearing them no grudge for their reaction, Jean-Noël preceded Odile up the gloomy, ill-lit staircase that led to his mother's room. Mlle Wurtzel had the attitude of someone who, out of tactfulness, pretends not to notice anything out of the ordinary in her surroundings; she climbed the stairs as if she'd been climbing them all her life. Mme Mercier's room was in a state of extraordinary cleanliness. The floor had been washed so recently that the grooves between the floorboards were still damp. A yellowed photograph of Jean-Noël was on the mantelpiece, next to a small branch of consecrated boxwood. Emile, who was standing motionless by the window, seemed to be present only by chance. Mme Mercier got up immediately and offered Odile a chair. She did not say a word to excuse herself for the poverty of her lodgings—not so much to make the visitor understand that she was not to be pitied, but rather that she asked nothing of strangers, and that if she was reduced to accepting outside help, one had, at the very least, to be worthy of offering it to her.

As for Emile, he was looking at Odile with an air both respectful and mocking, the look of someone who thinks that poverty is not synonymous with obsequiousness.

"I hope, Madame," said Odile, who wanted to show how kind she was, "that both you and your son will come to our wedding." Ernestine Mercier, touched and yet embarrassed by this invitation, nodded her head and blushed, not knowing what to say. As a result of having lived in the shadows, of having been shunned and repelled by everyone, she was moved whenever she was shown the slightest regard, and immediately suspicious. As for Emile, he replied in a ceremonious tone of voice that he might come, but that he could not confirm this, for it just so happened that he had an important appointment that day which he might not be able to reschedule.

His hands behind his back, Jean-Noël paced up and down the room. From time to time he would stop to make a comment, to approve of something his mother had just said, and then start off again, thereby giving his insignificant interventions a small air of importance.

Odile was watching him. Her only desire was to please him. She therefore avoided looking at anything that might humiliate him. One sensed that beneath her friendliness and obliging manner, she was lost. She was both intrigued and somewhat repelled by these peoples' past. The memory of Jean-Melchior flitted through the room like a tropical bird trapped in the hold of a ship. It explained Mme Mercier's craving for esteem, Emile's unsatisfied desires. The clothes hanging on the gray walls, the two beds, the basin sitting on a table, the entire room, in which there was only enough space for the body's most indispensable needs, seemed doomed to remain exacly as it was at this moment for all eternity, because the man who could have flung open the window was dead. Odile had the feeling that no matter what she did, she would always be considered the enemy here. Wishing Mme Mercier and Emile well would be to want to diminish them and make them like everyone else, to deprive them of their illusion that they were victims of a family drama.

On the third of December 1926 the weather was extremely cold. Jean-Noël woke earlier than usual in his hotel room, where nothing seemed to indicate that this day was going to be a significant one in his life. He dressed without the slightest emotion. The only thing which troubled him at all was the fact that his mother and brother were to be present at his wedding. Odile had gone back to see Mme Mercier. Her first visit had left her feeling terribly sad and disillusioned. As a result, she had gone back to see Mme Mercier nearly every day. She had spoken to her kindly, gently, hoping to transform her future mother-in-law into a person of whom Jean-Noël would no longer need to feel ashamed. In her inexperience, she had imagined that money was all that was needed to effect this miracle, that Mme Mercier's poverty was the only reason she was not fit for polite company. After one of these visits, she had even said to Jean-Noël: "But your mother is quite presentable. You had so warned me against her that I expected she was capable of anything." Jean-Noël had not replied, for he was torn between the desire to see his mother's lot in life improve and the fear that she would make him look bad. Before going to the town hall in the fifth arrondissement, where the "ceremony" was to take place, he sat alone in his room, which was somehow strange on such a day, wondering what his mother's and brother's attitudes would be. A few days earlier, again at Odile's insistence, Mme Mercier and Emile had gone to meet M. Wurtzel. Jean-Noël had not wanted to be present at the meeting, but he had some idea of how it must have gone.

His thoughts then turned to the wedding itself. Luckily, it was going to be an extremely simple ceremony, in spite of the fact that M. Wurtzel had wanted it to be a lavish affair. When he had realized that nothing would prevent his daughter from marrying Jean-Noël, he had wanted things to be done properly. It was only when he'd realized that his consent had not made Jean-Noël any more likeable that he had yielded to his daughter's wishes. She was only too well aware of the incompatibility between her family and her fiancé, and wanted as simple a ceremony as possible. Once he was ready, Jean-Noël went out. The day before, he had spent the afternoon in a cinema with Odile. When she had left him, she had said, "You'll have to be on time tomorrow," and he had nodded his head and replied, "Naturally." With that, he had left. She had called him back, however. "Make sure you don't forget to fetch your mother." Jean-Noël therefore went to the rue Mouton-Duvernet. As he climbed the staircase of the modest building, he suddenly felt unwell. In an hour's time, he would be getting married, and yet here he was in this house! He knocked at the door. His mother was wearing a house-jacket and an old skirt. "You're not ready?" he asked. Mme Mercier replied that she didn't know whether she was going to come to the town hall, that in any case he didn't need her, saying all of this without looking at her son, for in spite of everything she was in awe of him.

"And Emile, where is he?"

"He'll be along. He went out for a walk."

Jean-Noël then insisted that his mother get dressed. She obeyed, although not without making a fuss. A week earlier, Odile had arranged to have new clothes sent to her. But Mme Mercier had not even touched the parcels, which were near the door, as if someone were going to come and take them back. Shortly afterwards, Emile returned. He too had made no concessions where his appearance was concerned. Jean-Noël pretended not to notice.

At eleven o'clock, the three of them entered the town hall. Jean-Noël led his mother and brother to the room adjoining the one in which the marriage was to be celebrated, then went back outside. M. Wurtzel and his daughter arrived soon afterwards.

"Are my sons here?" asked M. Wurtzel.

"Not yet," answered Jean-Noël, who didn't dare mention the fact that his mother was already upstairs.

Just then, Simon's large red car pulled up in front of the town hall and the two brothers got out. Maurice was to be Jean-Noël's best man, for the latter had declared he had no friends close enough to stand up for him, which had surprised the Wurtzels most unfavorably. Finally, they all found themselves reunited in a large reception room. Mme Mercier and Emile, who were sitting off to one side, did not budge when they saw the Wurtzel family. M. Wurtzel pretended he had not seen them. "Papa," said Odile, "Jean-Noël's mother is over there." M. Wurtzel looked around and, as if he had just then noticed her, went to greet her. "I trust we aren't late?" he asked, in order to say something. Emile answered. He liked to seem well informed about practical matters, and answered, as if he was a regular visitor to town halls: "We are not late, Monsieur. There is another marriage still to be celebrated before my brother's."

It had been agreed that everyone would have lunch at the boulevard du Montparnasse, but Mme Mercier and her son took their leave of the others immediately after the ceremony. At two o'clock, Simon drove the newlyweds and M. and Mme Wurtzel to the church at l'Etoile.

TWENTY-SEVEN

There was no honeymoon for Odile and her husband. In M. Wurtzel's eyes, their wedding was merely a brief interlude. What mattered now was that Jean-Noël become aware of his responsibilities, that he organize his life before thinking of pleasures. Eager as she'd been to get married, Odile had not paid much attention to money matters. Like people who are ready to make any sacrifice as long as they have yet to obtain what they desire, but who come to their senses immediately afterward, as soon as she had settled into the rue de Babylone apartment that she said looked out over the gardens of a convent, using the plural the way Jean-Noël did when he spoke of doctors, she did her utmost to convince her husband that it was now necessary for him to enter M. Wurtzel's business. Hadn't some of her stocks recently stopped paying dividends? But Jean-Noël did want to hear about the family business. "I am still young. In a year, if I work hard, I can obtain my degree. Being successful in business requires special talents," he repeated every day, implying that he felt proud not to have any such talents. He did agree, however, to go and dine at the boulevard du Montparnasse once a week. On those occasions, he behaved like someone who bears an illustrious name and has been forced to marry for money; and yet this attitude did him no disservice. He was considered an original sort. No matter how disagreeable he might be, now that he was a member of the family his faults had to be overlooked.

Odile, meanwhile, grew closer to her father; a sort of complicity even sprang up between the two of them. She kept him
informed of all of Jean-Noël's plans, and he often advised her,
rather surprisingly, to obey her husband and not to criticize
him. She also grew closer to Mme Mercier. Jean-Noël might
well be ashamed of his mother, but he had to be touched that
someone was taking an interest in her. "Your mother can't go
on living in that room," she said to him one day. She took a
lease on a small apartment with a bathroom in a new building
and, as if doing nothing more than revealing her husband's
goodness, went to announce this to Mme Mercier. To her
astonishment, the latter refused to leave the rue Mouton-
Duvernet. She was too old for yet another change. She would
not know how to live in an apartment. She had always lived
in cramped quarters. If she were to accept and then Jean-Noël
suddenly decided to vanish, which was entirely possible—one
never knew what he was going to do—how would she ever
manage to pay the rent? In addition, Mme Mercier had a
persecution complex. She thought that, for mysterious reasons, they were seeking to isolate her. At least in the rue
Mouton-Duvernet she was safe. As for Emile, he was convinced that Odile despised both him and his mother, and that
her solicitude was only caused by the pride of a daughter-in-
law who did not want to feel embarrassed by her husband's
family. If people wanted to help them, there was a much
simpler way of doing so: by giving them money.

When Jean-Noël had abandoned his studies—something
it pleased him to blame, at least in part, on his love affair with
Mme Mourier—it had never occurred to him that he would
take them up again someday. Relieved of this concern and of
Marguerite at one and the same time, he had felt free, and
happy. What point was there in continuing to waste his time
on mimeographed course sheets when life in all its infinite
richness and variety was being offered up to him? It was only
now, three years later, that he understood how shortsighted
he had been. Against Odile's wishes, he decided to reenroll at
the Law Faculty. The desire to complete his education was

not, as he claimed, his only reason for doing so: rather, he needed something to replace the prestige that his implied association with Annie had brought him. Until March of 1927 he attended his classes regularly. Then he grew bored with putting on this act. Odile took advantage of this to begin badgering him again, her renewed vigor fueled by the increasingly gloomy visions of the future her father shared with her every day. Much to his surprise, Jean-Noël realized that the thought of becoming M. Wurtzel's associate was no longer so disagreeable to him. He refused all the same, for appearances' sake, claiming that he wanted to pass the examination for his degree in July.

Mme Mercier, who had finally agreed to move into the small apartment Odile had rented for her in a city-owned building at the porte d'Orléans, was a frequent visitor to the rue de Babylone. One day when she was alone with her son she said, "Be careful, Jean-Noël. I have the feeling something is being cooked up against you." This strange warning had been prompted by nothing more than a consultation between Odile and her younger brother, Maurice. M. Wurtzel, who was growing ever more anxious about losing his fortune and spoke constantly of "communism on the point of taking root in France," had for this very reason grown closer to Jean-Noël; for as the idea had gradually become implanted in his mind that soon everyone would be equal, he had come to the conclusion that he ought to take the initiative. It was then that he decided to offer Emile a job. Although Odile, who had played a large part in this decision, tried to make her husband understand that their finances would improve if he no longer had to support Emile and Mme Mercier, Jean-Noël flew into a rage. Only a few weeks earlier the news would have left him indifferent. But now, doubtless as a result of his daily contact with the Wurtzel family, he had, without noticing it, come to consider the interests of his wife's family as though they were his own. As a result, in spite of his constant allusions to his scorn for the Wurtzels, to their faded splendor, and to the brilliant future that awaited him, he had been unable to stop himself from feeling jealous of his brother. A few days later, when Odile told him for the hundredth time that he really ought to make up his mind to join her father's firm, he replied that she might well be right.

Jean-Noël took a certain pleasure in his newfound occupations. The sight of him arriving at the tanneries each morning produced a modest effect upon the workers and employees which flattered him. After he had worked as an intern in each of the different departments, M. Wurtzel, who intended to retire, appointed him to his new position on the first of June, when the annual cutback in production would make it easier for Jean-Noël to become familiar with his new responsibilities as director of the smallest of the tanneries, in the rue de la Glacière. He had lunch or dinner at the boulevard du Montparnasse nearly every day. Odile could not have been happier. Her brothers would come to fetch her at the rue de Babylone. Sometimes they all went to the theater together. Mme Mercier and Emile had stopped complaining. Nothing remained of the hostility everyone had once shown Jean-Noël. Since he was doing his duty, wasn't it right that in exchange they should all be grateful?

Nonetheless, there were times when he felt terribly sad. He would begin to think about his childhood, and it would seem to him that he had wasted his life. What would his father have thought if he could have seen him in the midst of such mediocre people? Hadn't M. Oetlinger been expecting something quite different of his eldest son, the son for whom he had shown such a marked preference? What use had he made of all the years gone by? They had succeeded one another like an idler's empty days, unconnected, purposeless. Rather than having improved himself, he had merely grown older. He had not made his life; it was his life which had made him. Would he have been any happier if he had completed his education? It was impossible to know, but he could have consoled himself with the thought that he had done what he could. Had Annie returned, she would have been delighted to find that he had become independent; instead, he was mar-

ried, the director of a tannery, and a daily guest at the Wurtzels' table. His admiration for his stepmother, greatly
enhanced by her absence, had done nothing but increase since
material worries had ceased to play a part in his existence.
Annie was a reminder of his entire childhood, and in contrast
to the drudgery of the life he now led, that time struck him as
having been exclusively happy. Like war veterans who make
pilgrimages to the very spots where they suffered the worst
agonies and who, standing where a trench once gaped, come
to miss those terrible years, he would have liked to have been
transformed into the young man who was filled with pride by
the mere presence of his stepmother. The faith he'd once had
in himself was gone. He could still remember it, however, and
when he reflected upon it, it seemed to him he might still
have it had not Marguerite and Odile, M. and Mme Wurtzel,
Maurice and Simon, his mother and his brother, crossed his
path. So when the concierge handed him a letter from Annie
early in July, announcing she was back in Paris and wanted to
see him, he suddenly had the impression that a breath of
spring air was entering his life. It was as if that chasm sepa-
rating him from the past had just ceased to exist, as if that
continuity whose absence made him suffer so had suddenly
been reestablished, as if the man he had become was no different from the man he'd been before. He went back up to his
apartment. Odile was in bed speaking to her father on the
telephone, which she did every morning. When she saw that
Jean-Noël had come back up, she smiled at him and made a
sign that he should wait a moment, giving him an inquisitive
look.

"I've just received a letter from my stepmother," said
Jean-Noël, as casually as he possibly could so as to conceal his
joy.

"Ah!"

That was Odile's only reply. Her face had gone from smiling to serious. The mere mention of the word "stepmother"
made her grow pale. Although it had been years since she had

seen Mme Oetlinger, her mistrust and jealousy of her had grown.

"She asks me to come and see her," continued Jean-Noël.

"Give me that letter."

He obeyed reluctantly, as if the very word "stepmother" were confidential and he was committing some misdemeanor by displaying her letter. Odile read it, her lips pressed tightly together, then returned it to her husband.

"You might as well go," she said, "if you think it's necessary. But perhaps you ought to wait a few days."

"Why?"

"You know perfectly well you have a great deal of work at the moment."

Odile had a lace mantilla draped over her shoulders. She was using the two pillows, her own and her husband's, as a backrest. She seemed to have already forgotten about Mme Oetlinger. Jean-Noël looked at her. Because he was standing above her, he thought her eyes were closed, though in fact they were only lowered. For a moment he felt alone. He took in the room, with its banal luxuries and comfortable appointments, the sofa-bed, the walls covered in plain beige paper, the tobacco-brown carpet, the deliberately unframed mirrors, the lamps, the furniture, the bathroom one glimpsed through the half-open door, where he and Odile took turns bathing, with the same little flurries of modesty each time. And in the midst of this décor, Odile had dared to tell him that he had a great deal of work, that she thought it best if he waited several days before responding to Annie's request.

"I think I shall go and see my stepmother today," said Jean-Noël.

"You should have told me earlier, while I was still on the phone. I could have told Papa."

The day seemed endless to Jean-Noël. He reread Annie's letter several times. One detail had surprised him: the address. His stepmother was staying at the Hôtel des Grands Hommes. Therefore she must be alone; otherwise why would she have chosen a hotel in which she had frequently stayed with Jean-Melchior, and of which she always spoke tenderly for just that reason?

It was half-past-six when Jean-Noël, who had walked, reached the place du Panthéon. The sun was still high in the sky, but the bustling in the streets and the relaxation on the faces he passed marked a day that was drawing to a close. Jean-Noël walked up the rue Claude-Bernard and turned into the rue d'Ulm, at the end of which that side of the Panthéon which was usually so lugubrious, that sheer wall of stone, had taken on the pinkish hue of churches illuminated by the setting sun. He was not wearing a hat. He was in a state of such high emotion that at times he felt as if an enormous drop of moisture was trickling through his hair, as though he had been walking in a forest after a rainstorm.

"Is Mme Oetlinger in?"

She had just gone out, but the hall porter thought she would be back soon, for he had noticed that she went out at this time every day. Jean-Noël walked around the square while he waited. So Annie had been in Paris for several days. She must certainly have gone to Mme Mourier's; how else would she have got his address? What had Laure said? Had she revealed that Jean-Noël was now married to Mlle Wurtzel? Suddenly, as he was drawing near the police station in the rue Soufflot, he saw Annie coming toward him. She had not seen him yet. Her eyes lowered, she was walking quickly, with that slightly mincing step he would have recognized anywhere, carrying two or three parcels in her arms and apparently paying no attention to the beauty of the late afternoon. Jean-Noël stopped, so overwhelmed he no longer knew what to do. In his memory she had always appeared to him alone, and seeing her now, dressed in dark colors, no different from the passersby in whose midst she walked, he was struck the way children are when they begin to realize that their father's authority extends only to their own family. A shadow of disappointment clouded his joy. Although Annie soon reached the spot where he stood, she still had not noticed him.

"Annie."

She raised her head, looked at her stepson, and cried out: "Jean-Noël, it's you! How nice you are to have come! I was just hurrying because I thought you might stop by this evening."

They walked up to the hotel together, speaking only of the pleasure each of them felt at seeing the other again.

"Wait for me a moment," she said. "I'm going to leave these parcels at the desk."

Above the half-curtain in the window, he watched Annie hand her parcels to a maid and then felt his heart tighten for an instant as she stopped to see if there were any letters for her.

"I didn't keep you waiting too long?" she asked shortly afterward.

He suggested that it might be amusing to go sit on the terrace of a café on the boulevard Saint-Michel.

"Oh, yes!" she replied, "your father used to love that so."

They walked down the rue Soufflot. The words that had gushed forth so spontaneously a few minutes before had been replaced by a slight awkwardness.

"Are you happy?" Annie asked Jean-Noël. She asked him endless questions about his ambitions, what he had been reading. She wanted to know if he had continued his studies. She admired the young people they passed on the boulevard Saint-Michel. Everything had changed. They were living in another time. Jean-Melchior would never recognize this neighborhood if he could see it now.

They stopped in front of a café. Annie let her stepson choose a table, call over the waiter. A man selling carpets approached them. A moment later, Jean-Noël had the impression that his stepmother was as moved as he was. Hadn't she apologized with the utmost seriousness for sending away the carpet-seller without having consulted her stepson? They smiled at one another.

"I heard that you married Mademoiselle Wurtzel," Annie said at last. "Is it true?"

Jean-Noël grew flustered and dared not reply. As if she hadn't noticed, Mme Oetlinger asked him if he was happy. He answered the first of her questions.

"It is true, but how did you find out?"

"From Madame Mourier," replied Annie, looking at her stepson in such a way that for a moment he thought she had not changed at all and was going to ask him, with that astonished air particular to her, if he had forbidden Laure to say he was married.

"I am very happy," Jean-Noël hastened to add.

Annie made no disagreeable remarks about the Wurtzels. On the contrary, she told him how happy she was that he was now living a more settled life, although she added that she did not entirely approve of his having left a woman as fine as Madame Mourier. She went on to ask him if his new wife was intelligent, if she took any interest in the child he had from his first marriage. He answered that Odile was very kind-hearted and that she regretted, as indeed did he, that the care of raising this child had been entrusted to Marguerite. Annie, too, seemed to regret it. How she had changed! Like people who disappear for a time and then feel like strangers when they return to a world that was once their own, she made no criticism.

Finally, Jean-Noël plucked up the courage to interrogate his stepmother. What had she done during the past year? Why hadn't she written to him? She adopted the expression she'd always worn when asked a question, however anodyne, about herself, an air which sought to convey that she was of no importance and that whatever concerned her was not worth talking about. "Oh!" she replied, "what goes on in my life is never interesting." Then, as if this focus upon herself had suddenly reminded her of certain obligations, she expressed a desire to go home. As they were making their way back, Jean-Noël was able to learn that she had been in Paris for a week, that she had no idea how long she would be staying at the hotel, and that if she found some peace of mind she intended to take up painting again. What emerged from these scraps of confidences was that Annie was somewhat at loose ends; that, at least, was the conclusion drawn by Jean-Noël. When he inquired at the hotel what she was planning to do with the rest of her evening and was told that she was looking forward to finishing a book she was reading, he could not help asking if she did not think it would be more pleasant for her to come and live at the rue de Babylone. She must have guessed what her stepson had been thinking, for rather than replying to this invitation, she told him that she had a charming room, and that she spent many agreeable hours there making her own tea and reading. As she was about to take her leave, Jean-Noël asked if she would like to walk a bit longer. Only the Panthéon's dome was still illuminated by the sun. The sky was a very deep blue; the air, still and sweet. She hesitated, then took hold of Jean-Noël's arm and said: "Right you are. Let's carry on. Let's walk down to the Luxembourg and back. This is such an exceptional day we're having."

TWENTY-EIGHT

"How is it," asked Odile one evening, "that your stepmother hasn't yet been curious enough to come and see where you live? If she loved you as much as you claim she does, it seems to me she would have been curious to see your apartment in spite of her fear of meeting me."

During the past week, Odile had pretended she found it natural that her husband was going to the Hôtel des Grands Hommes every day. It had even occurred to her several times that she ought to be going with him, if only out of deference for a woman who was older than she and who, in spite of everything, had been like a mother to Jean-Noël. But, like those intransigent people who become as docile as lambs when they have obtained what they want, ever since getting married she had taken to constantly asking her family's advice. In this instance, M. Wurtzel had pointed out to her that she was meant to be unaware of the fact that Mme Oetlinger was in Paris.

"Would you like me to invite Annie to lunch?" asked Jean-Noël. "I'm sure she would accept."

Jean-Noël had been so happy to see his stepmother again, he had never dreamt the Wurtzels might feel resentful that a woman about whom they had said so many unpleasant things had made no attempt to see them.

"We don't need to get down on our knees to her. If she wanted to come, she would come without being asked."

Jean-Noël sensed that it was not just Odile's pride which had been ruffled but that of the entire Wurtzel family.

"She was afraid of imposing," he explained. "It's my fault. I should have invited her, but I never thought of it."

Deep down, he had no desire for the two women to meet. He was afraid that they would rise up against one another, that Odile would deliberately hold her husband's hand and throw him meaningful glances while Mme Oetlinger was there. He felt ill at ease just thinking of the three of them sitting down to lunch together. He therefore carefully avoided extending any invitations when he next saw his stepmother.

"What is the meaning of this?" cried Odile.

"It means that I don't want to court a refusal," replied her husband.

"Your stepmother refuses to come here? In that case, I don't see why you go to see her. You have a wife now. Nothing could be more natural than for your stepmother to come and have lunch or dinner at your home from time to time. Or perhaps you've concealed from her the fact that you're married!"

"It's the very first thing I told her. Anyway, she already knew."

"Then why doesn't she come?"

Odile was pacing up and down in a state of great agitation. Wasn't this an affront on the part of Mme Oetlinger? Suddenly, she stopped in front of Jean-Noël.

"You're right," she said. "It would be more fitting if I went to see her first. I'll come with you tomorrow."

When Odile and Jean-Noël asked for Mme Oetlinger at the hotel desk, they were instructed to go upstairs. "There's no need to tell her that I lived here," said Jean-Noël as they climbed the stairs. As soon as she laid eyes on Annie, Odile rushed forward to greet her in the way a daughter might have done who was seeing her mother again after a long absence. Her husband, meanwhile, closed the door slowly behind him in order to allow time for this initial burst of feeling to pass.

"I learned from Jean-Noël," said Odile, "that you were back in Paris, and I wanted to see you at once."

"I am very touched," said Mme Oetlinger, pointing toward an armchair.

She was not in the least surprised by this visit, having been warned of it earlier in the morning by a telephone call from her stepson.

Odile had barely sat down when she began looking furtively around the room.

"This Hôtel des Grands Hommes," observed Annie with that expression of mocking respect she always affected when uttering the hotel's name, "is most inconvenient. But if you'd like, I think they would bring us up some lemonade, unless of course you'd prefer something else."

"Oh! Madame, I don't want to put you out. And in fact we've only stopped by for a moment. I wanted to ask you to come to lunch tomorrow, if you're free."

Mme Oetlinger seemed to be delighted by the invitation. She had a great deal to do, but she would make sure she was free. She accompanied the newlyweds to the stairs. As they went down the steps, Mme Oetlinger, standing on the landing, waved goodbye with her right hand and smiled, not at her stepson, but at Odile, with that delicacy with which she always kept her warmest farewells for whichever member of a group she had just been introduced to for the first time. But as soon as Jean-Noël and his wife had disappeared, her face became somber. She went back to her room, opened the shutters the maid had drawn shut, pulled her bed until it stood a meter away from the wall, and drew back all the curtains so that the windowpanes through which one could make out the starry sky reflected the room like a mirror; at night, she liked space. She lit a cigarette, picked up a book, and settled into an armchair.

Odile spent all of the following morning making preparations. She wanted to receive Mme Oetlinger with due dignity. Early in the morning, she had gone to see her father and ask his advice. He had called in his wife, who was always consulted whenever etiquette and receptions were being discussed.

At half-past-twelve, Annie arrived at the rue de Babylone. She was shown into the drawing room, where Odile came to greet her a few minutes later. It was a large room, with two sash-windows looking out over the street. The windows and the slightly sloping floor were all that remained of the room's original appearance. The wooden paneling had been removed, the walls decorated with painted frescoes, and the old doors replaced with thick panels made of lemon-wood. It was a gloomy, stormy day, and, as the apartment was on the second floor, a chandelier made of superimposed plates of glass had been turned on, casting an unpleasant, artificial light. Fortunately, the atmosphere was somewhat more cheerful in the dining room, from which one could glimpse a convent garden, but in spite of this a certain awkwardness reigned during the meal.

"We chose the apartment just for these gardens," said Odile. "They are so rare in the heart of Paris."

Immediately after lunch Odile rose, to show that she was someone who never lingered at table. Annie immediately followed her lead. One sensed that she had been applying herself to respecting every little bourgeois convention from the moment she had arrived at her stepson's. Although she loathed making small talk, during the entire meal she had not once tried to steer the conversation toward a subject that interested her. It was merely to be polite that she made a few compliments to Odile's taste. Jean-Noël sensed how much Annie found this sort of lifestyle incomprehensible, if not distasteful. Had he been able to, he would have told her that it had been forced upon him, so horrified was he at the thought that his stepmother, whose ideas and scornful respect for each individual's habits he liked to share, might think he was as proud of this style as was his wife. Mme Oetlinger, in fact, failed to understand how anyone could care about their comfort. When coffee was brought into the drawing room, Odile scrutinized one of the cups at length and had it replaced by another. The conversation resumed. Suddenly the front doorbell rang. Odile, who had remained silent to make it seem as if she'd not heard it, said: "My father has asked me to invite you to come see him. We've spoken a great deal about you."

"In fact, I was planning to go and see him."

Mme Oetlinger was not telling the truth, but as she had understood that what was expected of her was what would have been expected of one of the Wurtzel family's friends—that is to say, that she take seriously a relationship which meant nothing to her—she pretended, with that short-lived courtesy which was particular to her, to be very touched by everything being said to her.

At that moment the door opened and a servant came in, though she did not dare to interrupt their conversation. Odile got up, apologizing as she did so for being "constantly" bothered. She exchanged a few words with the servant, then came back, after having taken care to close the door. She turned her head toward her husband. Their eyes met, and he understood what had just happened.

Nine months earlier, when Jean-Noël had left Mme Mourier, the latter had suddenly grown close to Mme Mercier and Emile, in spite of having always kept them at a distance. She had judged that this would allow her to continue to play a part in Jean-Noël's life even though he had liberated himself from her influence, for she had often demonstrated that she set a greater value on remaining on friendly terms with all the men she'd loved than on the love affairs themselves. In spite of her mistrustful nature, Mme Mercier had been moved by her advances. She had discovered that she and Laure had certain things in common. Hadn't Laure suffered at the hands of Jean-Noël much as she had done at the hands of M. Oetlinger? The latter had passed all of his defects on to his son. But as soon as Odile had taken an interest in Emile and found him a job in her father's business, Mme Mercier had begun seeing Laure less frequently, then stopped altogether, as though Mme Mourier, having foreseen the favors that were to be bestowed upon Emile, had taken the trouble to remain on friendly terms with Mme Mercier only in the hope of collecting a few crumbs of those favors for herself. Laure had guessed the reasons for this sudden change. Although at the time she had felt nothing but contempt for them, she had remembered them when Annie had come to her looking for Jean-Noël's address. With feigned solicitude, she had warned Mme Mercier against the dangers that Annie's return could pose to Emile's job. Mme Mercier, who was already inclined to think she was being persecuted, had then thought only of protecting her child.

Following Odile's instructions, the maid had asked Mme Mercier, for it was she who'd rung at the door, to wait in Jean-Noël's study. Annie had noticed something was going on, and, eager to leave, she took advantage of the fact to rise. Jean-Noël and his wife showed her out.

"I was very happy," Mme Oetlinger said to Odile, "to see you again."

She broke off abruptly. Mme Mercier was standing motionless in the front hallway. In spite of the maid's insistence, she had stationed herself near the front door, suspecting that Annie was within.

"I hope to see you soon, then," continued Mme Oetlinger, as though nothing were wrong.

"Ah! It's you. Madame," cried Mme Mercier, pulling her arm away from Jean-Noël, who had grabbed hold of it. She was so agitated that she stammered as she spoke those few words. Although she had made no effort to see Annie in the last ten years, not a day had gone by in which she had not planned for the moment when she would tell her rival what she thought of her odious behavior, when she had not railed against the woman she called a schemer, a temptress, and far worse.

"I knew," she went on, "that fate would make you cross my path someday."

"Calm yourself, Madame," said Annie kindly. She had grown pale, and yet she did not look the way a person might who's just been accosted by a stranger in the street. On the contrary, she seemed to recognize that Mme Mercier had reasons to bear her a grudge, reasons that originated in her ignorance of what had really happened. In years gone by, although Jean-Melchior's feelings for her had always seemed entirely genuine to Annie, she had nonetheless always felt unwell whenever she had so much as thought of Mme Mercier. She was surprised to be feeling no inner turmoil at seeing her standing before her now, surprised and struck by her own indifference. Did this mean that the love she had felt for her husband was dead, too, if this woman was incapable of stirring up a memory?

"Ah! I knew all too well that I would meet you again someday," continued Mme Mercier. "The world's injustice would have been too great . . ."

"I beg of you . . ." said Jean-Noël.

"Let me speak. You are her accomplice. It would have been too great an injustice if I'd never been given the chance to tell you to your face that you killed him, my husband. For he was my husband far more than yours."

Mme Mercier had launched into her tirade abruptly. It was no longer the past which was giving her the strength to shout as she was now doing, but rather the feeling that, whereas those dramatic events had left her alone and bereft of resources, they had not modified Mme Oetlinger's life in any way.

"I think there is no point in our remaining face-to-face any longer," said Annie, whose calm demeanor served only to increase Mme Mercier's anger.

"And you didn't even love him," continued the latter.

Jean-Noël, who was utterly shattered by this scene, noticed that Odile had remained impassive, like someone who has decided ahead of time never to become involved in others' quarrels. She was not moving. At that moment Mme Mercier's fury abated. Throughout her life she had harassed Mme Oetlinger; throughout her life she had pursued her with her hatred; and she had come to imagine that, on the day she finally met her, she would reveal so many truths to her that her rival would be reduced to seeking her forgiveness. Even as it faded before her very eyes, this hope drained her of all her strength. A few tears rolled down her cheeks. For a moment, Jean-Noël thought that his stepmother would take pity upon Mme Mercier. Nothing of the sort happened. Annie ignored the woman. Had there been just one thing she could have done to save this woman, she would not have done it.

On the landing, Jean-Noël asked Annie if she wanted him to accompany her. As if nothing whatsoever had happened, as if she were taking her leave in entirely normal circumstances, she refused. She would take a taxi. She had a great many errands to run. "Come tomorrow evening, if you like," she added nonetheless. He watched her leave. She had already gone down a few steps when she turned and smiled at him with great tenderness, for the main effect of the scene she had just endured had been to make her reflect that it had truly been good of her to save her stepson from the sort of upbringing a woman like Mme Mercier would have given him.

When Jean-Noël came back into the apartment, he was met by an unexpected sight. Mme Mercier was sitting down, her elbows on a table, clasping her head between her hands. Odile was leaning over her, in that half-compassionate attitude that makes one place a hand on the back of a chair rather than on someone's shoulder, and speaking in hushed tones, obviously trying to comfort her. Motionless, Jean-Noël observed the scene for a moment. Without straightening up, Odile turned her head, revealing a face as calm as that of a nurse whose patient's modest origins in no way prevent her from doing her duty. This pseudo-charity served only to increase Jean-Noël's anger. He glared at his wife. She stood up straight and moved away, the way one does to clear the way for a more skilled practitioner. Upon seeing her son, Mme Mercier let out a little cry and hid her face once again. It had been years since Jean-Noël had seen his mother in such a state. It reminded him of scenes he had witnessed as a child. Those tears, that wringing of the hands, weren't they the same as those which had so frightened him years ago when, as a result of such scenes, his father hesitated to take him to Mlle Villemur's?

"Jean-Noël, you mustn't hurt your mother," said Odile, who pretended to believe that, above all else, her husband was a dutiful son.

She considered the fact that he had never spoken either ill or well of his mother as an acknowledgment of an affection which, however, she knew did not exist. When Mme Mercier left a quarter of an hour later, he was unable to contain himself any longer.

"Why did you leap to my mother's defense?" he asked.

"You know very well that I did not defend her," replied Odile, as if surprised that her husband could suspect her of acting in a way so contrary to his desires. "Don't you understand," she went on, as if seeking forgiveness for being so kind, "why I acted this way? Your mother is an unfortunate woman. One can't be inhuman. You mustn't hold this against her. Fate alone is responsible for their meeting today."

TWENTY-NINE

It was not without some trepidation that Jean-Noël returned to the Hôtel des Grands Hommes. When she had left, it had not seemed that Annie held him responsible for what had happened, and yet he was apprehensive that upon reflection, she might decide he had committed some fault. He was therefore relieved to find that he was received in the usual way, perhaps even slightly better. It was half-past-six. Through the open window one could see the Sainte-Geneviève library, some of whose windows were as fiery as the sun itself. Annie was sitting next to a little table she had moved in front of the window. A vase on the mantelpiece held three long-stemmed lilies whose scent filled the room.

"That fragrance is extraordinary," said Jean-Noël, whom it reminded of Nice and even of the studio in the rue d'Assas, which he remembered clearly and about which he had daydreamed so often while at the front lines.

"Yes, but I had all the trouble in the world borrowing that vase. Can you imagine? It seems that there weren't any at all in the entire hotel, and this is all they could find. Oh well, the flowers are in water. That's the main thing."

As she spoke these words, an expression passed over Annie's face that Jean-Noël loved; it was one she only let appear when she sensed she could trust the person she was with, the sort of false resignation we adopt when faced with a lack of taste.

"The vase is too small," observed Jean-Noël, without being entirely certain of this.

"Yes, I know, it's ridiculous. But let's talk about something else. I've given a great deal of thought to our lunch."

Jean-Noël was overcome with anxiety. Was Annie about to make an allusion to Mme Mercier?

"I find your wife very pleasant. You see, one should never be too quick to judge people. I don't know why, but I had imagined that a Mlle Wurtzel could not be anything other than a silly goose. I admit that I was wrong. Odile is charming, and I am sure she will make you very happy. She is very serious. She takes things to heart. She is exactly the wife you need."

If ever there was an assessment Jean-Noël had not been expecting, this was indeed it.

"Are you saying what you really think?"

Annie looked at her stepson with astonishment.

"Naturally."

"And yet you didn't like Odile."

"I didn't know her. And in fact that's not the reason. I've simply changed my mind. We're not the same person throughout our lives. Luckily! Life would be so monotonous if we never changed!"

Without once bringing up Mme Mercier, Jean-Noël and Mme Oetlinger continued their conversation for over an hour. He did not know what to make of his stepmother's sudden interest in Odile. Was she sincere, or was she trying to please him?

"You must be happy?"

"Oh! Yes."

Jean-Noël was more and more humiliated at being unable to do anything other than pass for the young man satisfied with his lot in life whom Annie seemed to see in him.

"Do you know that it is nearly eight o'clock? Your wife must be worried."

"She is never worried," he replied provocatively.

He would have liked to say that he was free, that he did not love Odile, but, just as on that day M. Wurtzel had come to get his daughter and Jean-Noël had been left alone with Denise, he felt that was impossible.

Mme Oetlinger put on her hat.

"I'm going to go have dinner. Come."

They went out. The rue Soufflot was very lively. One would have thought it was three o'clock in the afternoon. And yet a guard had already taken up his post outside the gates of the Luxembourg gardens, and the sun had just dipped down behind the museum whose exterior frescoes had so impressed Jean-Noël as a child. In front of a grillroom in the rue de Médicis, Annie extended her hand to her stepson.

"Don't keep Odile waiting," she said, pronouncing the name as if it was as familiar to her as those of her brothers.

Jean-Noël did not reply. He was so happy at his stepmother's side that at the thought of leaving her he felt he was being transported backward in time a few years, to that period when he had gone to the avenue de Malakoff as often as he could. Wasn't Annie leading an independent life, which was similar in some ways to the life he had been leading then?

"If you don't mind, I'll have dinner with you," he said, not in a pleading tone of voice but rather as if nothing could be more natural.

"You can't."

"Why?"

"And Odile?"

"Odile is not unaware of the fact that I'm with you."

"Well, you know better than I what you should do."

With her responsibility thus discharged, Mme Oetlinger immediately became more lighthearted. Like people who are too quick to believe you when you have lied to them so as not to spoil their pleasure, she avoided making any further mention of Odile. Nonetheless, the meal was marked by a certain awkwardness, for Annie and her stepson had never before met like this, in a restaurant, equals in the eyes of the world. At the end of the meal, Mme Oetlinger brought up Odile again. She had deduced from her stepson's silence that this was the only subject which interested him.

"We should have telephoned and asked her to come and meet us."

"She will certainly have dined with her family."

"Your marriage," she went on, "makes me very happy. This was just what you needed, a woman who has the very qualities you lack, a woman who knows what she wants, whose will is stronger than your own. I am very happy for you. As soon as my affairs are in order, as soon as I have resumed my routines, you and your wife will have to come and see me often."

Jean-Noël had grown increasingly somber. He was suffering because Annie's affection now seemed to extend to Odile as well, because he could not renounce his wife at the very moment when Mme Oetlinger seemed so well disposed toward him. The slightest unkind remark about Odile would have made a bad impression. He would have liked to talk about Odile in the way he suspected Annie would have talked about her had she not been convinced that he loved her. Instead, he was forced to play the role of the young newlywed in love, a role he despised, and to take part in a conversation that he could sense, by the silence his stepmother was observing on the subject of Ernestine Mercier or anything which concerned her intimately, was utterly conventional. How happy he would have been had his stepmother complained, had she confessed her worries to him! He would not have hesitated, then, to tell her the truth about his feelings for Odile. The understanding that would have arisen from such a confession would have made him the happiest of men.

"You will tell me when I should go to see Monsieur Wurtzel, because I would very much like to pay him a visit. I don't want your wife's family to think that I am avoiding them. They have been very good to me. The least I can do is thank them. And," added Mme Oetlinger, with a knowing look which hurt her stepson more than anything else had done, "it is useful that they know you are not alone in the world."

"I will ask Odile. But are you really determined to do this? I must warn you that they are not the most likeable people."

Annie looked at Jean-Noël reproachfully.

"One must never speak this way of one's family, my dear child. No one in this life is exactly what we hope for. Ultimately, people are only what we want them to be. Whenever we pass judgment on someone we are being unfair. We must be indulgent toward others if we want them to be so toward us."

"I wasn't saying it to be unkind."

"I know that very well."

Jean-Noël was surprised to hear her say this. Never before had Annie accorded her stepson's words such importance. Her "I know that very well" implied that she did not believe he could ever have bad intentions. Gone were the days when the most insignificant of his remarks had been misinterpreted. And yet Jean-Noël had the impression that in Annie's eyes he was but a stranger, and that it was only for Jean-Melchior, for the past, that she bothered to take any interest in him.

When they left the restaurant, he wanted to accompany his stepmother to the hotel.

"Today, I'll be the one who walks you home. You've stayed far too late as it is, and it's my fault," replied Annie, because of that habit she had of never wanting to be a hindrance which, a few years earlier, had made her fear that Jean-Noël was neglecting some far more important business every time he came to see her. "I'll go with you as far as your front door. That way I can make sure that you don't get home too late."

"But even if I get home at two o'clock in the morning, it doesn't matter," remarked Jean-Noël, unable to stop himself.

He had the feeling that a new era had just dawned; caught between his wife and Annie, he was more alone than he had ever been. In the past, he had struggled to get close to Annie and had always come up against a wall. He had been sustained, however, by the idea that he would someday prevail. Today, there was no more wall. No doubt because he was married, because she had nothing more to fear from him, Mme Oetlinger was no longer avoiding him. She was treating him with a benevolence that would have filled him with joy had the circumstances been different. She walked him to his door. She worried about his future. She had even told him that as soon as her life was more organized, he should come and see her often. And yet, in spite of all this, he had never felt her so distant. He suddenly felt weighed down. He had just realized that his desire to be loved by his stepmother no longer made any sense. Hadn't it been childish of him to think that nothing would change, that everything would remain as it had been in his youth, and to imagine that one could desire the same thing for years on end? Today, Annie had become a woman like any other woman, and he a man like any other man. For the first time, he had the impression that she was no longer the person whose faithful companion he had dreamed of being, that she was sincerely pleased that he had married Odile.

"This is the door, I think," said Annie, stopping in front of a building in the rue de Babylone.

"Yes."

She was about to ring when he stopped her.

"Wait a moment, wait."

She looked at him, astonished.

"Ring if you want to," he said, in a different tone of voice.

He had nearly abandoned himself to one of those sentimental outbursts Annie so disliked. He had nearly told her everything he had just been thinking: that he loved her, that he did not want to lose her, that Odile was nothing to him, that she was the only person in his life who mattered, that he wanted her to remain what she had always been, that he preferred her that way than the way in which she had just revealed herself.

Mme Oetlinger rang the bell and the door was opened almost immediately.

"Go up quickly," she said, her eyes already casting about for the taxi that would take her back to her hotel.

THIRTY

Jean-Noël did not manage to see Annie the next day, nor the following days. At mid-morning, he would telephone her. She would agree to meet him toward the end of the afternoon, but she would always be out when he arrived at the hotel. One evening, however, he found her there at the appointed time. As soon as he laid eyes on his stepmother, however, he understood that something must have happened. She was pacing up and down in her room.

"No need to close the door, we're going out," she told her stepson.

She picked up her handbag and her gloves, then walked over to the window to pull down the shade. But then, changing her mind, she put her bag down on the mantelpiece.

"I'll go out later," she said curtly. "It's better if I speak to you here."

"You have something important to tell me?"

Mme Oetlinger suddenly grew gentle.

"I'm going to hurt your feelings, Jean-Noël. I was going to write to you but decided that it would be best if I spoke to you after all. Oh, don't worry, it's nothing terribly serious. I was too presumptuous, that's what I had to tell you. Just after my visit to your wife, and in spite of what happened there, I thought that we could all see one another on a regular basis. I intended to rent an apartment. You could have come when it pleased you. As I told you, I found your wife very pleasant. I would have been happy to mold her tastes, to open her mind.

But then I gave it more thought. It's best if I tell you straight away that none of this is going to be possible."

Jean-Noël's gaze had been riveted on Mme Oetlinger's lips as he listened to what she said.

"Because of my mother?"

"No, not because of your mother. I will tell you why. But in a moment. You don't mind if we talk about something else?" asked Annie like a woman in love asking her sweetheart to think only of the present moment.

"Not at all," replied Jean-Noël.

"I have an extraordinary neighbor," said Mme Oetlinger. "Every night he reads aloud, alone, until two o'clock in the morning."

She told her stepson that she had made discreet inquiries to find out who the man was and what he was reading. Then, without telling him what those inquiries had revealed, she continued abruptly: "I love you very much, Jean-Noël, and were it possible for me to go on seeing you, I would; but there is your wife and your family. If she had not been so charming, you could perhaps have come to see me without her knowing it. But that's impossible. She makes you happy. You should not have to bear the consequences of the fact that she and I, her family and I, have nothing in common. I would rather draw back and leave you to your happiness. That is what I wanted to tell you. I have had enough experience in life to understand that if I do not do this now, not only would I come to regret it, but you could reproach me later with having had a bad influence on your home life."

Annie had said all this in a melancholy tone of voice.

"I don't understand," said Jean-Noël.

"Why not?" asked Mme Oetlinger briskly. "It's very simple."

"The other day, you were saying how much you were looking forward to getting to know Odile better."

"Indeed, but that was the other day. I have changed now. Since you don't understand, let me explain. Today, more so than ever, you see, I aspire to a peaceful life. Monsieur Le

Douaré was here again earlier today, reproaching me for not having agreed to marry him. It's becoming absurd. Circumstances thus all conspire against me. My own brother, supposedly because he is the guardian of my future and imagines that I am incapable of making my own way in life, is refusing to hand over my share of our inheritance. What have I done, why am I constantly having to defend myself, when all I ever did was wish well to the people whose lives touched my own? When I came back to Paris, I was looking forward to seeing you again. While I was away it had struck me that you might well be the only one who truly cared for me. I had even thought that, if you had become reasonable, we could work side by side. I am not criticizing your marriage in any way. You are old enough to know what you are doing. As I've already told you, I find your wife quite likeable and think she has many qualities to commend her. You're happy and that's the main thing. Nonetheless, I remain convinced that you could have become something more than an employee or the director of a tannery. I don't know exactly what position you hold: I'm not asking; it makes no difference. You have thus forgotten all the hopes your poor father had for you. Often, I can see him talking to me about you. He thought you would become a great thinker, a renowned professor. He would repeat whatever you said to whoever was willing to listen, even when it was nothing particularly intelligent."

"I'm only twenty-nine," ventured Jean-Noël.

"He was proud of you. And you—you married a Mademoiselle Wurtzel. Instead of work and struggle, you chose a nice, quiet little life, surrounded by people of no interest who think only about earning money."

At this point Jean-Noël was unable to restrain himself. To soften the impact of her words, Annie was looking out the window. He drew near his stepmother.

"I know very well," he said, "that I shouldn't have got married."

Annie turned slowly toward her stepson.

"Then why did you?"

Jean-Noël bowed his head. The one thing he could not say was that he had done it out of necessity. Nothing was more odious to Mme Oetlinger than marrying for money. The only possible answer to her question was to say he had married out of love. He therefore found it preferable to say nothing.

"You don't need to answer. I know why. You loved her, and you still love her. Nothing could be more natural. If there is one thing which cannot be held against you, that is indeed it. The mistake I made was to believe, perhaps because he repeated it to me so often, that, like your father, you had something in you which set you apart from other young people. I let you do as you pleased, I didn't supervise you, because I was sure that whatever happened would be a lesson to you, and that with time you would be able to bring forth what I thought you had within yourself. I was mistaken. Your aspirations are not those I had imagined. That does not make you a bad person; quite the contrary. Now that your life is mapped out, I have no more advice to give you. You must do what you think best. Be a good husband, and a good father later on. It's as good a way as any other of being happy."

Jean-Noël had sat down. Like a man condemned to death whose lesser sentences are being read out to him, he was no longer listening to his stepmother. With one hand on his forehead, he nonetheless seemed to be paying attention to what she was saying. He sensed the depths of Annie's scorn for him, for the life he was leading; and the fact that he could neither justify nor defend himself without transforming that scorn into anger filled him with a fear similar to that of a sick man who knows that he will continue to suffer no matter which side he turns himself onto.

"Let's go," said Mme Oetlinger.

He got up without saying a word and walked out ahead of his stepmother, who was about to draw down the blinds, moving with all the lassitude of a young man picking up a woman's gloves after the scene that has ended their affair. They walked down the rue Soufflot, moving swiftly the way

Annie liked to do after a day's work. At a street corner they were stopped by passing traffic.

"I hadn't seen your mother in a very long time," said Annie at that moment. "She did not seem unhappy to me. Does she come to see you often?"

"I don't know. I'm never there."

"I suppose Emile is also employed by Monsieur Wurtzel."

"I don't know."

It was not long before they had arrived in front of the grillroom where they had dined together a few nights earlier.

"Would you like me to walk on a bit with you?" asked Annie. "As we won't be seeing one another for some time now, I don't want to leave you like this."

They walked down the rue de Vaugirard, then the rue Bonaparte, until they reached the place Saint-Sulpice.

"I hope that you have clearly understood," continued Mme Oetlinger, "why I am asking for a little respite. Every day brings some new problem. I know very well that you don't deliberately cause me problems. And, in fact, all the people I'm worried about are just like you. That is why I've decided, I repeat, not to see anyone at all for a period of time. I feel no remorse where you are concerned; I know that you are happy, that you have married the woman you love."

As they talked, they had made their way back to the rue de Médicis.

"We must go our separate ways now, Jean-Noël."

He looked at his stepmother. He noticed that she was slightly flustered. Without even being aware of what he was saying, he heard himself asking if she wanted him to dine with her.

"No, my dear child, you must go home. Your wife is waiting for you. You mustn't make her suffer."

"It would make me so happy."

"You'll still have to leave me afterwards. I am tired. I need to be alone; whereas your wife, on the contrary, will be delighted to see you."

For a very long time, Jean-Noël had restrained himself

from saying what he thought of Odile. He now found he could hold back no longer.

"Don't talk to me about Odile anymore, I beg of you. You know perfectly well that I don't love her, that the life I am forced to lead with her horrifies me, that my only desire is to be free."

For a fleeting moment, it seemed to Jean-Noël that every sign of life had drained out of Annie's face, leaving behind just her features. She had not moved. Then the color returned to her face and her eyes opened wide. Without saying a word, she entered the restaurant, followed by her stepson, who was trembling at the thought of the consequences his confession would have.

"Shall we sit here?" she asked in the same tone of voice she had used when speaking of her need to be alone.

"Yes, that's fine."

As they ate, Mme Oetlinger never once mentioned Odile's name. And yet she never stopped talking, but exclusively about painting. One would have thought that nothing had happened, that Jean-Noël had remained exactly the same in her eyes, that she was utterly indifferent to what he had just told her.

After dinner, he accompanied her back to her hotel without any of the protests on her part there had been a few days earlier, or the slightest allusion to Odile. As soon as he was alone, Jean-Noël abandoned himself to his joy. As far back as he could remember, he had never been this happy. He pictured Annie again as she'd been when he'd told her he didn't love Odile, he pictured her afterwards, and understood he had a friend in her. While she might not have wanted to seem to approve, he sensed that at heart nothing could have made her happier than his confession. As he walked along, he wondered at times if he wasn't dreaming, if it was really possible that his stepmother, who was usually so strict where duty was concerned, really approved of him. Then he would start to worry, but the thought that Annie would not have hesitated to tell him if she disapproved would fill him with joy all over again.

It was not until midnight that Jean-Noël finally decided to go home. Odile was waiting for him anxiously.

"Where were you?" she asked.

He did not reply. Anything that was not Annie seemed unworthy of his attention. After leaving his stepmother, he had walked up the rue Denfert-Rochereau to the statue of the lion of Belfort. Coming down the boulevard Raspail, he had paused at the intersection of the boulevard du Montparnasse and looked up at the darkened windows of the Wurtzel's apartment. They were asleep. Nothing could have been more normal, and yet this had seemed to him an indication of their selfishness, their self-satisfaction.

"Answer me," continued Odile. "This is the second time this week that you haven't come home for dinner."

"Come," said Jean-Noël, taking his wife by the hand and leading her into their bedroom. "I need to talk to you."

They sat down on the bed. It had been turned down for the night. Odile's nightdress and her husband's pajamas were laid out side by side on the uncovered sheet.

"I am going to have to go away for a while," said Jean-Noël in that apologetic tone of voice more suited to people who, when we react to their unfaithfulness by refusing to see them again, assure us that they love us. He was not in the least emotional. In his eyes, it was so natural that his step-mother should come before anyone else that it had never occurred to him Odile might complain about it. It was therefore as if he were addressing a sister or a friend rather than a wife that he spoke these last words.

"But why? What's going on?"

Jean-Noël replied that nothing in particular was going on, only he sensed his stepmother was suffering from her solitude and needed someone near her. She had asked him to take a room at her hotel. He had no choice but to do as she asked, which, upon reflection, was of course entirely natural.

"Your stepmother seems to forget you're married. And yet she knows it. She saw it with her own eyes. I can't believe what you're telling me."

Because Jean-Noël realized at this moment that his wife was going to cast the blame on Annie, and because he preferred anything to that, he added, without the slightest embarrassment at contradicting himself, that Mme Oetlinger had not had anything to do with his decision, that it was he who had offered to keep her company.

"I wonder if you haven't gone quite mad. Well, do as you please."

Until that day, she had pretended to believe that love played a minor role in her relations with her husband. What bound them together above all were the battles they had fought side by side. They had been forced to overcome so many obstacles in order to get married that it was impossible to doubt their feelings for one another. While the idea of a separation was utterly inconceivable to her, she had nonetheless always pretended to believe that she loved her husband but demanded no such feeling from him in return. He belonged to her, like some province conquered in battle. Whatever outbursts of petulance, fits of ill humor, or capricious behavior it pleased him to indulge in, he would remain her husband all the same, if, of course, she did not make a habit of provoking him. He could do what he liked, she would always have the upper hand. That evening, convinced that this was nothing more than one of his usual outbursts, she therefore did nothing more than assume the expression of a punished child. But when she saw her husband rise and pursue his latest whim by fetching a suitcase, she began to worry.

"What are you doing?"

"I told you that I was going to have to leave."

For the first time since she had known Jean-Noël, the love she felt for him became apparent on her face and in her gestures.

"Please, Jean-Noël, that's enough now."

He continued calmly packing his suitcase. His wife came and grasped both his hands. He pushed her away gently, without looking at her, as if he were engaged in doing something that required all his attention.

"You're trying to frighten me, Odile."

As she could still not believe that her husband had really made up his mind to leave, she did not dare abandon herself to her grief for fear that, subsequently, he would know how much she loved him and be stronger as a result.

"Leave that suitcase," she said, standing in front of him this time and trying to force him to look her in the face. He turned his head away. Finally their eyes met. At that moment, she smiled as if both of them knew that this little display was only an act. But Jean-Noël's features were grim.

"What on earth is wrong, Jean-Noël?"

He was suddenly filled with pity. His wife's lack of tenderness had been the very thing which had given him the strength to leave her. He had just sensed that it was out of pride, because of everything she had done so that he would become her husband, that no sooner were they married than she pretended to love him only out of habit. The abrupt realization that, beneath her indifference, Odile cared more for him than she did for her own family had made him lose his composure.

"You know very well that I love my stepmother," he said, looking at Odile as if she had made him promises to which she was now paying no attention.

"I do know that, but I'm your wife."

For a brief moment, he thought he would not have the strength to leave. He was overwhelmed. He understood how childish he had been to imagine that Odile would not object to his leaving. How could he have believed that, after everything she had done for him? But then Annie's face appeared before him, and all of his hesitation vanished.

"I have to leave," he said.

Like a woman alone who takes fright in the middle of the night, Odile ran to the telephone.

"If you leave, I'm calling Papa," she said, though without picking up the receiver; for if there was one thing she dreaded, it was to see her family emerge victorious.

"Call him if you like," muttered Jean-Noël. He looked for

all the world like a man in the throes of some hallucination. Without saying a word, leaving his suitcase half-packed, he moved toward the door. Terrified, Odile watched him go, convinced not that he was leaving her but rather that he was having a nervous breakdown.

When he reached the street, he stayed close to the buildings as he walked so that his wife would be unable to see him if she went to the window. Although the evening was warm, he shivered. He himself did not understand how he had left, why his wife had not cried out or tried to hold him back. He felt no remorse. Rather, he felt free, light, as if several years had already gone by.

Twenty minutes later, a bit like a young man who does not yet know that everything changes with each moment that passes, and who comes running back to the spot where he'd left his friends, he arrived at the hotel. It was locked for the night and dark within. He rang. Only after a long wait did the night watchman come and let him in.

THIRTY-ONE

As soon as he'd closed the door of the little room to which he'd been shown, Jean-Noël threw himself, fully dressed, onto the bed. Try as he might not to think about Odile, he could not get her out of his mind. Perhaps she would be here in a moment, with her entire family at her side, begging him to come back. If he refused, they would all descend upon Mme Oetlinger's room. He so dreaded the latter possibility that he kept thinking he heard the sound of footsteps approaching. He got up. What would Annie say when she learned that he had abandoned his wife and come to live at the Hôtel des Grands Hommes? How would he react if she ordered him to go back home? He finally got undressed and fell asleep. At dawn, he woke with a start. The sky was an inky blue. He spent several minutes pacing back and forth in the small room, whose only window looked out over a narrow, silent courtyard. He got back into bed and closed his eyes. A minute later, he sat bolt upright. It must be noon. He looked at his watch. The hands marked six o'clock. Finally, he began to hear noises in the hotel. From his bed, he spotted a ray of sunlight on a building off in the distance. He waited until it was eight o'clock. He knew his stepmother was an early riser. His forehead covered with beads of sweat, he left the room in which the only trace of his passage was an unmade, barely warm bed, and made his way slowly down the stairs. When he reached Mme Oetlinger's floor, he began to tremble. Through a dormer window he could see a different angle of the courtyard he had contemplated at dawn. After hesitating for a long while, he finally started down the windowless hall, still illuminated by electric lamps, which led to Annie's room. He knocked at her door, and to give himself courage pretended he had just come from the rue de Babylone.

"Who is it?" asked Mme Oetlinger.

"Me."

"Come in, come in."

As soon as he opened the door he recoiled, dazzled. Annie's room was filled with so much sunlight that it did not even seem to be in the hotel. The window was wide open. A joyous cacophony drifted up from the square below. There were flowers everywhere. Annie was having breakfast, and the tray set in front of her made it seem that she was traveling.

"How early you've come," said Mme Oetlinger. "I didn't think I would see you before this evening. Perhaps you haven't had breakfast yet. Would you like me to ring the maid?"

"No, there's no need. Thank you."

He had only one thought in mind, to tell Annie everything that had happened between him and Odile, and tell her as quickly as possible, for he feared that his wife might arrive at any moment.

Mme Oetlinger did not appear at all surprised when she learned that her stepson had spent the night at the Hôtel des Grands Hommes and had no desire to go back to the rue de Babylone. She seemed to find it altogether natural that after having left her the night before, he had realized he could no longer live with his wife and had taken up residence here at the hotel. Jean-Noël was stupefied. He had trembled at the mere thought of this meeting, and yet everything was happening as if it were taking place in the most normal of circumstances. He had expected reproaches. He had thought he would have to provide reasons for his desire to be independent. He wanted to be free, not in order to burden his stepmother with his constant presence, but rather to make himself the man his father had so hoped he would become.

Although he had imagined he would have to put up a fierce struggle, he had been sure of emerging triumphant, unless of course the sincere affection he thought he had detected in Annie the day before had been only temporary.

"Do you approve?" he asked her.

"You are asking me a question to which it is very difficult for me to reply. I can neither approve nor disapprove of what you are doing without putting myself in a most delicate position. If you've done this, I assume it's because you thought it was the right thing. But don't ask me to take sides. You alone are the judge of your actions."

Jean-Noël no longer recognized his stepmother. Hadn't she been criticizing his marriage just yesterday? Hadn't she urged him to regain his independence? How could she now take refuge in such a neutral position? Was she afraid of what she referred to as unpleasant consequences?

"I thought that we would now be able to 'work side by side,'" he said, repeating an expression which had struck him when he'd heard his stepmother use it.

"We'll see," said Mme Oetlinger. "I must confess that I'm rather worried. I wouldn't want your wife to think that I had anything to do with this decision of yours."

In fact, Annie did not look in the slightest bit worried. She had never been so calm.

"I'm going to finish dressing," she said, and disappeared into the bathroom.

Left alone, Jean-Noël sat down near the window. For several minutes, he forced himself not to think about anything and let himself be distracted by the hustle and bustle in the square below. He sensed that his fate lay in Annie's hands and he was incapable of guessing what she was going to decide. Was she happy that he had come back or did it make no difference to her? He was asking himself this question over and over again as he watched the passersby when the little telephone near the head of the bed rang. He got up, then sat back down again. It was, without any doubt, Odile. She had come to get him. She was perhaps with her brothers, her father. What would Annie say? She would probably join them in asking him to go back to the rue de Babylone. What would he do? Should he give in?

"Can you answer that?" said Mme Oetlinger, opening the door a crack.

It was not Odile but M. Le Douaré. He was in the hotel lobby. He wanted to speak to Mme Oetlinger. As Jean-Noël put down the receiver, he realized that his stepmother was standing behind him, ready to go out.

"Did you tell him you would give me the message?" she asked.

"Yes."

She pressed both hands against her forehead, then sat down on her bed. Jean-Noël went over to her, filled with concern.

"Shouldn't I have said that?"

"No, it's all right, there was nothing else you could say. My God, when, oh when, is the world going to leave me in peace?"

Jean-Noël had heard her speak those very words so often because of him, he felt a sort of relief that this time he had not prompted them.

"He even comes to pester you here?" he asked, as though he would never have allowed himself to do such a thing.

"He comes all the time. He was here again yesterday."

Mme Oetlinger got up and walked toward the door. As Jean-Noël had not moved, she said to him, "Come with me."

He looked at her in surprise. Then his face lit up with happiness.

"If I tell you to come with me, that means you're not an inconvenience to me. Quite the opposite. I would like you to be there. When he sees that I'm not alone, perhaps he won't come back again."

When Charles Le Douaré saw Annie, he came toward her without even realizing that Jean-Noël was following her. He was obviously in a state of great agitation. As they were descending the last flight of stairs, Jean-Noël had caught a glimpse of him taking enormous strides as he paced up and down the hall.

"Annie," he said dramatically, "I have to talk to you. I have terribly important things to say to you. You refused to listen to me yesterday, but now you must."

"I can't listen now either. It so happens I have an urgent errand to run for my stepson."

At that moment, Jean-Noël came forward. M. Le Douaré, who had paid no attention to the young man, was momentarily taken aback.

"You'll have to excuse me, Monsieur," he said as if speaking to someone he had never met before, "but Madame Oetlinger must allow me to speak to her."

"That won't be possible. We have a very urgent errand to attend to," answered Jean-Noël.

"There, you see," said Annie, giving her stepson a conspiratorial look that filled him with joy while taking him by surprise. As far back as he could remember, his stepmother had never shown such trust in him.

"We have a very urgent errand we must attend to," he repeated, this time in a tone of voice which brooked no opposition.

"That makes no difference to me," replied Charles Le Douaré. Turning toward Mme Oetlinger, he added: "Annie, be it only in memory of our long conversations, of all the good you did for me, I beg you to hear me out. I saw your brother yesterday; he gave me his support; he reassured me."

"You went to see Henri?" asked Annie curtly.

"Yes, and he is going to come here."

"Let's go into the sitting room. Now, I am asking you to listen to me."

Out of discretion, Jean-Noël made no attempt to follow his stepmother. But it was she who asked him to follow her, as she had done earlier in her room. As soon as he entered the small sitting room, therefore, he thought it clever to say, "We're going to be late." Annie did not even answer him. She was in a state of rage that had nothing in common with those

Jean-Noël had witnessed so often in the past. This was not the sort of anger a son or family member might provoke, but rather that of a woman being harassed by a man she no longer loves, or has never loved. Jean-Noël could sense this, and it made him feel rather awkward. In spite of his happiness at feeling useful, he would have preferred to withdraw until the scene was over. That a man could demand that Annie hear him out, that she could be threatening in return, and all in his presence, seemed incomprehensible to him.

"I told you," continued Mme Oetlinger, "that if there was one thing which mattered above all else to me, it was that my family not be dragged into this affair. I understand your nature less and less. One would think you derive some pleasure from making yourself ridiculous."

"Your brother has always been a friend of mine. Even before I met you."

"I will go and see Henri this morning."

"How can you speak so harshly to me, Annie?"

"Good-bye."

Mme Oetlinger motioned to Jean-Noël to follow her. He obeyed, but not without feeling the embarrassment caused by an expression of friendship extended in circumstances in which it cannot be sincere. But M. Le Douaré caught Annie before she could go out the door.

"You won't hear me out?"

"I have already told you that not only do I not want to listen to you, I don't even want to see you."

"Are you really incapable of understanding," added Jean-Noël, "that you are insisting rather too much?"

This time, Charles Le Douaré attacked him.

"So you are taking up Madame Oetlinger's defense. I find that terribly noble coming from you, terribly noble and rather incomprehensible. Allow me to tell you that you have a short memory."

Jean-Noël blushed. He wanted to say something, but no sound came forth. At that moment, Mme Oetlinger turned and retraced her footseps.

"What did you just say?" she asked M. Le Douaré.

"I said that I shouldn't be surprised that you are treating me so cruelly, because that is how you have always treated everyone."

Annie looked M. Le Douaré straight in the eye. Then she turned toward her stepson.

"Come along," she said.

Maître Grimbert's offices were in an old mansion in the rue Saint-Georges. The name Grimbert was familiar to Jean-Noël, who had often heard Annie mention it. But when he saw it inscribed on a brass plaque, he was surprised, for he had always thought she was saying Rimbert and not Grimbert. The simple fact that he had learned the correct spelling of this name seemed a promise of further revelations, and he was already imagining himself intimately involved in his stepmother's life. After stepping through the door of the building, he and Annie found themselves beneath an imposing arch. In the distance, they could see a gravel-filled courtyard, which contained a bit of greenery, a tree surrounded by a circular stone bench, and a statue. The right wing seemed reserved for Maître Grimbert's living quarters. After having made their way through a long entrance hall lined with glass doors, Mme Oetlinger and her stepson were shown into a rather ordinary sitting room, then into a second one, which was more luxuriously appointed than the first.

"We won't have to wait long," said Annie.

Jean-Noël noticed she had that disconcerted air which people who are accustomed to showing they are active and decisive assume when circumstances constrain them to wait like the rest of us. She had not sat down.

"Did you notice the mechanism on the double door?" asked Jean-Noël, whom this visit reminded of other, similar ones he had made in his childhood, and who felt as if he had become a schoolboy again. The mechanism he'd noticed was a sliding rod that enabled both doors to open simultaneously. Mme Oetlinger did not reply. Since the moment she'd entered the premises of her family's solicitor, her stepson had seemed a stranger to her. Suddenly a person appeared whom Jean-Noël at first took to be Maître Grimbert himself.

"Maître Grimbert," said the newcomer with a bow, "asks you to please step into his office."

A man in his forties came forward to greet Mme Oetlinger.

"Dear Madame, how are you?"

"Isn't your father here?" asked Annie.

"No," answered the solicitor's son. "He was called out to the country last night. But rest assured, Madame, I am conversant with the matter at hand."

"My stepson," said Annie, when she noticed that Maître Grimbert was looking at Jean-Noël.

The solicitor greeted the young man discreetly, after which he went and opened a window. Jean-Noël could see the tree he had first noticed upon arriving, outlined against a nearby wall.

"I wanted to ask you," said Annie, "if you or your father had seen my brother. I am determined to settle everything as soon as possible."

"Your brother has not been to see us, but my father did write to him. We are awaiting either an answer or a visit from him. Whatever the case, you have nothing to fear. We are in possession of a precise list of the assets that belong to you. The only reason the distribution has not been formalized is that you were absent. In any case, I can assure you that within a fortnight you will be in possession of everything coming to you."

Annie looked at Jean-Noël with a smile and said: "I want to be able to have the use of what is mine. As you can see, I have responsibilities."

THIRTY-TWO

The meeting with Maître Grimbert had taken place about an hour after M. Le Douaré had begged Mme Oetlinger to hear him out. After leaving the solicitor's offices, Annie and her stepson lunched in a restaurant near the rue Saint-Georges. Afterward, they walked down to the Opéra. As many people had already left for their holidays, Annie suggested to her stepson that they go to the cinema in the afternoon. Then they took tea together. In the course of the hours they spent together, not once was an allusion made to what had just transpired. Mme Oetlinger seemed genuinely pleased to be in Jean-Noël's company. As for him, although there was an unpleasant tightness in his chest whenever he thought of Odile, he nonetheless felt utterly happy. His stepmother's attitude that morning showed that she was independent. This was the first time she stayed with him rather than dismissing him as she usually did when something was troubling her.

It was six o'clock when they decided to return to the hotel.

"What do you think I should do if Odile came while we were out?" asked Jean-Noël.

"I beg of you, don't ask me such questions."

Jean-Noël had not been wrong to fear that his wife would make an attempt to see him. As he passed by the front desk of the hotel, an employee handed him a letter, written in pencil. Odile informed her husband that she would be back at about five o'clock, that she had already come twice, to no avail. She asked if he would please wait for her.

"The lady who left this note with you has not come back yet, has she?" asked Jean-Noël when he noticed that it was past six o'oclock. Perhaps Odile had changed her mind.

"Would you read this letter?" asked Jean-Noël, handing it to his stepmother.

She took it, then returned it to her stepson almost immediately.

"That's a very sweet letter," she said, as if she had already read it. In the same indifferent tone of voice, she added: "I'm going up to my room. Would you like us to meet back here in about twenty minutes?"

Left alone, Jean-Noël reread his wife's note. Then, speaking again to the porter who had handed it to him, he tried to learn if Odile had seemed upset. It was then he was told that she had not been alone, that she had been in the company of a man who appeared to be her father, and that both of them had waited over an hour in the lobby.

He too was about to go up to his room, and had already walked up several steps, when he heard his name being called. He turned around. He saw the porter lift a sort of hatch to get out from behind his desk and point to the revolving door. A bellboy whom Jean-Noël had not noticed before but who had doubtless overheard everything cried out to him, "Here is the person who was looking for you."

A few seconds later, M. Wurtzel entered the hotel alone.

"Isn't Odile with you?" asked Jean-Noël, as though he was disappointed.

"Yes, yes, come with me."

He pulled Jean-Noël outside with him. A taxi stood in front of the hotel, all its doors closed.

"She's in the taxi?"

"Yes, but first I want to speak to you."

M. Wurtzel had not taken his eyes off his son-in-law. When he had learned what he had done, rather than feeling triumphant he had thought only of his daughter's suffering.

Against Odile's wishes, he had immediately wanted to use his skill and experience to intervene, failing to understand that only the married couple could effect a reconciliation. As soon as he found himself in the presence of Jean-Noël, however, he sensed that his efforts would be useless. This was why he now dared not take his eyes off the young man, a bit like the weaker of two animals.

"What on earth has happened?" he asked.

Jean-Noël did not answer. He ran to the taxi, not without thinking that if Annie was at her window she could see him, and opened the door. Odile was sitting in a corner. He got in next to her.

"What are you doing, Jean-Noël? You saw the state my father is in," she said, as if her husband shared her opinion of M. Wurtzel's intervention and thought, as she did, that it was ridiculous.

M. Wurtzel, who had approached the taxi, said "rue de Babylone" to the driver. At the same time, Jean-Noël got out. Odile did the same.

"Your actions are utterly incomprehensible," cried M. Wurtzel, in spite of the efforts his daughter was making to prevent him from saying anything.

Jean-Noël then explained that, ever since M. Villemur's death, his stepmother had been alone and that it was his duty to stay with her. She had raised him. He did not have the right to abandon her in her hour of need. These explanations made M. Wurtzel furious.

"Your behavior is unspeakable. I cannot believe that your stepmother is aware of your conduct and approves of it."

"I beg you, Papa, leave us."

Without being aware of it, to maintain their composure, they had gone back into the hotel. It was then that Annie appeared.

"I cannot believe, Madame," said M. Wurtzel in hushed tones, so as not to be overheard by the clients and personnel of the hotel, "that you can condone your stepson."

"I don't understand what you mean," replied Annie in a normal tone of voice.

"Let's leave, let's leave," begged Odile.

M. Wurtzel paid no attention to his daughter's plea. Irritated by the fact that Mme Oetlinger was treating him like a member of another generation although she was to Jean-Noël what he was to Odile, he struggled to make her understand that she was partly responsible for what had happened, and this in spite of being interrupted at regular intervals by Jean-Noël, who thought that doing so would win his stepmother's sympathy. He was mistaken in this, however; for each time she asked him to allow M. Wurtzel to finish what he had to say. When the latter had done so, Annie, like a person who has demonstrated her patience and must therefore be allowed to speak in turn, pointed out to M. Wurtzel that she was not acting on her stepson's part, that he was old enough to behave as he saw fit. Until the death of M. Villemur she had done everything she could to ensure that he learned to respect hard work and honesty. At present, Jean-Noël should follow only his own conscience. He had become a man. Even had she still had a certain influence over him, she would take great pains to avoid ever exercising it, for she did not consider it her right to modify a fully formed personality in any way.

"That does not change the fact that my husband left because of you," cried out Odile. "He just told us so himself, and you know it very well."

The disillusioned and yet self-satisfied smile which crossed Mme Oetlinger's face was that of a woman who is fully aware of her charm but pretends to believe others overestimate it. She turned toward her stepson:

"Jean-Noël, explain yourself, I beg of you. You can see that you're putting me in an unpleasant situation."

Addressing his remarks to M. Wurtzel and Odile in turn, in a sincere tone of voice which made him end each of his phrases with "Isn't that right?" or "Don't you think so?" Jean-Noël produced all the reasons he could think of to justify his desire to regain his freedom except the real one—Annie.

Every man had different ideals. It was only toward one's thirties that they were revealed. In his case, the ideal had proven to be just the opposite of what he had believed. He was cut out for struggle, for the unexpected, far more than for the tranquillity and safety of marriage.

While he was talking, Odile was looking at him with that incredulous air women adopt when the man whose every weakness is known to them endeavors to elevate himself.

"See here, Jean-Noël, how can you speak to me this way, to me?"

Her outburst was so sincere that Jean-Noël blushed. Wasn't Annie going to believe, as Odile clearly did, that he was putting on an act?

"I am speaking to you this way because it's the truth," he said, looking at his stepmother. She had drawn near M. Wurtzel.

"Don't you think," Annie said to the latter, "that we ought to leave them alone? They will be reconciled much more quickly . . ."

"You're right, Odile," said M. Wurtzel. "It would be for the best if we left."

By putting on a show of optimism at the very moment when a reconciliation seemed most impossible, Mme Oetlinger had struck him as having such a superficial mind and stony heart that he preferred to be done with it immediately.

"It's extraordinary," said Annie as soon as she was alone with her stepson, "that throughout my life I have always been considered responsible for the unpleasant things which happen around me."

The next day, Odile came back, alone this time; the following day, M. Le Douaré did the same. The unpleasantness of these visits was compounded, in the days that followed, by the necessary business Annie had to attend to at her brother Henri's and at Maître Grimbert's. A week went by this way. Mme Oetlinger, who in the past had taken out the slightest unpleasantness on her stepson, now treated him like a friend.

And yet he was not entirely overjoyed by this, for he had the impression that this trust was born of his stepmother's desire to show him she considered him a man rather than of any sincere affection she felt for him. From time to time she would speak to him of her family, saying far worse things about them than she had ever said about Mme Mercier and Emile. One morning, she handed him a letter from Mme Ville-mur in which the latter, without making the slightest allusion to Henri, begged her daughter to come and live with her.

"What are you going to do?" asked Jean-Noël, filled with anxiety.

Mme Oetlinger began to laugh.

"Haven't you guessed?"

If her father had still been alive, the question would not even have arisen. But to go back to the avenue de Malakoff today, to return to a family that understood nothing of her personality, would have been to renounce everything which was noble and generous in life.

The following day, she received a letter from Maître Grimbert. He asked her to come to his office the following Monday for a meeting with her brother. The quarrel between Annie and Henri had been settled. She showed no happiness over this. She even found it strange that the solicitor had written a bit as if he were announcing glad tidings. When the day of the meeting arrived, Jean-Noël was surprised at how very insistent Annie was that he come with her. The two thus went to the rue Saint-Georges.

"I would prefer to wait here," said Jean-Noël when they had arrived in front of the building, even though at heart he was dying to stay with his stepmother.

In the course of his first visit to Maître Grimbert, he had been offended by what he had perceived to be the unnecessarily cold way in which the solicitor had treated him. Mme Oetlinger became insistent again. It might seem strange that Annie no longer wanted to go anywhere without her stepson. And yet the reason for this could not have been simpler. Alone, with no other aim in life than to paint, and having, in addition, suffered at the hands of her family all her life and been accused by everyone of being heartless, she felt the need to justify herself in her own eyes. By taking Jean-Noël with her when she went to see her family, and indeed everywhere where she knew the young man's presence would startle people, not only was she affirming her independence, she was also proving to herself that she was not as harsh as people said. Although it was a cordial meeting, just as on the previous occasion no one paid the slightest attention to her companion. She noticed this. Several times, she made a point of turning toward her stepson to ask his advice, which made him blush furiously and stammer.

In the aftermath of this visit, Annie finally turned her attention to organizing her life. She would return to her studio, for, as she said, doing nothing tired her. But she carefully avoided asking Jean-Noël what he intended to do. He had nonetheless sensed that, in spite of the fact that his stepmother was asking nothing, all the same she was curious to know.

"I'm going to finish my law studies," he said.

"Very good."

That was all Mme Oetlinger said.

That day, they went to the rue Boissonnade. Annie had decided that, if it was possible, she would live in her studio. Meanwhile, they would try to find Jean-Noël a room, either in the same building, or in a lodging house or hotel nearby. He was bursting with happiness. This life he was going to lead at his stepmother's side was the life he had always dreamed of. Whatever Annie told him to do, he would do. The only thing that worried him was the monthly payment he was supposed to make to Marguerite. He was not terribly sure of how he would find the money. To ask his stepmother for it seemed impossible to him. Wasn't she unaware of the very existence of this obligation?

The concierge had the key to the studio. She was not in her loggia. Although Jean-Noël offered to go in her place, Annie herself went to look for her at the far end of the courtyard.

He followed a few paces behind. The concierge greeted Mme Oetlinger with that amiability which people of small account never fail to show someone who, although higher up on the social scale, is both simple and modest. She even called her husband to hurry out and greet their returning tenant. He arrived, cap in hand, bowing slightly, and although he was less loquacious than his wife, one sensed from the looks that he alternated between the latter and her tenant that he, too, was filled with respect and devotion. Annie motioned to Jean-Noël to come nearer.

"I have not come back alone," she said, "I have come with my stepson."

"We know Monsieur," said the concierge. "We saw him several times before you left."

Jean-Noël had never paid the slightest attention to the concierges. He now regretted this.

"I wanted to ask you," said Annie, "if you might not know of a room for my stepson."

"There's the gentleman's studio on the ground floor. He is about to leave."

"No, no, my stepson doesn't need a studio. And in fact it would be too expensive. What we want is a simple furnished room. The gentleman's studio would be far too big."

"I understand, Madame," said the concierge.

Jean-Noël blushed slightly. He found the conversation unpleasant. He could not understand why his stepmother, while not pretending to be poor, was showing she was concerned about money in front of people whose very amiability was prompted by her wealth.

"You ought to ask Madame de Vineuse," said the concierge to his wife. "She rents out rooms." Then, addressing Annie, he asked, "Would you like me to go see her?"

The house in which Mme Oetlinger's studio was located was a bizarre construction. The side facing the street looking a bit like a farmhouse. Upon entering, one found oneself in a vast courtyard along one side of which were the studios, a courtyard where Annie remembered having seen chickens before the war, when she had frequented the neighborhood painters. But on the right-hand side a little stone path led up to a four-story house, invisible from the street, isolated like a villa, and whose entrance, like that of a storehouse, was on the second floor. Two cement staircases, one leading from the right and the other from the left, were attached to the front of the house and came together in front of this entrance, where they formed a sort of platform.

"Those rooms may be very expensive," said Annie to the concierge, whose husband had gone off to make inquiries.

"I don't think so, Madame."

"We shall see. When your husband returns, tell him to come and find me."

Accompanied by her stepson, she walked up the wooden staircase that led to her studio. The furniture was covered with a heavy layer of dust. The walls were full of cobwebs; on one of them hung a pallette covered with dried-out paints. In this vast room, with its trunks, its tightly closed drawers, Jean-Noël felt the same emotion he had felt when he had arrived, alone, with his stepmother in Nice. It seemed to him now, as it had that day, that Annie alone existed in the world. She put down her handbag and opened the glass-paned door which led to a little wooden balcony. In spite of the dust that was flying about in the sunlight, in spite of the stifling heat, Jean-Noël looked at everything around him lovingly. Standing in this studio, which lacked any comforts, which was almost like a hangar, and in which he recognized certain objects he had known forever and which, for that reason, had tremendous value in his eyes, it seemed to him that from this moment forward he would never have another care in the world, that he and Annie would never leave one another, that they would each lead their own lives and yet be united, far from the world and happy.

"I'll have a curtain put up here," said Mme Oetlinger. "That way, you will have your own little corner where you can work whenever you want."

At that moment, there was a knock on the door. It was the concierge.

"Come in, do come in, Monsieur Gabin," said Annie. "So! Did you see this lady?"

The concierge replied that it just so happened she did have a room, which never happened to her, and that this was only due to the fact that the young German girl who had reserved it had just lost one of her parents. But Mme de Vineuse had more requests than she needed. It was necessary to go and see her at once.

"And what is the price of the room?" asked Annie.

"Three hundred fifty francs a month."

"Almost as much as my studio!"

"Yes, but the room is furnished."

Mme Oetlinger then said that she would think about it, and when the concierge pointed out to her that by the time she had made up her mind it might well be too late, she replied that in that case it didn't matter and that she would find something else which cost less.

After they had eaten lunch in a modest restaurant in the rue Campagne-Première, Mme Oetlinger and her stepson went to visit several nearby hotels, but the prices were either the same or even higher than what Mme de Vineuse was asking for her furnished room.

"I think," said Annie, "that you will have to take the room the concierge told us about."

Jean-Noël agreed unenthusiastically. He had spoken only grudgingly at lunch and had said virtually nothing since then, although he had been in high spirits all morning. This change of heart was due to the fact that he had suddenly noticed Annie was paying more attention to how much he was going to cost her than to his health and well-being. He would not have cared a fig for the latter if his stepmother had been in financial difficulties. It made no difference to him; as long as he was near her, he would live anywhere, eat anywhere. But what he found incomprehensible was that Mme Oetlinger was being so stingy at the very moment when her quarrels with her family had all been settled. Why, then, had she taken Jean-Noël to her meetings with Maître Grimbert? Was it natural for a woman who had been generous all her life to haggle over fifty francs for a furnished room? The only possible explanation was that she had suddenly become wary of Jean-Noël. Hadn't Annie always been afraid of being loved only for her money?

At the rue Boissonnade, Mme Oetlinger, who was pretending not to notice the sudden change in her stepson, asked the concierge if they could visit Mme de Vineuse's room immediately. He led her and Jean-Noël to the house. Mme de Vineuse was a woman who found herself in the sort of situation usually found among people who let rooms. She was a widow. She had suffered reversals of fortune. It was most unwillingly that she had embarked upon this small commercial enterprise. Having explained this in a conversation that took place in the drawing room, and in which Annie pretended to be very interested, Mme de Vineuse assumed her new role, which she filled far more ably than her conversation had suggested.

"This room," she said, opening the door a bit like a sculptor unveiling one of his works, "was my son's. Since he entered the Naval Academy in Toulon, he no longer uses it."

Mme Oetlinger and her stepson inspected the room quickly. It was clean, modest, filled with mementos.

As they came back downstairs, Jean-Noël, who had found the room sinister, rediscovered what he loved about his stepmother. The door to the room had barely been closed when Annie began to laugh, holding herself back so as not to be heard.

"No," she said, "no, it's impossible. I can't picture you living with Madame de Vineuse. We'll go look at the studio on the ground floor. It's really too lugubrious up there."

Jean-Noël was so moved by this change that the room which he would have been sick at heart to inhabit a moment earlier now seemed so beautiful to him that, after much insisting, he finally obtained Annie's permission to rent it.

THIRTY-THREE

Mme Oetlinger spent all of the following week making her studio liveable. Jean-Noël brought such zeal to the task of helping her that on several occasions she had forcibly to remove a tool from his hands. She took up her painting again before the studio was ready. While not a disorderly person, she liked it when her workplace resembled a building site. Jean-Noël sensed that his stepmother was irritated by his constant presence, although she never told him so, and he therefore got into the habit of not appearing until just before lunchtime. "It's noon already!" she would cry out, as if life was far too short to accomplish everything one hoped to do. Jean-Noël was therefore greatly surprised when Annie said to him one day, "I was hoping you would come down a bit earlier this morning."

"I was in my room. If you had told me, I would have come down right away."

She smiled at his answer. She did not think that because she herself tolerated being disturbed this gave her the right to disturb others.

"Do you see these paintings?" she asked, pointing to half a dozen framed canvases. "I'd like you to go hail a taxi. We'll move them together."

"Where to?" asked her stepson.

"To the paint store."

"Why?"

"That's the best sort of advertising, don't you see? Among

the people one passes in the street, a great many more are interested in painting than one thinks, certainly many more there than among society figures. This is a way of getting commissions to do portraits."

Jean-Noël then understood that his stepmother had once again succumbed to the vain ambition of becoming a "professional." While this desire of hers had been just barely excusable when they lived in Nice, it was utterly ridiculous now that money was no longer a concern for her.

"I don't understand," said Jean-Noël.

"You'll understand later," said Mme Oetlinger.

From that day forward one heard only about people who were coming to sit for their portraits. Sometimes it would be an old lady, sometimes a gentleman whose solemnity, she would say, was equaled only by his modesty. She would ask her stepson how he visualized these people, whom she mocked without malice and for whom she had that theoretical respect we feel for people who seem satisfied with their lot in life. In the evenings, just as they'd done after M. Villemur's death, the two of them would either walk home the little girl who had posed in the afternoon, or go wandering, what Annie called exploring. But Jean-Noël no longer derived the same pleasure from these diversions.

One morning he received a letter. The rue de Babylone address had been crossed out and replaced by that of the Hôtel des Grands Hommes, whence it had in turn been sent on to the rue Boissonnade. The letter was from Marguerite. She was surprised not to have received her maintenance allowance for the past two months and was asking Jean-Noël to send it to her by return post. He reread her letter several times. Although he had been expecting to receive it, he had hoped it would never come. He had been counting on Odile to continue paying Marguerite's allowance in order to maintain a connection with her husband, for he could not believe she no longer loved him. In his mind, time would fix everything. When he received this letter, however, he had the distinct impression that he had no more friends and that even Odile herself, whose devotion he found quite normal given the many instances of it she had shown, was now distancing herself from him. He was somewhat hurt by this. What was he to do now? At first he thought of admitting everything to Annie. But what would she say if she learned he had this responsibility? Finally, he made up his mind to go and see his first wife.

Three months after her divorce had become final Marguerite had left Saint-Cloud and moved to Paris, to an apartment in the rue de Vaugirard not far from the Luxembourg gardens, which she claimed to have rented "through connections." Although the apartment was quite spacious, it looked out over a tiny courtyard and was both dark and airless, in spite of which Marguerite seemed to think that her daughter was much better off there than in the suburbs. She took her out to the Luxembourg every afternoon, and had become acquainted with a group of mothers there. For, now that she was receiving a regular monthly allowance, she had begun to have bourgeois aspirations. Her only dream was to be a Left-Bank mother, a mother whose time is taken up by the need to take her child out for fresh air, and by department stores, in particular Le Bon Marché.

When Jean-Noël arrived at Marguerite's, toward noon so as to be sure of finding her at home, she received him like a person whose existence requires her total devotion. Although she had not seen her ex-husband since their divorce, she left him alone for a few minutes in a small drawing room filled with curtains and vases. Jean-Noël was thus able to reflect at his leisure upon the changes in Marguerite. She was still as unconcerned as ever about her appearance, but the former neglect and disorder in her surroundings had given way to a desire to provide an aura of stability to her situation as a divorced woman. Jean-Noël had already sensed this when the concierge had said to him, "Third floor, on the left." Finally, she came out to join him.

"Have a seat," she said to him, addressing him with a familiarity that suggested she had just seen him the day before. After sitting down herself, she got up abruptly and left the room, excusing herself as she did so but offering no explanation. This time, her absence was brief. "One hasn't a minute to oneself, with that little Annie," she said when she returned.

"This is a charming apartment," said Jean-Noël, who thought no such thing.

He felt somewhat ill at ease and had lost the desire he'd once had to astonish, to present himself as a man whom destiny has always favored and whose future could not be anything other than glorious. Marguerite was now a stranger to him, even more than a stranger, for he no longer felt either vanity or self-esteem when with her. This woman was absolutely nothing to him.

"Perhaps you'd like some lunch," she said.

"No, no, I only came at noontime to be sure of finding you in."

"If you want to eat, it's no problem," she continued.

It struck Jean-Noël then that Marguerite was proud of her independence, and that she considered the monthly payments she received from him something she was owed rather than a favor. "And what if I were to die?" Such an eventuality was the furthest thing from Marguerite's mind.

"You know," Jean-Noël told her, "that a great deal has happened in the past two months."

He told her that he had left his wife. Seeing that Marguerite's face had darkened, he quickly added that he was now living with his stepmother. He was experiencing temporary financial problems because the latter was in litigation with her family. But within a month, at the latest, everything would be sorted out and he would then send her the three payments he owed all at once.

She accepted this arrangement with unexpected good grace. She believed Jean-Noël now because, if he failed to keep his word, it would be so easy for her to make trouble for him.

Jean-Noël ate lunch in the neighborhood, but when he

returned to the rue Boissonnade toward three o'clock, he was utterly astonished to find that Annie was painting the portrait of a total stranger. The latter was sitting in an armchair, before a backdrop of irridescent fabrics, holding a book in his hands. He was a man of about sixty with crew-cut gray hair who'd been awarded the Légion d'Honneur, wore a jacket and waistcoat with braided trim, and who was taking his role so seriously that he did not even turn his head when Jean-Noël came in.

"Just a moment," said Annie, who continued painting.

Jean-Noël stayed near the door without moving a muscle. From there he glimpsed the little girl from the sewing-goods shop in the rue Saint-Jacques sitting on the floor near an open window, her hands blackened with charcoal as she, too, tried to sketch the unknown model.

Finally, Mme Oetlinger stopped working. She put down her palette, while the little girl, imitating her, put down her charcoal pencils, and said to her stepson, "That's all for today." But, changing her mind suddenly just as the stranger was about to get up, she said, "Please, if you don't mind, just a moment more." She then spent a long while gazing now at the man with the book, now at her canvas.

"My stepson," said Annie finally. "Colonel Meignier."

The latter had got up. As befits a man who has spent his entire life unaccustomed to hearing praise, he was embarrassed at having been the focus of attention for such a long period of time and kept repeating that, if the portrait was a failure, it would be because the model was too ugly. And yet at a certain moment he asked to see the result of this first sitting, but Annie, who was ordinarily so unaffected, put on theatrical airs whenever painting was the issue.

"It's impossible," she said. "All it would take would be for you to look at the start I've made, and I'd be unable to continue."

M. Meignier, who had sought out Mme Oetlinger on the recommendation of a local tradeswoman, and who considered it all but an honor that she had agreed to paint his portrait, knew that artists had peculiar habits which were often incomprehensible. He blushed, and to demonstrate his worldliness, added immediately that he would respect her wishes. "You will do me the honor, Monsieur, of having a cup of tea. You've certainly earned it," said Annie, with the air of the artist who, while she might well use someone, does not feel in any way obliged to discuss art with him. She disappeared into the corner where she kept a gas burner, some cups, an entire disparate collection of kitchen equipment, and was followed by the little girl, who was normally forbidden to go there because it was a "dirty" place but who took advantage of the fact that Mme Oetlinger was going there to do the same.

"And are you too a painter?" the colonel asked Jean-Noël. As the latter failed to make any reply, he went on to say that it was a talent which doubtless brought a great deal of satisfaction to those who possessed it.

Shortly afterward, Annie reappeared holding a teacup in each hand. One could hear the kettle beginning to whistle. Jean-Noël thought it was ridiculous that she had asked M. Meignier, who was here for the first time, to stay to tea. He looked at her. It had been a long time since he had seen her so engrossed in something. She fussed over the sugar, the milk, worried that her guest might not like toast. She disappeared again behind the screen. From Jean-Noël's position, he was the only one in the room who could see her. She took advantage of this to smile at him. All at once, then, his ill humor vanished. Her smile had been heavy with irony. It was the one we put on when professional obligations momentarily place us beneath people whom we judge to be our inferiors, for in spite of the pleasure she took in selling her paintings, Annie had no desire to be mistaken for a tradeswoman.

They had all gathered around a small table. Mme Oetlinger was expounding her ideas about art with the utmost seriousness, while her stepson listened and tried not to laugh, when a knock was heard at the door. Jean-Noël went to open it. He found himself face-to-face with a chauffeur, who asked him, cap in hand, if this was Mme Oetlinger's studio and whether she was in. Annie got up at once.

"Is my mother here?" she asked the chauffeur.

"Yes, Madame. Madame has instructed me to ask you whether she can come up."

"But of course. I'll go down with you."

She turned around to excuse herself and then disappeared.

"This must be Madame's mother, doubtless?" asked the colonel, without fearing for a moment that he was being indiscreet by staying.

Jean-Noël gave him a harsh look, in the hope of making him understand that he should leave now.

"Where's the lady?" the little girl asked at that moment.

Jean-Noël looked at her in the same way. Wasn't it ridiculous that this child, the colonel, and he should all be here in Mme Oetlinger's studio? He would have preferred to be here alone. When she saw these strangers, Mme Villemur would think that he played no greater role than they did in Annie's life. He heard the sound of someone coming slowly up the stairs. He rose, as did M. Meignier.

"Where's the lady?" the little girl repeated.

"Shhh," replied Jean-Noël, smiling at her.

He had moved away from M. Meignier. The latter drew nearer to the young man. Just then, Mme Villemur appeared on the threshold. Annie had not told her she had company. Had she done so, it would have seemed that she was warning her mother, and she intensely disliked doing that sort of thing. Mme Villemur therefore gazed with astonishment upon the bizarre group composed of the colonel, Jean-Noël and the little girl.

"Good day, Madame," said Jean-Noël, bowing.

The old lady, however, was always rather slow to recover her senses when startled by something.

"Colonel Meignier has asked me to paint his portrait," said Annie coldly.

"Ah! That's very nice," replied Mme Villemur, giving the colonel a smile, albeit a rather forced and distant one. Leaning on her cane, she crossed the studio and approached the little girl, who was observing her without saying a word.

"How pretty she is!"

"The lady has come back," said the girl, pointing at Annie.

"I suppose by 'the lady' she means you," remarked Mme Villemur.

Jean-Noël, who was standing perfectly still off to one side, could not help but feel hurt by Mme Villemur's indifference toward him.

"I don't wish to interrupt you," said Mme Villemur to her daughter as she sat down.

"I had already stopped when you arrived. Would you like a cup of tea?"

"No, thank you. I've only come for a moment."

A conversation began, in which the colonel took part, and whose subject matter was furnished by the remarks uttered by the little girl.

"I'm off to run an errand," said Jean-Noël, to show his stepmother he was not pleased.

"No, stay," Annie ordered curtly.

From time to time, Mme Villemur would look over at the colonel, anxious as she was that he should leave.

"I will come back to see you," she said, emphasizing each word, "since you're not free today."

Finally, the colonel got up. As soon as he had gone, Jean-Noël became the target of Mme Villemur's harsh looks.

"I have an important errand to run," he repeated.

"I asked you to stay," said Annie.

"But why don't you leave your stepson free to do as he wishes?"

"I didn't know you were in Paris," said Annie, without replying to her mother's question.

"You're the reason I came."

To disguise his lack of composure, Jean-Noël was trying to remove a paintbrush from the little girl's hands.

"Wouldn't you like me to take her home to her mother?" he asked his stepmother.

"Don't trouble yourself. We'll take her back together later on."

If Mme Oetlinger was so determined to have her stepson stay with them, it was because she sensed that her mother had not come with the kindest of intentions. It was clear that the main reason for the old lady's visit was her curiosity to see what use her daughter was making of the independence she had clamored for so insistently, and for which she had not hesitated to stand up to her brother. Annie, therefore, was determined to show that she had nothing to hide, and that if her stepson happened to be in her studio, it was because she wanted it that way.

"But who was that gentleman who just left?" asked Mme Villemur.

"My first customer," replied Annie in an ironic tone of voice.

Jean-Noël blushed. He looked at Mme Villemur. She had not reacted.

"Your first customer! I don't understand what you mean."

"He is my first customer. I hope to have others."

Mme Villemur stared harshly at her daughter, and then, as though she'd resigned herself to understanding nothing more of this particular mystery, she added, "Since you are so determined to have your stepson stay, I assume I can speak freely in front of him."

"Of course."

Mme Villemur then reproached Annie for the lack of trust she had shown in her own brother. Henri had involved himself in her affairs only to be of service to her, and not in hopes of gaining some profit. By seeming to doubt this, she had so offended him that he had sworn he would never see her again. Mme Villemur wanted to settle this conflict, which, as a mother, she found deeply upsetting. She understood that her daughter had wanted to have access to her inheritance, but it had been inelegant to have pretended to doubt Henri's honesty in order to obtain it.

While her mother was speaking, Annie looked over at her stepson several times as though he were an accomplice.

"This proves," she observed, "that I behave badly toward everyone. I have no heart. I am selfish. Throughout my life, I have thought only of my own interests, isn't that right, Jean-Noël?"

THIRTY-FOUR

Summer was drawing to a close when Jean-Noël received a letter that had been forwarded to him. The crossed-out and readdressed envelope reminded him of the letter he had received from Marguerite, and he opened it with apprehension. It was a letter from Mme Mercier. She told her son that, try as he might to hide, she would find him. M. Wurtzel had fired Emile. Because of Jean-Noël and that hypocrite Odile, she now found herself in an apartment whose rent was well beyond her means. All of this had been a plot. When he had forced his mother to move out of the rue Mouton-Duvernet, Jean-Noël had already known that he was going to abandon his wife and leave his mother in this situation. He was just like his father: he was infatuated with Annie. But there was justice on this earth. Mme Mercier would track down her rival, even if that meant spending every last penny she had and being forced to go to the police for help.

The letter, which arrived just when he was expecting to be taken to court by Marguerite from one day to the next, stunned him. For a brief moment, he thought of writing to Mme Mercier and telling her to be patient, that he would give her some money in the very near future. But what good would that have done? He then decided he would tell Annie everything as soon as she got in, but as she had still not returned by the end of the afternoon, he abandoned this resolution.

As Annie had not reappeared by suppertime, Jean-Noël finally went to the small restaurant in the rue Campagne-

Première alone. When he returned, there was still no sign of Mme Oetlinger. He set up his worktable, lit a kerosene lamp, turned off the electricity, and then settled into an armchair and closed his eyes. Moths came in through the open window and fluttered around the lamp. He could hear strains of music from a nearby studio. There was something infinitely peaceful about the evening. And yet it was merely a summer's evening like any summer's evening, imbued with that melancholy which fills the langorous last moments before sleep. From time to time, Jean-Noël thought about Marguerite, and the letter he had just received. What was going to happen in the next few days? Why had he heard nothing from Marguerite, in spite of the fact that he had not kept the promise he had made her? Would she, too, come after him at the rue Boissonnade? Though deep in thought, he nonetheless listened attentively to the sounds of all the footsteps echoing in the courtyard, to ensure he would have enough time to settle in at his worktable, for he knew that the sight of him sitting by his lamp with his books and papers in the middle of the night was one that would strike his stepmother's fancy.

Midnight had struck some ten minutes earlier when he heard the sound of an automobile stopping in front of the house, and then Annie's voice. A friend had doubtless given her a lift and she was thanking him. He then recognized her footfall in the courtyard and on the stairs. He had been sitting at his table for over a minute when, rather than coming in, Annie knocked. Without realizing it, he had locked the door. He got up grudgingly to open the door and turned on the electric light only after he was sure she had noticed that his only illumination had been the kerosene lamp.

"It's good to be working like this," said Mme Oetlinger with indifference.

She had long since grown weary of painting portraits of people like Monsieur Meignier, who had, in fact, begun to admire Annie's beauty rather than her talent just after Mme Villemur's visit. She was now reconciled with her brother. Little by little, she had begun seeing her old friends again. She had just now been out visiting one of these. But she had said nothing to her stepson of the changes that had taken place in her, doubtless because she did not want to distract him from his work.

"You say that without much conviction," observed Jean-Noël.

Whenever she came back from an evening during which she felt she had been particularly charming, she always waited a long while before getting changed. Without removing her gloves or the light coat she had draped over her shoulders the way Jean-Melchior used to do with his overcoat, she walked around the studio, silent but nonetheless agitated.

"You know, my dear Jean-Noël," she said, turning one of her canvasses back to front and examining it as though her art preoccupied her at every hour of the day and night, "that work rewards only those who love it."

"And I do love it."

"Very good. In that case, it will reward you."

Jean-Noël grew somber upon hearing this remark. Annie noticed it.

"You are tired. You must go up to bed."

As soon as he had reached his room, he was filled with an unutterable sadness. The house was quiet now, and the soft atmosphere of the summer's evening had vanished. The night in this banal room, where he was surrounded by photographs of strangers, was no longer serene. There were lights in the distance, and the sound of automobiles reached his ears. It occurred to him then that his stepmother had perhaps noticed that the zeal with which he had been studying was anything but sincere. As was her custom, she had said nothing to him, doubtless waiting to see before she made some irrevocable decision. And what would happen if Annie, who was already ill inclined toward him, learned that he was under a court order to pay a monthly allowance of two thousand francs, or that he was going to have his mother and brother to provide for yet again? Were these gloomy thoughts the result of the long hours he had just spent waiting in the studio? He did not know. His thoughts were jumbled, and yet he was hounded by the feeling that he ought to act. It was then that the idea of seeing Mme Mourier again came to him. She had always given him good advice. "If ever you have a problem, come and see me," she had said. She liked people to recognize that they owed her a debt of gratitude.

Feeling somewhat apprehensive, Jean-Noël went to the rue Laugier the following day. Mme Mourier might well be remarried. What attitude should he take if he suddenly found himself in the presence of a man he did not know? And in fact, what would be achieved by this visit? Each of us has a strange destiny. He had considered the years spent with Laure as lost, that someday soon it would be as if they had never existed at all, and yet here he was, about to seek comfort from the very woman whom he had judged unworthy of occupying a place in his memory.

When he arrived at the rue Laugier, the concierge, after having expressed a certain satisfaction at seeing one of his former tenants, told him that Mme Mourier had left the building and rented a much larger apartment in the avenue Niel, that she had come into an inheritance from her mother, who had died. This surprised Jean-Noël, for although Laure had spoken to him of this inheritance, she herself had never quite seemed to believe in it. He went to the address he had been given and was surprised by the grandeur of the lobby. So Mme Mourier had not lied to him. She really had come from a good family, and if there had been times when she had been forced to watch what she spent, this must have been even more distressing for her than it had been for him.

When he got out of the lift, Jean-Noël noticed immediately that there was only one apartment per floor, just as at the avenue de Malakoff. Laure could not be living alone. Finally, he rang. A maid opened the door, and when he asked to speak to Mme Mourier, she answered, "If Monsieur would like to wait a moment, I will go and see if Madame is in." Shortly afterward, she showed Jean-Noël into a drawing room, none of whose furnishings he recalled from the rue Laugier but where he nonetheless recognized some of Laure's tastes, in particular her fondness for muslin curtains and bric-a-brac.

A few minutes later, Mme Mourier joined him. The past two years had transformed her. Gone were the days when she had lived from hand to mouth, when she had attached no importance to furnishing her home and had cared only for going out, for dressing rather showily. Seeing her now, dressed soberly yet elegantly, Jean-Noël sensed that her attitude, too, had changed.

"Well, Jean-Noël," she said immediately, "at last you deign to come to see me."

She made a sign indicating her visitor should sit down and then, after having rung, instructed the maid to bring in an assortment of drinks.

"I heard," she said, "that you and your wife had separated."

"From Maître Préfil?"

"I can't tell you that." Then, in a different tone of voice, she added, "If you had come to me for advice instead of acting impulsively, you would never have married that young lady."

This reproach had little effect upon Jean-Noël. He sensed that Mme Mourier still had some interest in him, and that was all he cared about. She had, in fact, expressed herself in the manner of someone for whom the past has remained perfectly clear.

"You must be happy now," she said, "since you have achieved what you wanted."

"What do you mean?"

"Wasn't it always your dream to live with your stepmother?" Then, as if she took a real interest in Jean-Noël's fate, she added, "Is she at least treating you in the way you had hoped?"

"Yes," answered Jean-Noël.

He was most struck, in the course of this meeting, by the accuracy of Mme Mourier's memories. In spite of the change in her style of living, the particulars of his relationship with Mme Mourier remained as clear in her mind as if it had all happened yesterday. It was as if no time had elapsed. Jean-Noël was embarrassed. He could sense that this woman was proud of the fact that she had never tried to make trouble for him; everything in her attitude said that she was far from resembling an Odile Wurtzel. She was infinitely superior to the petty concerns of bourgeois life. Wasn't she receiving him with pleasure, as few women would have done, without any reservations whatsoever?

"You were right," he said. "I never should have married Mademoiselle Wurtzel. But, if you remember, I was in a dilemma."

"Not at all. If you had stayed on at Maître Préfil's, you wouldn't have anything to worry about today, which must not be the case now, isn't that right?"

"Indeed." He laid out his troubles. "And I can't say anything to Annie," he added, "because if she knew all this she would think I'm responsible."

"She would be right," said Mme Mourier. "Put yourself in your stepmother's place. She has done so much for you already. She's had to suffer so many things."

In Mme Mourier's mind, Annie had always been a victim of the people around her, not unlike the way Laure thought she herself had been, and most women were.

"That's exactly why I don't want her to know anything."

Jean-Noël had the impression that Mme Mourier was thinking only of Annie.

"It seems to me," she said, "that the best thing for you would be to have a frank discussion with your stepmother."

"That's not possible."

"Would you like me to talk to her?"

Since the beginning of the meeting, Mme Mourier had been casting about for a pretext to contact Annie. Although she had always pretended to pay no attention to Jean-Noël's stepmother, thinking he would take undue pride in the fact if she did, she considered Mme Oetlinger the sort of person who was made to get along with her. The difficulty had always been getting around Jean-Noël.

"I will write to your stepmother," said Mme Mourier, "and ask to meet with her. I will talk to her about you and," she added with a smile, "you know that I have a great deal of influence over her."

But if there was one thing Jean-Noël did not want, it was precisely this. He was wary of Mme Mourier's zeal. He sensed that she was deluding herself. But he could not tell her so.

"My stepmother does not want to see anyone," he replied. "At the moment, she is going through a rather difficult time, which is in fact the reason for my own troubles, for I dare not broach the subject to her now. Otherwise everything would have been settled long ago."

THIRTY-FIVE

A few days later, Jean-Noël was startled to learn that Annie had just spent a very pleasant afternoon with Mme Mourier. "She is charming, and I even find that she has much improved." He blushed. So Laure had paid no heed to his request that she not see Annie! The two women must certainly have talked about him. He could imagine Mme Mourier taking him under her wing, could hear her saying in a condescending tone of voice that he was an excellent young man, all the while having no idea of the awkward situation in which she was placing Annie. When he went back up to his room that night he wanted to cry. He had so many worries that this minor event had completely shattered him, and he alternated between viewing it as a plot against him or as further proof that no one cared about what he wanted, and that the people who were closest to him, and who should therefore be trying to avoid hurting him, in fact were thinking only of themselves and their personal satisfactions.

The next morning, out of some nameless desire to incarnate someone in distress, he smoked a cigarette as he got dressed, although this was something he never did. Was today the day the scandal that had been dangling over his head for weeks now would explode? The law allowed him to be up to three months late in paying Marguerite, but he had now reached the fourth month. And what did Mme Mercier and Emile's silence signify? In spite of his need to be active first thing in the morning, he came down the stairs slowly and knocked softly on the studio door. When no one answered, he turned the key that was in the lock and entered. Annie was sitting at her desk, writing. Jean-Noël guessed immediately that she was ill-humored; whenever she found herself obliged to write a letter, Mme Oetlinger was immediately reminded of her relations with businessmen, suppliers, landlords—all of whom were people she detested. He was in a state of such distress, however, that her ill humor did not upset him as it would have done ordinarily.

"Something very troubling has happened yet again," said Mme Oetlinger after having finished her letter, addressed the envelope, and affixed a stamp to it. "Your mother went to see Henri the day before yesterday and, incredible though it seems, he gave her my address. She may therefore turn up here from one minute to the next, whenever the fancy strikes her. What on earth can this woman want of me? Why doesn't she tell me once and for all what she expects of me! I will answer her. And then let me never see her again. It's just unbelievable that there are people whose only aim in life is to mind other peoples' business. Listen to me, Jean-Noël, I would like you to go see her and tell her that there is no point in her coming here, I won't receive her. All she will gain by coming here is to force me to leave. I really don't see what satisfaction that can possibly give her."

Just as on the day Charles le Douaré had come to the Hôtel des Grands Hommes, Jean-Noël was delighted by the fact that he was not the reason for his stepmother's ill humor. She was angry with Henri for having divulged her address. He was therefore quick to agree to do her this favor. But as soon as he had left the studio to go to the porte d'Orléans, his ardor vanished. He had not seen his mother since the notorious meeting at the rue de Babylone. He knew her well enough to know what sort of welcome she would accord him when she learned he had come bearing a message from Mme Oetlinger. "You only ever come to see me in order to defend that adventuress." She would certainly receive him with those words. She would reproach him for wanting to bring about her downfall, for being part of a gang—a clique, as she said—whose sole aim was to get rid of her. And that would be nothing compared to the far more reasonable and justified accusation that he had made her change her habits, only then to abandon her.

As soon as he entered the small apartment his mother occupied, he sensed that something dramatic was going on. Whereas at the rue Mouton-Duvernet Mme Mercier and Emile had spent their mornings cleaning the apartment as soon as they were dressed, going so far as to polish the slats of the Venetian blinds, he found them both dressed in the clothes they had not wanted to wear on the day of his wedding. The apartment, on the other hand, was in disarray. The furniture had been pushed up against the walls. Personal belongings that seemed to have no age, and no color, were strewn about everywhere. Although everything had been given to them by Odile, and therefore belonged to them, it seemed as though they were about to leave a furnished flat. They looked like people who have decided to take certain measures, who are prepared to defend themselves, and yet who are surprised by their own audacity when the time to act has come.

"In fact, we thought you would come," said Mme Mercier. "You're all the same. You only show yourselves when others get angry. If one trusts you, relies on the promises you make, you do nothing."

"I don't understand why you're saying this to me."

Mme Mercier turned toward Emile, who had made do with a casual wave to greet his brother, the sort of sign two young men might exchange, but one that in no way excluded his indignation.

"Are you ready?" she asked.

"Where are you going?" asked Jean-Noël.

"We are going to your wife's. We are going to ask her if the way in which she has treated us is proper."

Jean-Noël was stupefied as he realized that his mother and brother had not for a moment thought that he, Odile's husband, might be of any use whatsoever to them in the action they were about to undertake. On the contrary, he sensed from their decided manner that they feared he might offer to accompany them.

"I would like to talk to you before you go."

"We don't have time."

"I would like to talk to you about the visit you paid Annie's brother."

"You don't need to tell me that. I know that's why you're here. She's the one who sent you, isn't she? You're wasting your time. Emile wrote to her last night, to the rue Boissonnade, to tell her that we would be there tomorrow morning. And we will come. And if she isn't there, we'll wait for her."

"But what is it you want to ask her?"

"Me? I'll say nothing. Emile is going to speak. We've had enough now, do you understand, of being taken advantage of. Since the people who get everything in life are those who aren't afraid of making a fuss, well, we're going to make a fuss."

As he made his way back to the rue Boissonnade, Jean-Noël could not stop thinking of those threats. Upon reflection, what surprised him the most was that his mother had not held him responsible for Odile's behavior. He had expected he would be all but insulted, but apart from a few vague allusions to the way in which he fawned upon Mme Oetlinger, nothing disagreeable had been said to him. As he walked along, he tried to understand the reasons for this change in their attitude. It did not take him long to do so. Ever since he had left his wife, they had considered he was somewhat mad. He did not know what he wanted. He was under the spell of that Annie who, fully aware of the influence she had over him, did what she wanted with him. In exchange, she lulled him with promises. These were skills she had learned at the feet of a master, Jean-Melchior.

When Jean-Noël arrived at the rue Boissonnade, he found Annie had gone out without even leaving him a note, something she normally never did. He waited in the studio until one o'clock. He was hoping she would come and get him to go have lunch. He needed to see her. He was full of bitterness. The more he thought about the visit he had just made, the more sick at heart he felt. Hadn't he done everything he could for his mother, for Emile, whereas, had he wanted to, it would have been so simple never to have contacted them when he returned from the war? And yet today, simply because they thought he would never amount to anything, that he would never have any money (and Henri, with the aim of keeping Mme Mercier away, must doubtless have alluded to the impoverished life Annie was leading), they took not the slightest interest in him.

Shortly after one o'clock, he went to have lunch alone in the modest restaurant in the rue Campagne-Première, hoping that his stepmother would meet him there. He was eager to tell her about his visit to Mme Mercier. His mother's unbelievable change of attitude might well make Mme Oetlinger feel renewed tenderness for her stepson. She would certainly not be unhappy that he had been made to suffer as much as she herself by Mme Mercier and Emile. The entire afternoon slipped by without a knock at the studio door. Jean-Noël went to the corner of the boulevard Raspail several times without any fear of missing Annie, for the rue Boissonnade was a long cul-de-sac. He had gone out again toward the end of the day when he crossed a municipal police officer carrying a shoulderbag. He had a premonition that the man had come on his account. He followed him with his gaze the way one follows telegraph boys when one meets them as they are leaving one's home. He saw him stop in the middle of the rue Boissonnade, look at the numbers on the buildings, then disappear beneath an arched entryway. A few minutes later he came back and passed near Jean-Noël. The latter was pale. He retraced his footsteps. As he was passing by the concierges' loggia, he heard his name called. Feigning surprise, he turned around.

"This document was delivered for you."

He took it saying, "Ah! Yes, I know what that is," and put it in his pocket without opening it, as if it were a bill. But as soon as he was alone, he tore the envelope open with trembling fingers. It was a summons from the civil court, for it was customary, in cases where a complaint had been filed claiming a family had been abandoned, to make an attempt at reconciliation before further action was taken.

Jean-Noël did not dine that night. Although he had never doubted that Marguerite was capable of filing a complaint against him, he still could not believe that she had actually done so. What would he say to the judge? Where would he find the money he was being asked to pay? If he asked for a review of the judgment entered against him, he would still, in the meantime, be liable to pay the monthly amount to which he had agreed. For an instant the thought of calling Odile and begging her to help him, in memory of what he had once meant to her, passed through his mind. No, that was impossible. There was only one thing left for him to do: throw himself upon the mercy of his stepmother, admit everything to her. But when he thought about it, that solution seemed even more fraught with perils than all the others. Given Annie's certitude that she was not being told all the truth when someone opened their heart to her, such a revelation would seem proof to her that Jean-Noël was leading a dissolute life. If he wanted to lose her forever, all he needed to do was confess everything to her. There was still Mme Mourier. If he wrote her a desperate letter, and swore that she alone in the world could save him, she might lend him a sum of money.

At midnight Mme Oetlinger had still not appeared. Jean-Noël paced back and forth in the studio. Alone like this in the middle of the night, he trembled with fear. In the morning, which was now only a few hours away, Mme Mercier and Emile would arrive. If Annie returned in the next few moments and he warned her of this imminent visit, she would fly into a rage at not having any time left to take action, and everything would come crashing down upon him yet again. For an instant the thought crossed his mind of writing a letter and disappearing. But where would he go, what would he do?

All night long, he sat in an armchair waiting for Annie's

return, falling asleep and waking up by turn. Each time he awoke it was in the same way, with a start. While asleep he would forget everything; then, suddenly, after a few minutes, his situation would come back to him. He thought he recognized the voices of his mother and brother. They came in. Finding Annie was not in, they made themselves at home in the studio, opened the drawers, touched everything. He then imagined his stepmother's return, her surprise and her anger. So this was how he had acquitted himself of the errand she had entrusted to him! Rather than preventing Mme Mercier from coming, he had brought her back with him! And these were the circumstances in which he was going to have to admit to her that he had received a court summons. At dawn, in spite of everything, he fell asleep.

THIRTY-SIX

The studio had long since been flooded with sunlight when
the sound of voices woke Jean-Noël. They sounded joyful to
him. He even heard his name mentioned. There was talk of a
key, of the concierge. He heard the sound of knocking at the
door. He ran to open it. It was Annie, but she was not alone.
Mme Mourier was with her.

"What were you doing?" she asked. "We've been knocking for some time. Didn't you hear us?"

"I was asleep. I waited for you all night."

"Come in, come in," Annie said to Mme Mourier, who
had that reserved attitude one often sees in people whom one
has invited to one's home without knowing them terribly
well, after a party, for example.

"I'm not disturbing you?" asked Laure who, in view of the
fact that Mme Oetlinger had just spent the night in her home,
was being excessively discreet.

The day before, shortly after her stepson had gone out,
Annie had received the letter of which Mme Mercier had
spoken to Jean-Noël and in which, adopting an official tone,
Emile had announced that he and his mother would be coming to the rue Boissonnade the following morning. Mme Oetlinger had flown into a terrible rage. For a brief moment, she
had thought of vanishing on the spot, closing her studio, and
never again letting anyone know where she was. She had then
reflected that it was really too silly for her to complicate her
life because of people about whom, after all, she didn't care a

fig, and had thought long and hard about what conduct would be most appropriate in the circumstances. She had remembered Laure. Hadn't this woman been the very soul of obligingness? Hadn't she offered, a number of times, to do her any favor she required? Hadn't she even implied that if she ever found herself in need of support in delicate circumstances, she would find it a pleasure to provide it? Without waiting for her stepson's return, she had gone to the avenue Niel at once. She had not regretted it. No sooner had she informed Laure of what was happening to her than the latter had said: "You are going to do me the great honor, Madame, of accepting my hospitality tonight. Tomorrow morning, I will go with you, and you will allow me to receive these people for you."

"Good morning, Jean-Noël," said Mme Mourier. "You weren't expecting to see me?"

"Indeed, I wasn't."

"It's that Madame Oetlinger and I share some little secrets, isn't that right, Madame?"

Annie was smiling as she looked at her stepson. The bonds that united them were long-standing enough for them to understand one another without speaking. "No, there are no secrets, Madame Mourier is joking," read Jean-Noël in her eyes.

"Quite simply, my dear child," said Annie, "there is the fact that your mother is due to come here in a short while and Madame Mourier, in her extreme kindness, did not want to leave me alone to grapple with her. I don't know how to thank her; if it weren't for her, I think I would already have left Paris."

"It's the least I could do," observed Laure.

Mme Mourier had already shed the discretion she had shown when they'd first arrived. Like a home-nurse making her first visit who asks, immediately upon arriving, to be made familiar with the layout of the patient's house, and then gets changed and asks to be shown to a bathroom, she came and went in the studio, examined everything with a curious eye, and even glanced behind the screen, into the corner which Annie had arranged as a kitchen. She no longer seemed to recall the love she'd once felt for Jean-Noël. The familiar tone she adopted whenever she spoke to him, and the malicious looks she gave him, were those a woman of a certain age might adopt with a man who had once courted her but whom she had steadfastly refused, and who had since married an innocent young girl.

Half an hour after Mme Oetlinger and Laure's arrival, a knock was heard at the door.

"That must certainly be them," murmured Annie, staring fixedly at the bottom of the door, as if the people who were about to come through it when it opened would be physically as well as morally small.

"Do not be so upset, Madame. You will see that absolutely nothing unpleasant is going to happen."

Laure herself went to open the door. There indeed stood Ernestine Mercier and Emile. Without waiting to be asked in, they came into the studio.

"Good morning, Madame, how are you?" asked Laure. "It's been a long time since I've had the pleasure of seeing you."

Annie was standing, ramrod-straight, near the window, as though she'd been occupied looking out the window when she'd heard the knock at the door and had not judged it necessary to disturb herself. Because of Mme Mourier, it had only been at the very last minute that she had thought about how unpleasant this visit might be. Jean-Noël was looking at Mme Mercier and Laure from a distance, without seeing them, like an actor who has no lines to speak but whose part nonetheless calls for him to be on stage. A few moments after his mother and brother arrived he had suddenly remembered the summons he had received the day before, and had thought of nothing else since. As for Mme Mercier, she had immediately guessed the reasons for Laure's presence. Without answering her, she approached Mme Oetlinger.

"If you think that I'm not going to say what's on my mind just because there are other people here, you're mistaken."

Without turning around, Annie murmured: "I have nothing to say to you. Leave me alone. This is my home."

Mme Mourier stepped between them.

"Come now, come now, Madame Mercier. Do not abuse Mme Oetlinger's good nature."

At that moment, Emile came to his mother's rescue.

"We didn't come to see you."

Annie had taken refuge in the far corner of the studio. She was having to make an effort not to let her anger show. Although everything was happening in a manner which she could easily have predicted, she found this scene humiliating. No, she could no longer put up with these never-ending threats. This had to be put to a stop, once and for all. She rounded on Mme Mercier, forgetting all about the resolution she'd made not to say a word to her.

"I am asking you to leave now, Madame. You have absolutely no business being here."

"We aren't afraid of you," replied Emile.

Mme Oetlinger clenched and unclenched her hands several times, then suddenly spoke to Laure.

"Madame, I implore you, put a stop to this."

Laure intervened yet again. She was the one who had advised Mme Oetlinger to agree to this meeting. She did not want to be criticized for having done so.

"You must go, Madame," she said gently.

"We have no business with you," shouted Ernestine Mercier.

"Mind what you say. I don't have the same reasons as Madame Oetlinger to be patient."

Laure had uttered those last words in a slightly vulgar tone of voice, no longer speaking as one of Annie's friends but rather as to an equal, a bit as if, having grown weary of trying to convince Mme Mercier with kindness, she wanted to show her that, if it was going to be necessary to shout, she was prepared to do so. But neither Emile nor his mother paid any heed. There followed a confused scene which lasted several minutes. Mme Oetlinger, turning her back to everyone, had propped her elbows on the wooden balcony and was covering her ears with her hands. As if she had to execute the orders of a superior who has absented himself and wants everything to be over and done with by the time he returns, Laure now abandoned all pretense of pity. Whenever Mme Mercier or her son spoke, she replied unflinchingly that she had no time to enter into a discussion, that they must leave and never come back. Finally, Emile and his mother took their leave, though not before having uttered insults directed at Annie—insults which, in spite of the efforts she had made to stop up her ears, slipped through her fingers like water.

When Mme Oetlinger turned around at last, she looked like a different woman. There were red marks on her ears and temples where she had pressed her hands against them. The corners of her eyes were damp; her face was weary and mis-shapen, like a clay mask that has been handled before it was entirely dry. She was standing so straight that it was hard to believe she was the same woman whose stooped, rounded back had been visible a moment earlier.

"They won't be back," said Mme Mourier, surprised at the effect this scene had had on Mme Oetlinger. She had thought that Annie was merely awkward, that like most people of her class she was defenseless in the face of wickedness. She had wanted to extend her protection to her, to show her that women of whom it is said, somewhat scornfully, that they have too much cheek, can be useful in certain circumstances. "Let me take care of it," she had said with that pride which comes from feeling one has both feet firmly on the ground and is able to do battle with the most crafty and most clever, all the while letting it be understood that the trust she was requesting would only be needed for a moment, and that the mannish qualities she boasted of possessing would soon be replaced by others more appropriate in a pretty woman. She was surprised, therefore, that, rather than seeming grateful to her, Annie was not even looking at her. She sensed that something had happened, something which had escaped her attention.

Mme Oetlinger had not answered. She drew near her stepson.

"Would you like to make me happy, Jean-Noël? Make some tea. I am very tired."

"I'll do it, if you like," interrupted Laure.

"No, no, don't trouble yourself. Jean-Noël will do it."

"Would you like to sit here?" continued Laure, who didn't know what to do to make herself useful.

"Leave me. . . . Leave me alone."

Annie could no longer bear Mme Mourier. When she had received Ernestine Mercier's letter, her first thought had been to leave Paris. But after giving the matter greater thought, it had struck her that doing so could be interpreted as a capitulation, and that she would not have a moment's respite when she returned. She had then thought of turning to Laure for advice, and was now reproaching herself for having done so. Scorn and indifference were the only possible ways of responding to a woman like Mme Mercier; otherwise, one descended to her level. She now bore Laure a grudge, therefore, for having offered to arrange everything, for having persuaded her that, with her intervention, she would be rid of Mme Mercier forever, and for having thus led her to witness a scene as distasteful as the one that had just taken place in her studio.

"Aren't you making the tea?" she asked her stepson, who had just sat down next to her.

"Mme Mourier wants to do it."

Annie glanced at Jean-Noël affectionately and then, standing up, looked around for Laure. When she sat back down again, she took Jean-Noël's hand in her own and drew the young man toward her. Without raising her eyes, she murmured, "That woman is odious." Then she pushed him away, as if she had just entrusted a secret to him and they must now pretend they didn't know one another. This confidential revelation filled Jean-Noël with joy. During his mother's visit, he had felt utterly lost. In the midst of the raised voices, while his stepmother, the only person whose support he hoped he could count on, was turning her back to him, it had struck him that he would never have the courage to speak of the summons he had received, that he would be prosecuted, that Annie would hear of it and would never want to see him again. Seeing her now making an accomplice of him, and sensing she did not find him responsible for everything that had just taken place, he very nearly admitted everything to her on the spot. But wouldn't that have been a poor way of thanking the woman who had just given him such a token of her affection? Wouldn't it be best to wait a bit longer?

It was not until the following day that Jean-Noël told his stepmother that he was under a court order to pay Marguerite a monthly allowance of two thousand francs, that he had not paid it for the past four months, and that, since he had received a summons from the court, Marguerite had apparently decided to take action against him. He had, in spite of everything, been tempted to unburden himself the day before. But as soon as Mme Mourier had left, Annie had abandoned herself to a fit of anger. With the exception of Jean-Noël, no one had found favor in her eyes. The reason for this rather surprising exception stemmed from the fact that Mme Oetlinger, sensing she had been unfair toward Laure, whose only wrong had been to try to please her, was trying to give herself the illusion that she was not treating everyone unfairly. That afternoon, she had decided, most uncharacteristically, not to do any work. "We're going to go to the cinema," she had told her stepson. He had therefore chosen to say nothing. The next day, pretending he had just received the summons so that his stepmother would not accuse him of being a hypocrite for having kept silent the day before, he revealed all to her.

Mme Oetlinger was stripping a canvas to reuse it. Shortly before Jean-Noël had come down, which was toward half-past-eight, she had gone out to book a model for that afternoon. Mme Mercier's visit had deprived her of any desire to work. As a result, she had decided to start a new painting, since nothing made her angrier than having to neglect her work because of these sorts of preoccupations. She was now engrossed in stripping a canvas, doing so not to save money but rather in order to acquaint herself with the little material inconveniences as well as the joys of her art. She stopped working abruptly, and looked at her stepson with such a frozen stare that he lowered his head.

"What are you saying?"

Word for word, Jean-Noël repeated what he had just said. He did not realize that having memorized his confession this way gave it a rather premeditated aspect that would only irritate Annie further. She did not reply and went back to work.

"Would you like me to do that for you?" asked Jean-Noël, although he knew that his stepmother hated it when someone offered to take her place.

"No, thank you."

She continued cleaning the canvas as if nothing had happened. When she had finished, she asked Jean-Noël, who had been following her every move, what he had planned to do after lunch. He had grown so accustomed to making it seem as though he was thinking whenever his stepmother asked him a question that he remained silent. Finally, he answered that he did not think there was anything in particular he had to do.

"In that case, we'll spend the afternoon together," said Mme Oetlinger with unexpected tenderness. "I wanted to work, but I've changed my mind."

At noon, they went to have lunch in the rue Campagne-Première. Annie was in such high spirits that, rather than being overjoyed, Jean-Noël began to suspect his stepmother had not heard a word he'd said. She had asked him for no details. She would have been no different if he'd said nothing to her whatsoever. He began to fear that he was going to have to repeat that confession which it had been such an effort for him to make. His initial sense of relief had already vanished. He was as worried as he'd been before informing Annie of the problems he faced. He knew that she was capable of pretending to ignore them, and yet of answering him, if he reminded her of them, that she had understood him perfectly well the first time, without, however, doing anything whatsoever to help him.

After lunch, they went back to the studio for a cup of tea; Annie always said that the tea one was served in restaurants and cafés was brewed in the same pot as linden tea and chamomile and therefore tasted of those infusions. Afterward, although she had said she wouldn't work, she primed the canvas she had cleaned. Jean-Noël, who knew that his stepmother abhorred it when people did nothing on the pretext that they had only an hour free, took one of his law texts and forced himself to copy out passages from it. In part to show that time passes without one's being aware of it when one is working, Mme Oetlinger did not stop until four o'clock. They had some more tea. Then she told her stepson that she had several errands to run. While waiting for her, Jean-Noël might as well finish the work he'd begun.

"Perhaps you have forgotten that my summons requires me to appear in court tomorrow," he said in the same trembling voice he'd had that morning.

"No. I haven't forgotten."

Jean-Noël, who had no idea what to make of his stepmother's attitude and who was feeling increasingly tormented by his mounting anxiety, awaited Annie's return impatiently. Was she looking after him or had she no interest in what became of him? She returned at seven o'clock.

"Did you work well?" she asked Jean-Noël.

Annie's equable humor seemed a bad sign to him. He could not understand why the fact that he was being summoned before the court was having so little effect on his stepmother. Yet again, he wondered whether she had truly understood what he had told her.

"I worked fairly well," he replied.

They went and had dinner in the small restaurant where they had eaten at lunchtime. After the meal, Mme Oetlinger asked the waitress, while looking at the bill with great care, which was something she never did, whether anything had been left out. Then they crossed the place de l'Observatoire and made their way down the boulevard Saint-Michel. Although the evening was mild, there was already a hint of autumn in the air. It was like those evenings in Nice during which it had so pleased Jean-Melchior to go out with Annie and, sometimes, with his son. Lights were being turned on before nightfall. Although the chestnut trees along the boulevard were still in leaf, these were the last days in which they would begin to fall, one by one; you sensed that the moment was near when they would be gone, scattered. Jean-Noël was dreaming of his childhood, for he was incapable of taking pleasure from any aspect of life without relating it to others that had moved him, long ago.

"One could be in Nice," he murmured.

"I don't think so," replied Annie, to avoid any tenderness between them.

An hour later, they were back at the rue Boissonnade. They read and talked until midnight, but not once did the famous summons enter their conversation. Then Jean-Noël went up to bed. He fell asleep late. He did not wake up until nine o'clock the following morning. He immediately thought of the summons. Why had Annie made no allusion to it? Was he going to be forced to bring it up again in a little while? Filled with the same anxiety as the day before, he went to the studio. A piece of paper, on which Annie had written, "Get the key from the concierge," was pinned to the door. Jean-Noël felt a sense of relief. The note reminded him of many other similar bits of paper, each of which had afforded him the modest joy of knowing he was not forgotten. He did as his stepmother had ordered. But as soon as he had entered the studio, his attention was immediately drawn to a letter placed prominently on the desk.

He opened it and read as follows: "My dear Jean-Noël, I wanted to try a little experiment. I should have known that it would fail. But let's leave that be, it's behind us now. If I understood what you told me correctly, your first wife is demanding you pay her the sum of six thousand francs. I will ask my brother to have that amount delivered to you today. As for the monthly payments that follow, he will pay them directly to Marguerite or to her lawyer. That will be simplest. In addition, I have decided to give you an allowance for one year. As I have no idea how much a young man needs in order to get by and I loathe talking about money, you and Henri can come to an agreement on the amount. As for my studio, you can keep it if that makes you happy. For the moment, I no longer want to live there. I would like to ask you to please have my paintings and personal effects shipped to the avenue de Malakoff. Whatever is left you can give to the concierges, who are decent types. I am leaving you. Don't be surprised if I give you no advice. You know as well as I do that it's much better not to when one cares about someone's affection. I will doubtless go back to Italy. I have to work. I have lost too much time, too many years. Above all, let me know what you are doing. Write to the avenue de Malakoff, they will send on my mail. For I am impatient to know how you will use your freedom. I sense that the coming year will be a decisive one for you. You are at a crossroads. My dear child, I hope with all my might that you will choose the best road."